ELVENBABE

Adam opened the door, fumbled with the keys, and dropped them.

"Leave them," Moira said. She closed the door, and they stood silently in the main entrance for a moment. Then Adam looked up, put his arms around her, and closed his eyes.

The kiss lasted an eternity. Somewhere in the base of his spine a light exploded, sending shock waves through his body. She returned the passion, reaching around his back and running dagger fingernails up and down his inflamed spine.

Beyond his closed eyelids he perceived a flash of light, like a camera bulb. The kiss closed, and he leaned back, his eyes still shut.

"You've done this before," she whispered, her breath brushing against his cheek.

He opened his eyes a bit, and noticed something different in her blurred image. Their noses were touching; their arms wrapped around one another.

When his eyes opened all the way, he stared.

Her eyes, which were once dark blue, had become emerald with no whites. The pupils dilated, stretched vertically, in slits.

The rush of hormones leveled out and finally drained from his system, replaced ░░░░░░ a confused fear. Slowly, he drew ░░░░░░ her. Her arms relaxed, fell ░░░░░░ arms released her, b░░░░░ if he were clutch░░░ ░░░░░░ rounding her.

The tips of her ░░░ ░░░░░ two inches above her er░░ ░░░ ░pering to points.

OTHER BOOKS IN THIS SERIES

ELVENDUDE

Mark Shepherd

BAEN

ELVENDUDE

This is a work of fiction. All the characters and events protrayed in this book are fictional, and any resemblance to real people or incidents is purely coincidental.

A Baen Books Original

Baen Publishing Enterprises
P.O. Box 1403
Riverdale, NY 10471

ISBN: 0-671-87630-9

Cover art by Larry Elmore

First printing, November 1994

Distributed by Simon & Schuster
1230 Avenue of the Americas
New York, NY 10020

Typeset by Windhaven Press, Auburn, NH
Printed in the United States of America

To Ian

Prologue

The moment Samantha stepped from the Gate of light to the castle floor she knew that what the King had said about an Unseleighe invasion was true, and unexaggerated.

She stood unsteadily in the castle corridor, greeted only by the vertigo of Gating and a row of faerielight sconces along the wall. That no High Court elves greeted her on her arrival did not bode well. The Gate, a circle of yellow light large enough to step through, closed in on itself like a wilted flower, dimmed, then vanished altogether. Only a faint mist remained; this soon dissipated, leaving no sign of the temporary doorway between her world and the humans'.

This is not the reception I expected, even with the Unseleighe assaulting the castle with levin bolts, she thought, making her way down the empty corridor. Her anxiety grew as she wondered what had happened to their domain while she was away pretending to be a human.

A spider webbing of magical energy danced on the floor and walls, crackling like electricity, blocking her path. She'd seen this power before. Unseleighe power . . .

Levin bolt . . .

And she ducked behind a stone arch moments before an explosion ripped through the palace. The blast started at the end of the long hallway and swept its length with dust and rock.

"Great merciful Danaa!" Samantha shouted as the explosion knocked her backward. Though the blast slammed her against the rock wall, her only injury was a small gash in her leg. She struggled to her feet.

The healers can tend to this soon enough, she thought, eyeing the ceiling warily. *That is, if this corridor doesn't collapse. I doubt I could summon a shield strong enough to protect me from that.*

The blast confirmed her worst fears. The explosion's strength proved that it was not just a powerful levin bolt, but one sent from nearby. *The Unseleighe must have penetrated the outer perimeter. This is worse than the King said it was.*

She listened, but heard no others in the castle, and tried to remember how many layers of wall protected them. *Four, five chambers and a hallway. That bolt must have taken out the outer wing. Gods, how many of those have struck the castle?* From this she guessed the probable distance of the enemy to be within sight of the castle.

She clamored past portions of walls and ceiling, through a dusty tunnel that was once a spacious hallway, and peered into the gloom ahead of her. *Nothing. No movement, no sounds, save for the falling dust.* Faerielights flickered, threatened to go out. *Where is all the power going?*

After a few false turns, she came upon what was left of the King's chambers. She viewed the remains with cool detachment. Obviously, more than one levin bolt had struck the castle; one had rent a larger, gaping hole where the chamber's entrance once stood. Through this opening she saw that the entire wing had indeed collapsed. She gasped at the sight, hearing nothing except her beating heart.

When her initial shock subsided, she saw the first victims on the floor, some crushed by falling rock, some the victims of elf-shot. Fifteen in all. She checked the bodies for life, with little hope. Had they lived the King would never have left them behind. Among the dead she found a servant, a nobleman of the northern province, and a King's guardsman. Though she knew none of them, she recognized the guardsman, a loyal elder who trained many of the new recruits.

He probably died protecting the King, she thought sadly. *Where is the royal family?*

Through the crumbling hole in the castle's side she caught a glimpse of the domain of Avalon, then, occupying it in large numbers, the enemy. Her breath caught.

There are so many of them. How could they have summoned that many Unseleighe, and the Court not know it until now?

Over a stretch of rolling, emerald hills a vast blanket of Unseleighe elves swarmed like bees, preparing for the final charge. Their banners, black silken ribbons dangling from staffs, and flags with the Unseleighe black eagle crest, left no doubt in Samantha's mind who was behind the attack. What she first took for solely Unseleighe forces was a mixture of Unseleighe, Bane-Sidhe, gargoyles, and other creatures of unknown origin. *Mercenaries.*

Unseleighe mages gathered at the crest of a hill seemed to be summoning the power for another levin bolt hit. She did not recognize the family, or even the Court they came from; Unseleighe in general stayed away from Elfhame Avalon, so the Seleighe Court never became familiar with the vermin. Unseleighe kept to other regions of the elven lands, unless they planned an invasion, and had the means to carry one out. Clearly, to have gone this far, they had access to considerable power.

You will not win this one, she promised the Unseleighe. *They may win the battle, but not the war.* Despite her bravado, she knew the situation was grim, and unless something happened soon to turn the battle around, Samantha knew the survivors would probably have to flee Elfhame Avalon.

That's why they summoned me, she thought. *And at the last minute, too.* She searched the castle for her brethren, finding many bodies, wreckage, levin bolt damage. She sensed their presence somewhere in the castle, and her Sight took her deeper, to the lower levels of the castle, areas few of the Court ever saw.

She found two weary guards watching a stairwell, their

reaction disturbingly slow when they saw her. Blood stained their livery, a pale blue uniform with a cover of protective bronze mail. The two guards, young recruits, she noted from the shortness of their pointed ears, blinked at her briefly, as if wondering where she could have come from.

"Lady Samantha," one said. "I *thought* I felt the Gate," he added wearily. After hearing the pitch of his voice, she subtracted a few years from her original estimate. *They're employing elven children now?* "I am Iarbanel, humble servant to our crown. King Traigthren told us to be watching for you. We are to escort you to where they are waiting."

Waiting for what? A miracle? she wanted to ask. The other guard stepped forward. Samantha recognized her. *Ethlinn. She was once engaged to be married to a nobleman. Now, she's a soldier?* She stared openly, unable to believe their lot had fallen so far. Ethlinn looked too tired to take offense.

"Take me to King Traigthren," Samantha said, trying not to let her edginess show.

In silence Iarbanel and Ethlinn led her to a chamber she didn't even know existed. Deep underground, fortified with enormous flagstones, the room housed what remained of the Court. She doubted any harm could come to anyone inside, even if the castle collapsed completely.

Which isn't an unrealistic fear . . . It may yet become a tomb.

King Traigthren Tuiereann, Ruler of Elfhame Avalon, sat on a large high-backed chair. Evidently, it was serving as a makeshift throne. He was leaning over a heavy oak table with his head in his hands and a tattered ermine cloak pulled around him. His gold crown sat on the table. Guards sat around in various stages of exhaustion, one sleeping, one standing wearily at attention. Samantha counted five in all, including the two who had met her above.

Is this all that's left of Avalon?

In one corner on the floor a body lay wrapped in a golden cloth, with the Avalon emblem prominent in its center. *Queen Faldi.* Most of the Court was missing from the room; Samantha feared the worst. Prince Aedham, a mere elven child, sat forlornly beside his father, his eyes red with tears, wailing his grief into his father's cloak. Long, tightly curled black hair drooped over his shoulders, concealing all but the upper tip of his young elven ears. Broad of shoulder for one so young, the Prince resembled his father in other ways; on Samantha's last visit, she had learned of his mage potential.

Niamh, the King's Engineer, sat near an odd-looking weapon, tinkering with it madly, as if his enthusiasm alone would win the day. Samantha assumed that trauma had caused the poor elf to crack, and this was just another expression of elven insanity.

Two Counts from Highland provinces tried unsuccessfully to win the King's attention. King Traigthren ignored them. He reached down for his son's hand, who grabbed it and started wailing even louder. There were other elves, here and there in the shadows, some moving, some not.

Two bright faerielights illuminated the room from a high ceiling. Overhead, another levin bolt rumbled, and through the vibration of the floor, Samantha sensed the massive weight of still more rock coming down. Dust sprinkled from the ceiling. Faerielights flickered, dimmed.

King Traigthren looked up at Samantha. His expression chilled her. Even for an elf he had aged tremendously, and at that moment looked as if he was in his final century. A strip of bloodied cloth covered the tip of one of his pointed ears. His haunted eyes told her everything.

The King has given up.

"I thank you for coming to us in our final moments, daughter," the King said slowly, with a whisper that was heavy with defeat. He gently released his son's hand and pulled the cloak around him.

Daughter. The word, which he had never spoken to her before, sounded strange coming from his lips. No one in the room seemed to notice. By mutual agreement King Traigthren had never acknowledged his relationship with

Samantha, as she was the offspring from a previous, scandalous liaison. She easily forgot that she might have been Queen someday, had history dealt a different hand. Royal life never suited her, and even an elven existence proved boring once she came of age, this being the main reason she lived with the unpredictable, uncontrollable humans and their equally chaotic world. And, given the fate of the former Queen, it was just as well that history had omitted her from the royal succession.

The two noblemen turned and regarded Samantha with disdain. "You've summoned a mere *female* to take what's left of Avalon to safety?"

There it was. Now that her mission was no longer a mystery, she relaxed a little at the revelation. The snipe at her gender did not offend her. She had other things to worry about now.

"May I remind you both of the less than adequate job the *male* contingent of the Court did of protecting the nodes!" the King roared. Guards looked up. The noblemen looked away. Even the Prince had the presence of mind to stop crying at his father's outburst.

"How did the Unseleighe seize the nodes?" Samantha asked. "I didn't think such a thing was possible."

The King leaned back, the old wooden chair creaking loudly in the small, damp room. He looked at his hands as he spoke, a habit Samantha knew showed his embarrassment.

"Evidently, neither did our mages, none of whom are with us today. We acted so slowly when the danger was upon us. We'd received a message through the Oracle from Outremer. A warning, actually. Long ago, it now seems. This was during the new year's feast, the time of year we are least likely to be worried about anything, much less a confrontation with the Unseleighe."

Samantha's ears pricked at the mention of Outremer; her mother was from that Elfhame.

The King seemed to notice her interest. "Outremer tried to warn us. In fact, they *did* warn us, but in our arrogance we assumed that no Unseleighe had the power to conquer us. Our nodes were beyond danger, we thought. After all, had they not been in our Elfhame for millennium?" The King shrugged. "We all but ignored the message. We went about our affairs, sending only a few scouts to see if Unseleighe were gathering at the edge of our domain. Two of the scouts failed to return. We thought they were simply out exploring. That is, until we found their bodies. Or what was left of them." He glanced over at his wife's corpse, the pain and regret of his actions evident on his exhausted features. "We discovered the threat's true extent only recently. We attempted to communicate with Outremer, to inquire of the Unseleighe. Something blocked us. The message never arrived, and we assumed something had happened to *them.*"

Samantha nodded, understanding the complacency that had led to this situation. *Status quo. One of the reasons I left.* She looked away, down at the Prince who sat tiredly on the floor. The elfling nodded off for a moment, then jolted wide-awake.

Half brother, she thought. Then, *No, he's my brother. Brethren. Kin. And I'm to be his protector.*

"Even when the flow of one of the nodes ceased, we thought little of it at the time. This has happened before, particularly in the early days, and never proved to be permanent. What we did not know was that the Unseleighe had seized it, then used it to render their armies invisible to our Sight. Once the armies entered the domain, they set into motion the spells to seize the other nine nodes."

They might have prevented this, had the mages shown more . . . attentiveness, she speculated, but saw no need to mention this to the King. King Traigthren already knew, in the most personal way, that his Court had failed to protect itself.

Samantha shook her head, the fatigue and vertigo still hanging on. "Who are they? I didn't recognize any of the banners."

"*Zeldan Dhu,*" the King spat.

One of the guards groaned at the mention of the Unseleighe name. Fear masked the faces of those who remained quiet; evidently, they'd already acquainted themselves with Zeldan and his armies.

"They're not going to stop until we're *all* dead," the King said, glancing down at his son.

The elfling looked up, suddenly aware they were talking about him. The King stroked his head. "Don't worry, son. We're going to get you out of here. They will not get their hands on you. They'll have to kill me first. My death—" Another explosion roared, cutting off his sentence. This one felt closer than the previous one and stirred up a thick layer of dust. One of the faerielights flickered out, leaving them with only one. The group stirred, murmured frightened sounds. The King continued, "—is looking like a real possibility."

The dust settled, and the vibration rumbled to a stop.

"Have you decided where we will go?" Samantha said, though she had a good idea what the answer would be.

"The humans' world, of course. We must hide the Prince further, so that even if they see him in public, they will have no idea who he is."

Samantha frowned. "Of course, we have concealing spells. They give us the appearance of being human, and some ability to interact with them without practice. Sire, I've lived with the humans for many years. I have never once become suspect."

The King frowned. "Not good enough, my dear Samantha. They will not stop until they find every last one of the royal family. While one of us lives, they will never feel safe."

The King's request was becoming more and more disturbing; perhaps he had arranged some sort of surrender without telling anyone. Whatever became of this, he didn't sound like he would live much longer.

"The spell will activate when you and my son Gate back to the Earthplane," The King said, with finality. "The spell will not only give Prince Aedham the appearance of a human, he will . . ." The King's words trailed off as he looked down at his son, who had fallen asleep at his feet, curled up like a cat. "He will have the mind, abilities, and memory of a typical adolescent human male, thirteen years of age, with the regular growth spurts common to the species at that age. The Prince will remember nothing of the elven lands, Elfhame Avalon, his father and family, his dead mother, his mentors, his playmates, who have already died in this terrible battle. I will leave some of the details for you to work out once you both arrive."

Samantha wondered if the battle had touched the King's mind. This plan was, to say the least, extreme. *Total amnesia? No memory of Avalon?* She masked her doubts carefully. This was her King, and she was a faithful subject. Not only was it heresy to question him, the remaining members of Elfhame Avalon needed a single, strong ruler. They needed unity, now more than ever.

Survival. In its own perverse way, the plan makes sense.

"Your hesitancy," the King said slyly, "*is* understandable. But this is the only way I can be certain my son is protected. This total lack of memory will prevent any Unseleighe from reading his mind, if only by accident, and discovering his true identity. With the proper adjustments, he could be your son."

"It will be done," Samantha said without hesitation, although she didn't much like the notion of making herself appear older to become his human "parent."

The King stood, regarding the remaining soldiers of his Guard. "We must protect our youngest. Our children, even older children who are serving me in the capacity of adults, will go first. If we lose the nodes altogether, at least our most precious commodity will survive. You," he said, pointing at an elfling in full battle regalia, "and you. Step forward. Prepare to leave your heavy weapons behind. The less metal the better. And remove your chain mail. Yes, that's it."

Ethlinn and Iarbanel began stripping all metal from their battle dress.

"If we have the power, we will all go at once. If not, and if the rest of us survive," the King said, gesturing toward the remaining elves in the small room, "long enough to follow you in a later Gating, it may be several years, or decades, relative to yours and the Prince's arrival. Or possibly even before." The King offered his first smile since her arrival. "We might already be there."

"Yes," she agreed. Time to think about the consequences of *that* situation later. "Gating becomes inaccurate under these conditions," she said to assert her knowledge on the matter. *Better to let the King feel confident with who he's trusting his heir with.* "We do have two nodes left," she pointed out, "which is about double what we would need to Gate the survivors. *All* the survivors."

The King leaned over and gently woke his son, who rose with a start from his comfortable, curled position. He spoke in an undertone to the Prince, apparently explaining to him what was about to happen.

On Samantha's right, Niamh muttered loudly to himself as he diddled with what she perceived now to be a weapon of some sort. Its appearance suggested a cross between an AK-47 machine gun and laser light show equipment. Thick cables ran to what had to be banks of batteries, cradled by a backpack. Niamh looked up at Samantha and the King, his face aglow with success.

"Sire!" Niamh said, struggling with the backpack. Even for an elf, Niamh was small. "I think I have it this time."

"That's . . . wonderful news, Niamh," the King said. He did not sound excited. Apparently, Niamh had "had it" before. "We robbed it from the humans some time back," he said, waving absently at the weapon. "The mages thought they might be able to amplify magic, enhance our fighting capabilities. But in Underhill, the godsforsaken thing refuses to work."

"Have faith!" Niamh said. "There. That pebble." He pointed and aimed at a small stone in the corner of the chamber. Samantha stepped back in reflex; no one else bothered.

Niamh closed his eyes, squeezed a trigger. Samantha held her breath as nothing happened.

"If only we had a mage," Niamh said dejectedly. "I know we could beat the Unseleighe back, quick like."

"It worked in the humans' world," a new voice said.

Samantha turned to see Marbann, one of the King's knights. Marbann was easily the tallest elf in the chamber, strong and muscular, with blond curly hair and particularly long ears, even though he wasn't all that old. He wore the tunic and chain mail of battle, though the latter had taken some major hits. The tip of his sword was broken, the blade bent, his right arm bloodied. When he saw Samantha, his expression softened, then became sad.

Thank the gods, you're alive, Samantha thought as she ran to embrace him.

"We must leave now," Marbann said urgently, releasing himself gently from Samantha's arms. "The Unseleighe are crossing the moat now." The news did not seem to surprise anyone. As Marbann spoke, Samantha examined his injured arm, remembering her own leg wound when she saw the blood. Both wounds had stopped bleeding; they would both need more comprehensive healing later.

"Another node has gone over to the Unseleighe," Marbann said.

The King groaned and looked down at his son. "That last hit. We must get out of here now. While we still can."

"We'll have to go a few at a time," Marbann said. "Then, if it holds out . . ."

"Samantha, you take my son," King Traigthren said. "You will both leave immediately."

The Prince stepped backward, away from Samantha, toward the rear corner. "I don't want to go, Father," he said simply.

"But you must," the King said impatiently. "You have no choice!"

"I will be deserting the family!" he wailed. He stood resolutely with his arms crossed, with such apparent unwillingness to leave it looked like a direct levin bolt would be necessary to persuade him. "What will you do to protect yourselves if you cannot escape? You need as many adults here as possible."

"You are not an adult," the King said. The Prince

flinched at the insult. "And there is very little family left,"
he added, glancing at the shrouded body of the Queen.
"You are still a child, and you haven't even begun to explore
your magical potential. I suspect you could be a powerful
mage someday, but now is not the time for debate!"

"If you activate the spell to turn me into a human, won't
that divert power from the nodes?"

"Node," the King corrected. "We only have one left."

"My point precisely!" the Prince said. "This plan to hide
me with the humans . . . I have doubts."

Apparently he wasn't missing a thing when he "slept". . . .

"*Doubts* you may have, but say in it you have *not*," the
King said, his temper slipping visibly. "You are more liability than asset right now."

Samantha thought the argument would soon escalate
into a full battle; the elfling was trying to be a hotheaded
adult and succeeding nicely.

"You don't understand Zeldan Dhu the way I do," the
King insisted. "I know you're trying to be mature, but now
is not the time to grow up. Do as I say. You don't even have
to listen to reason. Just *obey* it."

The Prince's face changed slowly from anger and self-
righteousness to sadness and, inevitably, tears. The King
went to his son and held him for a long time, then whispered something inaudible to him. The Prince nodded his
reply.

"Farewell, Father," the Prince said. His shoulders
drooped, and his gaze dropped to the floor. In his own
moment of defeat, his posture mirrored his father's. Then
he looked up, jutted his chin out, and marched over to
Samantha's side, with a single tear trickling down his
cheek.

*He's trying to look so strong, and failing so completely.
He's crying inside so loudly the enemy can probably hear it.*

"We're ready," Samantha said. "Who will summon the
Gate?"

"I will," Marbann said. "With your assistance, sire," he
added, bowing deeply.

"Of course," the King said, and the guards cleared an empty space in the middle of the chamber. Marbann and the King stood facing each other an arm's length apart, then raised their arms, forming a circle. The faerielight dimmed as a low resonant hum began to vibrate in the floor, then reached up the wall. Several long moments passed with no visible sign of the Gate, and Samantha began to worry.

Gods help us all if they fail, she thought. *Have the Unseleighe already seized the remaining node while the King squabbled with his son?*

Light flickered in the air, but this was not the comforting arc of Gate light. Power popped and crackled and began dancing across the floor with the familiar power of destruction.

Not another levin bolt . . .

She instinctively grabbed the Prince and dropped to the floor. The wail of the incoming blast reached even their ears, deep below ground level.

"Everybody!" Samantha screamed, oblivious to royal protocol. "Get down! Levin bolt!"

Marbann turned toward Samantha, but made no move to follow her suggestion. His look was maniacal and desperate. The King remained standing, arms raised. He also seemed to be ignoring the approaching blast.

When it came, the Prince had covered both ears against the deafening wail of the bolt, the roar drowning out his screams. The room rose and settled as the concussion rippled through the castle like an earthquake, throwing everybody in the small chamber to one side. Except the King and Marbann; they stood in precisely the same spot, this time protected by the reddish hue of a shield, surrounding them in a sphere.

Then Samantha realized what Marbann had done, and why he had looked so crazed. He had reached directly for the incoming levin bolt, and siphoned off enough power to create a shield and protect their tiny room from harm.

Only a mage, or someone incredibly stupid, or practical, would do this, she knew. *We would have all died otherwise.*

The King and his subject visibly drew power from the levin bolt's residue, and trickles of red and yellow tendrils leaked through the walls and floor, and formed a swirling, circular cluster of light between them.

Samantha took the Prince's small hand and walked toward the Gate. Ethlinn and Iarbanel stepped close behind them.

Fare thee well, Elfhame Avalon, she thought as they entered the circle of light.

The vertigo returned, and the colors swirled angrily around her. She sensed the two guards close by, but they were only dim outlines in the light.

Please, King, come through now! she thought as she held the Prince closer to her. *The Gate will hold!*

But before the rest followed them through the Gate, Samantha felt another explosion. The Gate slammed shut, leaving them cradled in a web of light. She felt the change as they passed between the worlds, her own vision blurred by a cloud of gray fog; presently, she felt the solid ground of the Earthplane beneath her feet. Rich, moist earth. The smell of humus.

Unbalanced, she fell to her knees. The Prince was beside her, his eyes closed, unconscious. The two guards had fallen down as well and were crouched a short distance away. She looked frantically for the rest.

When it became obvious even to her scrambled senses that the others did not succeed in crossing, she let out a wail of grief that echoed throughout the forest that now surrounded them.

Chapter One

Lying sprawled on a wooden bench in a gazebo, Daryl Bendis woke to the sound of barking dogs and sprinklers. He blinked as bars of sunlight scorched his cornea through the ornamental roof. Groaning, he tried to sit up. When his head began to split open, he surrendered to the hangover, lay back on the bench, and closed his eyes against the supernova that had so rudely interrupted his sleep.

Why do tongues feel like roadkill after a good kick-ass party like last night?

Party. Yeah, he knew he'd been at a party. Somewhere. It took a few moments to orient himself, search his memory for clues to his whereabouts. He wasn't at home because they didn't have a gazebo, and anyway, he recalled telling Mum and Dad he was going to be spending the night at a friend's house. "To study trig." Such explanations generally granted him at least twenty-four hours of uninterrupted party time, and maybe a few hours more to sober up with, if he was lucky.

But which friend? Despite a strong desire to remain prone for a long, long time, he sat up. His head pounded with the worst headache of his life. When he was eleven, he'd microwaved a whole egg, just to see what it would look like when the shell finally exploded. This image appeared vividly in his mind now, as his throbbing head threatened to recreate the scene. He wanted to lie there at least another hour, while some of the drugs and booze filtered out of his body. One hour. That's all it would take, he knew from experience, before he was up and somewhat coherent, ready to do it all over again.

Once he sat up, he made a disturbing discovery. He was sitting in someone's backyard, near a kidney-bean swimming pool, with the beginnings of a sunburn glowing pinkly on his chest, wearing nothing but a pair of red Lee Wright briefs.

His clothes were nowhere to be seen on the finely manicured lawn. Instead, he found a trail of about four empty wine coolers, leading from his present location to the back door of a three-story mansion. A rhythmic heartbeat pounded away somewhere, mixed with the low electric whine of the pool pump.

Time to get into the house. Time to figure out where I am. Time to get out of this sun, he thought foggily. With every footstep, blood vessels threatened to rupture in his forehead. He hoped it wasn't too late in the day. And he hoped the day was either Saturday or Sunday. If today was a school day, he'd be up shit creek without a paddle, canoe *or* a life vest.

As he opened a set of French doors, a wall of new sound knocked him over. "Let the Good Times Roll" by Sheep on Drugs threatened to complete the microwaved-egg number on his head. Bone-jarring bass thundered through Earthquake woofers, plucking at his intestines with salad tongs. This was the heartbeat he'd heard earlier, muted by the mansion's architecture. Darkness, blessed darkness, as he closed the French doors behind him.

The music jogged his memory. *Steve threw the party. This is Steve's house. Steve's parents are in Cancún, slumming.*

Then, *This was my birthday party. I'm eighteen.*

I'm hung over.

Daryl burped.

Where the hell's Steve?

The phone rang. An irritating, wimpy, chirping sound. His eyes adjusted to the gloom, took in a high-tech kitchen with three hundred copper pots and pans hanging from a ceiling rack, a bank of microwave ovens, an intercom system, halogen track lighting dimmed to almost nothing. It reminded him of a biology lab: clean, sterile, and smelling of antiseptic. The music originated from the living room, a short hike down a marble hall. Thick black drapes concealed windows and French doors. *Steve's parents must like it dark, too.*

He padded across cold tile, chilled by air-conditioning turned down way too low. Then collided with a waist-high pyramid of empty and half empty beer cans, a carefully constructed work of art taking up a three-by-three-foot square of floor. The sudden and unexpected noise of tumbling aluminum and sloshing, stale Budweiser reminded him his bladder was about to burst.

"Hhmmmmph," he said, with little emotion. And suddenly he didn't want to answer the phone. *Why should I? It's not my phone. It's Steve's phone. But it's probably not for Steve, it's for his parents, and they're not even here. Probably some bitchy neighbor bitching about the noise last night. Hell, what about right now?* Though he didn't recall much of the evening, he assumed they had made enough noise to wake the dead. The condition of his central nervous system suggested as much. *Do they have a housekeeper?* The prospect made him uncomfortable, as he stood in the middle of the kitchen in his skivvies. *If they had a maid, how could we have a party? They must have sent her away or something.*

I gotta take a leak.

The phone continued to ring. If Steve was anywhere in the house, he was either unwilling to answer the phone, or unable to. He suspected the host was upstairs in his king-sized waterbed, with the girl or girls of his choice, passed out in never-never land.

In spite of the pressure in his groin, he felt strongly compelled to pick up the remote handset.

"Hello," he said tentatively, and began wandering through the house, looking for a rest room.

"This is Adam," said a voice on the other end. "Is Steve around?"

"Don't know. He's . . . I just got up."

A long pause. "Daryl, is that you? Are you okay?" Adam said, clearly concerned.

"Yeah, I'm fine. Just looking for the bathroom. I'm in the kitchen. Was."

"Find the utility room. There's a half-bath back there." Adam continued, as Daryl started that direction, "Is anyone around?"

"Nope. Haven't been in the living room yet. Music's still going. I fell asleep in the backyard."

"Music's still going because it's on a CD carousel. Random. Steve put it on last night before I left."

Daryl paid little attention to his friend. His bladder had reached critical mass. Little else registered until he found the bathroom and started relieving himself.

"That's gross," Adam said. Daryl sighed with relief. He noticed a bulge, right below his stomach, that had extended further than normal. Someone once told him that was his liver.

"What time is it anyway?" Daryl asked.

"One o'clock," Adam replied. "And you're just getting up?"

Now he wished he hadn't picked up the phone. This was not the kind of lecture he was in the mood for. *Jesus, I don't need parents. All I gotta do is call Adam. He'll do all the bitching for them.*

"*You* drank," Daryl whined.

"I had *one*. Then I left. You know that. I might as well have had a Sprite."

Which was one aspect about his friend he never understood. *What is the point of just having one?* He didn't like the way the conversation was going, the inevitable debate, which usually took place the day after a party. And since he couldn't recall much that would support his argument, he decided to end the discussion.

"Do you need to talk to Steve?" Daryl asked impatiently.

"No. I just . . . I dunno, I just had a bad feeling something happened over there. Guess you're all right."

He's just playing head games with me, like he usually does when I'm like this. Adam can be a real jerk sometimes. It wasn't always like this, though. He tried to remember when things began to change with them, counted back a dozen months, to their sophomore year in high school. Daryl once thought it was pretty neat that Adam's mother was a cop. When he started partying, though, and buying pot by the ounce, coke by the paper, and crack by the bottle, he didn't think her profession was very neat anymore.

In the next room, Sheep surrendered to KMFDM. In the brief transitional silence, Adam ended the conversation.

"Call me later, if you feel like it. I gotta go. Late for work," Adam said. "And oh, yeah. Happy birthday," he added, and hung up.

Daryl stared at the receiver, the dial tone somehow reaching his ears through the blast of *Virus,* an older KMFDM album from 1989. He hated this album, in general hated any music from the previous decade or earlier, no matter what it was. Had to be 1990 or later. And here it was 1994. *What are we doing listening to this old shit anyway?*

"Time to get out of here," he muttered to the phone. He shivered as goose bumps pimpled his flesh.

He returned the phone to its cradle and started down the hallway, toward the music, grabbing a cooler out of the fridge on the way. It was so loud he felt like he was walking through a lake of sound.

Then he remembered.

Jesus Christ, what a pipehead. We got out of school a week ago. It's summer vacation!

The revelation added bounce to his step. The music didn't sound so bad anymore, and when he entered the living room he walked over a body to turn up the music. The room was a wreck, but then it always was after one of

Steve's parties. The kid he stepped over was a freshman, just turned fifteen, who was the younger brother of Gina, one of the girls Steve used to boff. Steve and Gina had an argument the night before, something about Steve wanting to chase every girl in school but her, but he let Colm come over anyway, because he was silly and stupid when he got high and made everyone laugh.

Steve was passed out on the huge black leather pit group, a monstrous chunk of furniture that swallowed up the entire corner of the room. Two girls, partially clothed, lay more or less astride him, zonked out as well. Daryl didn't remember their names, but vaguely recalled one of them flirting with him at the party. One was in a black leather skirt, no top, and had smeared white-and-black Gothic makeup all over Steve's tank top. The other wore some kind of Spandex jumpsuit that might as well have been sprayed on. Steve was nineteen, but the two girls couldn't have been over thirteen.

Jail bait. The expression carried a stronger meaning for him today. *Not just for Steve, but for me too now.*

Wine and beer had stained the charcoal carpet, easily fixed since Steve had already made arrangements for the carpet cleaner to be in the next day . . . or was it today? It didn't matter anymore. It was summer vacation. Reality be damned.

He knew there were others at the party, and chances were they were in different places throughout the house, under beds, in beds, probably screwing this very moment. Suddenly he was glad he was the first one up—*is it really one in the afternoon?*—because now all he wanted was out. Being in the company of people, any people, held little interest. He twisted the cooler open and drank, wincing at the tartness; this one was more wine than the rest. Stronger. His stomach lurched, but he knew that if he could get a few gulps down he would be okay.

He found what appeared to be his socks next to the couch near Steve's head. A good start. It still didn't explain why he was half naked. *That would be a real bitch if I got laid last night and couldn't remember it.* It wouldn't be the first time that had happened.

His skin stuck to the leather couch, reminding him he had other articles of clothing to find before he could go anywhere.

A search of the house was beginning to look necessary, though he didn't really want to face any of the people who'd graced his party the night before, mostly because he didn't remember most of what he'd said or done. Whatever it was, it was probably embarrassing. Waking up mostly naked wasn't a good sign.

His eyes strayed to the contents of the big glass coffee table. Amid the debris of beer cans he saw Steve's glass pipe, a lighter, and several loose rocks of crack cocaine. His mouth watered. He reached for the rig but stopped halfway, remembering his semi-nudity. If he fired up the pipe now, he would have a harder time finding his clothes. Better to wait until he had at least found his pants.

He glanced out the big bay window that looked over the driveway and saw his red '94 Corvette blocked by a Camaro, a prissy little BMW, and a black Ford Mustang. Four other cars were parked down the drive, between the house and the security gate. What's more, he saw a black crease in one fender of his 'Vette. His blood started to boil.

"Shit," he said. Not only was he unable to hop in his car and drive away, his car was *damaged.* By some jerk driving a Ford. He couldn't remember whose car it was, but dammit, he would find out before he left.

Pissed, Daryl stalked back into the living room, where his companions remained, unmoving, and started powering off black boxes in the entertainment center until the music ceased.

"Steve, dammit, wake up," Daryl shouted. "Some asshole driving a Mustang dinged my 'Vette. *Who* is he? *Where* is he?"

Livid with rage, his hangover, which had started to subside with the cooler, bloomed in his cranium once again.

He stood in the middle of the living room, glaring down at his sleeping friends. They didn't move.

Daryl smirked as he considered devious ways to wake them, all of them involving ice water. His ears rang in the sudden absence of noise. And still, they didn't move.

"Okay, Steve. It's time to get up. Time to call the carpet cleaner guy."

Nothing. Daryl frowned. *They must have just crashed. Jeez, how late were they up, anyway?*

He went over to nudge Steve, and froze when he touched his arm. Not only was it white, it was ice-cold. Limply, it fell to the floor. Daryl reached for his wrist, started feeling for a pulse, though he wasn't sure exactly where it would be. When he couldn't find a rhythm there, he felt Steve's chest, recoiling at the coldness there. No beat, no nothing. Daryl was running out of things to check.

Maybe the girls . . .

He touched their shoulders.

Maybe not . . .

Daryl stepped back and regarded the scene numbly, never before feeling as devoid of emotion as he did then. *I am nothing, I feel nothing. Nothing happened. Nothing will happen to me. . . .*

He left the living room, first checking Colm, who was lying facedown in the carpet, and wondered why this didn't seem strange at first. Colm felt as cold and lifeless as the others; when Daryl turned him over, his eyes were still open. One pupil had withdrawn to the size of a dust speck. The other was wide open, blocking the iris completely.

There have to be others in the house. They can't all be dead.

There. He said it. *Dead.*

"Anybody up there?" he called up a long staircase. No one answered.

Daryl found himself at the top of the stairs, not remembering how he had gotten up there. The last bedroom upstairs belonged to Steve, but Daryl knew Steve wouldn't be in there.

A wall of bright light blinded him as he opened the door. The fluorescent desk lamp, turned upward, stared at him with its long, luminous eye. On the desk, which had a visible layer of dust on it, sat a pile of schoolbooks. *Steve's. There's the trig book we were supposed to be looking at last night.*

The phone trilled, this time a different, more annoying sound. The plastic receiver looked like it came out of a Cracker Jack box. Daryl sat on the edge of a waterbed and reached for the cheap phone.

"Yeah?" he said, making no effort to conceal his annoyance.

"Daryl?" Adam again. Over the phone loud music thumped away, something electronic. Adam had to shout to be heard.

"Christ, what time is it?"

A long pause. "Look, some of the guys who were over there last night are getting a little worried." Another pause. "You been there all morning?"

"Well, yeah," he said. "Some shithead blocked me in."

Then he remembered the horrible nightmare, in which he found those dead bodies. Including Steve's. But it was only a nightmare, he reminded himself as the blood drained from his face.

"Well, I thought I'd check," Adam continued. His happy, lighthearted tone was getting on Daryl's nerves. "I'm at the Yaz. You sure you're okay?"

"Yep. Listen, I gotta go. Say hi to your mom for me," he said, then hung up.

I gotta find Steve, he thought.

He went downstairs to the living room, where he saw Steve, two girls, and a boy named Colm lying dead.

Daryl sat on the floor, staring down at his feet, thinking, thinking. "Jesus Christ," he said to his dead friends. "How the hell did this happen?"

He tried to remember the events of the previous night,

his memories muddied with time and drugs. Grief lay somewhere deep in his throat, held back by the immediate need to cover his ass. He saw the drugs lying on the glass coffee table, which in itself was strange only because this was after the party, when everything should have been used up.

Wait a minute, wasn't there a weird group that crashed the party? He remembered the strange punkers in leathers and chains who rode up on Harleys and crashed the party uninvited. He still didn't know how they got past the gate, which could only be opened from the house. This was one of the reasons Daryl wanted the party here, because he knew cops couldn't break the gate down without a warrant, and video cameras would let them know who was knocking at their door long before that happened.

Steve tried to throw them out, but when they offered more drugs, he let them stay. About fifty people had arrived by then, and the newcomers began handing out vials of crack, for free, from a silk bag covered with hobbit runes and occult symbols and shit. The vials had black stoppers; other dealers used different-colored stoppers to label their product, but black was not one of the common ones. He remembered reaching for the bag, but had stumbled and fallen flat on his face. He had been so embarrassed from everyone laughing at him that he'd grabbed a six-pack of coolers and went outside to the gazebo. The idea was to return to the party after drinking the coolers. Instead, he had passed out.

Gotta call the cops. Gotta clean this place up first.

He grabbed a plastic bag and began cleaning, starting with the rocks and pipe on the coffee table. He searched everyone's pockets for more contraband, found an ounce of weed on Steve, pills of unknown type on the girls, and Tylenol 3's on Colm. He took three of the Tylenols for his headache, washing them down with warm cooler. Everything except alcohol went into the bag. He avoided looking into their faces, feeling like he was defiling them in some way.

In Steve's room he found more rocks and a backup pipe, but since it had apparently never been used he left it in the desk.

Sometime during the search of Steve's room, he remarked to himself that he should be feeling something, anything, right now. *Those people are dead. I even knew some of them.* He wasn't afraid of being arrested, but that was only because he was getting rid of any evidence that could be used against him. He felt no grief or even sadness over the loss of his friends. The codeine had kicked in, perhaps explaining some of this. He did feel a vague excitement, a thrill at outsmarting the police, but this was distant, clouded by the murk of a melting hangover.

In the bathroom he began disposing of the evidence in the toilet. Rocks and powdered coke went in first, followed by the glass pipe, which he smashed on the toilet sides. Then the grass and the pills, everything in descending order of legal liability.

About a grand in dope. Down the drain, he noted sadly as the swirling water sucked everything down. After everything had gone in, he flushed five more times, waiting for the tank to fill fully before flushing again, a technique he'd overheard his father discussing with a client.

Satisfied he'd completely covered his tracks, he went into Steve's room and reluctantly dialed 911.

Chapter Two

Officer Swink pulled his police motorcycle onto the North Central Expressway from Interstate 635, cranking the throttle hard to pull into the bumper-to-bumper traffic. He had another hour to go on his shift, and his unspoken but strongly implied citation quota had not yet been reached this month.

Before he had ridden a half mile, he saw a black VW beetle weaving down an on-ramp. The mere sight of the car was enough to get his dander up: the mag wheels and windows so tinted they looked spray-painted black were two strikes against the driver. The VW's driving habits didn't fare much better; the driver forced his way in front of a church bus, which screeched to a halt behind him. A textbook case of failure to yield. Swink was smiling so broadly his eyes nearly squeezed shut.

The bug was four vehicles in front of him, but right now it might as well have been forty miles away. Traffic had stopped completely, and on either side of him, portable concrete walls, the bane of traffic law enforcement, blocked him behind a Le Sabre with a serious oil-burning problem. Knowing he couldn't pull the bug over immediately, he made a note of the ramp's location.

Traffic crawled along for another ten minutes, then the retaining wall vanished, giving way to empty but unfinished pavement. Nothing his motorcycle couldn't handle, provided he watched for the protruding steel reinforcement rods still poking through the surface.

His single red light flashing, Swink zipped in front of the church bus. A flock of children in the bus applauded him, along with the old man driving it. Apparently the violation had irritated more people than just Swink.

Behind the bug, Swink tried to peer into the rear window. The oval was completely blackened; another clear violation of the law. Also, the bug's brake lights were not working.

There's three.

The bug did not immediately pull over onto the partially finished pavement, which irritated Swink further.

He shouted over his PA: *"PULL OVER NOW."*

The bug pulled over. Again, not as quickly as Swink would have liked. *I'm going to enjoy this.*

Jackpot. The bug had an out-of-state tag. California. And it was one of those vanity plates, which Swink hated. It read, simply: REPO.

As he pulled up behind he bug and stopped, flipping the stand out with a boot heel, he saw that he had misread the plate. It was actually an Oklahoma tag, IEX-1095, one he could call in. Given the black windows and the erratic driving, he smelled danger. *Better call it in,* he thought, reaching for the radio mike.

When the dispatcher responded, Swink blinked his eyes. The plate now was from Texas, QUP10-1, with an expired sticker. Blood vessels swelled in Swink's temples. Then he called in *that* number.

According to the dispatcher, the plate had never been issued by the state of Texas. *Bogus. That's four. And this one's going to jail.*

Swink called in a backup, and the dispatcher told him one was a minute away. He glanced back to the northwest and saw a Caprice cruiser about two hundred yards away, stopped in traffic. Another fifty feet and he would have unfinished pavement to drive on.

Swink approached the car, unsnapping his holster as he walked up to the window. He didn't like this; normally he'd be wearing a Kevlar vest, but he was sunburned from mowing the lawn the day before and had left it at home. He prayed he hadn't made a fatal mistake by doing so as he tapped on the driver's window.

The window rolled down slowly. Inside, Swink saw nothing but darkness and wondered briefly if there was another window, or a curtain, or something. The blackness was absolute. He saw nothing inside, the driver, the steering wheel, not even the door locks.

Swink was about to ask the driver to step out of the car when a deep, demonic voice rumbled from inside.

"You're blind."

Darkness poured from the car's interior, reaching out like a fist and wrapping itself around Swink's face; the cop staggered backward, held his hands up in front of his face, seeing nothing. Then he touched his eyes, which were open, but just not sending signals to his brain.

As he reached for his gun, the darkness briefly robbed him of his breath. When he regained it, he screamed in rage as he listened to the bug speed away.

On a late Monday afternoon, Paul Bendis left the Criminal Courts Building in downtown Dallas, near the historic West End District. He gave his briefcase a jaunty swing as he entered blazing sunlight, pleased with himself for helping his drug dealer walk away from an open-and-shut case of cocaine possession.

It doesn't get much better than this, he thought. *Who said lawyers were worthless?*

Earlier that day he had been a little down over the demise of his youth. *Today I turn forty-five. Today is going to really suck,* he remembered thinking when he got up that morning. He looked forward to the trial of Donald R. Wallbrook, a.k.a. Presto, with the same enthusiasm he reserved for root canal work. The best he had thought he could arrange for his client would be time in a minimum security prison, but something had told him to go to trial instead of plea bargain; he still couldn't put his finger on it, but despite what appeared to be good reason to bend over for the prosecutor, he fought it through.

He glanced over at his client, who was walking out of the building with him, a tall man in his thirties who could pass, with the right clothing, as someone ten years younger. Presto was smiling in the bright Dallas sunlight, his smile a flashing billboard for Paul's abilities.

Hell, yes, I'd be smiling, Paul thought. *I should be smiling too, but . . .*

The case had been dismissed, but the police would be watching them both for some time. He didn't like the attention, but being the number one criminal lawyer in Dallas County had its drawbacks. Not just that, but Bendis specialized in drug-related charges, which annoyed the detective division even more. Big-time drug related charges, the kind Presto had just squirmed out of, by luck more than anything else.

"That witness sure screwed things up," Presto said, still smiling.

Paul grunted, a sound that meant either amusement or annoyance. "You could say that."

In this case "screwed up" meant that the prosecutor's prize witness showed up in court so drunk he needed help getting onto the witness stand. Then he incorrectly identified Presto, pointing to the bailiff when asked if he saw the individual who sold him the coke.

Paul was about to tell him that the screw-up in question was the only reason he was walking free, but that would have taken away from the aura of omnipotence he'd been cultivating for years.

"Well, yeah, they didn't have much of a case anyway. Just a chance to let a rookie detective get his feet wet in the courts."

Presto snorted back, suggesting he didn't fully believe Paul.

"You just wait, buddy boy, they'll be after you again. Watch your ass a little more carefully. Use middlemen from now on. Get out of the line of fire."

They stopped at Houston and Main, a stone's throw away from Dealy Plaza, where Kennedy was assassinated. Tourists were swarming over it as usual, with the usual amateur sleuths looking for clues that several million other sleuths had somehow managed to overlook in the past thirty years. Presto glanced over toward the slow curve of Elm, under the County Annex building, where Oswald allegedly shot the president. Standing here with his guilty, yet unconvicted, felon felt somehow appropriate.

"Would you look at that," Presto said, shaking his head. "This ain't no place to be doin' that."

Paul looked over to what Presto saw. What appeared to be an old black man and his son were walking toward the Annex Building, smoking crack in a glass pipe. Paul looked away.

"So where'd you park that Beamer, Bendis?" Presto said after crossing Main. The dealer had a deep, raspy voice that added years to his apparent youth. Paul was running today, and he had happened to see an empty meter a few blocks from the courthouse. The usually skeptical lawyer had taken this as a sign that good things would happen to him all day.

"Down here on Commerce . . . yeah, there it is," he said. The new BMW had less than a thousand miles on it, but already it was an old friend. It had tinted windows that allowed him to do all sorts of secret things inside it. He was considering doing one of those things right now.

He frowned at the white glob of pigeon drop ornamenting the windshield, then climbed into the Beamer, glad to be out of the Dallas sun. Bendis loosened his tie as the car revved, and started the air conditioner, which cooled them off after the initial furnace blast from the vents.

Presto crouched into the tight space, his knees up to his chest, an angular, middle-class skeleton trying to look comfortable on leather upholstery.

"You got yourself a new one, didn't you?" Presto said, sniffing the car's new air.

Paul didn't answer him. He reached over and opened the glove compartment, looking for the brown bottle and minispoon.

First things first, the lawyer thought as he sniffed two

heaps of the white powder, one up each nostril. Then the sun rose on his afternoon, giving everything a pink tint. For the first time that day, he felt alive. The coffee he had for breakfast had done little to revive him, and as a general policy he didn't go into court coked up. It looked bad. Also, if he started doing that, he might become an addict and have to stop altogether and start going to those twice-damned Cocaine and Alcoholics Anonymous meetings, and he was damned if he was going to let a harmless little powder take over his life when he had so much going for him and was raking in three hundred grand a year from clients. Like. Presto.

His thoughts racing, heart pounding beneath his rib cage, he consciously slowed down his breathing. That was one side effect he didn't like from coke—sometimes it kick-started the old kicker a little too hard. *That will pass soon enough.*

He knew not to ask Presto if he wanted any. Presto didn't do coke. Or drink. Or smoke. Or even drink coffee. The man was an absolute health nut, eating acidophilus and psyllium husk pills like candy, along with dark green veggies, beta carotene, vitamin E, a walking "special foods" pharmacy. Privately, Paul thought he was a little nuts, but then almost all the dealers he'd ever represented avoided their own product. At least, the successful ones.

The cellular phone on the floor between them chirped, an annoying sound that, for some reason, he didn't find so annoying right now.

"Yeah, what is it?" Paul said.

"Oh, Paul," Yanni, his wife said, an edge of hysteria cutting through his euphoria. "Oh Paul oh Paul oh Paul . . ."

Paul grimaced, and forced calm into his voice, genuinely annoyed. "Yes, dear. What's wrong?"

His reply was not so much a question as it was an acceptance that he would have to listen to his wife for five or more minutes describe a completely mindless problem that had no hope of being solved. She did this only when he was in his car, never at his office when the call was relatively cheap. Half his carphone bill could be attributed to Yanni describing, in minute detail, how the clothes dryer killed the cat by slow-cooking it over a seventy-minute cycle, or how the paperboy came by and demanded payment in coke, or any number of situations a moron with an IQ of fifty could deal with. But not his wife. Not Yanni.

Since getting angry tended to multiply the length of the conversation by a factor of five, Paul tried to sound understanding. There was always the "whoops, I drove out of range" explanation for hanging up.

He listened to her sob for ten seconds, then sat up straight. *There might be something to this after all.*

"The police called," Yanni said, finally. "Daryl's in trouble."

Which can mean anything, he thought, biting his tongue. "Could you be a little more . . . specific?"

"The police called and said they were questioning him about some murders."

Oh, good God, Paul thought, getting angry. *That little worthless juvenile delinquent of a son would have to go and screw up like this.*

"When did this happen?" Paul asked patiently.

"Last night, or this morning. Oh, I just don't *know.* They want one of us to go over there, right now, and pick him up."

Paul groaned, his patience slipping. "Go *where?*"

"You don't have to shout!" Yanni shouted. "The phone works perfectly."

"I wasn't shouting," Paul replied. "Why don't you start from the beginning?" he said calmly, thinking, *before I defy the laws of physics and strangle you over the phone.*

"The police called from the Winton house. They are questioning *your son* about some murders over there. *Right now!*"

Paul rubbed his forehead. *Oh, boy.* "What was he doing over there, for crissakes?" He had to think a moment. *Where did that kid say he was going last night? Wasn't it over to Adam's house and study trig or some bs?*

"How am I supposed to know? He talked to you. He doesn't tell *me* anything."

"You said *murders*. Is that exactly what the police said: murder?"

"Ummmm," Yanni articulated. "Well, no. Deaths. Isn't that the same thing?"

Paul shook his head, glanced over at Presto, who was staring out the window.

"No. It isn't," Paul said.

"Well, anyway, they said they found several bodies over there."

"Is Daryl under arrest?"

"Well, no. I don't think so."

"Did you talk to Daryl?"

"I *said* he doesn't talk to me. No, I didn't."

"Give me their number."

He wasn't about to go over there in person. Cops, even homicide, had a way of knowing when one was on coke, even when there were absolutely no physical signs. But he couldn't just drop this, which was his first impulse: if Daryl was under arrest, the boy needed to be told to keep his filthy mouth shut until he sent someone from the law firm over to deal with it. If he blurted some kind of made-up confession, it could cost thousands of dollars and months of court time, which he didn't have right now to spend.

Yanni gave him the number, and Paul promptly hung up.

"What was that about murders?" Presto asked casually.

"Nothing." Paul grunted. "My wife doesn't know what she's talking about."

Paul called the Winton number. A male voice answered.

"Winton residence. Officer Demaret speaking."

Paul cleared his throat. "This is Paul Bendis. Daryl's father. What's going on over there?"

A pause, as the officer conferred with someone else, then, "It would be better if you just came over, Mr. Bendis. This is a serious situation."

"Well, that's kind of hard to do right now. I'm in a traffic jam and I have an appointment with a client in . . ." he glanced at his watch, "one hour." The latter half of the excuse was true.

"I see. Well, your son Daryl called the police this afternoon after finding his friends dead. There was some kind of all-night party, according to the neighbors."

"Dead. How did they die?"

Another long pause. "I think it would just be better—" the officer began.

"I told you, I can't make it right now. Is your superior officer there? May I speak with him?"

Moments later, another, older voice came on the line. "This is Detective Roach. Is this Daryl's father?"

"Yes, it is," Paul said, feeling his patience slipping away again. "Is my son charged with anything?"

"Mr. Bendis, this looks like an overdose. Your son could be very—"

"Is he charged with anything?" Paul cut in, and immediately regretted it. For a second there he forgot who he was talking to.

"Well, no. Daryl Bendis isn't charged with anything," the detective said, adding, "*yet*. We're still searching the house."

"You are, are you?" Paul said. He almost asked if they had a warrant, but thought better. *Just get Daryl out of there. The Wintons can clean up their own mess.* "Well, let me know if you find anything. I'll be there as soon as I can."

"Oh, we *will*, Mr. Bendis. Say, are you the attorney Paul Bendis?"

"Well, yes I am. Why do you ask?"

"Oh, nothing. We will—"

"I have to go now. I'm on a carphone, and the signal is getting a little . . ."

Paul hung up.

"Damn," he muttered at the windshield.

"What is it?" Presto asked.

Paul waved the question away, released the parking brake, and eased the Beamer into downtown traffic. "It's just a bunch of kids who don't know how to handle their drugs yet. My next client may be my own son."

Paul pulled onto 35E, dodging traffic, heading to Presto's house.

"Sounded serious. Your son okay?"

Paul looked up from the traffic. "What?"

"Your son. Is he okay?" Presto said with a strange, indecipherable expression.

"Hell, I guess so. He's not charged with anything," Paul said, turning his attention back to the evening rush-hour traffic.

Chapter Three

Adam McDaris hung up the phone in the Yaz's back office, for the first time realizing just how far apart he and his friend Daryl had gotten in just the past month.

Last summer was nothing like this, Adam thought. *He couldn't even think*, first angry, then depressed over how screwed-up Daryl sounded.

He picked up the phone and almost called back, but thought, *it would be a waste*. Besides, there were customers out front, with only one bartender besides himself working today. Adam sat at a brown pressboard desk strewn with accounting pads and a mountain of cash register tapes, wishing he could do something about his friend, but having the presence of mind to know he probably couldn't.

The traffic at the Yaz on a Monday afternoon tended to be unpredictable and varied, even in downtown Dallas, Texas. The juice bar opened only six months ago, but already a tight group of regulars had begun to frequent the place.

The Yaz began as a liquor bar, but as more and more bars sprang up throughout the scenic West End District, business began to dwindle. The owner, a second-generation Korean-American named Jimmy, decided to experiment with the after-hours/underage crowd. And business exploded.

The Marketplace shopping mall, an old four-story brick building that once housed the Sunshine Cookie and

Cracker factory, was already a haven for youth. The lower level housed a video/pinball arcade that looked like a carnival, boasting life-sized Western dummies in the laser shoot, elaborate holographic games, miniature bowling, foosball, and dozens of other ways to get rid of quarters on a Saturday afternoon. Upstairs was a miniature golf course next to a bar and restaurant, a cartoon art gallery, several fast-food eateries, an airbrush t-shirt shop, a Western shop, and an Irish shop. All set in a rustic atmosphere of wooden floors, restored oak beams and skylights, original equipment of the old structure, with no concrete, chrome, or stainless steel. Part of its appeal was that it didn't look like a modern mall; the building itself was an antique.

Which didn't explain its appeal to youngsters; perhaps it was just that it was different, particularly with the elaborate arcade. At any rate, Adam thought, it was a perfect location for the Yaz, whose time had certainly come.

He started working on the weekends last January, when it reopened as an after-hours. At first business was slow, but as word got around, the place developed a reputation as an alternative watering hole, where ID's were not needed and the latest in Techno and Industrial music played into the late hours of the morning. The money was good and the crowd not too overbearing, even the drunk ones who came in after two in the morning—with one or two exceptions. It was better than working fast food; here you didn't get burned with hot grease or have fingers removed by roast-beef slicers. In the nightclublike atmosphere, Adam felt a little more sophisticated and mature, more so than he would if he were flipping burgers and wearing a paper hat.

When Adam applied for work, Jimmy hired him right away. Now that the place was fashionable, there were two file drawers of applications, but Jimmy was about to throw them all out. The owner was particularly pleased with Adam, especially when the boy explained how his friends hated to pay two dollars for a soft drink but wouldn't mind so much a higher door cover: the change in pricing increased the profits by 25%, foot traffic by 50%. At the time Adam had just been looking for a place to work so he could make payments on his Geo Metro and the insurance that went along with it. The job ended up heightening his popularity with just about everyone.

The Yaz even found unpredictable but fairly steady profits by opening up early in the afternoon. The only stipulation required by Marketplace management was that they saved the loud, high-energy Industrial music for later hours. No problem. With a subtle changes in lighting and music, the Yaz was a laid-back cafe, specializing in exotic coffees and espresso. Adam was allergic to caffeine, but had no trouble preparing and serving the dark brews, as long as he didn't *drink* any of it.

Today was no exception; two preteens, a boy and a girl, were pretending to be romantic in a corner booth. The boy had ordered espresso, the "strong kind," and Adam had to fight to keep from laughing when the boy nearly gagged on it. A group of five girls from a private school had left the bar, and Spence, the other bartender, was picking up the cups. Spence was a year older than Adam, but instead of going on to his senior year in the fall, he would be held back a grade. Adam wasn't sure why, as Spence's grades were not that bad, or good, but he'd decided not to pry. Where Adam was well-defined and muscular, Spence was tall and wiry, with a crown of kinky red hair that, when allowed to grow, became a full afro. Others in school had pointed out they looked like brothers, but Adam saw no resemblance; their skin tones were completely different. Adam had French Canadian ancestry, and Spence's was clearly Irish. But they did share some of the same allergies, oddly enough, caffeine being one of them.

That left Colin, the kid sitting at the bar. Spence cast uncomfortable looks at him as he picked up the cups. He'd already replaced the cup Colin was nursing once. The boy shook so much he barely kept his coffee from spilling. Adam put on some Enya, hoping that would calm Colin down, but it had little effect.

Colin wore boots, a pair of jeans with a leather motorcycle jacket, and no shirt. He reeked of gasoline and booze, leftover booze from the night before. Here on the quiet side of the Yaz were several bay windows looking over a patio and street, and beyond one of these at the curb Adam saw Colin's bike, a fast and scary Katana 750 that looked like it was doing 120 sitting still. But Adam knew the bike had nothing to do with the reason why Colin was so rattled.

"He's still there," Adam said to Colin, who had looked up as he walked behind the bar. "Still stoned, but there."

"And?" Colin asked. The ceramic cup rattled loudly against formica.

"If something's wrong, he doesn't know it," Adam said calmly. He pulled four limes out of the cooler, laid them out on a plastic cutting board, and began slicing them into eighths with a Ginsu knife.

"Weird," Colin said, sipping the coffee, this time not spilling any of it. "Maybe I should just . . ."

"I think you should just go on home. Or go to a meeting. Look, just because you got drunk once doesn't mean it's hopeless."

"But dammit, I had a *year*," Colin said. He looked at the A.A. medallion hanging around his neck. "Thought I had it licked."

Adam didn't know what to say. Colin had just turned seventeen, had been an alcoholic since he was eleven, and had started going to A.A. meetings in his freshman year at high school. He might have been sober today, except that he'd gone to the same party at Steve's. Something happened, and he got drunk. And Colin was kicking himself all over the city today, first riding past Steve's house to see who was still there, then his sponsor's house, who he was too humiliated to visit, then a church where an A.A. meeting was in progress. He didn't stop anywhere except to ring the Wintons' gate, which went unanswered. Not wanting to be with the people he used to drink and drug with or the recovering alcoholics he knew in sobriety, he turned to Adam, who was neither, for an attentive ear.

At noon Adam opened the Yaz, and five minutes later Colin came in and told Adam he'd been by the Wintons' mansion. Ten cars remained parked in front of Steve's house, and short of breaking the gate down, he had no way in. Three of the cars belonged to friends who had to be at work that afternoon and had not yet shown up. The carpet cleaning people came and went, since no one answered the bell outside. Steve's parents were due at the airport at 9:00 P.M. And the house was a mess.

Colin is obsessed over everyone else's problems and afraid to do anything about his own, Adam observed. But he had to admit the situation at Steve's didn't sound right. He understood why Steve would throw a party—because the parents were gone—but he also knew Steve would go out of his way to make sure all evidence of the party was cleaned up. Adam also felt a strong sense of dread, a black, evil feeling when he envisioned the Winton mansion. Nothing more. Just a feeling of danger and of . . . death.

Adam shook his head, his Ginsu poised above his index finger, a half inch from carving a good slice out of it. *Back to reality.* He finished cutting up the limes and put them in the well box with the other pretty trappings for dressing up cocktails without the alcohol.

"What the hell," Colin said. "Freedom Recovery Group meets in fifteen minutes. Guess I'll go there," he said, dropping a dollar on the counter and leaving.

Through the bar's window, Adam watched Colin mount the bike. He had a different air about him, like he had a real purpose now and wasn't just killing time. *Now it's time for Colin to deal with Colin's problems,* Adam thought. *Now what about Daryl's? Is that something I should even think about right now?*

As Colin's bike screamed down the street, he caught a glimpse of Moira walking past, heading toward the front entrance of the Marketplace. She worked at a salon upstairs, a progressive shop called Skary Hairdos which catered to the Alternative music, Gothic and grunge crowd. She was evidently going into work, as she was wearing a black dress trimmed with leather and lace, large, frightening earrings that could double as shurikens in a pinch. She had big, tornado-proof hair that generated wind when she walked. She had been dressed more sedately with him last night when they went to Steve's party, more as friends than a true date, although Adam had recently taken a physical interest in her. She looked preoccupied with dark thoughts, as everyone seemed to be this afternoon. When she vanished from sight, Adam wondered what color, and how long, her fingernails were today.

He looked around the Yaz, mentally ticking off all the things he needed to do for Jimmy that day, finding that he'd accomplished everything except dusting the blinds. But that was a low-priority thing, busywork he saved up for when Jimmy was there.

Adam carried the Ginsu knife and a few other implements to the sink in the back, but before he got everything into the water he yelped as the Ginsu blade, which he accidentally touched, started *burning* his skin. The Ginsu clattered to the floor.

"You okay?" Spence asked, carrying a bus tub full of used coffee cups.

"Yeah, just touched metal, is all," Adam said, examining his skin where the blade had touched, leaving a slight pink patch. Spence picked the knife up by the handle and tossed it into the sink. If Adam had touched the metal any longer than that, it would have left blisters.

Spence nodded. No other explanation was necessary, as Adam's coworker was also allergic to steel. He didn't advertise the allergy to others, since he knew they wouldn't understand. His mother explained the allergy as a homeopathic ailment, a rare one which few people had, and even fewer doctors understood. His gut-reaction was to say nothing about it, except to others with the same condition.

He couldn't recall when he'd told Spence about the problem, and he didn't know when Spence told him about his. When they started working together, their mutual allergies seemed to be common knowledge between them.

After a few months, Adam assumed he'd known Spence for a long time.

Perhaps something psychic connected us, Adam had thought once, briefly, before the whole notion faded from his mind.

Spence carefully pulled on some black rubber gloves, the thick, industrial kind with almost no give, and began washing the utensils.

"Who died?" Spence asked, looking serious.

Adam frowned. "Am I that obvious?" he said, sorting out and separating the coffee cups. "You saw what it was like over there at Steve's last night."

Spence fixed Adam with steady gaze, as if trying to read more from his body language. "I told you how much he'd changed. His birthday party—his *eighteenth* birthday party—was guaranteed to be a drugfest."

Spence wasn't intentionally trying to throw the situation in his face, but that's what it amounted to. Adam had persuaded him and Moira to go over there last night, despite their suspicions it would not be an alcohol-only party. Adam knew he was feeling more embarrassed about it than was his due, but he couldn't help feeling remorse for dragging them along.

"At least no one got hurt," Spence said as he labored with the dishes. "I liked the way you bailed out of there before the drugs started going around."

"What else was I supposed to do? I don't like being around that stuff. And my mom's a cop. You all didn't have to leave. . . ."

"Yes we did, and you know that," Spence said. "Don't let it get you down. Daryl's an adult now. Daryl's responsible for Daryl."

"He's a *legal* adult," Adam corrected. "But he hasn't really grown up at all."

"Well, then, if you've done any maturing this last year," Spence said, his voice softening a little, "prove it by letting go of his problems and getting on with your life."

Adam shrugged, knowing Spence was right, but still

feeling emotionally connected to his old friend's problems. "I wish I could. We grew up together, we've known each other since . . ."

He tried to remember when they had met, but could only go as far as junior high, when he was thirteen. And before that, well, he'd moved down from Winnipeg, Canada, after living with his father for a few years. Daryl was new to the school, too, also entering in midterm, and that automatically created a closeness between them. The friendship weathered a minor jealousy over a girl in their freshman year, but she ended up spurning both of them, and the whole thing didn't really amount to much.

"Why don't you go talk to Moira?" Spence suggested. "I think I can handle this place for a while."

As Adam entered the Marketplace, he remembered the bet they made last night, that they would smell pot within an hour of arriving at Steve's. He forgot who bet what, but the wager had irritated him because it showed no faith in Daryl.

But then, does he really deserve any? he thought, taking the stairs to the top level of the Marketplace.

Adam glanced down at the arcade a floor below, the clanging and beeping of the games wafting up through the well. Just after lunch hour, the eateries were doing a bustling business with the suit and tie crowd, the downtown business district being only a few blocks away. On the top floor he passed the miniature golf course, the bar, several abbreviated eating places. He paused for a moment at The Future Image store, specializing in high-tech gizmos. Today in its front window hung a laser rifle, or what could pass for one. It looked more like an assault rifle wired for sound, or a light show.

Intrigued, Adam stepped closer to the window. The Ray Gun squirted a ruby red beam of light into a series of mirrors, angled to form a square around the toy, showcasing it. It retailed for three hundred and fifty dollars, and was recommended for children thirteen and older. Its blue steel surface looked like it could withstand an arc welding torch. The clip, which stuck straight down, was the battery that powered the Ray Gun. Then he saw the recharging rig, which had another clip in it. The Gun looked heavy, and Adam wondered if the average thirteen-year-old could hold it for very long, even with the shoulder strap it came with.

Stopping to window-shop was not something he did, particularly in a place he saw every day. Plus, gawking at a toy gun would not enhance the cool image he was trying to cultivate among his friends, who could happen along at any moment. But there he stood, transfixed by the weapon.

But it wasn't a weapon, it was only a toy. *Where have I seen this before?* he wondered. The Ray Gun was too small; he recalled something that was much larger, like one of those M50 rigs the Marines carried, and not as refined, almost like a prototype, with lots of exposed wires and components, itself a fragile instrument. . . .

The image vanished, and he shook his head. Without really thinking about it, he pulled away from the toy, the window, and the store. And walked over to Skary Hairdos, two doors down.

Adam saw her hair before he saw her. Bobbing about energetically in the shop, her mane announced her presence before she could; he wanted to curl up in that glorious hair, maybe weave a hammock for the two of them, or arrange it around them in a nest. *She could smuggle a Mexican family, a priest and two nuns in that hair*, Adam thought.

Neon framed the store's entrance, with deep green neon spelling SKARY HAIRDOS in an electrifying scrawl, superimposed over an acrylic painting of a zipper that changed to a set of poorly done sutures. Adam passed a pair of girls, one bald except for a two-foot thatch of bright pink hair hanging over her face, the other with a military flattop, both seeming very pleased with their new 'dos.

He suddenly felt out of place without his leather bike

jacket, which despite the warm weather appeared to be in style today. Even Moira kept one in the shop, though she seldom wore it in the summer. She was cutting the hair of a very young boy, maybe six, who was wriggling and screaming at the top of his lungs. The kid would have probably bolted altogether, except that Moira, or the mother who sat by impatiently, had tied the kid to the chair with a substantial length of nylon rope.

"This is about as good as it gets," Moira announced, the haircut apparently completed. She was perspiring; Adam had never seen her perspire before.

"I'm sure it's just fine," the woman said, but she started to look like a nanny taking care of a rich brat.

The boy cried relentlessly. Since he was still tied to the chair, Moira took a mirror and held it behind his head. "What do you think, Duane?" Moira asked, as the kid looked up. "I tried to leave as much length as I could. Shaped it up some."

The boy wailed in reply.

With the ceramic scissors, Moira snipped the nylon rope neatly in three places, and the bindings fell away. The nanny gave her a fifty-dollar bill and hurried the brat out of there.

"Please come again," Moira said, snipping the scissors at their retreating backs. This was a hostile side of Moira that Adam didn't get to see very often.

"Hi, Adam," she said, sounding weary. She put the ceramic dagger away and reached for a 7UP, sitting in the chair the boy had just vacated, the rope lying at her feet. "Talk to Daryl lately?"

Adam groaned.

"I'll take that as a yes," she said, meeting his eyes. Lately she'd been using a dark brown mascara and applying it with greater skill than what he remembered in junior high. Her eyes were tar pits, boy traps. His spine melted.

Adam sat in a vinyl chair under an old-fashioned hair dryer. An employee had sculpted a papier-mâché hand, complete with huge diamond ring, around the bowl of the dryer. When it was down, it looked like a giant was picking the customer up by the head.

"I drove by there today, on my way to work," Moira said. "There were cop cars in front of the house."

"What?" Adam said, jumping up. His head barely missed the dryer's right index finger.

"Sit down," Moira said. Adam sat. "You can't do anything about it now. Whatever went on over there, just be glad we weren't there when it happened."

"How many cars?" Adam asked.

"Four or five."

Then he remembered the dark feeling, which strengthened now with Moira's eyewitness account. "I knew we should never have gone over there."

"And that's exactly what you said last night when we left. And I'll bet that's what you've been saying all day."

Adam shrugged.

She pointed at him with her finger, its false, silver nail as long and menacing as a Bowie knife. "Well, get over it! You are not Daryl's keeper. Whatever grave he's digging is only big enough for one."

Adam looked the other way. "And my mother's a cop."

"Exactly!" Moira said.

"But that's not what's bothering me," Adam said, and turned to look at her. He felt very young and very vulnerable right then, as if her eyes had become the twin barrels of a shotgun. "I know it's best for me to just get away from him. Hell, he's even started pushing me away. On the phone today, he didn't even want to talk to me."

"That's not surprising," she said, examining her nail with ostentatious care. "He probably felt like shit."

"He sure sounded it," Adam said. *Cops?*

Moira pulled out a bottle of silver fingernail polish and began repairing a chip on her dagger. "Talk to your mom today?"

"No, and I need to. She might know what's going on over there. In a way, I hope she hasn't heard anything yet."

"Why?" she asked, blowing on the nail.

"She's in homicide."

"Oh," Moira said. "Anyway, since last night was such a bust, do you feel like doing something tonight?"

Adam stared at her breasts.

She noticed. "Besides *that.*"

He shook himself out of the trance, his face reddening with an instant embarrassment-rash. Moira giggled, a high-pitched trill that pierced .50-caliber holes in his young male ego. *She saw me staring at her! What else does she know about me?*

Gathering as much composure as was possible in three seconds, Adam said, "Come over after work and we'll decide. How 'bout . . . ?"

"A movie?"

"Or something. Anything besides a party." Adam rolled his eyes. "Had enough of those for a while."

A little old lady with a walker hobbled into the shop. "Time for me to get back to work," she said, blowing him a kiss.

Now what was that *supposed to mean?* Adam smiled, feeling a longing that started from his dry throat and reached down past his belly. Sweat broke out on his chest. He left before other portions of his anatomy betrayed him.

Filled with confusion, Adam left the shop and merged with the sea of humanity which filed out of the Market-place, now that happy hour was over. Soon, his own age group would start showing up at the Yaz. Perhaps, he hoped, with news of the situation at the Wintons'.

In the mall he bumped into a kid who, he first thought, was Daryl. He wore a black tank top and a bandana around his dark hair, which Daryl often did, but this boy was a few years younger, maybe fourteen, and more slender. He didn't react to being jostled. Then slowly, he looked up at Adam, his expression dreamy and distant. And smiled.

What is this kid on? Adam thought, disgusted. He tried to walk past, but the boy grabbed his arm with amazing strength. Instead of reacting the way he wanted to, which was to take a swing at him, he looked directly into his face.

I know you. Your name is Cory. You're not even in high school yet.

No one around them seemed to notice what was going on, not even the security guard who walked past. He felt invisible in the mall, which pulsated with people. He tried to push past the stoned kid, but his grip was like steel.

". . . it's like, the sky opened up, and Gabriel tore loose with horns of brass. And Armageddon was here. And the black Eagle saw the ruined castle, and all the dead within waited for the night to take the palace." Cory hesitated, then said, "And you were there. And you did not die."

Adam stared at him. His pupils were enormous. And the whites, for a moment, glowed.

Where is that security guard? Adam thought frantically. Cory released him, and Adam staggered backward a few steps.

"Is the bus here yet?" Cory asked. "I was out to lunch."

You're still out to lunch, Adam thought. Cory's breath stank of cheap beer and something else. Then, *this guy needs help. Why are all the addicts flocking around me today?* He remembered Daryl. *And last night.*

"Have some of this," Cory said, handing him a small glass vial with a black stopper. Adam didn't know what it was until he examined it. *Crack. Why the hell did he give me this?*

Then something about the black stopper triggered his memory. *Black stopper. Street name, Black Dream. Mom told me about this.*

"No, I don't think . . ." Adam began, but Cory started walking away.

"Hey," he said to Cory's back. The kid kept walking, till he vanished down the stairs. Then, *Hell, let him go. I don't want to give this back to him anyway.*

But what to do with it? A security camera pivoted toward him, and he realized the entire exchange was probably on tape somewhere. *Great. Now I gotta get rid of this.* If he didn't get rid of the vial, security might bust him.

The trash can was out of the question. *Doesn't really go*

anywhere. Nonchalantly, he started toward the rest rooms. *Damn you, Cory*.

The commode made a gratifying *sploooosh* as the contraband vanished into the Dallas sewer system. He flushed again to be certain. It occurred to him he might have hung on to it for his mother to examine, but if he were caught with it, he doubted she would be able to bail him out. Even if she could, it would be an awkward situation, one his mother didn't need. Being a cop was hard enough without having to fix charges against your son.

The hallway just outside the johns was vacant, and he concluded that no one was after him. They knew him here; he was clean, and he was, to the off duty cops who moonlighted there, family. *Still. Better safe than sorry*.

From the rest room, he should have turned right to return to the Yaz. That's where he needed to be. Instead, he hesitated and took note of his surroundings. The walls in the corridor were painted white, with blue on the lower half. The effect, he assumed, made the space look larger than it was.

Why am I going down here? he thought as he turned left. *I need to get back to work*.

The encounter with Cory left an acrid taste in his mouth. He felt tainted, as if whatever drug or drugs the boy was on had transferred to his bloodstream. Cory's breath had been foul, and he wondered if he had inhaled something evil, intoxicating; he felt a desperate need to take a shower, run laps, something, anything.

What's wrong with me? he thought. *This is crazy. There's no way he could have infected me*. But his feelings told him something different. He felt . . . poisoned. *Cory, what did you do to me?*

Got to get back to the Yaz. Biz is picking up. Spence doesn't even have the bank yet. Got to . . .

But he couldn't. He proceeded down the hallway with the white and blue walls, toward another area of the Marketplace, a large space that hadn't been leased yet. He'd seen it before, a nice large room with lots of exposed ducts and hanging lights, the ubiquitous concrete columns. Six large rectangular windows, eight panes, about a foot square, in each. *This would make an excellent nightclub, good dancing, even bet the acoustics are favorable.* . . . The place reminded him of an old gymnasium, with the high ceiling, wooden floors. Only thing missing was the basketball hoops. Here, in this unoccupied space, he smelled the age of the building, something he missed in the other shops, which had new equipment and furnishings and goods, all made in the last ten years. Ancient and earthy; Adam sensed something reaching from below, several floors down, past the basement.

His mind glazed over with a mixture of exhaustion, confusion, and a lingering surge of hormones from his talk with Moira. If perhaps he had caught some secondhand something from Cory, he could imagine how messed up the kid was. A lightness seized him, as if he were suddenly a hundred pounds lighter, or if he were drifting away; but no, his sneakered feet still touched the wooden floor. Though his knees felt like wet sponges, they firmly supported him.

Thin trails of smoke poured from the vents, but he didn't assume this meant fire; he found the sight tranquilizing, not alarming, as it might have been under other circumstances.

But what's happening now? he thought, and a small part of him told him it was nothing, this was as natural and necessary as the sun rising in the morning.

The smoke was actually fog, heavy fog, which clung to the wooden floor and spread out from several points. Sunlight pouring in from outside flickered, dimmed, as if dark storm clouds masked the sun. The round hanging lights simply ceased to be on, though he didn't remember when they switched off.

At some point the voice within him that fought against the change gave in and allowed him to go with this new experience. He felt comforted and safe, despite the strangeness of what he was seeing. What it was he saw remained vague, and at the same time he knew that he was not capable of comprehending any further.

Just below the surface of the fog, which continued to spread in a layer, lights flickered. A circle of small fires formed in the center of the fog.

He tried to count the candles, but found he could not focus long enough to do so. While the atmosphere felt safe and protective, he found that his mind was muddled beyond use. On a deeper level, the inability to use his mind disturbed him, but the reassuring inner voice calmed him, explained to him that it wasn't necessary to think right now.

He heard the thought, *I will understand when I need to,* and allowed it to become his own.

Adam closed his eyes, because that was what his thoughts told him to do. He was no longer in control, and nothing in him suggested he do anything but surrender. He found sanctuary in this sudden loss of control, knowing that whatever this power was, it would not harm him. With his eyes closed against the fog and the candlelight, he felt time drift, like a light breeze brushing against his skin.

He did not know how much time had actually passed. Staring at the empty room, Adam wondered if he imagined the entire psychotic episode.

Time to get back to work, he thought. *Weird doesn't even begin to describe what just happened.*

Chapter Four

To distract himself from the itchy rash which etched itself on his upper body, Daryl scribbled random words on a paper napkin with a number two pencil.

Detectives are pricks.

He erased the "pr" of *pricks* and was about to replace it with another consonant when one of the detectives came back into the dining room, holding a pen and notepad. Daryl had been sitting in the hard oak chair for hours while cops went over the Winton mansion, trying to amuse himself while praying to the gods they didn't find anything.

The several ambulances and fire department paramedics had left an hour earlier, after managing to load all the victims in the trucks; some openly wondered if they would have to make two trips. One boy wasn't quite dead, or so the medical examiner said, though he sure could have fooled Daryl. The CareFlight helicopter came and left with the one survivor, the fifteen-year-old kid named Colm. Everyone alive, or dead, was en route to the morgue or the trauma ward at Parkland.

Except, of course, Daryl. The police had many things they wanted to ask him.

From the kitchen he heard a cop retching his guts out, perhaps in the sink. Daryl frowned, annoyed.

They never seen dead bodies before? What gives? He yawned, and tried to get comfortable in the heavy dining room chair. No easy task, particularly when dealing with the early stages of a class-A hangover.

The detective calmly took a seat next to him, turning the chair out to face him. The man feigned patience, but Daryl saw the mask for what it was. For some reason the air-conditioning had quit working in the house around six that afternoon, and everyone inside had started to melt. Odors Daryl had never smelled before greeted his nostrils, antagonizing his already unhappy stomach. The detective wore a pinstripe business suit, but had shed the coat and vest soon after arriving, having apparently seen it would be a long ordeal. In his crossdraw shoulder harness Daryl saw an angry looking .45 automatic. Huge wet stains appeared under his arms, and while he could have been no older than thirty-five, he bore an uncomfortable resemblance to Daryl's father.

And his father had no patience, and would have resorted to knocking the crap out of him long ago to obtain the answers this detective now seemed to want.

The detective looked up, wearily, with perspiration pouring off his forehead. He glanced once at the paper napkin, wadded it up, and with no expression whatsoever, bounced it off Daryl's forehead.

The casual gesture frightened Daryl more than it should have. *Is this guy getting ready to beat me up after all?* he wondered. *Or is he just trying to psych me out?*

With a neutral, bored tone, the detective asked, "So tell me, Daryl, where's all the cocaine all you bad boys and girls were smoking and snorting last night?"

Daryl shrugged. "Beats me. We just had some wine coolers. I got drunk and passed out in the backyard. When I woke up, I came in here and found everyone dead."

The phone, which had been ringing off the hook since the cops arrived, rang again. Daryl knew they were trying to locate the parents of the dead kids, but were having little luck. They all seemed to be . . . unavailable.

Maybe this was one of them finally returning a call. . . .

The cop eyed him uncomfortably for a long, long time.

Daryl was impressed with himself at how long he was able to stare the man down without blinking.

"How do you know they're dead, Daryl?" The cop smirked.

"Guessed," he said. Through a bay window he watched a fire truck pull away. "Maybe it had something to do with the way they weren't moving very much."

The detective shook his head. "Godammit," he said. "Don't you feel *any*thing? They were your *friends!*"

Daryl's gaze remained fixed on the fire truck as it trundled down the long, long driveway to the automatic gate. "Not anymore," he said, with a yawn.

The cop stared at him. "You really don't feel anything, do you?" His face flushed red. "This isn't an act."

"I told you what happened. . . ." Daryl replied, getting irritated. *He's giving me a taste of the lecture I'm gonna get when I get home. Great. That stuff all over again.*

A uniformed officer stuck his head in the dining room. "Roach. Phone call. It's the boy's father."

Daryl snickered. "Roach. Pretty cool name for a cop, if you ask me."

"I'm not asking," Roach said. The cop got to his feet slowly. "The drugs have eaten your soul, lad. They really have. And you're only seventeen."

"Eighteen," Daryl corrected. "Yesterday."

"Oh, well ex*cuse* me. *Eight*een. All grown up and knowing everything. No more juvenile detention. When you go down, you go down in the big boys' jail." Then, apparently as an amusing afterthought, he added, "And they're gonna *love* you." He left the room to take the call.

Boy's father. Wonder if that's Winton. Then, a disturbing thought. *Maybe it's* my *father.* His stomach turned again at the possibility.

A few moments later, Roach returned, smiling. This made Daryl nervous. "Now I know who you are," the cop announced cheerfully. "I *thought* your name was a little too familiar."

Inside, Daryl groaned. He'd debated whether or not to

reveal the fact that his lawyer was also his father, and a high-priced one at that. But the police departments of Northeast Texas didn't like Paul Bendis, as he had so successfully defended an army of drug dealers in the past ten years, effectively keeping them on the street. So Daryl had decided to stay mute on the subject and leave the scene as soon as they let him.

As long as they don't find anything, they can't keep me. I at least know that much.

"Yeah, well, who am I?"

Roach looked around, and raised his voice when he said, "You're Paul Bendis' son. The lawyer. The crooked lawyer."

Three heads in the hallway looked up. "Say what?" one of them said.

"You all heard me. *The* Paul Bendis. This is his boy."

Paul suddenly felt like a black man at a KKK rally.

Another suit came over, one who had spent most of his time upstairs. This alone made him nervous, since Daryl hadn't gone over Steve's room very thoroughly, and this cop probably had. The detective was older, heavier, and louder than Detective Roach. He puffed on a long, obnoxious cigar that looked like a turd.

"Well, well," the detective said. "I was rather hoping to catch Bendis in the act, but I think his son will do for now."

"You haven't caught me at anything," Daryl said. "I know my rights. And my father knows them better than I do."

"Sure, sure," he said. "Looks like someone really went over this house with a comb. Say, I found glass shards in the commode upstairs. That wouldn't have been a pipe, would it?"

Daryl shrugged. "Don't know. You're the cops, you tell me."

Roach said, "Now that we know who Daryl is, I think we should go over the place just one more time. No telling what we might find."

"Yeah. No telling." They both started laughing.

Through the bay window Daryl noticed a charcoal-gray Chevy Caprice, the cop car of choice, pull in beside nine identical Caprices, five of them black and whites, in front of the Winton mansion. With the cars already out there from last night's party, cops were having to park on the lawn. It was getting a little full out there. Daryl squirmed, noting the time of day, feeling a little anxious. He'd started to come down big-time an hour ago, and he didn't like it one bit.

This one pulled in where the fire truck had pulled out. A well-dressed lady cop got out, a cop Daryl had known for years.

Sammi McDaris. Adam's mother. Daryl wanted to hide.

I smell the death already. Sammi grimaced as she pulled in front of the Wintons' mansion, finding the one parking space that wasn't taken by either a cop or a recently deceased teenager.

She had heard the report of nineteen overdoses, probable DOA's, over the radio. At least one of the kids survived and called the cops that afternoon. Several TV crews had set up shop in front of the gate, where a cop stood guard, letting only official people onto the grounds. "Not enough parking," he explained. The satellite city spread down half a block, an instant community of vans, trucks, satellite dishes, and well-dressed men talking into vidcams. Clearly, Sammi wasn't the only one listening to the cop frequencies that afternoon.

Sammi worked homicide, and even though this didn't sound like a murder, she called her commander and convinced him to let her check it out.

"I know some of the kids involved," she'd said. "I might be able to help. Sir."

What she couldn't say was, "and my son was at that party last night, and might have died along with them. I want to know what the hell happened. Sir."

Last night Sammi quizzed Adam on the "party," knowing it would be less than wholesome. Adam had replied that it was supposed to be drug-free, and she'd shrugged, and let it go at that. Her willingness to let him go had much to do with specialized spells she renewed on a weekly basis, which would alert her if he ingested any drugs, including alcohol. If the "alarm" went off, there were other things available to her, allowing her to spy or protect, should the need arise.

Adam returned unusually early from the party and told her the whole story, that drugs appeared and he just left, "bored with the whole thing," but she saw genuine disgust in Adam. Either disgust, or disappointment in Daryl.

She wanted to seize the opportunity to drive home the message that Daryl was slipping beyond their reach, and he would be doing himself a favor by cutting loose from him completely. But to do so might have alienated Adam. That was not a chance she wanted to take just at the moment.

Admitting her son's involvement in the Winton party at the household the night before would simply not enhance her image of being a good single parent. But what she *really* couldn't say was, "My son Adam is actually an elf, an elf *prince*, and I am his sister, also an elf. . . ."

As she got out of the car, she sensed not only death, but a hideous, dark magic at work here, a darkness that went beyond the evil capable of humans. She paused, fighting a wave of nausea.

The Unseleighe were here, she thought. *They must have been. And recently, too. Last night?*

When she entered the house, the feeling of Unseleighe power grew. *Adam should never have been here. Had they known who he was, they would have killed him.*

"What happened to the air-conditioning?" she said to the first officer she saw, who looked rather pale. She sniffed, and realized why.

"There were four bodies in that bedroom. Looks like some kind of orgy gone terribly bad," he said, gesturing across a broad marble hallway to what looked like a master bedroom.

"I'll say," she said, trying to hide her horror. *Adam was here last night. Gods, we've got to be more careful.*

The cop handed her a set of Polaroids. The detectives

usually took these in addition to the official crime scene photos, to show officers like herself who came in late. She stared, morbidly fascinated by the looks of terror on their faces, as if they had all seen the same dreadful apparition.

That's not a typical phenomenon of drug OD's, she thought, flipping through the photos. *Each bad trip is a little different, and they've never included "mass hallucinations." These kids died with their eyes open, looking in the same direction, in the same way. Very strange and disturbing, indeed.*

"Where is the young man who called this in?" she asked. "Where's Daryl Bendis?"

"Over there, in the dining room," the cop said, and shuffled off, leaving the photos with Sammi, who tucked them away in her purse.

Daryl didn't look up when she entered the dining room, an opulent setting with lots of crystal and silver, a traditional buffet, a lead crystal chandelier: all of the trappings of wealth.

The boy sat at the head of the table, shirtless with a blotchy sunburn, looking like he'd just wakened. He was also pasty pale, but this was a pallor he'd been working on for some time and not unique to this afternoon. Sammi suspected the boy's increased party schedule had something to do with it.

"So what goes, Daryl?" Sammi said sternly. "You're the one who called this in?"

Daryl looked up, sneering. "You already know, or you wouldn't be here," he said.

This human's insolence will soon kill him, she thought. *This human* child. *Who happens to be one of Adam's best "friends."* She shook her head.

Her voice lowered. "What the hell happened, Daryl?"

He looked down, visibly fighting annoyance. "Look, it happened like this. Steve threw this party for me, see, and I got a little drunk, went out to the backyard, and passed out." He pointed at his hairless chest, at the bars of pink flesh. "In the gazebo. The sun coming through gave me this burn. When I woke up, I came into the house and found everyone, well, dead."

Sammi nodded, figuring part of what he'd said was true. Over the years they'd had similar conversations over less serious issues; Daryl was an expert at telling the truth, and even better at leaving out important details.

"How did they die, Daryl?" She was trying not to sound confrontational.

"I don't know, ask them," he said, pointing toward the cops in the kitchen. "I'm already on their bad guy list because my dad's a lawyer," he added.

"Was it cocaine? Crack?" she asked, knowing this was probably the case. When Daryl didn't reply, she said, "Did you sell it to them, Daryl?"

"Nope," he said, looking out the bay window. "And that's all you're gonna get out of me, Mrs. McDaris. You're a cop, and your buddies have been giving me a pretty hard time. Leave me alone."

Samantha seethed, but held her temper. *I need to know.* "You don't know what a hard time is, Daryl. You will when you go to prison."

Daryl looked up. *"Huh?"*

"If they find so much as a *trace* of drugs around here, and we suspect you're not cooperating, you're going down. You're not a juvenile anymore. As of today, you're legally an adult. Am I right?"

Reluctantly, Daryl nodded.

"And if you take big boy chances, you can pay big boy prices."

The boy squirmed, and a bead of perspiration dripped off his forehead. "Well . . ." he said.

"Tell me what happened last night and I might be able to cut you some slack," she lied. This had nothing to do with homicide yet, and she doubted she could be very persuasive. There was a great deal of territory and turf-fighting within the department, even among the different munici-palities. One of the detectives working this particular scene, Roach, was not one she got along with too well, and therefore couldn't influence, except maybe with reverse psychology . . . and a little elven magic, if it were worth the trouble. She hadn't seen Roach yet, but heard him, shooting the breeze with someone else in the kitchen. She had the feeling he was intentionally ignoring her, which was just as well, as she wanted to talk to Daryl privately.

"Before I went into the backyard . . ." Daryl began, lowering his voice. He apparently didn't want anyone else to hear. "There were these weird dudes who showed up at the place. Steve didn't know how they got past the gate, because no one we knew had opened it. You have to do it from a button at the front door, or in the kitchen. There's a speaker for an intercom there, too. Anyway, they were in leather and chains, which really isn't our style, and looked scary. Steve tried to throw them out. They had this little bag of something, some drugs, and they spread it all around. Steve decided to let them stay."

"What was this stuff?" Sammi said.

"Well, I didn't get a good look at it. I didn't even touch it. But it was this little black-stoppered vial. Never seen *black* stoppers before."

She knew what he was talking about. *Black Dream. Were those Unseleighe elves who crashed the party last night?*

"Okay, Daryl, you're not in any trouble. But I need to know about these guys. I think they're passing bad drugs. How many were there?"

The boy looked around the corner, toward the kitchen. "Bad drugs? Never thought of that. Well, there were four, I think. One of them was big and blond, with chains connected to his wrist and waist. He had a pierced nose. Diamond stud in it. Something like that."

"You said four. Any names?"

Daryl seemed to really consider this. "Don't think so. I mean, I didn't hear any. I got pissed off or something right around then, that's when I went into the backyard." He looked up at her and said with conviction when their eyes met, "Honest, Mrs. McDaris. I didn't tell those other cops because they've been so shitty to me."

She saw, for a moment, the boy she once knew. The old Daryl stumbled through the druggy murk just long enough for some sincerity to leak through. And she believed him.

"Well, you'd better start being a little more cooperative," she said. "I know you have the right to remain silent, but if you start turning in some names right about now, it could go easier on you."

"Don't ask me to do that," Daryl said resolutely. "I won't do that."

"Yeah, I know," she said, standing. "They'll kill you if you do. Great friends you have there, Daryl."

Daryl squirmed so much she thought he would fall out of the chair. "Let me think about it. I might tell you, but not those guys. Think you could go see what they have on me?"

Looking out for his own hide, she thought angrily. *After nineteen of his friends just died.* She studied him for a long time, trying to figure out if he was being honest or had gotten much better at lying. She might have touched his mind with elven magic to get to the truth immediately, but to do so might alert any Unseleighe in the area. With no other choice, she assumed that for the time being he was on the level.

"I'll go see what they have," she said. "But if they haven't found anything by now, they probably won't. But this isn't your house, Daryl. How do you know you cleaned out everything?"

Daryl turned paler than pale.

Sammi went into the kitchen to talk with the others. Daryl heard her make a wry comment about the vomit in the sink and accused Roach of having a weak stomach.

Meanwhile, bugs started to crawl up Daryl's legs. He squirmed and scratched, and lifted his pants leg up to see if there really were bugs, but it was only the hangover. If he didn't go party somewhere soon, it would get much worse.

After the brief chat in the kitchen, Sammi left without confirming whether or not they found anything to charge him with.

A moment later, Roach came into the dining room and dropped a baggie of white powder on the table in front of him.

"Got any idea what that is, kiddo?"

Daryl eyed the baggie like a starving man would a steak.

That looks really good. Wonder if they'll let me do any of it?

The other, logical part of him started to get frightened. *Oh, no. I'm going to jail after all. Where the hell did his parents stash that?*

"Well, I'll give you a little hint. It goes with donuts."

Daryl eyed the baggie closer, caught a whiff of sweetness. *Powdered sugar.*

"You assholes," Daryl said without emotion. But the powdered sugar reminded him that he had an appointment Tuesday at one of his dealer's safe houses to pick up some *real* coke, lots of it. But that was a day away. *What am I going to do until then?*

Roach said, "You bet we're assholes. Professional assholes, you might say." The cops laughed uproariously. "Looks like the house is clean, sonny. This time, you managed to get everything. Truly remarkable."

Daryl got to his feet, a bold move, since he hadn't given him permission yet. "Can I leave now?"

"I suppose so," Roach said, acting as if he'd been deprived of some entertainment. "Looks like your dad's not going to show up."

No, I doubt it. Daryl thought. *Especially if he's coked up, too. Gets real paranoid around cops.*

"We know where you live. Since there are no witnesses to speak of, I'd say you're in the clear. But we have your number, Daryl. We'll be watching you. And we're going to get you."

Daryl found the rest of his clothes, which had turned up during the drug search, and got into his '94 Corvette. Since everybody else was driving on the lawn, as evidenced by several tire tracks in the grass, he no longer considered himself blocked in by the Mustang. He drove over the grass, a flower bed, and urged his beast onto the driveway. As he neared the gate, he gave the ghouls there the finger and sped on, ignoring the gaggle of reporters and vidcams.

He didn't want to go home. He wanted to go somewhere, anywhere, and get good and fucked up. After all, this had been a crappy day, and he deserved it. But if he did that, Dad would certainly beat the tar out of him. At this point, if he went directly home and convinced Dad he wasn't in trouble, he stood a fifty-fifty chance of avoiding injury.

His father's new BMW was parked in the driveway when he pulled in, and he considered driving on, but decided to go ahead and get it over with. He pulled up next to the Beamer and tried to make himself more presentable in his rearview mirror; he looked, and felt, like hell.

Depressed and shaky, he entered the house. In many ways it was much like the Wintons' mansion, except smaller. He made a beeline for the stairwell, which led to his bedroom upstairs. Before he reached the second step, his father's voice boomed from the living room.

"Daryl. Get in here."

Damn, he thought. His knees turned into marshmallows. The chances of making it to his room had been, to say the least, slim. But it had been worth a shot.

Paul Bendis sat on the sofa with a tumbler of scotch in one hand, a lit cigarette in another. Daryl came in and sat on a love seat across from him, and tried to look less hung over than he was.

He didn't fool anyone. "Son, you look like hell," Paul said, taking a large sip from the scotch. "What happened over at the Wintons' last night?"

Daryl got as comfortable as possible, resigned to his fate. *How much does he already know?* he wondered, searching his father's face for clues. Paul looked tired, but somewhat mellowed, due in no small part to the scotch. An empty bottle of Chivas Regal lay at his feet. A paper of coke sat on the mirror-topped coffee table. Traces of white powder remained, shadows of the lines now embedded somewhere in Paul's nasal passages.

Daryl's nostrils itched; his mouth watered. The bugs returned with a vengeance, crawling up one leg, then both.

"Did you *hear* me?" his father said, his voice rising. *"What happened over there?"*

Daryl shook himself from the trance the coke held him in. "Uhn, sorry. At the Wintons'. It was just a party. Wine coolers, beer."

"Any coke?"

"No, but I think there was Pepsi. . . ."

An ashtray whizzed over his head and smashed against the wall behind him. The object cleared his head by maybe an inch; he felt its breeze when it passed.

"Don't get *cute*," Paul said, now looking for someplace to put out his cigarette. He gave up and snuffed it into the glass top, as Daryl had seen him do many times when he was drunk. "I thought you said you were going over to Adam's last night. To *study*."

Oh, yeah, he thought. *Forgot about that.* "Well, we did," he added, hoping that this enhancement to the lie would dig his grave no deeper. *"Then* we went to the party." He became frantic as he tried to remember what happened before he went out, what he'd said, when he'd left. It was all a blank up until just before he went out to the Wintons' backyard and zonked out. And, of course, he remembered waking up and finding the bodies. But none of that really mattered now.

He remembered very little, and that made him nervous. These lapses in memory had recently become more frequent, but since his friends had them, too, he didn't really see anything alarming about it. *Unless you're trying to con your way out of a situation . . .*

"There were deaths over there," Paul said. "Lots of deaths. You'd better start remembering quick. I've had a bad day and I'm not in the mood for your childish crap."

You've had a bad day? Geeeez. Tell me about it!

"Okay, okay," Daryl said, thinking as fast as he could

under the circumstances. "I think they got ahold of some bad dope."

Paul nodded, as if he'd suspected it all along. "And?"

"And it looks like it did them in. I wasn't doing any of it. If I had, I'd be dead, too."

Which was true. He'd passed out drunk before he could do any of it.

Paul rubbed his face with his hands. "Good God, Daryl. Do you have any idea how much trouble you've caused me? Your mother called me in hysterics, said something about murders, then it turns out your friends just did some bad stuff. Really bad stuff. What did the cops say?"

"They looked everywhere," Daryl said, but something about his father's attitude was depressing him. No, not his attitude. What he *wasn't* saying. *Nineteen people just died, and I'm the only one from the party to walk away alive. And he didn't even ask me if I was okay.*

"Did they find anything?"

"Nope. Guess, well, I'll tell you what I did."

"I think you had better."

"I got rid of it all. Flushed it down the toilet. Went through the entire house."

Paul's eyes rolled upward, in apparent relief. "That's the first smart thing you've done all year. Evidently they didn't charge you with anything."

"They didn't *find* anything."

Paul shook his head, annoyed. "That only means they're going to be watching your young butt, son. What the hell are you doing with drugs anyway? You're too young to be doing that crap. If you ever went down for something, I'm the one responsible, not you, not until you turn eighteen! Where are your *brains?*"

Eighteen? he thought. *Doesn't he know my birthday was yesterday?*

"Dad, I turned eighteen yesterday," Daryl said, getting a little angry. Dad had completely forgot.

Paul glanced at his watch. "You did? I thought . . ." Then he shook his head. Now, he was smiling. "So you're *not* my problem after all. You're an adult now. If you screw up, you get to pay for it."

"That's right," Daryl said. "I pay for it. Why are you getting so uptight about it?"

"Don't talk back to me, Daryl," Paul said, his voice even and low, menacing. "You're still living under my roof, eating my food, with my rules, and if you keep this crap up, my hours!"

"Okay, Dad, you're right." Daryl looked down at his feet, feigning humility. *Don't you dare lay a curfew on me!*

"I know I'm right! I'm always right, and don't you forget it. I don't care what you do, but stay out of trouble with the cops, and stay out of jail! It's getting harder to defend drug cases these days."

You would know. "I'm sorry. It was just, well, my birthday party, that's why I went."

"Yeah, I know. But you were stupid to go anyway! The *Wintons'* house? You might as well have waved a banner!"

Daryl didn't know what he meant by that, but didn't ask.

Yanni, his mother, came in to the living room. She wore a pair of tight jeans and a halter top, and held a large bottle of Valium.

"Let's just have some meds and calm down, boys," Yanni said, yawning. "You don't have to get all upset over nothing, do you?"

"Honey, we're having a talk. Do you mind?" Paul said, waving her away. Right now, a few of those Valiums looked pretty good to Daryl, but he was a little nervous about asking in front of his dad. He was just so damned unpredictable. He had no idea what his reaction would be.

"Whatever you say, dear," Yanni said, shuffling out of the living room.

When Yanni was gone, Paul said, "If you get thrown in jail, don't bother calling me. I won't come get you." He finished his drink and left the room. Moments later, Daryl heard the BMW start up.

Great. I hope he wrecks it, Daryl thought, getting up to look for the bottle of Valium. He found it next to his parents' bed, where his mother was sound asleep. She'd spilled some of the yellow pills on the table, and at first glance it looked like a suicide attempt. But he knew it wasn't; this happened all the time.

He scooped up three or so of the little pills, knowing it would take at least that many to kill this particular hangover. Normally he would have taken two, but today was a special occasion. Besides, he had a good reason to get good and loaded. Half his friends had just died. He grabbed a 7UP from the fridge, washed the five or so Valiums down, and started for the bathroom to get cleaned up.

Halfway up the carpeted stairs, the universe dropped out from under him.

Chapter Five

"Adam, what's *wrong* with you?" Jimmy said for the second time as Adam counted out the drawer from the first shift. Usually Adam's employer wouldn't hover over him while he tried to do his work, but today was an exception. Spence and Jimmy exchanged looks, which unnerved Adam even more.

"Nothing, just a little tired, is all," Adam said, wanting to believe his own words. Jimmy shook his head, which for him might have had ten different meanings.

The owner seldom showed up on a slow day like Monday, but today was unusual in that it wasn't slow. Adam thought Spence might have called him about the hour lunch he'd inadvertently taken when he went to see Moira, but wasn't sure. They tended to cover for each other when necessary, and calling the boss for any reason was not something Spence would normally do. But then, today had been anything but normal.

Jimmy was nearly forty, but possessed the perpetual youthfulness of many Asians; tall and wiry, he sprinted about the bar at his usual frenetic pace, pouring drinks, making coffee, running the espresso machines. The register had run out of paper, but since it was close to ten anyway, he went ahead and zeed it.

"I'm fine, really," Adam insisted, but a little of his annoyance slipped through his teeth. *Something* is *wrong. I just don't know what it is.*

The missing time bothered him, more because Spence suffered, working a heavy bar alone for an hour, when he should have been there with him to help. As to the incident itself, he felt vaguely disturbed, but not alarmed.

Now he had trouble counting money. As soon as he thought he'd counted a stack of fives, they were actually tens, and he had to start all over. Either the numbers blurred all by themselves or his eyes weren't working. On the fourth attempt, he managed to count all the bills.

Then his steel allergies kicked in with a vengeance. The coins started getting warm, no, *hot*, so much that he had to lay them out on the shelf under the bar and count them with a pencil eraser. Adam had never bothered to tell Jimmy about his steel allergies, as it never seemed necessary. But now the boss gave him strange looks, which made him lose count.

"You know, there is a flu going around," Jimmy said good-naturedly as he untwisted the espresso dispenser. "Working a job like this, I'd bet it'd be easy to pick up."

Adam felt bad, but it wasn't a flu; not that he'd know it if he had one, since he'd never been ill. A few times the Dallas heat made him a little dizzy and dehydrated, but a few minutes in an air-conditioned environment cleared that up. No, it wasn't influenza. *But what the hell is wrong with me?*

"Maybe you'd better go on home," Jimmy said. "I've got a lot of nervous energy today. I can handle the bar tonight. These ten-hour shifts you've been doing might not have been the best idea anyway," Jimmy said, his expression friendly but firm. Jimmy was not making conversation, he was telling him to do something. And he had better do it.

But when Adam looked up, Spence stood a few paces behind Jimmy, gazing at the boss. Spence's eyes glazed over, daydreaming or just plain tired. Adam had seen his friend's zombielike expression before, usually associated with working long hours, but not quite in this context. Sure enough, as Jimmy told him to go home, Adam saw Spence's lips moving silently, mouthing the same words, as if reciting a script for Jimmy to read.

Adam blinked, and what he thought was an odd scene now was not odd at all. Spence shuffled off to the back room. Jimmy poured espresso. A pinstripe-suited businessman read a newspaper at the counter. Music from Pink Floyd's *The Division Bell* trickled softly over the sound system. Business as usual.

Great. Now I'm getting paranoid, Adam thought. *Maybe I'd better go home after all.*

"I don't want to leave you hangin' like this," Adam began. "But at least I finally got the drawer counted. Thought I'd never get this thing tallied."

"Don't give it another thought," Jimmy said as he loaded more paper into the register. "You're doing a terrific job. I don't want you to burn out. You're my head man down here."

"Yeah, well . . . ." He wanted to argue. He didn't feel good about leaving work like this, and under normal circumstances he would argue further. After all, he had car and insurance payments to make. But something within urged him to go home without complaint.

"*Go,*" Jimmy said. "We'll survive."

Adam nodded and winced at the headache he felt coming on, the kind usually brought on by proximity to caffeine, but he hadn't been anywhere near it. *Allergies are in overdrive. Never this bad before. What gives?* Adam frowned, wondering what this might mean for his continued employment at the Yaz.

As he left the Marketplace, he ran into Moira coming back in. She looked frantic, and perhaps a bit pissed off about something, but at that moment, incredibly sexy.

"My pile-of-junk car won't start," she said suddenly, waving a plastic key ring in the air. "Can you give me a lift home?"

Adam smiled as many different scenarios sprouted from his active imagination.

"Sure," he said. "I'm on my way home now."

"This early?"

Adam shrugged. "Boss let me off," he said, not going into

any detail. *If she thought I was coming down with something, which I'm not, then* . . . He considered telling her about the missing time, but thought better of it. Adam wanted to put the whole incident behind him and get on with his life.

"Want to come over for a while?" Adam ventured. He was taking a gamble that Mom might be there, but she tended to work until at least ten or eleven. Of course, Moira had been over before, for dinner and movies, as a friend. His throat dried up, and his heart pounded in his ears as he considered something beyond that.

If Moira noticed, she pretended not to. "Well, we were going to go do something, remember? I don't have to go home."

"You look just *terrific*," he said, hoping he wasn't being too obvious. "What about your car?"

"I've got a mechanic coming over tomorrow to look at it. I'm about ready to drive it off a cliff. Empty, of course. If it can even *make* it to a cliff."

Adam nodded, grateful she hadn't asked him to look at it. He knew one thing about cars, and that was that the engine blocks were one big chunk of steel. Poking around under a hood would be the equivalent of sticking his hand in a blast furnace.

Adam's car was a new Geo Metro, a three-cylinder with a turquoise paint job. The door handles were plastic, as were most of the surfaces inside, a main selling point with him. It was the least painful for him to drive, easily insured despite his age, and the most affordable in payments and gas. Since he always went to full-service gas stations, to avoid handling the metal gas spouts, he needed to milk as much mileage out of his car as possible.

Moira had a little trouble getting her huge hair into the tiny car, mashing it against the car's roof in order to fit.

"How's your car holding up?" Moira said as she fiddled with the vents. "Must be nice having air-conditioning."

"It still feels new," he said. "Gets me where I need to go."

Adam dropped in a Blancmange tape, wishing he had bothered to put in a more impressive sound system, the one thing about an automobile that would have impressed Moira. She didn't much care for the large muscle cars or even slick sports cars, but she did love music, Blancmange in particular.

"So you went and got this," she said, looking over the cassette case. "Like it?"

"Love it," he said, really meaning it, even if he originally bought it in the event he drove her anywhere.

"Ever talk to your mom?"

Adam had forgotten all about calling her. He now realized that, since the weird experience in the empty mall space, he'd forgotten about the whole incident at the Wintons'. "Not yet," he replied.

With Moira so close to him, and catching occasional whiffs of her perfume, he forgot about Daryl and the whole sordid mess at the Wintons'. *It's not my problem,* he thought. *Daryl can take care of himself.*

"Moira, we've been friends for a long time." Adam heard his mouth working, and was uncertain where the words were coming from. "I don't know how to tell you this, except that I think you're really attractive."

Moira turned to look at him slowly, resolutely. He felt his male ego and other things withering under her look, like an African violet in direct sunlight. And he immediately wished time travel was possible, so he could recall the words.

"I don't know what to say," Moira said, obviously flustered. "I'm flattered. I'm sort of surprised. I mean, I thought you might have had something for Spence."

What?

"Spence is a good friend," Adam said quickly. "But I don't think about him, well, *that* way."

"Oh," she said. "But you do like me. *That* way."

He was about to say something, but his throat constricted. Had he spoken, it would have come out a squeak, and he knew it. He made do with a simple nod.

They rode in a terrible silence. A string of firecrackers going off in the backseat would have been a welcome relief of the quiet that fell between them, despite the music.

The tape switched over to side B before she said, "We are going to your house, aren't we?"

"Do you want to?" he said nervously. Then quickly amended, "Go to my house, I mean."

She gave him a sly, mischievous look that made the hair on the back of his neck stand up. "Only if you have condoms."

Stunned, Adam focused on the road. *Did I really hear that? Did she really say that? I don't believe it!* The smile that spread on his face threatened to squeeze his eyes shut. *Sure am glad I got that box of condoms to practice with. . .*

"Don't look so surprised," Moira said casually. "You've been doing some, well, growing in the past year. And I've noticed."

He pulled into the drive of their modest home in the burbs, a four-bedroom brick house on Doucette Street, a few blocks off Cedar Springs. In an otherwise older section of Dallas, a developer built a whole street of new homes, each unit a mixture of contemporary and 1940's architecture. Their driveway was a horseshoe of brick, which swung around to a garage on the side. The house itself was white stucco with an oriental roof of white tile. Though not as luxurious as some of the older, larger homes a few blocks to the north, their home was above the standard of the average police officer. His mom's Taurus was nowhere to be seen.

As sex became an immediate prospect, Adam's knees threatened to buckle when he got out of the Geo. Moira grinned, reminding him of a predator, swooping in for the kill.

"Looks like your mom's somewhere else," Moira said, taking Adam by the arm. The gesture seemed to support him as much as anything; he felt dizzy suddenly. Dots clouded his vision.

"You're not a virgin, are you, Adam?" she asked.

"Huh?"

She giggled and pulled him closer. "You heard me."

He dropped the keys in front of the door. Picking them up, he said, "Yes."

"Good," she said. Adam didn't understand that reply at all. In fact, he didn't understand anything right then, as his brain had seized up completely.

He opened the door, fumbled with the keys some more, and dropped them.

"Leave them," Moira said. She closed the door, and they stood silently in the main entrance for a moment. Then Adam looked up, put his arms around her, and closed his eyes.

The kiss lasted an eternity. Somewhere in the base of his spine a light exploded, sending shock waves through his body. She returned the passion, reaching around his back and running dagger fingernails up and down his inflamed spine.

Beyond his closed eyelids he perceived a flash of light, like a camera bulb. The kiss closed, and he leaned back, his eyes still shut.

"You've done this before," she whispered, her breath brushing against his cheek.

He opened his eyes a bit, and noticed something different in her blurred image. Their noses were touching; their arms wrapped around one another.

When his eyes opened all the way, he stared.

Her eyes, which were once dark blue, had become emerald with no whites. The pupils, dilated, stretched vertically, in slits.

The rush of hormones leveled out and finally drained from his system, replaced now with a confused fear. Slowly, he drew further from her. Her arms relaxed, fell to her sides. Adam's arms released her, but remained in position, as if he were clutching a thick force field surrounding her.

The tips of her ears extended a full two inches above her enormous hair, tapering to points.

Adam stared. He stopped breathing, afraid to speak, afraid to move. No coherent thoughts formed as he stared at Moira, her eyes, her ears. Frozen in place, he felt the blood draining from him, the strangeness of the situation spraying ice water on his fire.

"My name is Ethlinn," she breathed, a slight smile creasing her alien features.

Light clouded his vision, and he became vaguely aware of his body folding into a heap on the floor. She grabbed his arms, breaking his fall, seconds before he passed out.

Presto pulled his '82 Camaro with the bashed-in front fender into the hidden recesses of a dark, empty alley, parked, and turned the engine off.

"I *said*, he'll *be* here," he said to the kid sitting next to him. "Do you think you can shut up for at least a minute?"

"Yeah yeah yeah . . ." the boy said, sounding bored. "Look, I told you, I've done this before. I know what I'm doing." His hair was long and matted, and his eyes wild and crazed. Presto hadn't wanted to take this kid under his wing and make him his new middleman, but his former lieutenant, Monk, now in jail for unpaid tickets, said he was clean and never did product. Presto had doubts, and expressed these to Monk, who replied offhandedly that Mikey was just naturally insane.

"But you don't *know* this dude," Presto said. The boy irritated him. He reflected that it would be easier to make the exchange himself, go home, and start stepping on a ki of coke by himself, without Mikey's help. But he needed to train a middleman, if only a temporary one, and acquaint him with his supplier. Until Monk got out of jail, he would have to make do with temps.

He even considered recruiting Daryl Bendis, one of the few regular customers who appeared to have a brain, but figured he'd be watched after the fiasco at the Wintons' mansion. *Maybe later,* he thought, *after things cool down.*

That is, if he didn't kill Mikey first. The boy started humming a few bars of an Ozzy Osbourne tune, tapping his feet on the rusted floorboard, and playing drums on the dash. *Not cool. Simply not cool.*

"So what's he going to be driving, huh, boss?" Mikey chirped, peering down the darkening alley. He had an annoyingly high voice for a boy, but then he was only sixteen. Maturity, and intelligence, had not occurred yet.

"You'll see," Presto growled. *Wonder where Daryl is right now?* "It'll be here in a minute."

From one end of the alley came a strong gust of wind, sweeping litter past the Camaro. Mikey stopped all noise and movement. He stuck his head out the window. "There's not a cloud in the sky. This a storm or what?"

"Sit tight," Presto said, grinning sardonically. "It's almost here."

A jet-black Volkswagen beetle with blackened windows pulled in behind them, drove past, and proceeded to the end of the alley. As usual, the driver was invisible.

He's going to crap his pants when he hears this guy, Presto thought, trying hard not to laugh.

The beetle parked, but its engine remained running. Thick gray exhaust clouded around the vehicle.

"That's him," Presto said, pulling a shoebox full of fifties and twenties out from under his seat. "Give him this. He'll give you something. It's that simple."

Mikey said nothing as he climbed out of the Camaro. He gave a Presto a nervous, worried look, and for a moment looked like he was about to bolt.

"What's wrong?" Presto said evenly.

"Uh . . . nothing. Just smells like something *died* in this alley," he said before he walked up to the bug.

That could be arranged, Presto thought as he opened a bottle of Evian.

Adam woke in his bedroom, fully clothed, lying on his bed. He wanted to believe that what he saw was a dream; no, not a dream, a nightmare.

I was trying to get laid. And Moira turned into an alien.

Voices filtered in from the living room. Moira's, and another, a male voice.

". . . should have waited until after Lady Samantha broke the spell before dismissing the glamories," the man said with an actor's voice that reverberated throughout the house. "But at least you brought him here, to the Gate. Does he know anything yet?"

Adam propped himself up on his elbows. *I just woke. Or did I? This sounds like part two of* Nightmare On Elm Street. *Or* Close Encounters of the Third Kind.

"I don't think so," Moira said, her words softer and difficult to hear. "I've been with him since the King Gated us to this human realm, and from the first moment we assumed our identities, he was completely ignorant of his elven identity. I just hope he recovers soon."

Adam moved to his feet and silently crept to the door. "Lady Samantha works effective spells. Where is she now?"

"Dealing with a potential Unseleighe infestation," she said. Adam understood none of it. *Mother's a cop, not an exterminator. What in the world are they talking about?*

They whispered something among themselves, then became silent.

"Adam. Come in here," the man said loudly. "We have a great deal to discuss."

Geez! How did they know I was awake?

He considered bolting through the window, but by the time he got the outer screen off, they would have caught him, or whatever. Besides, he wanted to know what was going on. *Moira and a stranger are in our house. I'm going to find out how he got in here, and what he wants.*

"Adam, there is an explanation for what you saw," Moira said. The hair on the back of his neck stood erect.

Taking a deep breath, he walked down the hallway and stopped at the edge of the living room, then peered around the corner.

Moira and a strange man sat on the couch, opposite the home theater system. Neither seemed particularly alarmed that he was awake. In fact, they seemed eager to talk to him. Moira's eyes and ears were the same as he remembered from the nightmare. The stranger, who was a large blond man, had the same features, though his pointed ears looked to be much longer. He seemed older, too, as did his dress. His right arm had been bandaged with gauze between the elbow and shoulder, and a bit of blood showed through. Aside from that, he looked like he'd just walked out of a fifteenth-century portrait.

The rest of the living room seemed normal. In the center, facing each other, were two gray couches and a matching chair. The coffee table was a solid cube of granite, decorated with a vase of lilies and a china tray of empty lead crystal liquor decanters. An antique buffet with its usual collection of art deco bric-a-brac lined one wall, and a long mirror framed with flowery Greek columns hung over it. Overhead a 1930s ceiling fan turned placidly on its lowest setting. The room had its usual cozy charm, which was spoiled by the two aliens now occupying it.

He closed his eyes, leaned against the hallway wall, and slid down into a crouch.

"I'm not seeing this," he moaned to no one in particular.

"*Adam*," Moira said sharply. "Quit being silly. Get in here."

"Lady Ethlinn," the man gasped. "Dare you speak to King Aedham that way?"

"This is a drastic situation. He will understand, once he returns to his normal self."

Adam opened his eyes against his will, stood, and entered the living room. The man and Moira sat comfortably on the couch as if they belonged there; he felt a twinge of jealousy that, given the strange circumstances, seemed completely out of place.

"Sit," Moira said.

"No," he said resolutely. "Not until you tell me what's going on." He peered at Moira and rubbed his eyes. "What happened to you?"

"Perhaps we should tell you," the man said, "what happened to *you*."

As the man spoke, Adam realized he simply could not be a human being. Not only did he speak with a deep, bass voice, it had a metallic ring to it. *A robot? An android? A Vulcan? What is he?*

The man turned to Moira, looking annoyed. "Lady Samantha should be here to dismiss the spell. As long as he remains human, it will be impossible to convince him who he really is."

"I know it would have been better," Moira said apologetically. "But she simply could not be here. Remember, we are having to maintain our human covers, as well as watch for the Unseleighe. Samantha was doing both."

Are they talking about my mother? he thought. *She's the only Samantha I know.* Then, *Someone must have slipped me some LSD. This is a very real, vivid hallucination, caused by drugs.* He focused on the man's pointed ears. *It's the only explanation.*

"This isn't real," Adam said simply. "I'm going to close my eyes. And when I open them, you're going to be gone."

Adam closed his eyes. When he opened them, they were still sitting there.

"Young King," the man said, "I know this must be a shock, but please listen to me." He stood, towering above Adam like a giant, having a good six inches or more on him. Adam took a few steps back, then stood firm. This was, after all, his house, and this man was an unwelcome intruder. But this intruder wore a period costume, straight out of the Middle Ages, or perhaps from the distant future. The tunic was a light tan, with tight-fitting sleeves pulled back over his thick, muscular forearms, and folds that covered his waist. A thick leather belt secured loose trousers of the same, linenlike material. His boots were black leather, and gold embroidery trimmed the edges of sleeves and boot cuffs; in all, a striking outfit. But in Adam's home, it was completely out of place.

At first glance the intruder reminded him of Prince Valiant in the old Sunday edition cartoons. He had a strong, handsome face, with all the stereotypic lines of a heroic figure. His eyes were emerald and slitted, just as Moira's continued to be. Pointed ears protruded from his blond, shoulder-length hair like antennas.

Moira looked on with concern, all the sexiness she'd radiated during the ride over here now gone, replaced by this insane mixture of stage costuming and special-effects makeup.

"Please believe me," the man said, his arms spread in a gesture of pleading. "While I don't expect you to remember, I am Marbann of Avalon, faithful subject of the Tuiereann Crown. I fear I come with sad news." He looked down, his posture radiating grief. "Your father is dead. The Unseleighe murdered him shortly after they invaded the castle."

Adam laughed. "My father is in Canada. Marbann of what? Avalon? What is that, an insane asylum?"

Marbann ignored him. "Since the King is slain, you are the new King of Avalon. I have come to serve you."

Adam crossed his arms and regarded him with cool skepticism.

"The Gate through which I passed is located in yon glass screen," he said, pointing to the Sony TV.

Yeah. Right. "So where's the hidden camera?" Adam tried desperately to find humor in this whole thing, and failed miserably. He'd seen complicated stage makeup before, including good prosthetic Spock ears and contact lenses, but this job was as good or better: there weren't any seams. *If I'm not hallucinating, this must be a joke. But why today? Why not April first or Halloween or some other traditional day for practical jokes? But this guy's not a kid; he's at least thirty, and he looks very serious about all this.*

He must be psycho.

"I don't think he believes us," Moira said. "Perhaps we should contact Lady Samantha now?"

Marbann looked thoughtful. "Perhaps you're right."

"If I am the King," Adam said, "and you are here to obey me, then obey this. Get out. Both of you. This isn't funny anymore." He turned to Moira. "What's going on here, Moira? Is this a joke? I thought you . . . liked me."

Moira looked hurt. "I do, my King," she said. "But it's not the same anymore. Perhaps if we'd had more time as humans, I might have fulfilled your desires."

"My what? Oh, that. So what's changed, aside from the fact that you've turned into an extraterrestrial?"

She crossed her legs, a very Moira-like gesture, and regarded him with surprise. "But my King, we have not been properly wed. We're not even betrothed!"

That did it. "I'm calling the cops. You can play your games with someone else. This has been a really crappy day. I'm not in the mood for this elaborate joke." He paused, reflecting. "You know, someone sure put a lot of work into those outfits."

He reached down for the phone and put the receiver to his ear. Nothing. He tapped the hook several times. No dial tone. The phone was dead.

Adam slammed the phone down. "Cute. You disconnected the phone."

"Your Majesty—" Marbann began.

"Oh, Marbann. Give it up. He'll never believe us as long as he's human," Moira said, and sighed. "Lady Samantha did a remarkable job in blocking his past. She's the only one who can bring him back."

Adam started walking backward, toward the front door. He reached in his pocket, but his keys weren't there. *There, on the floor. Where I dropped them.* He picked them up by the plastic handle.

"You must believe me!" Marbann pleaded, following him into the entrance hall, moving with amazing swiftness. Adam thought he was going to tackle him, but he stopped just short of running him over. "This is no prank!"

"Get away from me!" Adam shouted. The man was just too *big* to move that fast. Confusion surrendered to fear as he bolted out of the house.

I've got to call the cops, he thought as he pulled the Geo out of the driveway, the little three-cylinder engine showing surprising power in the Dallas heat. He drove down Cedar Springs at breakneck speed, hoping a cop would pull him over, but he saw none as he sailed past nightclubs and a Chinese restaurant. He squealed into a convenience store, parked, ran for a bank of pay telephones, and dialed 911.

After the bell tone came a hiss, a crackle, and a familiar voice.

"My King, please come back," he heard. *Marbann?* He looked into the receiver, half expecting to see the intruder's face there.

He dropped the phone, picked up the next one.

"Adam, if you have to call the cops, call your mom." *Moira? How the hell are they doing this?*

He reached for the next one, which rang before he touched it. *Pick it up or not?* Not.

Back in the Geo, he pulled back into traffic, driving a little slower now. It would do no good to contact the police by causing an accident.

But when he looked in his rearview mirror, he saw Marbann sitting in the backseat.

He slammed on his brakes. Behind him, a pickup screeched to a halt. Profanity followed a loud horn blast. He turned to look in the backseat, which was empty.

Maybe I'm on acid after all, he thought. *Should I even be driving?* Cars and trucks honked as they passed him. *Or should I sit here and block traffic?* His hands and legs shaking, he urged his car forward, taking deep breaths, calming himself. *I didn't see that. I didn't see that at all.*

As soon as he felt collected enough to drive, he found the expressway and drove at a sedate 55 mph to the police station where his mother worked.

Upstairs in Homicide, the girl working the desk smiled and waved him past. Everyone knew him here, although it had been weeks since he'd visited his mother on the job.

He walked into her office and closed the door behind him. Sammi was talking on the phone and peeling an orange at the same time.

She looked up, saw Adam, and said to the receiver, "I've got to go now. Let me know about the tests."

Adam began rattling off the encounter. "Mom, you're not going to believe this, when I got home with Moira, there was this guy sitting in the living room, well, no, I went to bed or actually took a nap, *then . . .*"

Sammi held a single hand up, a gesture which silenced him.

"Hold it right there," she said as she peeled the orange. "I didn't understand a single thing you just said. Sit down and start at the beginning."

Adam sat in the plain wooden office chair and tried to relax. *Where do I begin? What do I tell her?*

"I think I'm seeing things," he said, hoping he wasn't tripping on LSD after all.

"I see things all the time," she replied simply. "For instance, I'm seeing this orange. I see you. Can you be a little more specific?"

Adam frowned, accepting the likelihood that anything he said would seem insane anyway. "I've had a really crazy day," he began, deciding to leave out the part about the missing time at work. *Let's start with Moira. . . .*

"Jimmy let me off early today, and when I was leaving I gave Moira a lift, since her car wouldn't start. When I got in the house she, she . . ."

"She what?" Sammi asked.

Tried to rape me? No, not quite. "She grew ears. And her eyes changed color."

"You mean that all this time she didn't *have* ears? I guess under all that hair . . ."

"No, no," Adam said, shaking his head. *This is coming out all wrong.* "Let me skip that. There was this guy in the living room of our house. He said his name was Marlboro of Avon or something. I asked him to leave and he wouldn't. And he kept calling me King Aid Him or some shit."

"Watch your mouth, young man," Samantha admonished.

"I don't know who he is, or why he was there. Moira

knew him or something." He hesitated before asking the next question, ransacking his memory to make sure he had it right. "They said you would know what was going on."

His mother looked grim. "Did he say his name was 'Marbann of Avalon' by any chance?"

Adam's eyes became very big. "Yes. How did you know? Do you know why they were there?" Then, "Who *are* they?"

She met his questioning look, asked him, "You don't recognize him?"

Say what? Adam leaned forward in the chair, his hands fidgeting. "Should I?"

"Then it has happened," she said softly, but Adam had the distinct feeling she was not speaking directly to him.

Sammi stood and holstered her Glock. "Did you drive here?"

Adam nodded. "Who is he, Mom?" he asked plaintively, hoping she could somehow explain all the weirdness away.

"I don't have time to explain," she said, picking her purse up. "But this Marbann is a friend. I'll explain everything when we get home. You follow me."

"But . . ."

"No buts. I'll tell you later. This office is no place for explanations."

During the ride back to the house, Adam tried not to think about *anything*. But his mind continued to spin. *She knew about Marbann, at least, knew he was 'of Avalon.' What in hell's name is going on here?*

He resisted an urge to turn off and start driving anywhere, as far as he could. In the little Geo, which still had a full tank, this would be quite a distance, particularly with the twenty-dollar bill he had in his wallet. New Mexico was within driving range. But something urged him to stay behind his mother, proceed to the house, and see what this was all about.

They both pulled into the drive, parked, and started for the house.

"Mom, don't you want your gun ready or something?" Adam said nervously.

"Don't be silly," she said. "Marbann would never harm either of us." She paused at the door, added, "You, in particular."

It's all probably a big joke. If it is, Mom looks like she's really into it.

Adam followed his mother into the living room, where Moira and Marbann were still sitting. Marbann sat on the couch, calmly reading a *Newsweek*. Moira was buffing her nails and didn't seem to notice them when they entered.

"My lady," Marbann said, standing. Then, bowing briefly to Adam, said, "Thank the gods the King is safe."

Adam rubbed his eyes, studied his mother's face. No answers yet.

"Marbann," Sammi said, and embraced him. The man, or whatever, kissed her on the cheek.

Now Mother looked afraid . . . or was it grief? *What is she grieving over?* Adam thought frantically. *The loss of our sanity?*

"They have finally slain the King," she said sadly, in a tone of voice Adam had never heard her use before.

Adam stepped closer, not liking the idea of this creature being so close to his mother. "Mom, what the hell are you talking about?"

"I'm afraid so," Marbann continued, glancing at Adam, who flinched when their eyes met. "The Unseleighe have assassinated the royal family, seized the palace, and are now searching this human city for Prince—no, King Aedham." He bowed again, this time more elegantly, before Adam. "I am at your service, Your Majesty."

Sammi turned to Adam and said, "The time has come for an explanation, young King."

Adam started walking backward down the hallway. Then he turned and fled into the bathroom, slammed the door shut, and locked it.

Wonder what kind of LSD it was, he thought morosely as he sat down on the closed toilet lid. *Who did it, and when? Was it in the 7UP I had this morning? Product tampering? Practical jokes by the clientele of the Yaz?*

Then he saw the chain mail vest, which looked like it had been blown open by a shotgun blast, lying on the floor next to the john. In the sink lay bits of bloodied cloth. He remembered the stranger's bandaged arm.

He sensed their approach to the bathroom door. "This isn't going very well, my lady," he heard Marbann say from the other side.

No, it couldn't have been at the Yaz. Spence wouldn't drug me. Maybe those weird chicks in the leather who were leaving Skary did . . . something. But what? Did they prick me with an LSD-tipped pin when I wasn't looking? Wouldn't I have felt something?

"Adam, come out here this *instant*," his mother said angrily.

"Not until you tell me what's going on," he said, starting to sweat in the windowless bathroom. "If this is all an elaborate joke, I think you've had your fun by now. If this is *Candid Camera* or *Totally Hidden Video* or something entirely new, you've had your laugh." He looked around the bathroom, checked the medicine cabinet. "Nope. No camera in here. Looks like it's out there somewhere."

"Aedham, this is not a human prank," Marbann said.

"It's useless to reason," Sammi said. "I'm just going to have to . . ."

The little lock on the doorknob popped out, then the knob started to turn. Horrified, Adam looked on. *How are they doing that?* Then, *How did she find a screwdriver that fast?*

He grabbed the blow-dryer and held it up, like a club.

The door opened. Marbann and Sammi stood there, looking at him with—what, pity? Then he saw his mother in the darkened hallway. Like Moira, she now had pointed ears and green cat's eyes.

Adam stepped backward, pulling the blow-dryer's power cord taut.

"Get back!" Adam screamed, and turned the blow-dryer on.

"Or what?" Moira said from behind the both of them, sounding amused. "You're going to style our hair? Got any gel?"

"I mean it!" Adam said, then felt suddenly silly. *But if those prosthetic ears are wax, then—*

He stepped forward with the blow-dryer and turned it on "HOT—HIGH," grinning as he waited for Marbann's ear to melt. His stomach curdled as he caught a whiff of the man, an acrid but clean smell, definitely not human.

"Don't be ridiculous," Marbann said, plucking the blow-dryer from his hand. "You still think you're a human. How terrible *that* must be."

Adam pushed his way past them, started running down the hallway, intent on getting into his car. *New Mexico looks pretty good right now.*

But as he reached the end of the hallway, a bright light flashed past him. Something hit his back and caused him to stumble, but whatever it was cushioned him as he rolled into a wall.

He lay there, unable to move for several moments. Moira, Marbann and his mother stood over him.

"Are you hurt, Your Majesty?" Marbann asked with sincerity.

"Uh . . . I don't think so. But I can't move."

"The effects of the low-level bolt will wear off," his mother said. "Marbann, would you carry him to his room?"

"Certainly, my lady," Marbann said, then scooped him up in his arms as he would a load of laundry and started down the hallway, sideways. "My, young King, you have grown even as a human," Marbann said good-naturedly as he deposited him on his bed.

Adam said nothing, resigned to the long wait it would probably take for the hallucinogens to filter out of his body. *And when I wake up, I'll either be in prison or an insane asylum.* Under the circumstances, he looked forward to those prospects.

"Now, young King," his mother said, leaning over him.

"You will go to sleep. Then I will conjure a spell to *break* a spell."

Against his will, he did as he was told.

Chapter Six

He stood in what had once been a great hall, overlooking the ruins of what was once a great castle, wondering who he was and what he was doing in this particular place. Jagged, fallen walls reached for the sky with tortured fingers. Death lingered in the air, along with the acrid stench of a recently fought levin bolt battle.

He made his way through the ruins, wondering how he was connected to the carnage that had taken place here. The dead bodies he found offered no clues to his identity, except that the victims had long pointed ears like his own. The victims wore various grades of silver and gold armor, portions of which were mangled beyond usefulness, or blown completely away from the wearer. They were mostly young males, with a few older elves fallen as well, still clutching weapons: clubs, bows, blades. This battle must have been a last stand, a final showdown before the conquerors prevailed and the owners of the castle died, or fled to places unknown.

Still, he remained ambivalent. *Did I live here, or was I somehow related to those who died?* he wondered, but these questions were unimportant now; his main purpose was to wander and explore, get in touch with his soul, and then, if within reach, his past. His ears, he knew, were a clue.

Would my ears, and eyes, seem strange to me in another life? he thought, and the more he pondered this, the more he felt certain this was so. Why they were odd, he didn't know.

I have no name, he realized. *I don't know who I am.*

His lost memory did not alarm him as it might have in another life. He would learn his name when he was ready, but now was not that time. He walked past the bodies, down a short flight of stairs that remained intact, though significant chunks had been blown away by some fearsome weapon.

Levin bolts did this, he knew, and shuddered at the strength these bolts must have been to bring down the castle. He had a dim recollection of mages, and their ability to wield these weapons, but the images were shrouded in murk. *The present is what is important. Examining my past must come later.*

He examined the impact the levin bolts left. The pocked craters penetrated a hand's breadth into the stone and mortar. A residue of the magic remained, trickling from the crater like blood from a wound: a dark, evil power, alien to his touch. He recoiled from the damage, as from a hot flame.

I know this was a palace, but how do I know that? He looked up at the mound of boulders and mortar, dotted with an occasional standing wall, and imagined what this palace looked like before the battle. Magnificent, it must have been, covered with brilliant white limestone, though little of the facing remained now. He felt sorrow, not because of any personal loss, but only because such a beautiful structure had been destroyed.

He wanted to know who destroyed the palace, and where they were now. The ruins stood on a high peak, which jutted from a plateau of gently rolling hills covered with emerald grass the texture of velvet.

In the distance stood a ridge of mountains. This natural barrier, he knew, formed a political boundary as well, and the conquerors, whoever they were, came from the other side. He did not understand why they would defeat these people and then move on. Perhaps nothing worth claiming remained after the battle, or maybe they wanted to kill for the sake of killing. Hate still lingered in this place, as thick and tangible as the fog that burned off in the morning heat.

As he proceeded down the side of the hill, the fallen rock and debris from the palace became less frequent. The moat encircling the palace was completely dry and growing with grass and wildflowers. The sight puzzled him at first, until he guessed that the owners of the palace must not have expected an invasion, in fact hadn't worried about the possibility of one for some time. The bridge crossing the moat, at least what was left of it, was overgrown with thick vines, securing it more or less in place.

Dreaming. This is called . . . dreaming, a voice spoke from deep within him. The voice belonged to another entity linked to his past, but still a part of him, a fragmented portion he sensed wanted to become whole with him again. The message came through as a thought, but odd, runelike symbols represented the phrase: Dreaming. In this alien language, dreaming was not isolated to one word. There were different kinds of Dreaming, and this was only one of them, but when he tried to remember what the other forms of Dreaming were like the memory eluded him.

Above an eagle circled. It dove a short distance, pulled up, and circled some more. He watched it for some time as it meandered through the sky, turning in wide, lazy circles, growing larger as it descended. It was no ordinary eagle, or any eagle he was familiar with in any of his lives, as it was jet-black with no other markings. Also, not only was it larger than he was, it was larger than four of him laid end to end.

Talons extended, the eagle plunged toward him.

He didn't react at first; fear froze him in place. One of those talons was longer than his hand, he saw with sickening clarity as the bird attacked. Then the voice urged him to action, and he ran for the bridge, diving under it moments before the eagle struck. Talons pierced the bridge, sending splinters and boards flying everywhere. The entire structure shifted as the bird struggled to unhook itself.

Finally the eagle dislodged itself and flailed away, its shriek of rage a deep, terrifying scream that vibrated his very bones. He looked up through the holes left by the talons, knew then that the bridge would not protect him a second time.

As the bird gained altitude, he bolted out from beneath the bridge and ran up the stairway's remains. *Somewhere, up here, there is the entrance to an underground hallway.* The memory fragment offered itself reluctantly, the voice doling it out cautiously, grudgingly. He saw the passageway clearly in his mind, or rather how it had appeared before the invaders destroyed the palace.

The eagle passed over him as he reached the ruins, urging his legs to move faster. In the remains of the great hall he found a gaping hole in the floor, the only protection he saw. The eagle might trap him down there, but it would not be able to follow him.

He plunged into the darkness, and moments later the great bird struck at the entrance, sending a torrent of pebbles and dust after him, but no more. The eagle shrieked after him. The darkness became absolute, but he didn't care; he'd escaped death. He proceeded further into the passage's depths, feeling the walls for guidance.

He found a room at the bottom of the stairs. A thin veil of fog shrouded the floor, and beneath it glowed lights—candles or lanterns. He tried to count them, but his mind drifted, and he lost count.

He closed his eyes, because that is what the voice told him to do.

This is Dreaming. And the Dream is about to end. . . .

His stomach lurched as his universe shifted around him, and for a moment he was in free-fall; in vacuum, in darkness. His feet found solid ground, and he was standing upright again.

When he opened his eyes he was standing in his living room, with Lady Samantha on one side, Ethlinn on the other, and Marbann off to one side, kneeling, head down.

Adam wore a comfortable, knee-length velvet robe,

embroidered with a complex pattern of silver thread. The garment hung loosely on him, the long tubular sleeves fringed with silver lace, with a thick ermine collar which extended down the front. Beneath the robe he wore a silk tunic and hose, and on his feet were leather boots with long, pointed toes.

Around his neck hung a heavy silver pendant, inscribed with the same runes the voice used: symbols of a foreign language, alien, but now familiar. He removed the crown that sat coldly on his head, saw that it, too, was made of silver, with rubies adorning thirteen silver points.

"Your scepter, my lord," Ethlinn said, handing him a long silver staff crowned with an enormous ruby the size of his fist.

He put the crown back on his head and took the scepter, a heavy, gaudy object. The moment he touched it, a surge of power passed through his hand, up his arm, and into his body; he sucked his breath in sharply as the power coursed through him. The ruby pulsed with a dull red glow, which sharpened to an intense, hot light.

The voice spoke again, and this time he knew where it came from, who it belonged to. The voice was his own; his elven voice, speaking to his human side.

You've been a human for a long, long time. . . . the voice said. *Are you still elven, or have you forgotten what it's like to be immortal?*

Adam recalled that last horrible day in Underhill, the scene branded into his memory.

I remember all of it, he thought, cringing at the recollection. *It's like it just happened, and this is a mere moment later.*

"Marbann," he said, turning to the large blond elf kneeling on the floor, "please stand up." Marbann stood to his full height, his head down. "What happened after Samantha and I Gated to this world?" he said calmly, still trying to grasp what had happened to him, then and now.

"Forgive me," Marbann said softly. "I have failed you. I

have failed all of Avalon, to be sure, but you and your family in particular."

"That's nonsense," Samantha said. "You did everything you could, and then went further and accomplished the impossible. You held Zeldan's forces at bay. You gave the rest of us enough time to get away."

King Aedham looked with repulsion at his royal scepter, the robe, the reflection of his new crown on the Sony entertainment center screen, knowing now what this meant.

Father's dead.

Then, with a vague sense of dread, he realized, *I'm the King of Elfhame Avalon now.*

"The Gate succeeded," Adam said. "Why didn't *everyone* escape?"

Marbann looked away. "We tried, Your Majesty. Once you were in the Gate, another levin bolt struck. I could not control the magic of this one. I lost the Gate." He hesitated before going on. "That last bolt killed the King. I tried to shield him, but I was already focusing my energies on the Gate, not our shield."

"He might have made it over, then," Adam said sadly.

"Perhaps," Marbann said. "I constructed a second Gate, though one not nearly as stable as the first, using energy from our last remaining node. Then we escaped."

The royal finery felt heavy on him, and he looked up at Samantha. "I don't want to wear Father's royal robes yet."

"Of course," Samantha said, and a bright ball of light formed in her outstretched palms. The robe, the clothes, the crown and the scepter began to glow a golden yellow, then turned to vapor, circling around him in a brief flurry before collecting in her hand. Adam looked on as the light concentrated in a single sharp point in her palm. Then the light blinked out, leaving behind a gold ring bearing the rune "T."

Adam found his human clothes, the jeans, the t-shirt, the sneakers, lying on the couch, and wordlessly began putting them on. His movements were slow and deliberate as he fought back the tears, and he contemplated finding a private place to grieve.

No, he thought. *I've been away from my kind, in heart and soul, for too long. I must be with them now.*

Samantha gave him the gold ring, she opened her arms, and he welcomed the offer. They sat on the couch, with Samantha holding him as a mother would, and Adam began to cry without shame.

Zeldan stood with his army at the crest of a hill, overlooking the remnants of the palace of Elfhame Avalon. The levin bolts had all but leveled the palace, but he sensed the Seleighe, at least some of them, still alive. They'd called off the levin bolt attacks and started sending troops in, mostly armored warriors with short swords, spears and shields. The mages would soon follow. It was nothing to Zeldan to sacrifice an entire battalion for the life of a single mage. Warriors were replaceable. Mages were *not.*

Zeldan Dhu closed his eyes, again feeling Avalon's magical energies at work, tangible through the very ground he stood on.

"They have Gated again," said Mage Japhet Dhu, Zeldan's son. Zeldan was pleased he had chosen to stand at his father's side in their moment of victory. Japhet wore a robe of black silk, with a long, pointed hood that reached to the ground, as did the sleeves. It was an awkward garment to wear under most conditions of battle, but this was no ordinary day, and no typical battle.

"So be it," Zeldan said, his disappointment evident. "If the family escapes, I will follow them. *Wherever* that happens to be."

His son nodded, apparently keeping his thoughts hidden. Zeldan would have preferred knowing what his minions were thinking, but had never pushed the subject with Japhet. His hood concealed whatever facial expression might have revealed his thinking. That mage abilities had skipped a generation was unfortunate, but Zeldan had confidence in his son's loyalty. He was, after all, the mage who had seized the first Avalon node, and with that first success had nurtured the complete takeover of the magical matrix.

With hardly any physical effort at all, Zeldan's army had crushed Elfhame Avalon, due in no small part to his son's efforts and the complete surprise the attack had been. The royal family had taken flight below ground, like the rodents they were.

At least some of the Seleighe had Gated to places unknown, like cowards. Now Zeldan sought to seize the last node of magical energy and trap whoever remained in the bowels of the palace ruins.

And my guess is the King did not survive long enough to escape.

Zeldan studied the palace, or what was left of it, and smiled a grim smile. A subtle shifting in power, governed by other mages on a nearby hill, announced their success.

"And now the final node is ours," said Japhet. "They can Gate no more."

Zeldan Dhu waved his comment away. The Unseleighe ruler towered a good seven hands above his son, and today had chosen black leather armor trimmed with silver and rubies. As easily as the war had gone, Zeldan doubted he would see any combat himself, so he wore his finest, without fear of its becoming damaged.

"Come," Zeldan said smugly to his son. "Let us see who is left *alive.*"

Chapter Seven

Adam cried until he had no more tears to shed. Curled up on the couch with Samantha, he grieved until his chest ached, and his face stung. Samantha held him gently, rocking him like his mother would have; anyway, it felt the same, and he found it easy to imagine his mother holding him like this. The grief drained him, but once it was out he felt better, if weaker.

Now his sorrow had mutated to *anger.*

The Unseleighe must die, he seethed. The anger was a hot, bubbling mass, boiling over the rim and hissing violently over red hot coils. *Slowly, painfully. My family is dead. They've taken everything! They deserve a long death.*

He wanted to smash everything in sight, to scream and shout, pull his hair out, but he held back, knowing this wouldn't look very royal. Also, he would feel obligated to clean up the mess, whether or not Samantha told him to do so. This would waste precious time, something they had little of right now.

I'm in charge of these elves now, and everything I do from now on will be scrutinized. Behaving like the human teenager I once was will not win me favor in this new Court. And I will not shame my father by behaving irresponsibly on my first day of rule.

"Marbann," Adam said, "who else came through the Gate when you did?"

Marbann nodded, then went to another part of the house, to what sounded like Samantha's bedroom.

"Come with me," Adam heard him say.

He returned, holding the hands of two small elven children, a boy and a girl. The boy, Petrus, was small and frail, and dressed in a vaguely effeminate way. He wore his hair long and curly, and had unusually long ears for someone so young. Wenlann, the girl, looked like a frightened mouse. She seemed to be afraid of her new surroundings, Adam in particular.

"Prince *Aedham?*" Petrus said, clearly surprised, as he came over to Adam. "How long have you been here? You've grown so much since the last time I saw you. Which, by my reckoning, was only a moment ago."

"He is King now," Marbann said gently. "You must address him as such."

"Five human years," Adam said. "And yes, I have grown. But I'm still the same Adam you knew." *Am I?* He regarded the group, and felt a terrible weight fall on his shoulders.

Am I up to leading these people? he wondered. *Not only must I deal with my own fate, I am in charge of theirs.*

"Ignore me, will you!" an elf said from the hallway. Adam remembered him. Niamh. He had teeth like a gopher and a nose like a potato, and looked far younger than he was. He was really much older than Marbann, though Adam didn't know by how much. Niamh looked dazed and muddled, but then he usually did.

"'Twas only a slight tap on the head," Niamh said quickly, rubbing the back of his head. "Where are the Unseleighe? I will rip their throats out, I will!"

"It's okay, Niamh," Moira soothed. "We're safe now." She felt the back of his head, and Niamh flinched. When she pulled her hand away, it glistened with fresh blood.

"You are more hurt than you thought," Adam said. "To the sickbed with you. Mo—Samantha, do we have bandages? Gauze, and the like?" *I almost called her Mother,* he thought, pained.

"The weapon," Niamh groaned, holding his head. "We left it behind."

Samantha and Adam turned, and the King said, "What weapon?"

"The . . . rifle, the thing we stole from the humans years ago. I almost had it working, I did," Niamh, clearly pained at the loss of whatever it was.

"Oh. *That*," Samantha said. "It was a science project the Elfhame appropriated from a school in California, years ago. We never spent much time with it because we never got it to work, and besides, there was no threat." She paused. "Until now."

"What we need is a *healer*," Moira said, feeling the rest of Niamh's scalp for more wounds. "None survived the attack. Bandages will have to do for now."

Adam and Marbann gently guided Niamh to his bed, and urged him to lie on it facedown. He looked ready to object, then complied.

"The bleeding has stopped, but we need to close that wound somehow," Samantha said. "Adam, would you—" She stopped herself, paused, rephrased. "No, I will get it myself. You are not my son now. It may take a while for me to get used to that."

"Don't worry, Samantha," Adam said. "Even though you raised me as a son, a human son, we hardly know each other as elven siblings." He grinned, a little embarrassed that his mother was his sister all along. "I promise to be a King you cannot offend easily."

"Well said, young King," Marbann said, arranging a blanket carefully over Niamh.

But Adam was paying little attention; at the mention of bandages he felt the palms of both his hands turn warm. At first the warmth became uncomfortably hot, then receded. Thin tendrils of yellow light crackled and sparked over his fingers. The tendrils increased in brightness and number, bathing his hands in yellow light.

Marbann gasped, as did Moira, who stood in the bedroom doorway.

"Your Majesty," Marbann said, stepping back. "You have the *gift*."

Adam stared at his hands as if some foul substance had coated them. "What gift? What's going on?"

"Don't you feel it, Adam?" Samantha said, her surprise turning to evident pleasure. "The *gift*. The healing gift. Your father was right."

"I don't understand. . . ." he started to say, then suddenly understood clearly. Without taking any conscious actions, his hands went to Niamh's temples. His fingers flared with yellow light, so bright he had to squint to look at them. It looked like he was on fire, but somewhere inside Adam knew all was well, this was as it should be. His hands moved around Niamh's head, over the wound; through the glare he saw the wound closing, changing color. They watched the flesh heal until only a patch of pink remained. The blood surrounding it had dried to a fine pink dust. When Adam blew, the blood dust vanished, cast to the winds.

"The King is a *healer*!" Adam heard Petrus shout in the living room. The entire Elfhame had gathered at the door, looking on in awe, their faces filling the doorway; it looked like the whole stack would fall if the bottom row shifted.

"*I am a healer*," he thought, but the thoughts didn't feel like his own. A wave of exhaustion fell over him, and he fell to his knees. The yellow power that bathed his hands dimmed, then became a faint trickle. As the last of the power left him, he felt dizzy, and weak, and just a bit nauseous.

"Good gods," Samantha said. "He hasn't been trained. The healing was too much. . . ."

He lay on the floor of his bedroom, his stomach churning, feeling horrible, until he saw Niamh's face join the others who were looking down on him; when he smiled, the dizziness subsided. Adam sat up.

"To the sickbed with you!" Niamh said, mimicking Adam's words and voice perfectly. Marbann hissed at him, with a full elven ear quiver: a remarkably hostile expression.

Adam found Niamh's comment amusing, managing a grin as they helped him to his bed.

"You'll need water," Samantha said, and Moira dashed out of the room, temporarily upsetting the elven pyramid blocking the door.

"You'll need more than a drink," Marbann said, looking into Adam's eyes, first one, then the other. "So far you've managed to avoid healer's shock. Next time, you may not be so fortunate." Marbann stood to his full height, and his head threatened to touch the ceiling. "I made a promise to your father that if our escape ever succeeded, as it has, I would teach you in the ways of the elves. You father said you would forget much, and now it is evident that you've forgotten more than we've bargained for. No mage would have handled that much raw power without protection."

"It seemed the thing to do," Adam said. "Niamh, are you well already?"

"I am, I am, Your Majesty. Your most capable hands have healed me completely."

Moira returned with a Flintstones jelly glass full of water, which Adam gratefully drank down. He was thirsty; when it was finished, he gave it to Moira, who went off again to refill it.

Marbann continued, "My education is a bit sparse when it comes to mage powers. However, I believe you have forgotten some basic concepts."

Adam's first reaction was to deny this—after all, wasn't he the King? Even before today he caught himself assuming he knew it all, a common trait among teenagers, elven *and* human. But he still hadn't quite recovered from healing Niamh, and if Marbann had advice to offer, he was going to listen to it.

"Will you please show me?" Adam said. Marbann seemed to bloom with the request. The big elf beamed proudly and extended his hand. Adam took it and, with some effort, got to his feet. "I have my memories, but other things, basic abilities, I've lost. I don't know how to turn myself into a human, and as you've seen, I don't know how to protect myself from my own power." He had a raging headache, he discovered when Marbann helped him to his feet. "And my head hurts."

Marbann chuckled. "That I don't doubt, young King."

"And another thing. I think I should insist that everyone should call me Adam, even if we are among ourselves. I don't feel like a king yet, and the title makes me feel distant."

"When I am through with you," Marbann said as they made their way through the living room, "you *will* feel like a king."

Someone had turned the entertainment center on, and Moira was showing Petrus how to channel-surf. The young elf held the Sony remote as if it were a live animal that would bite him, and the other elves were gazing at the screen, awestruck. Of course, they had never seen a TV before, Adam realized, much less one this big. The elves jumped when the surround-sound blasted through from a fight scene from *Terminator,* and one of them looked behind the couch, apparently looking for hunter-killers.

"Moira, maybe you should order more pizza," Adam said. "Looks like we have the makings of a party here."

"Might as well," Moira said, making herself comfortable on the couch next to Petrus. A surge of jealousy flared in Adam, then quickly subsided, knowing that Petrus was far too young for her.

"Marbann, why don't you both go out in the garage," Samantha said, taking control of the remote from Petrus, who was all too willing to surrender it. Niamh was fascinated with the techie toys all lit up on the console, and was poking at the receiver's illuminated dial. "Niamh, don't touch *anything* yet," then, to Adam, "I think I'll stay here and give our recent arrivals a crash course on the human realm with the help of cable TV. There's a big clear space out in the garage with lots of privacy."

"Which is precisely what we need," Marbann said. "Cold iron will get in the way, but I suppose now that we're in the human realm this is unavoidable." He turned to Adam.

"And another thing. When I am teaching you, and only when I am teaching you, you are no longer the King, and I am not the royal subject. You are the student, and I am the master. Agreed?"

Learning, or relearning, the elven ways in a suburban garage in a human city seemed a bit ludicrous to Adam, but they were in hiding for the time being, and there was no other place. Since he never felt like a king in the first place, Marbann's conditions were easy to swallow.

Besides, if I make a mistake, I'm not likely to destroy anything valuable, he reasoned.

"Let's go," the young King said. "Now's a good a time as any."

Adam had started keeping the two-car garage fairly tidy once he'd bought his Geo, so that it and Mom's Taurus would both fit without banging the doors. At the end toward the house was a set of aluminium shelves, the gas heater, and the hot water heater. On the shelf was a set of metric sockets, a power drill, a fire extinguisher, and a heavy-duty staple gun. Next to the shelf was a portable wooden worktable with adjustable clamps, which was handy for working on things you didn't want moving around. Then there was the smoker, a crude piece of work, made of quarter-inch steel plate. Its steel content made it too uncomfortable for either of them to use.

The garage was easily ten degrees hotter than it was outside. Adam turned on a ceiling fan, but that only stirred up the hot air.

"Do you think it's hot in here, Adam?" Marbann asked.

"It's hotter than hell in here," Adam replied, gazing at the ceiling fan forlornly. "Maybe this wasn't such a good idea."

Marbann shook his head. "You're still thinking like a human, and this is something you must stop doing. Elves do not let their environment rule them—elves rule their environment. Granted, there are specialized problems here in the human realm. However, a hot garage is *not* one of them. Observe."

Marbann closed his eyes, and Adam felt something *change* in the garage. His ears popped as the air pressure increased, and the temperature began to drop quickly.

"It's comfortable now," Adam said. "How did you . . . ?"

Marbann continued with his work. The temperature continued to drop, until Adam saw his breath fog before him. The ceiling fan slowed, as the grease and bearings inside it became cold, and its whine was a little deeper. Frost formed on the floor, the shelves, the worktable.

"Marbann! It's cold enough in here. It's below freezing, at least!"

Marbann opened his eyes. "Cold, is it? I thought you said it was too hot."

"Well, it was, but now . . ." He ran his finger along the wall, leaving a line in the frost. "Is this how you like it? Cold enough to freeze your . . ."

Marbann was grinning wickedly. "If you don't like the temperature, then *you* change it to your liking." He folded his arms. "Well. I'm waiting."

"I don't know how to do that," he said. "You've got to show me. . . ." He began to shiver, and he hugged himself against the cold. *It's got to be ten degrees in here!*

"I'll do no such thing. At least, not directly. You healed a rather nasty wound in there. With no training, I might add. Bringing the temperature up a few degrees in here is nothing compared to that."

"But I *had* to do something! He might have died."

"Precisely. So tell me, how *did* you heal Niamh in there? Tell me quickly. Or don't tell me at all. I can wait all day."

Adam didn't like this one bit. Marbann had suddenly turned the tables and was toying with him, like he was a child. *Compared to him, I am a child. I should go along with this, I guess. . . .*

"I reached inside, and it, well, just happened."

"Then make it happen again. It's not getting any warmer in here."

Marbann was right—it wasn't. The older elf was still

making the temperature go down. The ends of Adam's nose and ears were getting numb.

"We're going to freeze in here!"

Marbann smirked, which, despite the cold, made Adam's blood boil. "No, *you* are going to freeze in here. I'm doing just fine, thank you."

He's making a fool out of me, that's what he's doing! He doesn't like the idea of my being King, and he resents it, and now he's playing with me. Damn him. . . .

Adam hardly noticed his own clenched fists, clutched at his sides, as the anger boiled up within him. Then, something began to happen. He visualized his anger, imagined it turning to heat. He sensed Marbann letting go of the situation, the older elf's expression turning from ridicule to anticipation.

"That's it," Marbann whispered. "It's like grabbing a rope and then pulling on it. But if you pull too hard, it comes free, and you have to start all over again."

As the temperature stabilized at what had to be around seventy, Adam let go of the "rope" and looked at Marbann expectantly.

"Well? How did I do?"

"You did fine," Marbann said, "though I have to admit that I set you up."

Adam tested the floor, finding it damp from the recently melted frost, but safe to walk on. "What did you do?"

"Anger is one of the primal emotions of our kind, and of the humans, as well. It is an emotion that protects, and defends. Magic-using is also instinctive, but since it's been blocked for so long in you, I had to get to it a different way, through emotion."

Adam reached for the power, now closer, accessible. It was like a recently hatched eagle, young and awkward, but no longer sealed off by its shell.

Marbann went on to the next lesson: shields. Adam had a bit more trouble with these, mostly because of the distance between him and the nodes, which were miles away. But once he established the link between himself and their prized power source, the shields went up practically by themselves.

"These shields are malleable and can be concentrated on certain sides, depending on the direction of the attack. For example," Marbann said, standing in the center of the garage, "like this." When he closed his eyes, the shield formed around him, a humanoid block of blurry ice that reminded Adam of a cubist painting. The shield contracted, then appeared to melt from behind and reform before him.

"If you are certain your enemy is nowhere behind you, you can concentrate your shield elsewhere." Marbann's voice had changed timbre and sounded like he was speaking through a long metal tube once the shield was up.

Adam tried several times before he successfully copied the move, first forming the full shield, then focusing the energy on a flat area before him.

"The shield, in this state, is much stronger and will withstand more from your opponent," Marbann said. "The disadvantage, of course, is that your arse is vulnerable. Now. I'd like to demonstrate a helpful aid, commonly referred to as *bridging*."

Adam glanced over at Marbann, who seemed to be tapping into the nodes as well. The King felt the subtle change in the flow he was receiving.

"Even an experienced mage cannot use the full potential of power in a node cluster the size of this one." His mood turned visibly dark. "This is how Zeldan seized our nodes. Instead of his best mage taking on the nodes alone, they spread the power out over several mages. This formed a web which, when focused on a specific point, generated levin bolts of horrendous strength." The teacher paused before continuing. "It was one of these bolts that killed your father."

The King said nothing in reply, instead focusing on extinguishing the new anger that surfaced. His shield flickered during the brief lapse in concentration.

"Bridging can be useful, then," Adam said, when he'd

regained some of his composure. "With the help of my people, I shall return the favor to Zeldan."

Marbann bowed, a signal for Adam to do the same, and dropped his shields. The protective fields evaporated, and Adam's teacher came into sharp focus once again.

They went on to the next lesson: offense. Marbann began with the basic attacks, starting with paralyzing moves reminding Adam of Vulcan neck pinches, moving up to the more lethal weapons of their magical armory.

"The energy for levin bolts comes from the same source as shields. The main difference is that the bolts are highly concentrated in a tight area and are focused outward. As you are a mage, your capacity is greater than the average elf, but it will, like everything else, take time to master." Without concentrating much on what he was doing, Adam tried to randomly generate a bolt; too late, he realized he had given the blast nowhere specific to go.

"Adam, no, *wait*. . ." Marbann began, but it had already begun. Adam felt node energy race from the souls of his feet through his body and blast from his palm. Marbann ducked as the searing white arc flared past his head and plowed into the metal shelves against the garage wall. The blast threw them both sprawling backward; Marbann fell into the wall, and Adam landed gracelessly on his rear end.

Adam sat on the floor, dazed, an eerie silence having fallen on the garage. With Marbann's assistance, Adam crawled to his feet, and his hearing gradually returned, the blast having temporarily robbed him of it.

"What are you two boys doing out here?" Samantha admonished from the garage doorway, hands on her hips, evidently trying to look angry. The grin on her elven features gave her away.

"Nothing to worry about, my lady," Marbann said quickly, as Adam brushed dust off his jeans. "Just a little levin bolt practice."

"I'll say," she said. "It's past nine. Here in the human realm, we can't make noise that attracts attention to us, much less noise that occurs at this hour. I might be able to cover for us once or twice if my coworkers at the police department show up, but if this becomes a habit, it might look a little weird."

"Yes, my lady," Marbann said. "Perhaps we should take a rest from tonight's practice and resume tomorrow?"

"Marbann, that is a *splendid* idea," Samantha agreed. "There's something inside here I'd like to show you."

In the kitchen, Adam found Moira cutting hair with a pair of ceramic scissors she carried around in her purse for emergencies. Niamh sat at one of the informal dining room chairs with a pink flowered bed sheet around his neck, scowling most unhappily about the whole thing. Several hues of elven hair lay at their feet.

"Marbann, you're next," Moira commanded, snipping the scissors in his direction. "You need something a little more human."

Marbann looked pained. "But, my lady, this is my mane, my badge of honor. . . ."

"Which no longer applies up here," Moira came back.

"But how are we to hide our ears?" Marbann protested weakly. Moira gave him a *look*.

"Don't give me that," she barked. "You know as well as I do that glamories will hide just about anything. I cut the hair because it takes too damn much node energy to hide eyes, ears *and* hair."

"Look out," Samantha said as Petrus zoomed in from the entrance on a fat skateboard, nearly colliding with Marbann in the process. Petrus wore a black ball cap and an oversized t-shirt with the Tasmanian Devil huffing and snorting on the front. The boy came to a stop, then expertly toed the skateboard so that it leapt into his arms.

"Whatcha think?" Petrus said without a trace of elven accent. "New look. New do. I can even skate circles around people with this thing."

"I thought we'd go for the pre-teen hip-hop look," Moira said. "Baggy shorts are in style." Adam noticed the cap with an "X" on it, turned backward. "Trendy. The 'X' is a little out, but no one will notice. I left a tail on the back of his head. Pete, take your hat off and show us your do."

"Pete?" Adam asked.

"My new *cover*," Pete proclaimed proudly. "Petrus don't sound too cool." He took the hat off, showing a nearly shaved head with a thin layer of blond fuzz, with a long, dangling tail reaching halfway down his back. "We might even dye it blue or something."

"Cool," Adam said. "Where'd all these clothes come from, anyway?"

Samantha stepped into the kitchen, and Pete squealed away. "I had a box of clothes put away for just such an occasion." She gestured them to follow her. "There's something else you probably don't know about."

In the garage she pulled down the wooden ladder which led, Adam had thought, to the attic. Instead, there was something else.

"Before the rest got here, young King, I had additional living space built," she said. "You wouldn't remember it because I made sure you wouldn't. Didn't want you and your little human friends hiding up here to play doctor."

They ascended the steep wooden stairs, and entered an apartment.

"I didn't know this was up here," Adam said, confused. "All this time . . ."

"I put a mild glamorie on the ladder to make you ignore it. I can dress the place up with magic if we so desire, but by itself it makes a suitable living space for our guests."

Adam counted eight beds in the attic apartment. The walls and floor had been covered with new carpet and still smelled unused. In the corner was a bathroom and a kitchenette.

"No need to hide everyone in the house. That would be dangerous, with all the unwanted visitors that might come by. Door-to-door peddlers, in particular. The only problem is that it's only accessible from the garage, from the pull down ladder we just climbed. Not the most elegant way to ascend to the new place, but it will be discreet."

They climbed back down, and Sammi raised the ladder. From below it looked like any other unfinished attic space over a garage.

Everything was happening fast, too fast. He knew it was real but it didn't feel real. Samantha's transition from mother to sister was still unnerving; perhaps it was his human side, hanging on to his elven self.

He asked her about this. Samantha replied, "Given the circumstances, you will probably always have a little bit of human in you. Which isn't such a bad thing, provided you use the good part of your humanity."

"You would know, I suppose. You've been here, living as a human, for a long time. What did you find so interesting about this place?"

Samantha looked thoughtful for a moment, as if carefully considering the question. "The world here is in a constant state of change. Avalon was too . . . utopian, I guess would be the proper human term. I was bored." She regarded him with a hard look that wasn't altogether unfriendly. "I've always been your sister, and it's going to be interesting, switching to that role."

"But if you're my older sister, then why aren't you the new ruler and not me?" He tried not to sound accusing; the throne was, after all, his responsibility, and he didn't want it to sound like he was trying to avoid it.

Samantha laughed softly, looking much younger than she had in years. "We have different mothers, Aedham. Yes, I am Tuiereann. But my mother, she was from Outremer." To Adam's confused look, she added, "I think our father was trying to establish some sort of alliance with the other elfhame. And for whatever reason, it didn't quite work out. We remained distant from Outremer." She looked past Adam, as if trying to remember something. "I never knew my mother. *Our* mother was everything I ever needed. I loved our parents dearly, Adam. Please don't forget that."

The serious turn the conversation had taken felt uncomfortable. As they walked back to the house, Samantha subtly changed the subject back to the situation at hand.

"Since it's summer, we won't have to worry about putting anyone in school. If anyone asks, I'd suggest the following: relatives from out of town. The Haight in San Francisco. I have an address we can use, if needed. While you and Marbann were practicing, I showed them our tape of *Encino Man*. Looks like Pete's already picked up on some of the slang already."

Adam groaned. "He doesn't need to be going around sounding like Pauly Shore. I think it would drive me *nuts* after a while."

"Just think what a good disguise it would be," Samantha pointed out.

In the dining room, Moira stood over an empty chair, and with the scissors waved Marbann to sit down. "Your turn, Marbann. And speaking of disguise, did you ever show our King here how to hide his elven features? He can't be walking the street looking like *that*, you know."

Marbann held his arms up in a gesture of surrender before Moira fastened the sheet around his neck. "I leave that in your capable hands, my lady," he said. "He knows basic self-defense. This I thought would be most important to learn."

"Basic self-defense and how to nearly level a house with an uncontrolled levin bolt," Samantha said sardonically. "It doesn't look like any structural damage is done," she added, eying the ceiling suspiciously.

As it turned out, learning the human glamorie was simpler than building the basic shield and required less energy. Since Adam's hair was already styled to blend in with the human population, all he had to alter were his ears and eyes; it was like wrapping a miniature version of the magical shield around his face and wearing it like a helmet.

"There. Now you look presentable," Moira said.

At the door came a knock. Adam looked up at Samantha, who had a mischievous expression he couldn't quite fathom.

"Well, King Aedham," she said, "shouldn't you go answer it?"

Chapter Eight

My, Bridget is a big girl, Peter Pritchard thought wryly
as his two o'clock appointment walked into the New You
Fitness Center. A severely overweight woman in her mid-
thirties lugging a shopping bag squeezed in through the
front doors. *If they get much larger than this, we'll have to
install a garage door.*

Before approaching her, Peter caught a glimpse of himself in the mirrored walls. He was a big hunk of a guy with
short blond hair, a forty-two-inch chest and a tropical tan,
wearing Spandex shorts and a New You Fitness Center
t-shirt. *I should make quite an impression,* he thought, grinning at his stunning reflection. *I always do. She may even
want to bed me before I say the first word.*

Yesterday Bridget had called to find out what the New
You had that other health clubs didn't. Peter suggested
she bring workout clothes for a free session. From the
looks of the large shopping bag, she'd brought an entire
wardrobe.

"I'm here to see Mr. Pritchard," she said to the recep-
tionist at the counter, but Peter was already on his way to
greet her.

"Ah. Mrs. Bridget Palmer. Pleased to finally meet you,"
Peter said, offering his hand.

On her rounded, sour face perched a pair of horn-
rimmed glasses. The puce polyester pantsuit, worn thin in
many places, threatened to rip where her compacted flesh

filled it a little too tightly. She looked him up and down suspiciously, then blushed.

As expected, Peter thought smugly to himself. *She can't take her eyes off me.*

Finally she shook his hand. He crushed hers. He loved doing that, to prove both his strength and innate superiority. No one ever complained, male or female. It was expected from a strapping specimen of manhood such as himself.

"The ladies' locker room is through there," he said. "While you get changed—"

"I was rather hoping you would show me the club first," she interrupted, glancing past his large frame, toward the equipment room. "So far I haven't really seen anything, um, unique about this place."

Peter held back the laughter that threatened to burst past his lips. As he put his arm around her shoulder and gently led her to the locker room, he said, "Ah, but you will see, soon enough, what our club has to offer. It would be much better to try the equipment firsthand. Explanations do no justice to what we have. Twenty minutes of your time, that's all we ask."

"Twenty minutes?" she said hopefully. "Is that all?"

"Trust me," he said. And she disappeared into the locker room.

Moments later, she emerged wearing a pink Spandex leotard, the price tag still dangling from the sleeve, looking for all the world like a giant wad of bubble gum.

"Okay," she said. "Where do we begin?"

"This way," he said cheerfully. "First, we must weigh in."

She made a face. "Do we *have* to?"

Peter flashed his famous placating grin. "How else are we to know how much progress we've made?"

She stopped, looked up at him with an arched eyebrow, her suspicion renewed. "In *one day?*"

Peter replied, "I told you we were different. What do you have to lose?"

The scale creaked and groaned before the needle finally settled. She weighed in at 285 lbs. And a half.

"My God!" she wailed. "I gained *a pound and a half*!"

Peter chuckled despite himself.

She glared at him. "What's so funny?" Bridget shrieked.

"You will lose that pound and a half, and more, before you leave today," he assured her.

"In twenty minutes?"

He smiled. "Trust me."

For twenty minutes precisely, she walked on treadmills, marched on StairMasters, pedaled on Aerobicycles, and sat in on the last five minutes of a group aerobic workout. Literally. After everyone else had left, Peter found her sitting forlornly on the carpeted floor, sobbing.

"I'm never going to lose weight!" she wailed. "Besides, it *hurts*!"

"Of course it does," Peter said, standing over her with his arms crossed. "You know the expression: no pain, no gain. In most clubs, it's just pain with no gain. Here, you get both." He held a hand out. "Come. Let's weigh in. I think you'll be pleasantly surprised."

With great effort, and with both hands, Peter helped her up. "This is pointless," she muttered. "I think I'm going to have the lipo done after all."

"Perish the thought!" Peter said, shaking his head. "You don't even know how much you've lost today!"

"I haven't lost a damn thing," she said. "I can tell. I never do. This whole health club nonsense is just that . . . nonsense."

She grumbled and moaned and bitched and raved like that, all the way to the scale. Then she stepped on it.

Bridget stared at it. "No. This can't be right."

"Oh, it's correct, my dear. In just under twenty minutes, you've already lost eighteen pounds."

The scale read 267. And a half.

"It can't be," she said, but her smile threatened to squeeze her eyes shut. "Eighteen pounds? Eighteen . . . *pounds*? Eighteen eighteen eighteen eighteen *POUNDS! I don't believe it!*"

She leaped off the scale and gave Peter an enormous bear hug. Afterward, he had some trouble breathing.

"Eighteen pounds! In twenty minutes!" She moved around with more energy now than she had during her entire visit.

Peter beamed. "See. I told you it was different here. And what's more, and I haven't shared the good news yet: you can eat absolutely anything you want to! Lasagna. Cream pies. Twinkies. Ho-Hos. Cookies. Corn dogs. Scrambled eggs, bacon, sausage. *Pizza.* Pepperoni, hamburger, anchovy, cheese lovers, meat lovers, Canadian bacon. Oh, my dear Bridget, you can eat all the pizza you want to. And then some!"

She sighed. "This is heaven. Where do I sign?"

"Right this way," he said, leading her to his office. "This will take no time at all."

Peter Pritchard watched Bridget's retreating back as she left the club, noting with some frustration the bounce in her step, the jaunty walk. She even said hello to a total stranger coming in. Unfortunately, the human actually felt good about herself, an unpleasant but unavoidable by-product of their operation.

She won't be feeling too good about herself tomorrow, when she comes in to do it all over again, Peter thought. *And next time, it won't be nearly as easy. I'll see to that. And she'll only lose two pounds. Then we'll see how much she likes herself then!*

With elven magic, one could remove as much fat as necessary. Or as little, depending on the circumstances. Peter mastered the technique, a method of un-kenning that he stumbled across by accident, a year before. This was the secret of the New You Fitness Center. The workouts served *other* purposes.

Time to see how the synthetic nodes are doing. . . .

Peter left the main exercise floor through a locked door, behind which was a flight of stairs. Locking the door behind him, he descended into darkness.

The stairway led to a dank hallway, illuminated by red light bulbs and an occasional flickering fluorescent. Peter and his kind preferred artificial darkness, with just enough light to do their work. Since no humans were permitted down here, they weren't too concerned about being discovered; the building inspector had come and gone for that year, and the health inspector never made surprise visits, at least during the year they'd been in operation. No one asked to see the basement. The building itself was a defunct two-story office complex, a victim of the eighties recession, located in a vast warehouse district in western Dallas. Its extensive basement once housed a vast data library and mainframe computer. All that remained was the raised floor, cables and other IBM bric-a-brac.

Rathand sat at a crude control panel composed of illuminated crystals, hand-carved oak knobs, and a set of crude capacitors made from thick glass jars. He wore a severe black business suit with the tie loosened and hanging limply around his neck. The elf made minute adjustments with one of the knobs, watching the light travel up one of the long fingerlike crystals. Peter saw from the primitive dial that Bridget's negative energy during the grueling workout had been strong.

They used the rig to collect negative energy from the fitness center, as well as other places in the city. The contraption was a purely Seleighe invention, put together and understood only by Rathand, which Zeldan reluctantly admitted the need for some months back. Mutant technology such as this, which implemented elven magics along with other physical rules of the universe, human and elven, was not something Zeldan felt comfortable with.

The pain and unhappiness Bridget just supplied us with should fuel us quite handily for the next few months, Peter thought with glee.

One of the unfortunate by-products of the invention was that it made reading Rathand's mind very difficult. But since Rathand was a slave of the Unseleighe, and had shown no signs of breaking his conditioning, Zeldan felt confident enough to put his tools to use. And to keep Rathand on the "payroll."

As a double guarantee, Zeldan had implanted a red crystal in Rathand's head. The crystal was connected directly to the elf's pain centers, and would, if Zeldan were ever killed, result in Rathand's death as well. This made it very much in Rathand's best interest to protect Zeldan and to do his bidding. The pain from the crystal was quite severe.

"Most excellent," Peter said, savoring the moment. He opened his eyes without realizing he'd closed them.

Rathand whirled around. "*Zeldan.* I didn't hear you come in." Grinning broadly, he tapped the dial on the console. "Who was that, anyway? We haven't had this much negative power to tap since that accountant went on that shooting spree in the mall in Plano!"

Peter, or Zeldan, now that he was down here in the lab, nodded in agreement. "A most disturbed, and angry, human being. We need more like her. Perhaps a special advertisement in the paper, fifty percent off for people weighing over two hundred pounds."

Business at the New You had been good but needed improvement. A building of this size had a great deal of overhead, and lately Zeldan had barely been breaking even. They needed more money, and more negative power. The more mistreated the human, the more negative power they had to offer the artificial power nodes. Granted, these nodes were no replacement for those he left behind in Underhill. Once tapped, they tended to deplete quickly and had a limited time before they began to weaken without recharging. But they were better than nothing.

"This society of humans must truly be demented if they treat these people with such cruelty." Then, with a wicked smile, Zeldan added, "I'm starting to actually *like* it here."

Finally, after spending a human year searching for that thrice-damned King Aedham! Zeldan thought. *I've found something worth staying around for. Human pain.*

His inability to find Aedham Tuiereann, and his periodic fits of rage over this failure, was something he'd much rather forget. The only clues to the potential whereabouts of the Avalon elves was the discovery of nodes beneath the West End Marketplace.

Those nodes might have served Zeldan's purposes, had they not been so polluted with human energies already. The humans had been at the site for a few hundred years, and during the last century the factory had left a residue of human thoughts that, given Zeldan's hatred for the race, was too distracting.

The power they preferred generally resulted from pain and, in extreme circumstances, torture. Zeldan kept tabs on the West End nodes, but had found no sign of the Seleighe. Spell signatures unique to the Avalon clan had failed to turn up. They were either not here or in clever hiding. Zeldan thought the latter more likely. Failure was an embarrassment, and when it became clear that Adam would not be an easy elf to find, he turned his attentions to other pursuits.

He might have returned to Underhill to rejoin his tribe of Unseleighe, but he had yet to find the last Tuiereann. Gating back and forth required more energy than he had and would prove a considerable drain on the nodes he'd seized at Avalon if he ever wanted to return here. His clan thought him mad to stay in the humans' realm for so long, but then they were not bound by their family's vow of revenge. He had unfinished work here; the fall of Avalon was not yet complete.

A Tuiereann still lives somewhere in this human city. If I have to stay here for a century to find him, then so be it!

For a time, he and his four Unseleighe warriors lived in hiding, masquerading as homeless street people, feeding on the humans' pain. He discovered crack cocaine and heroin, and the powerful grip they had on humans. They learned to feed on this particular kind of human pain, renewing their dark souls with the suffering of humanity, but it was a hit and miss arrangement, and often they simply had to do without. In short order, living on the street became tiresome and made his search for Aedham more difficult. Zeldan was a King himself, and he grew weary of living like a pauper, even if it meant the occasional banquet of an addict dying of withdrawal. Then he had an idea.

For a time he made drug connections with dealers on the street, kenning huge amounts of human currency, gold, and silver, and within months he was buying from one of the biggest cocaine brokers in South America, Rodriguez Cruz.

Cruz had been in the business for a long time and seldom had let someone like Zeldan into the fold until they had proven themselves, usually over a period of years. But Zeldan was elven, not human, and worked his magics to penetrate his layer of safety, convincing his lieutenants that Zeldan was legit and for real, and not a cop. They liked being paid in gold, which was fortunate, as this was one of the easier substances for Zeldan to ken. Gold was a basic chemical substance, and much simpler to forge than a detailed hundred-dollar bill with serial numbers. In less than ninety days, Zeldan was a trusted partner in their distribution network.

Cruz owned ten or more cocaine factories in Colombia, which produced pure cocaine hydrochloride. With four refurbished DC-6's, and four U.S. pilots down on their luck and looking for easy money, Cruz ran a three-pronged pipeline from Colombia to West Palm Beach, to Miami, and to a tiny town called Tempest, Texas. Every few months Cruz flew in two hundred kilos of Colombian cocaine to a clandestine landing strip near Tempest, approximately fifty miles from the United States-Mexican border. Cruz had grown weary of the ground crews he hired out of Tempest, who usually smoked pot and drank cases of beer while waiting for the DC-6 to land, and often were next to useless by the time the plane landed. They needed to move fast and efficiently, and in their condition, neither was possible.

Zeldan had an idea. He offered Cruz his crew of Unseleighe workers. Cruz agreed, having everything to gain. Zeldan's minions moved quickly and had the plane unloaded in ten minutes. The DC-6 was back in the air before the engines had time to cool off.

Zeldan's quality work crew enhanced his position with Cruz, and the drug lord started cutting him some lucrative deals in return for transport of the merchandise within the United States, the riskiest part of the trip.

Soon, Zeldan's elven minions were selling coke in quantity. Their business expanded, and with their elven magic, they stayed out of police trouble most of the time. He might have kenned all the money he wanted and lived like the true king he was, but it would have cheated him of the human pain that went along with drugs, the pain his tribe thrived on.

Zeldan gained confidence in his abilities to control, and began including humans in the drug sales. Certain humans were all too happy to do the chore—and take the fall that went along with it. Not only would humans do the dealing, they would even stay off the stuff for the sake of the money they earned. This amazed Zeldan; he knew that most humans were utterly weak, but there were a few exceptions. And these exceptions were making him rich.

Still, collecting the negative energy they lusted after was a problem. Cocaine dealing, while useful in destroying human lives, supplied only a marginal amount of the force they required. They needed a central location where people would go, and return to, time and again. He also needed a means of storing, beyond the Unseleighe's own dark souls, these powers.

To find the tools he needed, he made a brief trip back to Underhill. The Unseleighe had long been allies with several tribes of dark demons, evil entities that were more spirit than flesh.

Morrigan, a solitary Unseleighe witch and governess of demons, offered a plan: certain quartz crystals, available in Underhill mines their clan controlled, possessed the properties Zeldan sought. These he could use as reservoirs of dark energy. Morrigan even offered a bonus: a captured Seleighe Duke they had succeeded in turning to the dark side of their work. Morrigan suggested that Rathand, a former Duke of Outremer, might be able to improve on the crystal storage system.

Once Zeldan explained his drug operation, she had asked

him, "How would you like an elixir to add to this drug and create an Underhill version of it? One which will inflict untold anguish, make the humans surrender their souls to you, and still be nothing like the drugs the humans have ever seen?"

Such a substance would have advantages from a practical standpoint as well. An alien substance would baffle the humans' law enforcement. "New" drugs, altered versions of existing vices, entered the drug market all the time under street names, such as Dragon, Lucky Seven, Clown and Mister D. And if the drug were appropriately addictive, it would not only crack the drug market, it might create one of its own.

Zeldan named the new drug "Black Dream." Morrigan offered Black Dream elixir, access to the mines, and a limited supply of crystals. For a price.

Morrigan's tribe had run into the same vacuum in Underhill as Zeldan's forces had: no new challenges. Also, her people thrived on negative psychic energy more than the Unseleighe, and felt the deficiency much more than the elves. So in trade, she wanted a cut in whatever power he harvested from the pathetic humans. A pipeline, so to speak, from the human well. With enough Black Dream to guarantee an ample supply of agony.

They had sealed the agreement over a decapitated Avalon elf, a symbol of their mutual hatred for the Seleighe.

That had been only a year ago, human time, and while the Black Dream project provided an enjoyable diversion, the Avalon elves remained at large.

Rathand said, "I believe Morrigan is going to call us through the Terminal."

"She is?" Zeldan said, mildly annoyed. In the room's center was a rather large crystal, surrounded by a geometric pattern of smaller ones. They referred to this as the Terminal, which served as a direct line of communication to Underhill. It worked on similar principals as the Gate, but used far less energy and was nowhere near as disruptive to the senses. Morrigan had been calling more often lately, leading Zeldan to wonder if she was checking up on him. While he liked the benefits of their business deal, Zeldan suspected that she wanted far more power than she originally asked for.

The Terminal flickered to life, much like a television screen, but the image extended over four different facets of the huge crystal, giving her face a fragmented look. Morrigan had the power to choose whatever appearance she liked, and why she chose this particular look confounded Zeldan from the very start. Her face was round with fat and a double chin, and she had a nose that might be mistaken for a beak. Bright red hair circled her face with a crimson halo, with wild, flaming eyes to match. And this, Zeldan guessed, was a good day, since he heard no victims screaming in the background.

"Zeldan," she said brusquely, with a voice like a chainsaw. "The next shipment of elixir is ready for transport. I trust all is well with your end of the operation?"

"Oh, indeed it is," Zeldan said, stepping closer to the Terminal. While on his end of the link he had the psychological advantage of looking down, he knew it would have no effect on her, since she was looking down on *her* end. He found her assumption of command of him unnerving, and had to constantly reassure himself of his superiority.

She's not down here in the trenches like I am, shoveling this shit heap called the human race. She'd better be damned glad I've got the courage to take these chances for the both of us!

"We have three new employees of our little organization, human employees, who are practically begging to be pawns," he said. Zeldan knew she had never liked the idea of employing humans and made no secret of it. She distrusted the humans simply because they were an inferior race, and it amused Zeldan to annoy her in this way.

Morrigan made a sour face, all the more hideous in the crystal facets; it looked like her face had been broken and glued back together clumsily. "You know I dislike those silly apes. At least they're expendable; if they cause too much trouble, I will have to insist you get rid of them. In the most permanent way possible. If one of them finds out what's going on . . ."

"It will never happen," Zeldan said. "They think they're working for a human. They know nothing of the fitness center. And as for the business itself, the New You Fitness Center just passed scrutiny by the highest authority in this land."

This seemed to surprise her. "The police department?"

Zeldan shook his head. "The IRS. Our taxes came back with a clean bill of health. We had to pay several thousands of their dollars, but it was worth it. We'll more than make up for the loss with our product."

She smiled a carnivorous smile and laughed. "I should say so, King of the Unseleighe," she said with a hint of sarcasm. "Our supply of pain and sorrow runneth low here in Underhill. Are you ready to deliver?"

"Certainly, my dear Morrigan," Zeldan said, turning to Rathand. "We have quite an ample supply, courtesy of a pathetic human named Bridget."

Zeldan nodded to Rathand. "Send bank alpha through the pipe," he directed, and to Rathand's questioning look, added, "Yes. All of it."

This should keep the bitch happy for awhile, he thought. This was the part of the agreement he didn't care much for. Had he held out more, she would have threatened to withdraw the elixir necessary for Black Dream, forcing him to fall back on the human standby: crack cocaine. Crack had its uses, but was not nearly as addictive, and destructive to the human psyche and soul, as their particular brew.

Rathand pulled two crystal levers, and the computer cabinet storing bank alpha came to life. Yellow phosphorescence seeped through the panel cracks, vibrating the frame as a loud whine issued from within.

"We will have to send it over in packets," Rathand said. "The pipe can't handle the full force of what's in there now."

Zeldan frowned in annoyance. "Then, so be it." *I was hoping to shake their receptors up, damage them, even. But if we disrupted the path needed to send the stuff to Underhill, that would have fallen on my head.*

Rathand fiddled with the console for a moment, then the Terminal went blank, replaced by the static of a television tuned to a dead channel. Bank alpha shuddered, then spat forth the first packet of pain and sorrow.

Down in the Unseleighe chamber, wind rose, ripped at the walls and the hung ceiling, dislodging panels. A wide beam of yellow power, streaked with black, blasted directly into the base of the Terminal, where the pipeline port to Underhill was located. The port was a cluster of crystals, fused together with much use. The Terminal displayed images of the power, red pain, icy steel agony of Bridget and countless others. Behind the pain of the workout was a deeper sorrow, displayed in the Terminal as tortured faces screaming back at high school taunts. Shame, utter shame, embarrassment to be seen in public, on the beach, in swimsuits. Then came the dark purple of self-loathing, bathing the room in a deep violet light. Crowning all this agony was the frustration of gaining weight, grimly superimposed over the pain and struggle of trying to lose it.

The first packet complete, the port now glowed a dull red, and the crystals, molten, semiliquid, threatened to surrender their matrix.

Rathand scurried over to the port, examined it, and gave Zeldan a pained look.

"Well?" Zeldan said, joining him at the base of the Terminal. "Can it take more?"

"I don't know yet," Rathand said, his brow dripping with sweat. The tips of his pointed ears were flushed, a sign of anxiety in most elves. The wind had died down in the chamber, and the packet had dwindled to a pencil-thin stream, but the Terminal was still hot to the touch. "The port crystals are starting to fuse more. We may have to replace them."

"How many more packets do we have left to send?" Zeldan demanded.

"Four. If we wait, the port may cool sufficiently for the rest."

Morrigan came back on the Terminal. She seemed dazed, stunned even; from the looks of her hair, Zeldan had broadcast their windstorm along with the power.

"Good *gods*, Zeldan," she said, with an addict's gleam in her eye. "That was the strongest dose of human pain yet! Where did you *get* such power?"

"The usual channels. The fitness center . . ." Zeldan began.

"You didn't use *torture* this time, did you?" she said with a grin. "If you did, then shame on you." She laughed explosively. "And keep up the good work!"

Zeldan shrugged, remembering the argument they'd had over the pros and cons of torture. Zeldan insisted it wasn't necessary and created more trouble with the humans' law enforcement than it was worth. His plan, tapping into the physical pain in the fitness center, had led to other rich reservoirs of agony: that which the humans hid in their subconscious.

"No torture needed," Zeldan said casually. "It's all quite legitimate, so far as the police are concerned."

Morrigan beamed at her partner, but Zeldan didn't know if it was envy or contempt he read in her face.

With her, the two emotions are often inseparable.

"I have more to send, if it pleases you, my dear Morrigan," Zeldan began. "*Much* more."

This seemed to surprise her. With a raised eyebrow, she said, "That wasn't an entire bank?"

"Dear, no. Only a packet." He glanced over at Rathand, who shrugged, resigned. "Sending it all at once would have destroyed the port and the pipeline. I think our equipment can handle—"

Morrigan shook her head vigorously. "No, Zeldan. Do not send it now," she said slowly and deliberately. "Our crystals haven't recovered from the last transmission. There will be a festival tonight, since this is the richest lode we've received in . . . well . . ." She paused, reflecting. "The richest lode I recall *ever* receiving."

Zeldan saw her trying to maintain her acid personality, but her complete satisfaction, at least for the time being, leaked through.

"When we are ready for the rest, I will let you know. We are sending the elixir now," she said, killing the transmission.

Zeldan gazed at the blank crystal Terminal for several long moments before Rathand turned it off from the console.

"It's a good thing she can wait for the rest," Rathand said, looking over the port at the base of the Terminal. "This matrix would never have handled another surge like that last without cooling off first."

Zeldan wanted to feel relieved. Morrigan was satisfied, much more than she admitted, and the Black Dream elixir would arrive unimpeded for awhile longer. But the satisfaction wouldn't last. With four more packets of artificial node energy in store, he figured she would be satiated for a few days, at least.

"We'd better get to work constructing another port," Zeldan said. What he really meant was that Rathand had better get to work. "Make for us a crystal port which can withstand more than we transmitted today. I don't know how to do it, but do it. This is your area of expertise." Zeldan considered something disturbing, which made him praise Bridget—and curse her at the same time. "I have a feeling Morrigan may expect this level of power each time she asks it. We might have just raised our own standards without realizing it."

"Yes, Your Darkness," Rathand said, with bitterness behind it. Rathand clearly didn't want to get to work; his posture gave him away.

Zeldan smirked to himself, enjoying this play of power on not only a subordinate but a captured Seleighe. When Morrigan was pleased, Zeldan Dhu was especially pleased, and even this mild form of complaint from Rathand did not change his good spirits.

He left his minion to do his work, and stopped next door

at the Factory. This was another room built and outfitted for the specific purpose of manufacturing Black Dream. Before cutting his particular deal with Morrigan, Zeldan and his people had mastered the relatively simple task of making crack cocaine. Presto, now one of Zeldan's human lieutenants, had been most helpful in showing them how to make rock.

One evening Presto invited Zeldan over to his apartment. The elf had no reason to suspect Presto was any wiser to his true identity; Zeldan had always met him in human seeming, disguised as the properly pumped-up health freak, Peter Pritchard. At his apartment, Presto showed Zeldan how to increase his cocaine profits by "stepping" on the coke. The result was a greater quantity of an acceptable grade of coke, ready for peddling on the street.

"What about crack?" Zeldan asked. "That's what everyone wants. How do you build a crack factory?"

At this point Presto started to act a little suspicious, and Zeldan had to lay a spell on him to dispel any doubts of his intentions. In a zombielike trance, Presto took the ki he had just stepped on, dumped it into a shallow pot on the stove, and proceeded to make a batch of crack.

"You don't need a factory, man," Presto said, holding the pan out for his inspection. "All you need is a stove and a pot. This here's a motherlode of *crack*. That's all there is to it."

Not only was crack more lucrative, it was more addictive than the original agent. The final step boiled away most impurities, leaving behind nearly pure, smokable coke.

The result of this meeting was the drug lab under the fitness center, constructed with the help of Presto and Rathand, though Presto, nor any other human, had not ever set foot in the basement. Rathand quickly mastered the technique for making crack and was soon turning out their own street version, which they called Black Dream.

Along one wall was the equipment, a series of vats and gas burners, used to cook the cocaine. Each batch received one drop of Morrigan's potent elixir.

On a long table in the middle of the room were several cases of tiny vials. The vials had black rubber stoppers to identify the product as Black Dream. On another table were ten ki's of raw cocaine hydrochloride wrapped in neat, butcher-paper packages.

In a corner of the room was another Terminal, without the central crystal. This Terminal was a receiver only, with a circle of crystals on the top of it. And in this circle was a clear vial of elixir, which Morrigan had apparently just sent.

"Ambrosia," Zeldan whispered, gently picking up the small vial, which was about as big around as his finger. The elixir was the color and consistency of used motor oil. He stored the vial in a small safe, which Rathand would open up when he got to work on the next batch of Black Dream.

We'll have to watch the dosage a little closer, next time, he remarked to himself. *That last batch was a bit too strong.* On the news he had seen the coverage of the nineteen deaths at the Wintons'. Fortunately, the police suspected no deliberate foul play.

If only they knew . . .

His crew of Unseleighe had gone over to the party to test a newer, more potent batch of Dream and handed sample after free sample to the kids. This batch produced some impressive fear, terror, and hallucinations in the humans who took it, and this power now resided in Rathand's bank number four. Unfortunately, the humans died of heart failure before Rathand siphoned off the bulk of their terror; the rest vanished with their souls to whatever realm the humans went in the afterlife.

This situation might have created complications for their operation, and might yet as the humans fumbled about with their investigation. But since human kids died frequently enough from drug overdoses, he doubted the humans would cast much suspicion on anyone.

As Zeldan left his domain and entered the humans' world as Peter Pritchard, he remembered another task he had to do himself. Presto had recently avoided jail with the help of a human *lawyer,* in spite of the fact he'd been caught with enough crack to put him away for decades. Zeldan already knew of these professionals called *lawyers,* hired negotiators human criminals used to avoid imprisonment, but only recently learned that some lawyers were better than others. They cost more, too, but that was not a problem for the Unseleighe. Zeldan anticipated an increase of Black Dream distribution, and with that, an increase in arrests. The situation at the Wintons' might yet develop into a full-scale problem, or might even recur somewhere else. Though the human helpers he had were expendable to an extent, he needed to keep as many as possible. Replacements took time *and* elven resources.

Presto had given him a business card of the lawyer, one of the best in the Dallas-Fort Worth area.

He regarded the card, with its raised golden letters, with some skepticism.

It may be worth my time to give this Paul Bendis a call.

Rathand watched Zeldan leave the basement, his human seeming flowing back into place as he exited. The moment he was out of sight, he exhaled a sigh of relief.

That was close, Rathand thought, touching the red crystal installed in his temple. *I must be more careful than that.* Satisfied Zeldan was far enough away, he returned to the console of crystals and resumed his act of sabotage.

The technology Rathand had assembled for his master was less than perfect, but it had something in its favor, something that would make the entire system his ally.

I'm the only one who understands how this creation works!

Rathand wanted nothing more than to be rid of his master, but to do away with him would be suicide. And a painful one, at that; he wasn't prepared for such martyrdom. With that in mind, Rathand had looked for other ways to foul up Zeldan's plan, and his solution was simple: he found subtle ways for the artificial nodes to act against themselves.

Crossing the lines from the Terminal to the banks was one way. This had caused a short in the power flows, and half the banks had, over a period off weeks, slowly drained themselves of the artificial node energy. So far Zeldan had not detected the short, but given time, he would have to. That it might well result in the destruction of the device didn't matter to Rathand.

I hope it takes him if it does blow, he thought, retracing his work, making certain the short was in place.

Perhaps there is a way to hasten the process. . . .

Chapter Nine

At the door came a knock, and when Adam answered it, Spence came in, without his human seeming.

"Your Majesty," Spence said, bowing. "I am Iarbanel of Avalon, and I wish to be of service. Sire." The elf wore a maroon Bugle Boy shirt, slacks, casual shoes—his usual attire. The only thing noticeably different about him were the pointed elven ears. His bowing seemed odd, alien, uncomfortable. But it was something Adam would have to get used to.

"I'm glad you've decided to join our little party," Adam said, dispensing with the royal formalities and giving Spence a hug. "I'm only recently, well, re-elfed, I guess. This is still new to me," he added, dismissing the glamorie and returning to his full elven splendor.

Spence nodded, as if he'd expected the reply. The moment felt awkward to Adam, since he'd looked up to Spence and his wisdom in spite of his youth. And now, Adam was his King.

Take it slowly, Adam thought. *Just because I'm the ruler now doesn't mean I can't still look up to him. Didn't Father say that wisdom was part humility, and knowing when to seek advice?*

Adam now saw that, since his arrival in the human realm, he'd been surrounded by elven guardians. His "mother" Sammi, Spence, Moira . . . when school was in session, they had been inseparable and made excuses or explanations for each other's "allergies." When Adam started working at the Yaz, Jimmy hired Spence the same day, even though there were several applicants more qualified.

Hmm. Looks like my best buddy has already been using elven magic to influence the human realm. Maybe that's why he made straight A's when I had a B average.

I'm going to have to talk to him about that. . . .

They seated themselves in the living room, Adam on the chair, the others on the couches. Spence took a seat to his left, looking grim, a disturbing sight on his otherwise light-hearted features.

"Something happened over at the Wintons' mansion last night," Spence began. "I don't think you've learned of it yet, and I wouldn't mention it now, except that it has a bearing on this Court."

Sammi leaned forward, glanced at the others, and said, "Adam, you didn't know about that?"

"About what?" he said. He didn't like the look his mother had at all. Moira looked interested, too. Apparently she hadn't heard the latest. "I knew there was a big party over there last night," Adam said, feeling like he'd been left out of a big secret. "We were there until things started getting a little out of hand."

"'Out of hand' is not the phrase I would have chosen," Sammi said. "I was over there this afternoon, saw the results of last night." She looked at Adam, hesitating before continuing. "You wouldn't know what had happened, I suppose."

Spence said, "Several humans died. Steve was one of the victims."

"Died?" Adam said, horrified. "What *happened* over there last night?"

Sammi rummaged through her purse, pulled out some pictures, and handed them to Adam. "*This* is what happened. Not long after you left."

Adam took the pictures, started going through them. He got halfway through the stack before he stopped looking.

The ones he saw sickened him; he had even known a few of the now-dead kids.

"Nineteen dead," Sammi said. "Or was it twenty? Your friend Daryl was the only survivor." She shook her head. "It wasn't a homicide, but I paid a little visit anyway, in part because you were involved, or almost involved. Good thing you left when you did."

Adam shrugged. "I never would have done the drugs in the first place," he said. "Neither would Moira or Spence."

Sammi's grin was wicked. "That's right, you wouldn't have. But if you had, I would have known. Spells. Like little alarms. I would have heard them a thousand miles away." She paused, reflecting. "I'll bet human mothers would appreciate something like that."

Adam didn't know what to think about those particular spells, but was glad Sammi had the foresight to place them. *As a human, I would have human weaknesses. No telling what might have happened if I'd been a little less resolute.*

"I'm not concerned with the drugs, per se. Yes, they killed the humans. And yes, you were in the same house, but—"

Marbann interrupted, "The humans are not our concern. We are their superiors in every way," he said. The comment brought strange, accusing looks from all assembled.

"We have lived among the humans for some time," Spence said. He seemed visibly angered by Marbann's statements, but appeared to be holding it in. "We have even *become* humans, to a degree. It has been five human years since we Gated here. You have only arrived today."

"The humans are very much a part of our world now, Marbann," Sammi said. "It has been many years since I arrived here, but I do remember what my first impressions of this race are. I didn't much care for them. They enslaved their own kind, the ones with dark skin, though they later fought a great war over it. Slavery ended. The race improved. They are far from perfect, mind you, but . . ."

Sammi's words trailed off, as if she were seeking the right words to express herself.

"What I think Samantha is trying to say," Moira said, "is that humans are not the lesser race we once thought them to be."

Marbann didn't look convinced. "Are you telling me they are our equals?" he said, and looked around, seeking support for his side. He found none. "They only a live about hundred years. They have *no* possession of magic. They scoff at our existence, or anything else that doesn't fit neatly into their narrow sciences. They are cattle, so far as I am concerned." Marbann folded his arms resolutely.

"You forget, my dear Marbann," Sammi said ominously, "that King Aedham Tuiereann has lived among, and believed himself to be one of, these cattle, as you so indelicately call them. Where does that leave our new ruler?"

Flustered, Marbann replied hastily, "I meant no insult, Your Majesty. It's just that . . ."

"It's just that you're repeating the same line of *caca* we were taught in Underhill," Moira said. "We've been here long enough to know there is much to this race, which our kind has ignored for too long. Now we have been forced to learn about them, and we have even learned to appreciate them, in the course of our own preservation. Tell me, Marbann of Avalon, have you ever met a human? Have you even seen one?"

Marbann said nothing for a long moment and looked down at the carpet, avoiding everyone's eyes. "No, I have not," he said grudgingly. "I've only just arrived here." Then, "I have much to learn."

Adam remained quiet during the discussion, his mind returning to the previous evening at the Wintons' mansion. *It was Moira, Spence and I. Daryl was having a birthday party. The place felt wrong from the beginning, but we stayed anyway. I had a wine cooler. As the evening progressed, the human children starting acting stupid, which often happens at such parties, but there was something else underlying the stupidity. I knew then something bad was about to happen. Today when I talked to Daryl, who couldn't find his ass with both hands if he had to, I knew something bad* had *happened.*

He regarded the Polaroids as if they were some sort of time machine; they had nothing like photography in Underhill, and even though he'd been in the human realm a few years, and photography and video had become commonplace in his human life, the technology seemed alien now. *All those humans dead. No, there's more to it than just an overdose of recreational drugs.*

As he reviewed the events, he recalled some other strange occurrences the last few days, aside from his raging hormones and his lust for Moira. There was that stoned kid in the mall, and that black feeling he got from him. And then the experience in the vacant store. *The lost time. What happened back there? What else happened that I don't remember?*

While Adam's thoughts trailed off, the conversation became chaotic, with everyone speaking at once. But he heard through the chaos something which seized his attention.

"Is it any surprise that the Unseleighe followed us here?" Samantha said loudly, clearly.

All conversation ceased.

"Go on," Adam said, intrigued. "I think you now have our ears."

Moira groaned, as if in response to a bad pun. But Adam had intended none.

"You do not know Zeldan Dhu as I do," Samantha said acidly. "Before our late King died, he told me of Zeldan and his family. Our ancestor killed his ancestor long ago. Our great-great-grandfather fought against his. They had been plotting the invasion for centuries. Zeldan Dhu had vowed to kill every last one of the Tuiereann family and will not hesitate to come here, to the human realm, to do it."

Marbann didn't seem convinced. "They could not have traced us back to this human city in this human time. The spell our late King and I wove was not detectable. It left no trails for our enemy to follow." He stubbornly folded his arms again, an action which was becoming irritating to Adam.

Is he forgetting who's King here? Adam thought, holding his tongue and temper.

Spence said, "If the Unseleighe have pursued us here, what evidence have you?"

Again, that terrible silence fell in the room. Adam wondered if he should attempt to exert some royal influence to calm things down, assume a leadership role, but at the moment he didn't feel much like a leader. The transition to his true self left him a bit muddled, and he still didn't feel, well, *royal.* Not yet. His only link to royalty was his family, who were all dead except for Samantha. *Things were so much easier when I was a human kid. . . .*

Samantha continued, "At the Wintons' mansion I felt Unseleighe magic."

Marbann stood up, his height towering over the others. "Certainly not here, milady . . ." he said, amid gasps of disbelief in the room. "We have only just arrived. I doubt the Unseleighe's ability to find us in a year, much less a day."

"We don't need Unseleighe to have evil around here," Moira said haughtily. "Humans do just fine all by themselves! Besides, there were enough bad boys and girls at the party last night to fill a prison. Losers. Troublemakers . . ."

Samantha calmly held a hand up, gently urging all to be silent and listen. Once the gesture restored order, she continued, "Granted, evil forces exist in abundance in the human world, but these forces are of a different flavor from Unseleighe evil. They are . . . human. For all the good humans do, they have their evil as well. As a human, I am an officer of the law, a profession I have chosen so that I can study the humans. With my authority, I have access to records that most humans do not. I can use this access to cover my elven identity should I need to. In this profession, I investigate crimes, murder mostly, and I am very good at it." She gestured toward the room, the house in general. "This is an above-average human abode. And none of this has been raised by magic. I earned it all, the old-fashioned human way."

"'Abode'?" Marbann said, clearly confused.

"This *home*. This . . . *elfhame*. Our new one, for now. While I was at the Winton mansion, the magic I sensed was not human. It was Unseleighe."

"*Zeldan?*" Moira whispered.

"I don't think so. More likely a minion. I doubt he would have the courage to show himself, though I don't know how long they've been here in the humans' world."

Last night's close call made Adam shudder. Not only had he been a defenseless human, he was an oblivious one as well.

Perhaps they would have discovered me, perhaps not. The risk is still too great to repeat. But then, that was the whole idea of hiding my elven identity under a wrapping of humanity.

"Where *are* they?" Spence asked. "Among us?"

Then, it all became clear to the new King. "They're here, all right. In Dallas."

Samantha stared at him. "Do tell, young King," she said. "Have you encountered them already?"

Adam straightened himself up in the chair; he had begun to slouch. While he did this, he gathered his thoughts. *How to put this?*

"I think that what I encountered was their results," Adam said. "First, I ran across a young human, stoned on some drug, in the Marketplace. He said, and I think I have this down correctly: 'It's like, the sky opened up, and Gabriel tore loose with horns of brass,'" Adam began, feeling his voice change to match that of the stoned boy's, a pitch higher, and slurred. "'And Armageddon was here. And the black Eagle saw the ruined castle, and all the dead within waited for the mighty to take the palace.'

"Then he looked at me, and said, 'And you were there. And you did not die.'"

Adam considered this, remembering something now that he didn't before . . . because it hadn't happened yet.

The black Eagle. Ruined palace . . .

Fear rippled through him. *He couldn't have known!*

Adam leaped to his feet.

"Gods, Samantha. That boy described the Dream. The Dream I just had! How did he—?"

Marbann said, "Do not confuse time, young King. What is before and after, here in the human realm, does not fall necessarily in that order in Underhill."

"He's right," Sammi said softly. "Was he Unseleighe? Would you have known?"

"No, I . . . don't think so." *The boy was Cory, and I've known him for years. But I guess that doesn't really mean much.*

Samantha looked uncomfortable, as if a disturbing thought just came to her. "You said the boy was stoned. On what?"

Adam returned to his seat, feeling reassured, though he did not quite grasp the time concept Marbann was trying to explain.

"Black Dream," Adam said. *The black-stoppered vial.* "The boy was on Black Dream."

Samantha exhaled loudly. When Adam looked up, she had her face in her hands.

"That's the drug you warned me about," Adam said. "Was that the drug that killed all those humans last night?" It was a wild guess, but his hunch was unusually strong. *I knew there was something different, evil and magical, about that envelope.*

"So that's *why,*" Samantha said cryptically. "It's been on the street for a year, but it has to be."

"My dear lady, you are making little sense," Marbann said. "If this is a human *drug,* it is a human *problem.*"

Samantha glared at him. "There lies the problem. *It isn't a human drug.*"

"The Unseleighe," Moira said. "Zeldan. That's his style, all right. A *year,* you say?"

"At least. Narco has been going crazy lately with a new wave of the stuff, particularly after last night at the

Wintons'. I think Black Dream is responsible for the deaths. And Black Dream has been around since last summer."

Marbann of Avalon yawned.

"A year," Adam said. "The time—"

"—doesn't matter here," Moira said. "The human realm doesn't intersect with Underhill on any level. Five human years ago, relative to you, you Gated. Marbann has only just arrived, but left immediately after you and Samantha did, am I correct?"

Marbann nodded. "You are. For me, the King . . . died only moments ago."

"So it is possible," Adam said, "that the Unseleighe have been here not only a year, but perhaps longer."

"The Unseleighe," Samantha corrected, "have been here for *centuries.* Zeldan is the newcomer. He may have arrived shortly after you did, young King. Or a month ago."

"What matters is that they are here *now,*" Moira said. "Gods, I didn't think it had already happened."

"Moira," Adam said, approaching this from a new angle, "did you notice anything odd last night about the party?"

Moira considered this carefully, taking a several moments to respond. "I wasn't particularly aware of anything Unseleighelike, though I always sense evil when I see humans abusing their minds, souls and bodies. But then, *I'm* not a mage."

Samantha hissed, her ears quivered, and her slitted eyes widened and glowed momentarily with an energy of their own. Her elfing-out totally like that was a frightening sight. Adam curled up into the chair like a cat, protectively.

"What? What did I say?" Moira asked, but she sounded like she knew she'd let something vital slip out.

"Samantha, what's a mage?" Adam asked. He had an idea. He wanted to be sure.

Samantha sighed in resignation. "I suppose it is well past the time we should keep anything from you, Adam," Samantha said.

Adam realized he preferred to be addressed as Adam instead of King, or young King, or even Your Majesty, but now was not the moment to bring that up. *Later.*

"A Mage is an elf with exceptional magical abilities. Humans occasionally have mages sprout up randomly, but the occurrence is so rare it is not worth concerning ourselves with right now. Or, maybe, ever. Zeldan Dhu is our problem. Not mages."

"I see," Adam said, uncertain if he did. "Let me adjust to being an elf, first. That's . . . taking some getting used to. I've been a human a long time." He reached up and touched his ears. "These still feel weird."

"Our plan precisely," Samantha said, casting a warning look at Moira. "But I suppose no harm is done."

"There was something else," Adam said, hoping to break up the awkward moment by changing the subject, "that happened after this incident I described. Now *this* was weird."

Even Marbann sat up attentively.

"The boy I mentioned, he gave me a vial of—you guessed it—Black Dream. And walked off. Security cameras are all over the place there, so I thought, 'Hey, this looks like a drug deal,' so I started looking for a place to ditch it before I got busted. I went straight to the men's room and flushed it. It went all the way down."

"You flushed twice. Good boy," Samantha said. Marbann grimaced. *He is the King, not a child!* his look seemed to say.

Adam continued, "After I left the rest room, there was this unleased space to the left. And I was like, I dunno, hypnotized by something. The room filled up with fog. Lights appeared under the fog. I must have zoned out or something."

Moira seemed delighted. "So you were Dreaming, even under the spell." She turned to Samantha. "You felt it too, didn't you?"

"But what happened there?" Adam asked. He felt like he'd been excluded from yet another secret, and they were teasing him with it. "What were those lights under the fog?"

"Don't you know?" Moira taunted.

Adam held his tongue.

"Those were the *nodes*," Samantha said. "Powerful ones, too. Deep underground, at the very spot they manifested. The human realm has them as well. Only, they're wasted here, unless an elf comes along and puts them to use. Why else do you think our kind would bother coming to this chaotic place?"

Moira seemed to be enjoying this. She said, "The Marketplace was built on the site of three power nodes, long ago. Originally the building was a cookie and cracker factory."

Adam groaned as cookie-making cartoon elves flashed through his mind. "Give me a break," he said, smiling just a bit in amusement.

"It's for real. Well, most buildings would have been knocked down when they outlived their original usefulness, but someone decided this one was worth saving. Maybe it was the nodes, influencing the humans subconsciously. Anyway, the presence of the nodes is one of the reasons we were drawn to the Marketplace. It's a natural place for us to be."

"The Marketplace," Adam said, bemused. Then a dark thought came to him: "If the nodes attract us, won't they attract the Unseleighe as well?"

No one said anything for quite a while. Then Samantha spoke up, "Most likely they would , as unappealing as the prospect is."

Hunger was not among the physiological differences between humans and elves. At some point during the dark discussion, Adam realized he hadn't eaten much that day and now had a craving for pizza.

In Avalon, of course, there was no pizza or any of the processed foods humans enjoyed. Fruits and vegetables grew abundantly on the palace grounds, with the aid of magic. In his particular elfhame, Adam had learned that to create food, or *ken* it from nothing, was not polite. Kenning food was something the Unseleighe did, Adam had been told while growing up, but he knew that other Seleighe elf clans kenned regularly. It was just a matter of etiquette. While it was acceptable to urge the natural growth of vegetables along with spells, "acceptable" food went through the stages of normal growth, more or less.

Game was also in abundance, though servants hunted it for the royal family instead of raising it in pens, as Adam had grown accustomed to seeing out in the country in Texas. Servants did most of the hunting, but occasionally the royal family would indulge in a bit of sport, hunting deer with the crudest of bows and arrows, and *no* magic whatsoever. Neither Adam, nor anyone else in Avalon, had never been hungry. Food was always available, in one form or another. There had never been a drought, a famine, or a flood.

The Unseleighe were the only scourge in Avalon, and in less than a day they had taken everything from the rightful owners.

Adam found himself in a quandary. While it had been five years since his last experience with the war, Marbann had just stepped out of it, and was no doubt famished. Moira, who'd mentioned she'd eaten no breakfast or lunch, was probably starving, too. Other elves were on the way as well, and might arrive anytime. But this was the human realm, with no elven food to speak of; food here was all grown without spells, and was highly processed, seasoned, and garnished.

On the floor was a stack of newspaper with the coupon section on the top. "Unexpected Guests? Order a Two For One from Dominique's Pizza," one ad announced. *Dominique's makes the best pizza in the universe. And I'm King. That's what we're having.*

"Anyone hungry?" Adam asked. Everyone was.

While the new King called in the order, Samantha went scavenging in the kitchen for other eatables. Since she wasn't expecting out of town guests either, at least on this particular day, she came up empty-handed.

"Looks like it's pizza tonight," she said from the kitchen doorway. "Time for a shopping trip to SAM'S."

Marbann looked puzzled. "What manner of beast is a *pizza?*"

Adam stifled a smirk and said, "Several kinds," he said. Samantha brought in a pitcher of lemonade and five glasses. "You're all probably parched," Samantha said. After filling the five glasses, Adam noticed the pitcher was still nearly full.

I guess a little kenning is acceptable, if done surreptitiously, noted Adam as he downed his drink.

Presently, the pizza arrived, and Adam went to the door to pay for it.

"Ah, wait a minute," Moira said, following him to the door. "Aren't you forgetting something?"

Adam paused, with his hand on the doorknob. "Like . . . what?"

"Are we having a costume party here, or are you trying to pass yourself off as a Vulcan?"

Adam felt his ears. "Geez, of course." As Moira had shown him, he replaced the glamorie, and immediately noticed the difference between elven and human perceptions. His vision was not as sharp, and he didn't feel as strong. Moira stood back, out of sight. When he opened the door, he must have been presentable to the pizza human who was standing on the front steps with their dinner in a big vinyl box. The Dominique's guy didn't seem to notice anything amiss as he counted out the change.

Adam closed the door, and as he stood there, holding the two-for-ones, Moira changed him back. His vision sharpened, and his energy returned. *I'm not going to like going back to being a human, even temporarily,* he thought morosely.

Adam entered the living room and announced, "Dinner is served."

"That smells sooooo gooooood," Samantha said, holding a stack of plates and forks. "I never did get to eat that orange at work."

"Your hired servants put the kill in *boxes* before they present it to you?" Marbann said. "Most odd, these human ways."

Adam set the pizza down on the coffee table and opened the long cardboard box. The vultures descended on the kill.

All except Marbann, who gaped at the pizza, openmouthed. He picked up and examined one of two little plastic table thingies used to keep the box lid from touching the pizza. He held it up and exclaimed, "How did they manage to kill this strange beast with one of *these*?"

Moira almost choked on her slice. "Marbann, this is not an animal. It is a combination of ingredients, part pig, and part . . . well, pig. Something like a boar. Sausage and Canadian bacon. And cheese, made from milk. The red sauce is made from a vegetable. The crust is, a—well, never mind. It would take too long to explain baking."

Marbann shook his head. "Why go to all that trouble? It is much easier to cook the boar on a spit, and the vegetables taste much better by themselves."

As Spence devoured his slice, he said between mouthfuls, "It has been a long time since I've arrived from Underhill. I remember thinking the same thing, but after awhile I grew to like human food. Humans don't have magic, remember, and they have to go to extra trouble to make their meals enjoyable."

"I can't imagine life without pizza," Samantha said. "For humans, too much of this causes fat to build up around their stomachs. Elves have no such problem, you see."

"Humans gain fat when they eat?" Marbann was aghast. "Then why do they eat this *pizza*?"

"Because, my dear Marbann," Samantha said, "that is the way of the universe. Humans have little control over their lives, their physical surroundings. And *no* control whatsoever over the sacred pizza pie."

Marbann tried a piece of Dominique's finest and recoiled violently.

"Humans also like their food very hot. Be careful," Moira said belatedly.

"Thank you for the warning," Marbann said, then frowned, regarding the slice of pizza as if it were poisonous. "I'm not so certain I'm going to like the humans' world."

"It will grow on you," Adam said, already reaching for another piece. "What should we do about our human covers? Should we go in hiding somewhere, or retain our human identities? If Zeldan is looking for us, might it be in our best interests to go somewhere else? Overseas, perhaps?"

"I've always wanted to go to Ireland," Spence said. "I remember my father talking about it in the old days, how easy it was to be elves there. No glamories, no secrets."

"And those days are gone forever, I'm afraid," Samantha said. "I've been giving it some thought, especially recently, since I've suspected we would soon learn the outcome of the battle we fled. It is not easy to go into hiding in the humans' world now. So much is explored. Although the humans don't have magic, they do have advanced technology that can record and track us, if they so desired. When I arrived in the new world over a hundred human years ago, this land was largely unexplored, and an elf could live in relative isolation because so many of the humans here did.

"Now it is much easier to hide in plain sight. I don't think we'll have any trouble staying here for awhile. With our magics we can make do with this abode for some time. What do you think, Adam?"

It was unusual for his mother to ask his opinion of important matters, but she was not his true mother, and he was, after all, the King.

Time to act like one.

"Perhaps it would be best," Adam said, "if we stayed here until we find out more about Zeldan Dhu, and what he's up to. I don't like the idea of spreading out just yet. I think we're all in danger." *Black Eagle. Unseleighe. Zeldan Dhu . . .*

"They're after you, not us," Spence said. "Don't kid yourself, Ad—I mean, Your Majesty."

"But they won't hesitate to kill us all. That means we all

need a *sanctuary*," Adam said. "And if we're going to go on living like humans, it would look a little odd to keep calling me 'Majesty.' Call me Adam. Like you always have."

"Well, not *always*," Moira said.

"Those of us with human covers should stick with their human names," Sammi said. "If anything, to keep *us* from getting confused."

"I'm inclined to agree," Marbann said. He'd eaten one slice and was starting on a second, this time without hesitation. "Zeldan is out there. And we must stay here until the others appear, since I don't know how to move a Gate once it's established. Gating is not my specialty. Those capable of moving a Gate are now dead."

"Alas, 'tis true," Samantha said. "But no matter. We are safe here, for many reasons. My cover is secure with the police department, as is the King's at his place of employment."

"The King, doing *manual* labor? Is this appropriate?" Marbann said, but he seemed more interested in the pizza, talking around his piece most impolitely.

"What better way to keep an eye on the Marketplace?" Adam said, eyeing the vanishing pizza with distress. "If Zeldan and his people show up there, we would be in the best position to notice it." *Maybe we should have ordered more.* "And if Spence and I suddenly disappear, that would seem strange, even suspicious. Anyone familiar with the Yaz would notice. Jimmy would be left running the entire place, and he's been fair to us from the very start. I think he deserves the same in return."

"I agree with the King," Samantha said. "At least for now, I think those of us already living in the humans' realm should go on, business as usual."

"Hey, I *like* cutting hair!" Moira exclaimed. "*Most* of the time. That little brat today . . ."

Marbann finished his pizza and reached for another, but there was only one left.

"Don't you even think it," Moira said, eyeing the piece. "I've only had three."

Marbann looked hurt. "Well, I've only had *two*, madam," he said, then his expression softened in evident surrender. "But since I am a gentleman . . ."

While Marbann and Moira discussed the fate of the last piece of Dominique's, the piece glimmered momentarily, then vanished from the tray. They stared at the empty space for several long moments, then looked around.

"Okay," Moira said, accusingly. "Who swiped it?"

And as one, the elves turned to their King, who proudly held up his sausage and Canadian bacon prize.

"I think our King is starting to remember his magic," Marbann said with a hint of pride in his voice.

Samantha had also turned back to Sammi McDaris, the human lady cop. "And now, young man, it's time for you to go to bed. You have a busy day ahead of you," she said, urging him toward his bedroom.

"Aw, *Mom*," Adam said, half in jest. He was tired and had been ready for bed for the last half hour. That screw-up with the levin bolt happened because he was tired. After a full night's rest, he knew he would control one better, if not perfectly. Learning one element of magic had triggered some recall of the other forms. "Do I have to go to bed *now?*"

"Yes, you do. Now turn around and march," she commanded. "Moira and I will tuck in the rest of the Folk in the attic."

Adam paused at his door. "Good night, everybody. Sleep as late as you want. *I* have to be at work tomorrow."

The young elven King flopped down on his unmade bed and promptly fell asleep.

Chapter Ten

Daryl figured he must have zonked out for a few minutes, since he woke up from a sound sleep on the ruins of his bed. The hangover was better, nearly nonexistent; he had energy and his head didn't threaten to explode as he stood up. He stripped and climbed into his shower, turned it up as hot as he could stand it, and spent a good half hour luxuriating in it. By the time he emerged, he was ready to go out on the town and party all over again.

Standing in the bathroom doorway, drying himself off with a towel, he surveyed the wreckage of his bedroom. Despite his mother's partial attempts to keep the place picked up, the room looked like a bomb had recently detonated. Clothing, some of it actually clean, covered the floor, forming a mound capped by his waterbed. The bed itself was a nest, with clothing and blankets arranged around a vaguely Daryl-shaped cavity. Having already made good use of it, he was up again, ready to go out.

"Where you goin'?" Justin, his little brother, said brightly from the hallway. He stood there, shirtless in a pair of jeans, much as Daryl had been most of the day. Justin had found a recent musical interest in, of all things, the Alan Parsons Project, which had begun cutting albums around 1975, years before the kid was even born, for crissakes.

Justin's only fifteen. An instrumental cut from the *I Robot* album flowed in from the other bedroom. Little brother had unfashionably long blond hair and stood almost as tall as Daryl, having grown nearly six inches in the last year. His voice had stopped cracking, and could with effort be as deep as Dad's. Daryl had even caught him shaving one morning, and it wasn't make-believe. Uncertain why, Daryl found his recent growth spurts distantly threatening.

"Nowhere," Daryl replied shortly. "Not tonight." Ignoring Justin, he approached the sink and fumbled for the hair dryer.

Justin followed him into the bathroom. "Yeah, you are. I know that look on your face." Daryl glared at his brother's reflection, his additional height distressingly evident as Justin looked down from behind his right shoulder. The blow-dryer roared to life, but wasn't loud enough to drown out Justin, who seemed determined to talk to him no matter what. "You don't bother to get cleaned up unless you're out looking for *punta*."

The word took him by surprise. "For *what*?"

Justin grinned and shut the bathroom door behind him. "You know, *punta*. Piece. Girls."

"Oh, that," Daryl replied. Sex was, oddly enough, the last thing on his mind until Justin mentioned it. Lately his member had become so shriveled with cocaine use as to become almost useless for anything but urination, but the mention of girls made him twitch a little. Now, the prospect added a rosy glow to his plans. *And Justin would only get in the way. Sorry, kiddo . . . If you tag along, there'd be no chance in hell. No way.*

Justin said, "Can I—"

"No!"

"—go with you?"

Daryl finished drying his hair and went into the bedroom. Justin followed him, and Daryl continued to ignore him as he rummaged around for some jeans. He found some 501's that were mostly clean and slid them on.

"Why not?"

Daryl frowned. "Sorry, you're on your own. You shouldn't have any trouble scoring. Hell, you're almost as big as I am. And it's Monday night. Nothing's going on Monday night."

"*Monday?*" Justin looked like he was about to laugh. "Monday was yesterday, you dolt! You don't remember anything, do you?"

Daryl fixed what he hoped was a hard, cold look on his brother, but in the past several months this had become next to impossible. *How can you stare down someone who's taller than you?*

"You passed out on the stairs. Good thing I carried you in here. Dad would've shit if he saw you."

He's just screwing with my head, Daryl thought, glancing over at his clock. It read five P.M. About the time it should.

"You slept all night and day," Justin insisted. "Mom went out. Dad went to work this morning and hasn't been around since."

"Tuesday," Daryl said distantly. "It's fucking *Tuesday*. I'm still going out. Alone."

Justin frowned, but even at his advanced age it still looked like a pout. "Okay, then, how 'bout—"

"No!"

"—turning me on to some pot?"

This question, too, took him by surprise. Suddenly Daryl's little brother had grown up overnight, while he wasn't looking. Little brother had no more of the baby fat, was now lean and wiry as a whippet, with a washboard stomach starting to form. Only yesterday, it seemed, they were staying up all night playing D&D, drinking Pepsi, no drugs, not even weak beer.

That was only a year, or a few years, ago. When's the last time we played D&D anyway?

And now, Justin wanted some of the action Daryl had learned to take for granted.

"You're too young to be doing that stuff," Daryl said uncomfortably, searching the floor for a shirt. He found a black KMFDM shirt he'd whacked the sleeves off of, and slid it on.

His brother was staring at him.

" 'Too young?' Oh, gimme a break."

"You're only fifteen!" Daryl said, debating whether or not to tuck the shirt in.

Justin looked hurt. "No, brother. I'm sixteen. I turned sixteen *last week*."

Daryl looked away. "Oh. Guess I forgot. Well, still, you're *too young*."

Justin started pacing. "Oh, come on! Why don't you ever turn me on to some pot or something? My friends can get their stuff from *their* brothers!"

They were getting loud, and Daryl held a finger up to his lips. "Shut the fuck up!" he whispered. "Dad doesn't need to hear this conversation."

"Dad isn't here, and if he was, he wouldn't *give* a fuck. You know that! That's why he didn't go get you from the Wintons' yesterday."

Daryl stared at a bare patch of carpet as his body surrendered to a cold shiver. *Oh, yeah. Steve's. The cops. Sammi. Steve, the girls, the others . . .*

The entire grisly scene surfaced from the fog of semi-wakened mind, focused, and presented itself with morbid clarity.

He had almost forgotten the waking nightmare at the Wintons', and he wondered if he would have remembered it if Justin hadn't said anything.

"You know about that?" Daryl demanded.

Justin laughed. "Who doesn't? You know Mikey. His brother died over there last night, and I knew Colm, the one they took to Parkland. He didn't make it, by the way."

"Colm. Oh, Colm. Christ, I thought he was already dead."

"Yeah, well, word's gotten all around. What was it, some bad coke or something?"

"I don't know." *I'm alive because I didn't find out.*

"You didn't do any of it, did you?"

He didn't want to go into detail about how he'd gone and passed out in the backyard in his skivvies. That would present an uncool image. By the same token, he didn't want to become his brother's dealer.

Hypocrisy. Isn't like me.

Seeing his little brother on drugs felt wrong, wrong, wrong. He was suddenly grateful he hadn't taken Justin along to the party. His little brother would have probably died along with the rest of them.

"Forget it," Daryl said. "You're too young to be fooling around with that stuff. Any stuff. You can't handle it."

Justin sulked off to his room, slammed his door, and turned the stereo up as high as it would go. Somehow, *I Robot* turned up didn't have the same violent effect of, say, Nine Inch Nails, Daryl thought as he started down the stairs.

A blast of humid, Texas heat greeted him outside, and Daryl soon discovered his 'Vette was now an 'Oven. The black seats burned through his jeans, toasting his backside and exposed shoulders, but once he got the car started and the aircon going, the temperature began to drop. He slapped a Ministry CD in the player and put the car in reverse.

Daryl loved his 1994 Chevy Corvette. For him, this was the only car to drive. Dad had a Corvette when he was in college, and in a drunken stupor had gone down and bought this one for his son and paid for it with a cashier's check. The gesture struck Daryl dumb. Dad had never bought him something so lavish before, but he was not going to argue. But when Dad came to after the blackout, he had forgotten about buying it himself and accused his son of stealing it, then of selling drugs for it; it wasn't until Daryl persuaded him to call the dealership that he realized that he had indeed bought the car, lock, stock and barrel.

Dad threw his arms up and said, "What the hell, you might as well enjoy it. Since I've made such an ass of myself, I'll even get the tags for it."

He bought the tags, but not the insurance. Normally the tag agency wouldn't issue the tags without insurance verification, but with the hundred-dollar bribe, the criteria became unimportant. Nevertheless, Daryl knew he would need insurance, and other things like gas and maintenance, and started looking for ways to make money. Big money, quick money. Meanwhile, he drove the car around uninsured. He had no other choice.

It was a perfect car, except for the goddamned dent the Mustang put in it back at the Winton mansion.

The owner deserved to die, Daryl seethed with satisfaction, feeling little else.

His coke stash was gone. He used up the last of his crack at Steve's party, and that was not one, but *two nights ago.* His palms, formerly dry, began to sweat, making the steering wheel slippery.

Was I supposed to pick something up today? he thought in a panic. He didn't remember. Seemed like there was something important to do today, but he had no idea what.

He drove for fifteen minutes before he remembered.

Now I know. I'm supposed to go over to one of the safe houses to talk to Presto. He's supposed to line me up with some product to deal.

It was three in the afternoon, and he had to meet him at four. He wiped sweat off his forehead as he changed lanes, hopped the expressway for Presto's spare apartment.

Daryl had sold small amounts of coke and crack for Presto at school; lately the demand had swung more toward crack, which was cheaper and smaller and easier to get rid of in a hurry. But it never amounted to a whole lot of money, just enough to keep him supplied with his own stash. Since school was over, his number-one market, impulse purchases in the hallways, was gone. He had been hoping to reestablish his clientele at the party, being the birthday boy and all, but the evening had gone horribly wrong. He didn't want to work for some of the other dealers, and wasn't "big" enough to try to move in on someone else's turf without it being a suicide mission, so he'd stuck to Presto, hoping something would come through. Perhaps something had; he was on his way to find out.

I need to sell quantity, he thought. *That's the only way to make any money. None of this nickel and dime bottle*

ELVENDUDE

bullshit. I've been driving this Corvette for the past three months without insurance. If I get pulled over for anything, it's over.

Presto hated the 'Vette and made no secret of it.

"Get rid of it," Presto had said. "If you're going to work for me, you drive the bug."

The comment stung. Daryl was proud of the car, even though it had been handed to him on a silver platter. He couldn't deny the 'Vette screamed "Drug Dealer," but he didn't care. Girls paid attention to him, and he'd gotten laid strictly because of the car at least five times since he'd started driving it. Steve Winton, who had always wanted a 'Vette for himself, had envied him for it, so much that he threw the lavish party for him when his parents were away. For the first time in his life, he was popular, all because of a hunk of metal and plastic.

But Presto hated the car. "I've seen more people busted because of a flashy car. Busted with *quantity.* And besides driving what they were driving, they'd done nothing wrong. Obeyed the rules. Went by the book. And now they're doing time because they attracted attention to themselves when they should have been invisible."

Daryl told him he'd get something else, something bland, like a station wagon, but just hadn't gotten around to it yet.

The safe house was an apartment in north Dallas, just off Highway 635. It was a large, wealthy place, with two huge pools and lots of expensive cars. Daryl pulled his 'Vette up between a Lexus and a Dodge Stealth, wondering what the fuss was over *his* car.

Anything *but* a flashy car would stand out here.

Presto opened the door before Daryl knocked. Wordlessly, he let Daryl in and closed the door behind him.

The apartment was designed to look like it belonged to a poor person living well above his means. The apartment itself was expensive, but the furniture was cheap. Presto had put in enough used furniture to make the place look lived in, but he didn't live there himself. The older man flopped down on a beat up old futon in couch mode, and Daryl situated himself in a lumpy papasan that a cat had sprayed profusely. Multiple launderings of the cushions left behind a stale cat spray and Bounce scent that wasn't entirely unpleasant.

Presto gave Daryl the creeps. The man was just too pale to be alive, and looked like he'd just walked off the screen of *Night of the Living Dead*. His appearance reminded Daryl that he'd been in court the day before and assumed it had gone well, since he was here and not in jail. He'd lost even more hair since the last time Daryl'd seen him, and was now, for all intents, completely bald.

Daryl knew better than to ask. When Presto spoke, it was never an answer to a question.

The old dealer pulled a shoe box from behind the futon and placed it on a glass-and-chrome coffee table between them. It was full of black-stoppered vials of crack.

Oh, Lordy, look at all that beautiful rock, Daryl thought, salivating. If Presto knew Daryl did the product he sold for him, he didn't seem to care. But he did care if it was done in his presence; that he knew from Monk, an even stranger individual than Presto, who was in jail.

"Think you can turn these for me?" Presto said hollowly, with that half-smirk Daryl knew was more challenge than amusement.

"Sure I can," Daryl said flippantly. "I've sold everything else, haven't I?"

Presto reached down and plucked a pair of glasses from the immaculate black carpet. They were round and silver, and looked rather cool on Presto, who had the kind of rough face needed to pull it off. Most younger kids looked dorky with round glasses. When Daryl tried some on, he thought he looked like a cross between a pseudointellectual jerk and a periscope. On Presto, the glasses made him look wise.

"It's not your usual crack," Presto said softly. "Be careful with it. It's potent. If you do any of that shit yourself, stay away from driving is all I can say."

Daryl glanced down at the box, guessing there were

about a hundred bottles. At ten dollars apiece, that was a thousand bucks staring at him.

"Sell them for ten, give me eight. Keep the profit. And don't smoke it all. You don't look so hot today, kid."

Daryl shrugged, wondering if he should mention the Wintons' mess. Then he decided against it; Presto might suspect him of cooperating with the police.

"Put it in this," Presto said, pulling out a rusty old *Jetsons* lunch box, sans thermos. "Try the Yaz. I hear there's action down there."

Daryl knew what the Yaz was like or, more specifically, the Marketplace. Security cameras everywhere. He would have to watch out for those, maybe even limit his time inside. There were other, seedier places he might try later if he struck out at the juice bar.

He shelved these secondary plans for his immediate pressing need to get loaded. When he pulled out of the apartment parking lot, tires squealing, he caught a glimpse of Presto looking out a window, shaking his head in disapproval.

As he got back on the highway, he reached under his seat and pulled out a small glass pipe. The water had shaken out of it, but he didn't care. He'd smoke the stuff directly on his tongue if he had to.

One-handed, he popped open a black-stoppered vial, loaded a single rock into the pipe, then stuck the pipe between his teeth where he held it. With the same hand he found an economy pack of Bic lighters, pulled one out, and lit the pipe. During the entire procedure, his speed never dropped below eighty.

The rock hissed and cracked as he sucked the vapors down, down, burning all the way down through to his lungs because there was no water in the pipe to cool it. As soon as the drug hit his lungs, it flashed through his entire nervous system.

Then he knew why Presto had advised against driving under the influence of this particular crack.

The 'Vette began to fly. It began as a lightness in his feet and hands, then he felt the front two wheels leave the pavement. Then, as wind rushed under the 'Vette, the rear wheels levitated, until the car evened out. He glanced out the window, figured he was about a foot or two off the pavement.

He cruised along like that for several moments, watching the other traffic drop behind him. No one seemed to notice the flying Chevy in the lane next to them. He might as well have been invisible. When he passed an eighteen-wheeler, his window was even with the driver's, who was drinking a Bud and smoking a Marlboro, never once glancing left to see the flying 'Vette beside him.

I must be invisible.

When turning, the car responded as if it were on the pavement. Sluggishly, at first, then with its usual tightness, the car turned and switched lanes with ease. The wheels, Daryl speculated, must be acting like rudders. Since the Corvette was not designed for air travel—at least to this degree—it was the only explanation that came to him.

Should I file a flight plan somewhere? he thought whimsically. *Get a pilot's license?* These were the only things that came to him as he sped down Highway 75 south.

Sitting on the passenger's side, a deep green gargoylelike thing with long, pointed ears and eyes as black as charcoal reached across and touched Daryl's right arm.

The pipe fell from his teeth and clattered to the floor.

He would have believed the creature to be a hallucination, brought on by the new version of crack coursing through his system. And for that matter, the flying phenomenon as well, since Corvettes didn't fly. Not really. But the thing had touched him, and that made it real, and Daryl wanted to scream.

Instead, he just kept driving. His new passenger was smaller and thinner than he was, with long spindly arms and legs, and not much of a torso. It wore some kind of black Spandex shorts, and a black tanktop that said "New You Fitness Center." The leg warmers, hugging ankles no wider than Daryl's wrist, looked like elastic snakeskin.

"Don't you think a seat belt is in order, young human?" the creature asked, with a wicked grin that gave him the willies.

"Yeah, uh, sure," Daryl said, pulling the belt over and buckling it. He avoided looking at the creature directly.

The situation was fearfully bizarre, the creature hideous, but he found no terror in himself. Either numbed by the drugs, or hypnotized, or controlled by a mind-ray, he simply was not afraid of his uninvited passenger. The fear and anxiety seemed to leak away as soon as his brain manufactured it, as if something siphoned it off before his consciousness felt it.

Afraid or not, he wanted to be as far away from the creature as possible.

"Presto warned you not to smoke our creation while operating heavy machinery," the creature lectured. It reached over to his CD box and started sorting through it, pausing to look at this or the other, finally selecting *Machines of Loving Grace*.

"If I were *Unseleighe*," the thing said as it deftly operated the CD player, loading the disc, selecting *play*, "I wouldn't know how to do this. I would be afraid of this *thing* of technology. I'm just an agent like you, working for the Man."

"So what do I call you?" Daryl said, but *Machines* drowned out his words. "You're not a Colombian or anything?"

"Oh, no," the thing said, evidently hearing him over the first raspy cut anyway. "Let's see . . . you can call me Mort. That would be suitable." Mort's lips curled over bright, white incisors, punctuating the black face with ferocity. "I think you've had enough of *this* chapter," Mort said cryptically. "Turn the page. Time for round two. Guaran*teed* to get that little ticker of yours going pitty-pat."

In the 'Vette's rearview, a red and blue light bar came to life. It was the new, brighter disco light show version the cops had started using lately, brilliant and flashy enough to land a 747 on a dark pasture. Daryl was usually more observant of black-and-white paint jobs, but hadn't noticed this one until it was at his back door.

"I believe the correct human response is, 'Oh, *shit*,'" Mort said.

At some point during the brief pursuit, the Corvette apparently remembered it was a car and not an aircraft, and had returned to the pavement. Daryl nudged the vehicle down to seventy, sixty, then a sedate forty. And, yes, his heart was pounding away at his sternum, threatening to blast through his chest like the critter in *Alien 3*. But he wasn't particularly afraid, at least didn't feel any of it, in spite of the fact that he had no insurance, was going at least ninety in a sixty-five mile an hour zone, had a dirty pipe and a hundred vials of crack cocaine in a *Jetsons* lunch box on the floor.

"I'm going to jail," Daryl said woodenly as the Corvette rolled to a stop.

"Probably," Mort said. "How do you drive one of these things, anyway?"

Daryl sighed. "They'll probably tow it. Or confiscate it. Yeah, that's what they'll do. They'll throw my ass in jail and do something weird with my 'Vette, like turn it into a show-case black-and-white or some stupid—"

The cop tapped Daryl's window with a nightstick.

In a way, he was grateful to be arrested. He didn't think his new passenger, Mort, was legit, and was probably doing things to his mind that were unhealthy. But then, smoking crack wasn't healthy, either. *Crack doesn't turn into a gargoyle and go through your CD collection. Or does it?* At any rate, he would be separated from this creature, unless they arrested him, too. This presented problems as well. How does one explain this to the judge?

"License and proof of insurance," the cop said. "You were doing ninety. Where's the fire?"

Usual cop shit. Daryl fumbled for his wallet, which he wasn't even sure he had, having tossed it into the growth of clothing on his bedroom floor the night, or two, before.

Mort leaned over and said in a loud, baritone voice, "You don't need his license. Or the insurance."

The cop didn't seem to notice the apparition as he penned his ticket, confirming his suspicion Mort was a hallucination, induced by the crack. *But crack is not a hallucinogen,* he thought, maddeningly. *What the hell's going on with my head?*

"On second thought, never mind," the cop said. He ripped the pink ticket out of the book and tossed it over his shoulder.

"Tell me, sonny, what's that in the lunchbox?" the cop asked.

Daryl looked down at the *Jetsons* lunch pail, which sat precariously between Mort's thin, knobby knees. The lid was open, the hundred or so black-stoppered vials in plain sight. It was exactly what it looked like.

"Uh, nothin'," Daryl said weakly.

"Never you mind about the lunchbox," Mort said, closing it. "It's a government secret."

The cop shrugged. "Son, you might want to slow it down a bit. You were going at least a hundred. If you hit anything in this car, you'll get a big eight-cylinder Chevy engine block shoved through your chest."

"Okay," Daryl said, as a bead of sweat dripped off his nose.

"Drive careful, now," the cop said, smiling. He climbed back into his cruiser, turned off the lights, and took off. Daryl waved as he passed.

"That was weird," Daryl said, cranking the 'Vette back on.

"To the Yaz. We have goodies to sell," Mort said, yawning. "He's lucky I didn't blind him."

When they got to the Yaz, Daryl smoked down the last rock from the vial he'd already opened, out in an auxiliary parking lot near some railroad tracks. He hadn't come down yet from the first hit, but he knew he would, particularly after the close scrape with the cop. Mort even lit his pipe for him.

"You're not coming in, too, are you?" Daryl asked.

Mort gave him a hurt look. "You don't want to be seen with me in public?"

"Well, no . . ." Daryl said, fumbling for the words, the right words. "I'm going to be selling. You would, let's say, attract attention."

Mort didn't bother to open his door; he oozed through it with a sucking gelatin noise that made Daryl flinch. *That sounded painful.* "I'm more spirit than flesh. You're the only one who can see me."

"Oh," Daryl said, feeling silly. "So you *are* a hallucination."

Mort held his palms open, a gesture of acceptance. "Only in that you are the only one who can see me. I do exist." He gave Daryl a look, one eyebrow upturned. "I did get that cop off your back, didn't I? Where's your gratitude? Typical human. If it weren't for me, you'd be sitting in jail making your one phone call to Daddy."

Daryl groaned. "Don't remind me. I'm already in deep *caca* at home."

Mort giggled obscenely. "When *aren't* you?"

Daryl felt that he should be angry at the insult, but again an unseen force diverted the feelings, pulled them off somewhere else.

For a Monday—no, Tuesday—evening, the West End Marketplace was unusually busy. There was the usual electronic loudness erupting from the arcades below, and a thick mass of people winding up the stairs and escalators. Daryl went directly, but nonchalantly, as if he had no real destination, to the Yaz.

The juice bar, also, was packed—or what passed for packed on a Tuesday night. Adam and Spence were tending bar, as usual, but that weird Korean guy who owned the place was nowhere around. He surreptitiously scanned for cameras, hidden or not, and once he was satisfied there were none, strolled into the Yaz.

The crowd consisted of a mixture of goody-goody types and his friends, or at least people he recognized. There seemed to be an invisible rope dividing the two groups, right down the middle of the bar, where kids sat and stood around booths and tables, sipping Cokes, espressos and exotic coffees. The lighting was subdued, it being the early evening hours, and the dance floor was dark and empty. Still in cafe mode, the Yaz had yet to switch to disco.

Daryl ordered a cinnamon coffee from Spence, who was polite but said what he usually said when he was there: nothing. Adam had vanished into the back for something, and Daryl didn't know if he should say anything to Adam or not.

He turned from the bar and went back to the corner, where he spied a girl he recognized from another of Steve's parties, months back. She wasn't at the last party, and he remembered wondering why.

"Daryl!" she said, when she looked up. "I thought . . ."

At the two booths, where seven or eight grungy teens in ripped up clothing sat and smoked unfiltered cigarettes, heads turned up and regarded him with surprise and— what was *that* kid thinking?—distrust. He wondered if he'd made a mistake by coming here. The paranoia such a scenario would usually invoke was strangely absent. He sensed Mort at his elbow, urging him along, but he was more spirit now, a dim outline in the smoky Yaz.

"Hi, ah, Sharon," he said, quickly remembering her name.

"Naw. Try Tina," she replied.

Or not. "Mind if I sit?"

At the table sat a boy wearing a black trench coat and a pair of shorts and sandals, an Asian in a Cardinals uniform, and Tina, in a fashionable black miniskirt and leather vest. They stared at him as if he were a ghost. Then it occurred to him that's precisely what they thought he was.

"Weren't you at . . . Steve's the other night?" Tina said.

Daryl sat next to her and met her eyes. He didn't find the black lipstick all too appealing, but the rest of her was a knockout. Then he remembered how long it had been since he'd gotten laid. He moved closer.

"Well, yeah," he said, wondering if he should say anything, since the police were all over the place the next day.
But the news was out, and if he denied anything that would
look suspicious as well.

"We thought you *died,* man," the Asian boy said. Daryl
had no idea what his name was, though he had met him at
one time or another. The name on the uniform said *Li.*

"What happened over there?" the boy in the trench coat
asked. He looked paler and warmed-over deathlike than
Daryl ever had, then Daryl saw that he'd used light base on
face and chest to achieve the effect. "We heard all sorts of
stuff."

Tina put her hand on his thigh, distracting him momentarily.

"Bad stuff," Daryl said. "Everyone got a hold of some
bad rock."

Li sneered. "Then why ain't *you* dead?"

Daryl opted for the truth. "I passed out in the backyard.
All the stuff went around before I got to it."

"What about the cops? Didn't they bust the place?" the
other boy said. Tina's hand crept higher. Daryl squirmed.

"They gave me a hard time, but they didn't find anything,"
Daryl continued, his voice a bit higher and cracking. "I got
rid of it all before they got there. Assholes dropped a baggie
of powdered sugar on the table in front of me, scared the
crap out of me, but that's all it was: powdered sugar."

Li and the others laughed. "That's all that happened?"

Daryl noticed the people in the booth behind, and in
front of them, were all staring at him.

"Guys, this ain't cool," he said softly. "I'm holding."

The others turned away. He now had less of an audience
in the middle of what looked like a guaranteed market. He
knew that look, the hungry eyes.

They've been going without these past few days, too.

"All the rock dealers shut down for a few days, 'cause
what happened," Tina said. "*You* got rock?"

"Enough. For a price. Ten dollars a bottle. Primo."

"Well, shit, man, let's *go,*" Li said. "I'll buy ten right now."

Yeah, and thrown in for free, you get a little black gargoyle to keep you company and shoo the cops away, he thought giddily.

"In the bathroom. Can't deal this in the open. Send them in one at a time."

If what Tina says is true, this rock's gonna go fast. Better dump it and get out of here. He looked around for Mort, who had vanished. *Mort's gonna get real busy soon.*

Then, like a load of crashing bricks, came the realization that he was selling Dream, *the* Dream, that killed his friends three nights ago.

Black-stoppered bottles. It had to be the same stuff. Why didn't Presto say anything about it? Wait, now, he did say something about it. This was a potent batch or something. Well, if I didn't die, must be a different lot. What the hell. Black Dream it is.

As he made his way back to the bathroom, weaving through natural wood tables, another row of booths with high backs, and past the bar, he still felt a little sickened by what he was selling. Then Mort appeared directly in front of him, and he stopped.

"You can just walk right through me, if you want," Mort said. Instead Daryl walked around him, trying to look inconspicuous, and continued to the bathroom, Mort following. "I know what you're thinking. That this batch of rock is the same that killed your friends the other night."

"I don't think, I know," Daryl whispered over his shoulder. He paused at a cigarette machine, made a pretense of digging for coins. "Were you involved with that over at the Wintons'?"

"No, and no," Mort said. The little demon reached over, touched the machine, and a pack of Marlboros dropped down. "And what you have is not the same batch. It didn't kill you, did it?"

"Well, no," Daryl said. He paused before reaching for the pack, assuming they were a hallucination like Mort, but when he touched them they were real. "But it did add you to my life."

"You don't sound pleased with my company," Mort said with a hint of anger. "I can be a great help to you. While you're in there, dealing your rock, I'll stand out here and be lookout. What a deal, huh?"

Daryl put the cigarettes in his pocket and glanced around again. Half a dozen hungry eyes were turned toward him.

"Okay. Stand guard. I'll make this quick."

Daryl went into the bathroom, a row of stalls on one side and four sinks beneath a long mirror on the other. Like the rest of the Marketplace, the rest room was appointed in natural wood floors, walls and ceiling. Even the stalls were a rustic pine. He looked in the mirror and saw death staring back at him, and suddenly he didn't feel very well. Stars clouded his vision and his head became light and fuzzy. He wished he had a chair to sit on, but made do with the sink counter.

He noticed he wasn't alone; someone was in one of the stalls. The toilet flushed, and out walked Adam McDaris.

Chapter Eleven

"Hi, Daryl," Adam said as soon as he saw his friend sitting on the counter. "How're you doing?"

Daryl grunted in surprise. An unpleasant surprise, Adam figured from the wide, fearful eyes. Daryl looked like hell. He sat there, legs dangling, in grimy blue jeans and an oversized cut-off t-shirt. His damp hair hung over his face in a messy part. A thin layer of perspiration glistened across his pale and pasty forehead, even though the Yaz and the bathroom in particular was cooler than the rest of the Marketplace. It was probably sixty-nine degrees in there, but still Daryl was sweating like a pig.

"Awlright, I guess," Daryl said finally, but his voice was barely a whisper. He avoided Adam's eyes and looked as if he was up to something. Adam had an idea what it was.

If he's dealing out of the Yaz, he's in for a rude surprise.

Adam also noticed a distant, vague look in his eyes, and knew he was on something. His pupils were dilated, despite the bright fluorescent lights in the bathroom.

"I saw you come in earlier," Adam said. He tried not to let his uneasiness show; if Daryl needed help, he wouldn't open up to him if he looked uncomfortable.

Easy, now, Adam thought. *The Unseleighe may be near, and Daryl may be involved with them.* Moira was upstairs at Skary, and Spence was at the bar. The rest were at home, hiding out.

If anything happened, the two could be at the Yaz in

seconds. He should have felt pretty safe, but when he saw Daryl, and the condition he was in, he didn't feel safe at all.

If they can get him, they can get me, he thought, though he knew how irrational that really was. *I have more protection than he ever will, particularly today, with bodyguards all over the place.*

Only, the bodyguards don't know I'm in here talking to Daryl.

The kid in the Cardinals uniform came in, took one quick look at Daryl and Adam, and left. Daryl rolled his eyes, confirming Adam's suspicions.

Looks like I screwed up at least one sale, he thought, trying not to smirk.

"So what happened over there at Steve's, Daryl?" Adam asked. "I hear you're the only one to come out alive."

Daryl shrugged and shook his head. "I dunno, Adam. I went in the backyard and crashed. When I got up, everyone was dead."

It sounded like a speech he'd been reciting repeatedly, which more likely than not was the case. Adam wondered how much he should push, and if it would get him anywhere. Lately Daryl had been retreating into a shell, closing himself off from his old friends and hanging out with the dopers and grungers. He'd even begun to mimic the other crowd, shuffling around, slouching, looking perpetually pissed off. He dressed like them, too; they wore angry clothing—ripped jeans, chains, metal studs. That was the crowd at Steve's party, and Adam wondered why he'd bothered to invite someone like himself.

Daryl was becoming one of them, but hadn't quite metamorphosed completely. He looked bad, and at least some of his diseased appearance was not an act. Despite the demeanor he was trying to affect, he still looked like he came from a wealthy family. The drugs had got to him anyway, Adam saw, and it had nothing to do with what he wore or who he hung out with. He'd aged five years since the party at Steve's. Daryl looked used and worn out before his time, like an expended racing tire.

Now he's trying to carve a niche in their society by sell-ing them drugs, Adam knew. *Question is, where did he get it, and who are they?*

"I gotta go," Daryl said, and started for the door.

Adam grabbed his arm. Daryl looked back, surprised, then angry. When he pulled back, a vial fell out of his pants pocket.

Adam picked up the black-stoppered amber tube, held it up to the light. Daryl reached for it feebly.

"Give me that," Daryl said, but made no serious move to retrieve it.

"What are you doing with this shit?" Adam said. "What is it, Black Dream?"

Daryl looked surprised. "How'd you know that?"

"My mom's a cop," Adam reminded him, and Daryl flinched.

"C'mon, don't turn me in," Daryl said. "You wouldn't, would you?"

Adam eyed him directly, until Daryl met his eyes. "I would and I will, if I catch you dealing out of the Yaz again. No, don't deny it. You're trying to sell shit out of this bath-room."

Daryl looked away. "Yeah, so what if I am?"

"Take it somewhere else," Adam said. He didn't know what else to say; Daryl's look of determination said it all. There wasn't anything Adam could do or say to make Daryl give it up and get clean.

Hell, he's probably addicted so badly he'd need a hospital to come down. No wonder the Unseleighe got into the crack business.

"Just go," Adam said.

Daryl turned and stormed away into the noise of the bar.

"Oh, give me a *break*," Sammi said as she stared at the photographs. "Is this a joke or something?"

They sat at Detective Roach's desk, one of about twenty gray metal desks manned with an exhausted staff in the Narcotics division of the Dallas Police Department.

Though not her usual turf, Sammi had exerted a little influence—and a bit of elven magic—to get transferred here, where she thought she would be of more help to humans and elves alike. Black Dream seemed to be the key to finding Zeldan Dhu, and the closer she was to the action, the better.

She hadn't expected *this*, though. On her second day on the new job, Detective Roach dropped a bombshell on her lap.

"I kind of wish it were a joke," Roach said. He had finally gotten a decent night's sleep—seven hours—and still looked like death warmed over. Roach looked far older than his thirty-two years, a common trait among law enforcement, uniformed or not. His scruffy auburn hair needed to be cut, but such improprieties in hygiene were seldom pointed out in this department. Neatness was not something easily asked of cops who worked twenty hours a day, six days a week.

Sammi leaned back in a squeaky metal chair. "Where did you say these photos were taken?"

"About a hundred miles east of Laredo," Roach said as he drank his second cup of cold coffee. "Desert, sand, cactus. Perfect setup for a drug drop. Just wish whoever took these had been more specific about the date."

Sammi looked through six 9 x 11 black-and-white glossies. In the grainy photos, four individuals were unloading bundles of what was probably raw cocaine into a beat up 1943 Ford pickup. Rain had recently fallen, and even in the photos the subjects were clearly soaked to the bone. Each of the four had unmistakable long, pointed ears.

Unseleighe.

"So who are they, Vulcans?" Samantha said. "I don't get it."

"I don't either. Hey, I just got these yesterday. The DEA agent said an informant took these sometime around January. They sent these to us in case we might be able to identify any of these creeps."

Samantha chuckled. "Looks more like an elaborate practical joke to me. I'm surprised they passed these on."

"They insist they're legit," Roach protested, but his defense of the photos sounded weak.

"Those ears. Could it be some kind of gang trait? You know, like tattoos or body piercing?" Samantha knew she was reaching for ideas, but Roach seemed to be entranced by the pictures. This made her a tad uncomfortable.

"Nope. None that I've heard of. Piercing, huh? You know, I saw a guy with a barbell through his—"

"Did you ever run a check on that truck tag?"

Roach peered over her shoulder. "What tag?"

She looked again. Sure enough, there wasn't a tag on the rear bumper.

"Guess they figure they'd be the last ones transporting half a mil in coke with an illegal vehicle," Roach said. "Or something. Sure would be helpful to know what *color* the damned truck was. All they had were these lousy black-and-whites."

Sammi put the photos back in their ragged manila envelope and frowned. The same question kept rolling around in her mind.

When did Zeldan Dhu Gate here?

Given the time discrepancies, it was impossible to guess. An exact date, or even an approximate one, might give her an idea what he'd been up to, and where he might be now. These pictures answered at least one of those questions.

"What about the lab results of those kids?" she asked. It had been less than a week since the autopsies, but she thought she'd ask anyway.

"Nothing yet. Wasn't garden variety coke, which they would have found right away. All they know is that they all died of heart failure."

That sure narrows it down, she thought grimly. "What about the other earlier samples of Black Dream?"

"Have a look yourself," Roach said, tossing her a coffee-stained file. "I'm gonna go take a leak."

"You do that," she murmured, opening the file. *Disgusting humans.* Lab reports were not her specialty, but she poured over the technical jargon anyway, hoping to glean important clues to what they were dealing with—and what Zeldan was selling. All the samples came packaged the same way, in black-stoppered amber vials. Black was not a color commonly used by drug traffickers in their area, so its color was thought to be significant, perhaps suggesting its lethal qualities. The drug was cocaine with something added to it, something that changed the cocaine into something else, something that still had their lab techs scratching their collective heads.

One detective had scribbled a note in the margin of one of the lab reports. "This stuff's not of this world," read the barely legible script.

She closed the file. *Of course it's not of this world. It's from Underhill. Courtesy of Zeldan Dhu.*

From her purse she took out the Polaroids from the Wintons' mass death. She shuddered whenever she saw them, in part because the King nearly ended up as one of the bodies. Or perhaps not; she didn't know what effect Black Dream would have on elves. She doubted it would be anything harmless.

On her desk next to Roach's she studied the photos, along with the ones taken by photographers at the scene, and read the reports over again. The only recurring fact that struck her as odd was that Daryl survived, and practically everyone else at the party hadn't. She remembered the dialog Daryl had had with Roach, who had repeated it to her early that afternoon; the kid didn't look the slightest bit disturbed over what happened, and he didn't seem too concerned about the consequences.

With a father like his, who would?

When Roach returned, he sat down next to her and propped his feet up on the desk. "By the way, Sammi, did you hear about Swink?"

The name rang a bell, but she wasn't entirely sure if she recognized it. "I guess not," she said. "What happened?"

"Swink was one of our best motorcycle cops. Some asshole in a Volkswagen threw acid or something in his face when Swink pulled him over. Blinded. For life, the doctor says."

Sammi stared at him. "Blinded?"

"Yeah, funny thing was, they didn't find any acid burns or anything. They're thinking it might have been some kind of laser weapon or something. Still—"

"In other words," Sammi interrupted, "nobody really *knows*."

"That's my guess," Roach said. He looked as if he was about to doze off. "Perps still at large. Black Volkswagen bug. No tag."

"That narrows it down," she said grimly.

When Sammi finally came home, it was past midnight and Adam had just arrived with the others and was putting the young ones, Petrus and Wenlann, to bed in their new digs. Moira had arrived with a carload of possessions, having decided that she needed to be with the others for security reasons. Besides, it made no sense for her to live alone, now that Adam knew who he was and what was going on.

After some discussion, the group had decided that Spence, who had been living in an apartment less than a mile away, would not be moving in. Too many young, teenage kids moving in with a lady cop would be too difficult to explain to Sammi's supervisor, if it ever came to his attention. The four new arrivals from Avalon would be enough to deal with, and explain, as it was.

Once the two littles were in bed, Adam and his horde gathered in the kitchen. Samantha, Moira and Marbann sat at the kitchen table, while Niamh scavenged in the refrigerator for something to munch on. Adam had left Spence to close up at the Yaz.

The King watched surreptitiously as Niamh pulled out a bottle of ketchup, then a jar of olives. Then he examined a roll of raw biscuit dough packaged in a cardboard tube, scrutinizing the label. Apparently the heat from his hands caused it to pop open explosively. The elf squawked and dropped the dough, stepped away from it, eyeing the Pillsbury tube fearfully.

"Okay, Niamh," Samantha said, the noise having attracted her attention. "Out of there. You don't know what you're doing. Human food can be *frightening*."

"The game is still alive!" Niamh cried as he backed up against a cabinet. "Shall we behead it?"

Adam snickered, trying his best to show no amusement. *Good gods, I'm glad they laid that human spell on me when I got here. Figuring this stuff out by trial and error must be terrifying.*

Niamh raised a Nike-shod foot and made ready to stomp on the dough.

"Don't you dare," Samantha said as she rescued the prey from the floor. "I'll bake these if you're still hungry. I just *cleaned* this place."

"Aye," Niamh said, shaking his head. "The humans have certainly gone out of their way to make eating complicated, they have."

Once the biscuits were laid out on the Teflon pan and placed in the oven, Samantha and the hungry elf came back to the table for the meeting.

"So tell me dear, how did your day go?" Samantha said lightly, but behind the lightness Adam sensed some dread.

Adam turned serious, which was difficult to do with the vision of the exploding biscuit roll still playing in his head. "Daryl Bendis is dealing Black Dream," Adam replied emotionlessly. "He was trying to unload some tonight at the Yaz."

Sammi let out a low whistle. "So. He's finally graduated to selling. I shouldn't be surprised, but I am. How do you know?"

Adam told her about the incident in the Yaz bathroom and the black-stoppered vial.

"You're sure it was Black Dream?" she asked.

"Black stoppers. All I know. Daryl was a waste, as he usually is these days," Adam replied.

"I hope you chased him out of there," she said. "The last thing our clan needs is police involvement at the place you work. Then there's the other probability."

"Which is?" Moira asked.

"This is connected with the Unseleighe."

She told him about the DEA pictures and the elven subjects. And only Unseleighe elves would have anything to do with something as dark as cocaine trafficking.

"Which further supports my belief that Zeldan is behind Black Dream production," Sammi said.

"If you find the source of Dream, then you find Zeldan," Adam said, and the prospect was more terrifying than he had first thought. He was careful to keep his fears hidden; he didn't want his Court to know he was afraid. "Lady Samantha, you're a cop; you're in a good position to do this."

"It won't be that easy," Sammi admitted. "The Unseleighe are good at staying hidden. Remember, they are elves."

Adam thought about Daryl, and what was happening to him. *Maybe this is how I can help him,* he considered. *By taking down his supplier.*

When he looked up, Samantha was looking directly at him. "I think Daryl will be better at finding Zeldan than the cops will be. He is, after all, closer to him. And it would appear that he's working for him as well."

"Yeah, but . . ." Adam said, but his argument stopped there. *I'm not so sure I can use Daryl that way.* Daryl was still his friend, and it didn't feel right taking advantage of him. "He wouldn't tell me anything if I asked." Perhaps his human side was still trying to protect him. *This is getting confusing. Why do I have to be a teenage human on top of all this!*

Adam wanted to change the subject. "Zeldan, Zeldan, *Zeldan!* He captured our palace, killed my family, and is probably looking for me. Why? What did we ever *do* to him?"

Marbann and Samantha exchanged looks. "It's a good

question," Marbann finally said. "We never told him before, did we?"

Samantha shook her head. "We disposed of the Unseleighe threat so long ago that we had quite simply forgot they were a threat."

"They're a threat now," Adam pointed out. "What happened?"

Samantha took a deep breath, and Adam prepared himself for a long story. "Zeldan Dhu's clan was originally part of a larger Unseleighe group which our Outremer brothers defeated in a long, senseless battle. Some wanted to continue the battle to the end. Admitting defeat, the majority of the Unseleighe threw the troublemakers out. One of these outcasts was Zeldan's grandfather, Zantor, the leader of the new splinter clan.

"Zantor set out across uncharted and unknown regions of Underhill, just like our ancestors did, but for entirely different motives. They destroyed and killed everything they encountered. They were nomads and looters. Lone Underhill creatures by the score fell under their blade.

"Their victories came so swiftly and decisively that they became overconfident. When they encountered Elfhame Avalon, by then well established, and having been warned by Outremer, we were ready for them. Zantor didn't know this. He and a small party attacked the palace at night, expecting an easy slaughter. Aedham the First, your grandfather and King of Avalon, was ready.

"There was indeed a slaughter, but of Zantor and his people, not ours. Grandfather Tuiereann personally slew Zantor with a dagger tipped with Death Metal. Zantor was armed with a sword likewise poisoned. Grandfather won despite the disadvantage in weapons.

"Then, once the raiding party was killed, Avalon warriors spread out and attacked the Unseleighe camp. The Unseleighe knew something had gone horribly wrong, and when they realized their leader was slain, they had no will to fight. They fled, beyond the mountains, to regions unknown. Over time,

Avalon had forgotten the threat. There had never been a serious one in the first place."

Samantha calmly got up, put on some oven mittens, and pulled the pan out. "Anyone hungry?"

Niamh stared wordlessly at the repast set before them. In addition to the biscuits, which now served as mere garnish, there was a small roasted ham, with apple slices around it. Potatoes, onions and carrots shared the pan. The food's steaming aroma made Adam's stomach rumble.

During all the brouhaha, I'd forgotten I hadn't eaten in a while, Adam thought as he helped serve dinner to the others.

"Under the circumstances, I think that kenned food would be acceptable, don't you think?" Samantha said, as Moira brought a stack of plastic plates and utensils to the table and began passing them out.

"Don't care," Niamh said. "I'm hungry."

"I'll take some up to the littles," Moira said as she disappeared into the garage with a plate of ham and vegetables.

"Anyway," Samantha said, as the group dug in hungrily. "*That* is what happened."

The Unseleighe killed my family, Adam thought, his rage now renewed. "We were only defending our home."

"Forget about finding reason in the Unseleighe's actions," Marbann said. "We've tried for millennium, without success."

Sammi nodded as she rubbed her face tiredly. "We have a link, now. If Daryl's selling Dream, then perhaps we can follow him back to the source. What are the chances of his returning to the Yaz?"

"Good," Adam said, feeling a little tired himself. "I doubt my threats to call the cops had any effect on him. I don't think he believes me. We've been friends for—"

"Too long," Marbann pointed out harshly. Then his tone softened a little, and he added, "We can't cure humans of all diseases."

"Then perhaps we should wait for Daryl to slip up,"

Moira said. "When he leaves the Yaz tomorrow, provided he arrives, let's follow him."

"We wouldn't even need a concealment spell," Sammi pointed out. "Though it wouldn't hurt. He knows what that car of yours looks like."

"Let's sleep on it," Adam said. He didn't like the idea of using Daryl to get at Zeldan, but at the same time he saw no other way. "It's been a long day. I believe that when we awaken, the solution will be clear to us all."

Chapter Twelve

Nightfall in Dallas.

"Tell you what," Li said, as he rode with Daryl in his Corvette. "I'll buy enough rock to get us both good and fried, then I'll show you where you can take the rest of the product. I owe someone a few favors, anyway."

"Sounds good," Daryl said, trying not to sound depressed.

"Look in the *Jetsons* lunchpail down on the floor."

But Li was already into it. He even had his own pipe, and this one had water in it.

Snap, crackle, pop. Li handed him the pipe.

Daryl took his turn and buried himself in the ritual silence, and Li did the same. When he tuned in the Edge, "Radioactivity" from the Kraftwerk Mix album poured through the speakers. Coaxing his 'Vette up to 80 mph he sailed down Highway 75 south, which eventually led him out of the Dallas area and into less traveled lands. Daryl didn't care where he went, and neither did Li, apparently.

Every few miles or so, Daryl glanced out at the road to make sure it was where it was supposed to be, and not three yards beneath the car. Though the flying car phenomenon had been kind of neat at the time, he preferred a car that stayed on the ground, particularly when he was smoking rock. Too many things might go wrong. It was probably why the cop pulled him over in the first place.

Li said little during the ride, apparently cooked by the rock. Daryl glanced down at the gas gauge, which read E.

"Shit," Daryl said. "I need to pull over and fill up."

"Okay," Li said, grinning at something. Or nothing.

Daryl pulled the 'Vette off at the next ramp. In the distance he saw an Exxon station, but he would have to drive a ways to get to it. The ramp and the streets it led to were in the process of being resurfaced and widened. Fluorescent orange and yellow plastic drums lined the road on either side. The only visible light was the Exxon station, still about a mile away, and a billboard advertising a motel ten miles away.

"Hey," Li said. "You're still going about sixty. How fast *can* you drive this thing?"

Daryl grinned. *Does he really want to know?* he thought. *Maybe's he's never been in a 'Vette before. Well, if that's what he wants* . . .

Daryl floored it, and the hand of God pressed them back in their seats. The orange and yellow barrels became a blur, the white striped line now a solid one. The motor sang as he shifted back up into fifth, the eight cylinders protesting little, wanting to go faster.

He wasn't expecting the orange and yellow barrels to veer across his lane, forcing him to switch abruptly over to the other side of the road. Even as he started the turn, he knew he wasn't going to make it.

For a moment the universe was eerily silent as the car left the pavement; on impact, everything went black.

Hissing steam woke him, then pain, searing pain, as hot metal burned his right side.

He opened his eyes, and when he blinked a hot fluid that smelled like Prestone dripped into them. He didn't know where he was, or what had happened.

Antifreeze soaked his shirt and face. Daryl squirmed, finding himself wedged into an impossibly small space, his head crammed into a bent steering wheel. Something large and hot and smelling like gasoline now sat in the passenger's seat. Once his eyes adjusted, he saw that it was the car's engine.

A slow, creeping dread spread over him as he began to comprehend that he'd wrecked his 'Vette but good. It still felt like a bad dream that he would wake from any moment. But instead of waking up, his body began talking to him in vague and disturbing ways. His right leg was somewhere under a twisted mass of plastic and a spaghetti tangle of multicolored wires, plastic hoses, and the startling clarity of an exposed CD, shimmering with rainbow colors in the dim, reflected light of a nearby billboard. The windshield was gone, neatly popped out and nowhere in sight. His ruined 'Vette continued to hiss and sputter, the horrid death noises of a car mortally wounded.

A strong stench of gasoline reached his nostrils.

I've got to get out of this thing, he realized. And Daryl discovered how much fear was possible in a human being when he imagined the car engulfed in flames.

As he struggled to free himself from the car, he lost control of his bowels.

Please oh God don't let me burn to death in this thing! his mind screamed. His teeth clenched against the pain in his right leg, his mouth refused to let him moan. He reached over to the driver's door, which still seemed to be intact, sort of. He pulled on the handle and the door popped violently, then gave a few inches when he pushed. Metal screamed as he pushed harder, and a sharp pain shot through his right leg.

Daryl crawled through the foot or so of clearance between door and car. A jagged piece of metal caught him in the middle of his chest and carved an incision to his waist as he wriggled through; he hardly felt it in his panic to get out. Outside the gasoline scent was stronger; when he put his hand down on the ground, he found a puddle of it.

Oh God oh God oh God get me outta here I'll never smoke crack again. . . . he prayed. *I'll make it up to you. I'll—*

The ground was not ground, but concrete. The car had struck a retaining wall, and from the crumpled condition of the roof, he figured it must have rolled a few times. His right leg refused to work, but he got up halfway anyway, hobbling away from the wreck, finding a network of steel reinforcement rods sticking up irregularly from the edge of the concrete road.

Daryl had crawled and hobbled about seven yards from the car before it burst into flames.

The heat and brightness brought a scream from Daryl's mouth. He dropped to the pavement and covered his head with his arms, waiting for the fireball to engulf him.

He felt only a wave of heat, no more, and sat up to regard his burning car.

I'm alive. For now. But how long will I live after Father finds out?

Then, another thought.

Li.

He was still in the car. Or was he . . . There was a motor there, where Li had sat.

It must have crushed him. He was under the motor. He must already be dead.

The flames leaped higher. Then the car exploded, showering the ground with falling, burning fiberglass and plastic.

I hope he was already dead.

The explosion cast a wider circle of light. Daryl looked down the road, saw the bend he failed to negotiate a considerable distance from him. He must have rolled more than twice; the bend was a quarter of a mile away.

Li's dead. But why am I alive? he wondered. Daryl knew he shouldn't be alive, not after a wreck like that. Nobody would live, much less walk, or even crawl away.

From somewhere off to his right, a moan.

Li?

Hope flared. Peering down the road, Daryl sought the source of the moan.

"Li," he called out, wiping antifreeze from his eyes. But the boy's name came out as a croak, which he hardly heard himself.

He got up on his good left leg, dragging his right, and

started down the road. *It came from down here somewhere,* he thought as he put distance between himself and his burning car. The night became colder and darker as the flames receded behind him, and his shadow became a tall slender giant, passing over a white sea of new concrete, punctuated with skid marks and broken glass.

When he saw Li, Daryl wished he *had* died in the fire.

The Cardinals uniform was a bloody rag, wrapped around a limp body, lying on his back. Li moaned again. Daryl hobbled closer and looked down at him.

He had no face.

Daryl recoiled, tried to scramble away, succeeding only in falling back, sprawling on the new concrete. He began to whimper, the horror of what he saw now showering him with grief.

I killed him, he thought.

Li moaned again.

I might as well have killed him, he corrected himself. *All that blood . . . how is he still alive?*

Daryl sat there for an eternity, afraid to move, afraid to stay where he was. The flames of his burning car died down, casting a lambent, orange light over the area. When he looked down at his right leg, he saw a bone sticking through the shredded jeans.

"No wonder it doesn't work," he whispered. *This must be what shock feels like. Lots of nothing.*

A flame flared suddenly from the car, then was gone. The acrid stench of burning tires washed over him. He straightened his leg with his right hand, and watched the bone disappear into the flesh.

I'm in hell, Daryl thought, and screamed.

Someone kicked him in his side. When he opened his eyes, he was looking up at Li, who stood over him, holding the glass crack pipe. He still had no face.

"Come on. *Get up,*" Li said, kicking him again. "How are we supposed to keep this little trip going if you don't stay high?"

Daryl sat up, and Li sat down next to him. The billboard cast a bit of light even at this distance. His car was now a burning ember, barely visible down the road.

"Me first," Li said. Daryl watched passively as Li held the glass pipe to his head, approximately where the mouth used to be, and lit it. The light from the lighter revealed a grisly pulp where his face once resided, with bits of teeth and skull poking through.

The pipe hissed and popped, reminding Daryl of his dead car.

Without complaint, Daryl took the pipe and inhaled as Li lit it for him. He took an especially long hit, which he felt he deserved, under the circumstances.

"You know, we were going about a hundred and ten when we flipped," Li said conversationally. Despite his injuries, his voice came through loudly and clearly. "Looks like you banged yourself up a bit. Don't worry, smoke that and you'll feel better."

Daryl handed the pipe back. "How long have we been here?" he said absently.

"Oh, a couple of hours, something like that."

Daryl looked up at the highway, saw no cars, no lights.

"We're alone here, you know. Look," Li said, pointing to a point beyond the burning car. "Even the Exxon station's closed."

"Terrific," Daryl said. "Maybe we better just . . ."

"Just what?"

What? Call a taxi? Just start walking?

"This can't be real," he finally said. "Are you dead? Are you a ghost?"

The head turned toward him. Remaining bits of muscle contorted enough to mimic a smile, revealing white, undamaged teeth. Daryl's stomach threatened to turn inside out.

"Does it matter?" Li said, lighting the pipe again. When he was through he passed it back to Daryl. "We have enough rock here to last at least a few days."

Daryl tried to find fault with the logic and gave up.

"I'm right and you know it," Li said, with a touch of anger. "Now, tell me, how do you plan to get out of this little scrape? My father's gonna raise hell when he sees what happened to me. The cops, if and when they decide to get here, will probably not be too pleased with the situation either. Especially with all that crack in the front seat. The lunch box will probably protect most of it from the fire."

Daryl eyed Li suspiciously and frowned.

"Good thing your dad's a lawyer," Li added. "Looks like we're going to be in court a long, long time."

Daryl's suspicions strengthened. *That voice. That isn't Li. Not anymore.*

That's Mort.

When the apparition handed the pipe back to Daryl, he slapped it out of his hands. It crashed and tinkled amid a small shower of sparks several feet away.

The apparition stared at him.

"You're not Li," Daryl said, crawling away from him.

"I'm not?" it said, inching closer. "Then who am I, human?"

Mort. Transfixed on the apparition, Daryl saw the ruined body of Li shimmer briefly, surrounded by a glowing mist. The mist swirled about the bloody Cardinals uniform, slowly at first, then whirled with increasing speed, until it was cocooned with light. Then, with a brief flash, the light was gone.

Mort stood there, hands on his hips, looking down at Daryl, looking extremely disgusted.

"Get up," Mort said. "There's nothing wrong with you."

Daryl kept crawling, now with a little more urgency. Mort walked up and kicked him in the ass.

"I said *get up,* human," Mort repeated. *"There's nothing wrong with you!"*

"But my leg!"

"What about your leg?"

Daryl rubbed his eyes and examined his leg, which now appeared to be undamaged. The pain was gone, replaced by a rawness in his palms where he had rubbed them against the concrete. He felt his body, now dry except for perspiration, with no hint of antifreeze or gasoline.

He stood shakily, taller than Mort, but that made no difference. The little creature terrified him now.

Mort looked up at him and started laughing.

"Oh, my young human, you look soooo pathetic," Mort said, then doubled over with laughter. "Drugs do terrific things, don't they? If you don't like your own reality, you can trade it for something else, for less than the price of a CD."

Daryl was baffled. "How did you *do* that?"

"Do what?" he replied, between laughs. "Heal your bone?"

"Yeah, and—" He looked down toward his burning car, saw only a dark shape, and nothing else. The air had cleared of the burning smell, replaced by the ripe, fertile smell of rural countryside at night. "You put the fire out."

"What fire?" Mort shrieked, now rolling on the pavement, laughing uncontrollably.

"My car . . ." he murmured, and started walking toward the shape.

Halfway to the Corvette he saw there had never been an accident, except for the demise of one plastic barrel he'd run over, and a two-foot scratch of black his tires had left on the new pavement.

He looked inside, found his keys in the ignition, and no one sitting in the passenger's side.

He walked around the car, twice, dumbfounded. The 'Vette didn't have a scratch on it, except for a slight blemish on the nose where it connected with the barrel. And of course, the black ding left by the Mustang at Steve's.

Mort caught up with him, leaned over, and examined the blemish.

"Yep. Now, *that's* real," Mort said, running a finger along the scratch. "Shame. That's about two hundred dollars there."

Daryl wasn't paying any attention to what he was saying. His confusion now turned to anger.

"You little shit. You made the whole thing up!"

Mort looked up with mock dismay. "Would *I* do such a thing?"

Daryl reached for his neck, and Mort dashed away, quick as a bunny. Daryl dashed after him, chasing him around the 'Vette in tight rectangles.

"Oh, my. Oh, no, the human's pissed, *I'm afraid now!*" Mort cackled, doing flips and handsprings as Daryl ran after him. "I'm in trouble! I'm done for! Human's gonna kill me now!"

"That's right, I'm going to kill you, you little bastard, if you slow down long enough! I thought I was dead! Where's Li?" Daryl shouted as he ran.

"Oh, you stupid human. Don't you know an illusion when you see one? Li went home long ago. It was just little ole me, orchestrating the whole thing."

"I'll KILL YOU!"

But before Daryl killed Mort, he ran out of breath. He stopped on the passenger's side of the 'Vette, leaning on it for support.

"You will?" Mort said, over the roof of the 'Vette. "Looks like you're going to have a heart attack before you do that."

Daryl glared at him, his blood boiling over.

Behind them a pair of headlights appeared. The new arrival distracted him momentarily as it pulled up beside the 'Vette. What he thought was the outline of a cop car turned out to be a black Superbeetle. It didn't sound like a regular Volkswagen, and he assumed it was modified.

"Just remember this," Mort said as he opened the passenger door on the bug. "We can wreck your precious car and kill your friends anytime we want. For real. This was just a sample of what we can do to you. Just so long as you keep smoking our product, we have you by the balls."

Daryl shook his head. "No, you don't." Then, softly, "I want out."

Laughter ripped through the air between them. "You want out. You want *out!* Surely you jest!"

"I'm not kidding. I want out."

"Well, tough shit, sonny!" Mort shouted. He got into the bug, which started to pull away. Daryl walked after it.

"You have no say in the matter," Mort said as the bug pulled away. "You're working for us now."

Daryl walked after the bug, then broke into a trot as it sped off.

"And remember this, human," Mort yelled. "If you fuck us, we'll kill you!"

Daryl watched the bug pull away, get onto the on ramp, and take off down Highway 75.

He considered chasing it down. In his car, this would be no problem, no matter what kind of nonstandard engine the bug had in it. But he knew such a move would be pointless, that everything the little demon had said was true.

"They have me," he said to the night, his eyes welling with tears. "They have me by the balls and they're not going to let go."

Chapter Thirteen

Adam and Marbann sat in the King's Geo, several yards away from Daryl and his Corvette. On their right was a desolate concrete graveyard, beneath ribbons of more concrete, forming the junctions of various highways. On their left was the historic district. It looked almost as if a time line had been drawn, dividing the two areas neatly with asphalt.

Adam had pulled the Geo across the rough gravel beyond the parking area, a strip of crumbling asphalt next to an old train station boarded up with plywood. About twenty cars were lined up on the strip, most belonging to the teenagers who came and went, purchasing Black Dream from Daryl at their leisure.

They were rather close to him now, and they saw without a doubt what the others were doing. If he had called out in a loud speaking voice, Daryl would have heard him.

But he would not have seen them. With little help from Marbann, Adam cast a concealment spell that rendered the little car and its occupants invisible. After the initial spell was in place, Adam tweaked it so that the Geo cast no shadow, left no tire tracks in the gravel. Marbann pointed out the obvious danger of this sort of concealment, that while the car was invisible it still existed on the human's plane, and if anything like a truck or a bus struck it at a high rate of speed, the results would be the same.

So they sat within a stone's throw of Daryl, watching him

deal his drugs. The amount of currency his friend was accumulating amazed Adam; in the short time they had parked there, at least a thousand dollars changed hands.

"He's got to run out sometime, you know," Adam said. "Unless the car is filled to the ceiling with those damned little amber bottles."

The King tried to keep the mood light, but the more he watched, the grimmer his mood became. Daryl acted like a hunted animal, hawking his dark wares with an urgency that chilled Adam's blood.

No. Not a hunted animal. A hunted zombie. There is absolutely no emotion in his eyes. Despite his best efforts, his heart filled with sadness.

Marbann seemed to understand. "Don't let it rule you," he said softly, touching Adam's right arm. "We can help him, if you want, when our own lives are not in such peril."

"We must," Adam said. "I feel responsible."

Marbann gave him a hard look. "For what? His addictions?"

"Well, in a way, I suppose," Adam said. He didn't really know what he felt responsible about. There was only a distant feeling that somehow Daryl's problem was his own.

"That is incredible arrogance, young King," Marbann said mildly, turning his attention back to Daryl, his car, his clients. "To think that you have so much power over his life. And you didn't even know you were an elf, much less an elven *mage*."

Adam glared at Marbann and checked his anger. *What is he telling me, that I'm a fool?*

Marbann continued his lecture. "Did you tell him to start drinking himself silly? To smoke cocaine until his lungs bled? I think not. These were all decisions he made on his own, and as much as you would like to view yourself as a god in his world, you had nothing to do with those decisions."

Adam fumed. "How do you know? You've only been here a few days. You don't know the humans like I do.

Gods, until recently, I've been a human, for *years*. In this short time, how have you become an expert on the situation?"

Marbann yawned, deliberately, it seemed. "It is amazing how much is the same. How elven and human psychology can be so different, and at the same time eerily familiar. If you think about what I've said, I believe you will see some truth, if only a glimmer."

Adam returned his attention to Daryl, wanting to change the subject to anything else. He felt his control of the discussion slipping, and he didn't like that.

Easy, now. Is that the arrogance Marbann just got through warning me about? I think it might be.

As he considered Marbann's words, he began to understand them a little more and admitted part of what he'd said. *No, I didn't make him do what he's doing. If anything, I'm trying to make him stop.*

And that's not working, either. . . .

"Look sharp, young King," Marbann said. Adam snapped out of his musings long enough to see Daryl get into the Corvette and drive off in a cloud of dust. "It would appear he's run out of his supply."

Adam started up the Geo and followed Daryl, but his friend seemed to be in a big hurry. His little Geo, with its fuel-efficient but underpowered engine, sounding like a lawn mower when he floored it, simply did not keep up.

Riding in moving vehicles horrified Marbann, particularly when he drove faster than a running human or elf, so it didn't look like he would be much help with what he had in mind.

"Marbann, are you belted in?"

He was. Adam reached . . .

Uncertain what the powers would do to his motor, he eased his way back into the power nodes, difficult to do with his eyes open, and siphoned some off. The weak stream went into his engine, transferred directly to the wheels and the rubber.

The car lurched forward on the highway traffic, quickly

passing a two-trailer Freightliner, a Yugo, a Volkswagen Thing.

"Young *King!*" Marbann squawked. "Remember, we are not visible. If a craft decides to pull into us . . ."

"Oh, ah, yes," Adam replied. "I *knew* that," he added, though he hadn't remembered.

The speedometer lay dead and buried on the right side of the dial. All he knew was that he was going faster than ninety. Much faster.

The little Geo didn't handle those speeds very well, so he diverted some of the power into the steering, hoping he wasn't about to kill himself.

They caught up to the Corvette just as it was exiting at a ramp. Adam signaled out of habit, then remembered the car, the signal, and the passengers were still invisible; at least he hoped they were.

"Where are we, young King?" Marbann wanted to know. "I don't recognize this place."

Adam pulled into the parking lot after Daryl, found an isolated and empty section of pavement off to the side no one would likely park in, and turned the crazed little Geo off.

"Well, I'll be damned," Adam said, scratching his head. "He's going into an athletic club. What kind of drug dealing is going on in *there?*"

After unloading the *Jetsons* box of Dream in the parking lot of the West End District, Daryl congratulated himself on making it through most of the day without encountering Mort. *I must be doing something right,* he thought. *But there's still time for him to show up.*

In anticipation of selling all of his stock, Daryl phoned Presto to let him know he would probably need some more at the end of the day. Presto replied with an offer which, at first, sounded too good to be true.

When he pulled into the parking lot of the New You Fitness Center, it was beginning to look like it *was* too good to be true.

"This sucks," he said, looking around. Not a fancy car in sight. Old beat up GM's and Japanese and Korean products, no Beamers, no Lexus, no Mercedes. Not even a *Cadillac*, for crissakes.

Presto must be nuts to think he can make any money selling Dream in this hole.

Resigned to at least checking it out, and with the evening's haunting memory of the car crash that never was, he forced himself to open the door and walk into the fitness center.

As predicted by the nearly vacant parking lot, the club wasn't all that busy. In the reception area was a counter island with a bored but good-looking lady sitting there, talking on the phone. In the background he heard the steady *clink, clink* of weights, the whirring of a few exercise bikes and StairMasters. The place smelled like sweat and chlorine.

This really sucks, Daryl thought, and he turned to walk out of the place.

Before he got to the door, a deep voice boomed behind him.

"You must be our new employee," the man said. He was a big, blond, Nordic athletic type, who looked like he'd never touched a drug or a drink in his life.

"You must be mistaken," Daryl said, but suddenly felt compelled to stay.

The man smiled broadly, showing a perfect set of teeth. *Predator's teeth,* Daryl thought.

"Did Presto send you?" the man said.

Daryl looked away, unable now to look directly at him. "Yes," he said, finally.

"Well, then, that's excellent!" he said, stepping forward. "My name is Peter Pritchard. I'm the general manager of the New You Fitness Center. And you must be Daryl Bendis."

"Yeah," Daryl said laconically as Peter crushed his hand.

"Come this way. I have *so* many things to show you."

Daryl stifled a groan as Peter put a large beefy arm around him and led him to his office, closing the door behind them. Though he'd never been in a health club before, the degree of luxury he found was not what he expected. It resembled his father's own well-appointed workplace, the one downtown, not at home. The desk was a dark wood, probably mahogany; the interior design lavish, with lots of natural wood paneling and glass, giving the place an aura of wealth. As Daryl sat, the leather chair squeaked under him, and smelled new.

Peter leaned back and regarded Daryl through steepled fingers. "It seems to me this isn't what you had in mind," he said, with a hint of anger behind his voice. It was the same sort of ominous tone Mort had used with him, and it got his attention.

Daryl cleared his throat, which had constricted to uselessness. This man frightened him, and his body was letting him know it. "Tell me the deal," Daryl said, trying to sound brave. His voice's cracking on the last syllable spoiled the effect.

Peter chuckled, shrinking Daryl's ego even more. "Ah. The direct approach. I like that. Well, the 'deal' I assume you're talking about is the dealing of drugs."

Daryl nodded. "Uh-huh. Presto sent me. Presto told you what I was here for."

"Presto works for me," Peter said bluntly. "And you'd best not forget that. So whether you realize it or not, you've already been working for me for some time now. It just wasn't necessary to know who I was. Until now."

Daryl gulped. *Jeez. The Man. Why the hell didn't Presto tell me?*

"It occurs to me," Peter said, leaning back in the enormous leather chair that looked more like a small couch, "that you haven't gotten rich selling ten-dollar bottles for Presto."

Daryl shook his head, but held his silence.

"That car of yours, which you have insisted on hanging on to, must cost a fortune to operate. We know your father bought it for you, in a blackout drunk, without benefit of insurance or tags."

"He bought the tags," Daryl said. "The insurance, well . . ."

"Is taken care of," Peter said, pulling a drawer open. He presented Daryl with a large manila envelope. "Consider it a down payment. If you're going to be selling quantity for us, it would not do for you to be arrested for driving without insurance."

Daryl cautiously opened the envelope and pulled out the forms. Two insurance verification forms fluttered out.

"All you have to do is sign," Peter said, handing him a fountain pen. "Then we get down to business."

Ten minutes later, Peter was showing Daryl the locker rooms. "There's not much going on this time of day," Peter said, glancing at his watch. "It's only three. Around five, when everyone else gets off work, the place will be full."

Daryl hated locker rooms, as they reminded him how alien the athletic world was to him. He'd never been comfortable in sports at school and dropped gym after the ninth grade. There had been a major row with Dad then, who expected him to be a football star before he was eighteen. Since then, the subject of his masculinity had occasionally come into question, particularly when he got into scrapes in school over drugs and alcohol.

"Look, we're not asking you to become a Mr. Universe. Since you're young, you still have a naturally defined build that half the people in here are working their asses off to achieve."

Daryl was beginning to see what Peter was getting at. *As long as he doesn't try to seduce me or some shit like that*, he thought, but that didn't seem to be a real possibility. Even though Peter was masculine and straight-acting, he knew from experience that was no proof of orientation. No, Daryl knew the vibes, and Peter was not sending them out.

"Presto's known you awhile now. He tells me you're a good con."

Daryl shrugged. "I do what I have to."

"Well, then," Peter said, flashing that blinding grin again. "Do this. So far as your cover job is concerned, your duties are to keep the men's locker room stocked with towels, mop it at the end of each day, and keep your eyes open for undercover law enforcement. They've never been here, but there's a first time for everything."

"But what about . . . the real job?"

"Okay, here's how it works," Peter said, entering a hallway, which led to an indoor swimming pool. "Once, sometimes twice, a week we get customers from out of town. We don't deal quantity to locals yet, because we haven't been around that long. We will give you a package and a key to a certain locker. After our customers disappear into the club for a half hour or so, you go in and put a workout bag of product in the locker we tell you. You won't be able to screw up because the key we give you will only fit one lock."

It sounded too good to be true. He was on the front line, and the first person to be busted should the deal go awry, but this looked like a pro operation. After all, Peter was the Man. And the Man didn't get busted. Ever.

His Corvette had seemed too good to be true at the time, too, and it turned out to be real. Sometimes good things happen, every so often. But one crucial question remained.

"How much do I make here?" Daryl asked.

"That's the best part. One hundred dollars a day. Five days a week. With or without a shipment."

Daryl felt like he was going to fall over. "In cash?"

"If you like. The IRS isn't interested in our books, if you know what I mean."

Daryl didn't, but nodded in understanding anyway. "I believe you got yourselves a deal," Daryl said, shaking Peter's huge hand. "When do I start?"

Peter produced a pair of shorts, a shirt, and an expensive pair of brand new Nikes, with the New You Fitness Center logo embroidered on it all. Daryl didn't notice the items before and had no idea where they came from. From thin air, it seemed, but he was past the point of caring. *One*

*hundred dollars a day. Cash. And my insurance is already
paid for. It's party time!*

"Come in tomorrow, around ten. Don't stay out partying
too late tonight. It would never do to have you show up
wasted." Peter's eyes narrowed, and he lowered his voice.
"Do we understand each other?"

"Oh, ah, yes sir," Daryl said. "I'll see you tomorrow." He
turned to leave, and made it almost to the door, when Peter
said.

"And Daryl? One more thing."

Daryl turned around in midstride.

"If you fuck us, we'll kill you. Now go home and get
some sleep. You look like hell."

Shaken, Daryl nodded uncertainly and started out the
door.

"Here he comes," Marbann said, but Adam had already
spotted him walking down the hallway.

Daryl got into his Corvette and drove off. Adam looked
over, saw a tall blond man standing in the entrance of the
center.

"Who is that?" Marbann said.

Despite the fact they were still invisible with the concealment spell, the man was looking directly at them.

Their eyes locked, though Adam wasn't certain if he saw
them or not; in that moment, he saw the terrible depths of
pain this being had linked to his magical powers. He shivered, catching a glimpse of this power and comparing it to
his own feeble grasp of magic, and knew then he was no
match for this Unseleighe.

Adam turned the Geo on and pulled out of the parking
lot. The elf with human seeming watched them as they left,
his eyes tracking their course out of the parking lot and
onto the adjoining street. When Adam glanced back, the
man was smiling at them, his arms crossed in an air of
defiance.

"Zeldan," Adam said, his hands shaking. "That was
Zeldan Dhu. And he was looking straight at us."

Marbann hissed, and Adam sensed strong shields snapping into place around them. "As a human he looks even more disgusting. Is he following?"

"I don't think so," Adam said, after glancing in the rearview mirror. "How good was that spell we used to hide ourselves?"

Marbann took only a second to consider this. "The very best. He may have sensed our presence, but I don't think he saw us. . . ."

"We don't know that," Adam said, feeling vulnerable despite his powerful company.

Rathand stared at his work, unable to believe what was taking place.

Great Danaa, he thought, mystified. *The nodes are healing themselves.*

It was the only explanation he could find as he poked around in one of the cabinets, checking for signs of his sabotage. Instead of finding drained nodes, he found, among the tiny rivers of energy running from the capacitors to the Terminal, a bybass of node power that had definitely not been there before. It was as if these artificial nodes had a mind of their own, knew they were in trouble, and had taken appropriate measures.

He closed the cabinet doors, disturbed at what he saw, more disturbed at what it implied.

Does Zeldan, or even Morrigan, know what I'm up to?

Chapter Fourteen

Zeldan watched Daryl climb into the Corvette and snickered to himself when he remembered the fright-trip his minion Mort pulled on the boy the night before.

He will be a good little pool of terror, he thought. *And he's still relatively sane. We should be able to throw all kinds of horrors his way before he finally snaps.*

Until his mind became useless, Daryl promised to be a faithful servant, acting as a front for their larger coke transactions when he wasn't mopping the locker-room floor. And during those inevitable moments of weakness, when the miserable human indulged in Dream, the horror show would begin.

He chuckled to himself as the Corvette drove out of the lot. Then, in another corner of the parking lot, he sensed the presence of something else. Zeldan's eyes focused on the spot, and he reached out with his magics, but not with much force, as he didn't know quite what he was dealing with yet. Just a tentative pass, enough to tell him that something was out there.

His smile didn't waver, but the discovery bothered him. Then, the presence moved, and Zeldan saw the vague outline of an automobile, but nothing else: a small car with an unknown number of passengers.

They think they're invisible, Zeldan thought. *I will make them think otherwise, whoever they are.*

His eyes fixed on the blur, which resembled shimmering

heat waves off hot pavement; a slight quiver in the fabric of the human's realm, where agents of Underhill dwelled and spied on him. He didn't know who they were, exactly, but he had a good idea.

Avalon elves. Perhaps even the King himself.

Zeldan resisted an urge to fling a levin bolt directly at the moving vehicle, partially because it would have attracted a lot of unwanted human attention, and also because it might be agents of Morrigan keeping tabs on him. Instead, he gazed after the concealed vehicle, pretending to be able to see it completely.

Seleighe maggots, he spat, as soon as the vehicle was gone. *I look forward to crushing you, Tuiereann. Now, let's go see what Rathand has cooked up from our little friend's nightmare.*

Down in the basement, Zeldan found Rathand studying the contents of an artificial node, supplied the night before. On the crystalline Terminal, Zeldan recognized the crushed remains of the Corvette, the mutilated face of Li-who-was-Mort. The multifaceted images flashed by swiftly, as if Rathand were holding down a fast-forward button.

"Mort does good work," Zeldan said, and Rathand grunted. "The boy had no idea it was all an illusion."

Rathand turned and stared at Zeldan with an attitude the Unseleighe didn't find appealing. "He does good work, all right. The boy almost died of heart failure during that little trip you put him through."

Zeldan stepped within an arm's reach of Rathand. "Yawn," the Unseleighe lord said sarcastically as he surrounded himself with the magics needed to turn from human to elf. Peter Pritchard underwent a brief but drastic metamorphosis: skin darkened, ears and nose lengthened, a robe replaced the yuppoid outfit of the New You staff. The Unseleighe lord glanced down at the cowering Rathand, who looked like he regretted everything he'd just uttered.

"You were saying?" Zeldan said.

"It wouldn't have mattered," Rathand murmured, turning back to the console. "What's another human life?"

"That's better," he said. "You will see, in due time, how dispensable these cattle are. Provided it is not a senseless waste. These banks," Zeldan said, walking over to the computer cabinets, "house our livelihood. When they are empty, we go hungry. If we can milk enough terror out of an eighteen-year-old human to fill one of these banks, it is well worth his life. There are many, many more where he came from."

"Yes, Zeldan," Rathand said. On the console, a crystal lit up. When Zeldan noticed it, he groaned. "Let me guess. The *bitch* requests an audience."

"It appears so," Rathand said. "Shall I—"

"No," Zeldan said, waving his hand in a gesture of dismissal. "Put her through. I'd rather deal with her now. And while you're at it, would you ready bank delta?"

"Yes, Zeldan," Rathand said, going over to one of the banks. "I've already upgraded the port with larger crystals. The old one was ruined during the last transmission." Rathand opened one of the cabinets, its interior illuminating him briefly as he glanced over the fully charged crystals. "Aye, delta is ready to send." He closed the cabinets and regarded Zeldan with pride. "Since delta is the largest of our banks, and the most fully charged, it would be perfect to test the new port. I doubt we'll have the same trouble as last time."

Zeldan hadn't noticed the old, fused port until then, set off in the corner. It had cracked as it cooled, and now resembled awkward ice sculpture that had been left out too long, and was slowly disintegrating. The replacement port, placed near the banks where the old one once stood, bristled with new, larger crystals, and looked like it could handle just about anything they had to send through it.

Zeldan jumped slightly as the Terminal flickered to life, and Morrigan's face appeared in its full hideous splendor. Rathand looked away, apparently not wanting to witness the exchange about to take place.

Morrigan sneered briefly before she said, "To date, what you have done with our product is only producing half what I anticipated. What will it take to increase the return?"

Zeldan stared at her, confused. *She had been ecstatic over that last transmission,* he thought, *and now she's saying it's not enough? She's starting to act like the addicts to whom we sell Black Dream. Will it* ever *be enough?*

"My dear lady," Zeldan said, forcing a smile. "I was under the impression you were pleased with the last delivery."

Morrigan grimaced, then snorted. "Well, yes. And no. Once I saw what was possible, I desired more, and more of it. Not that we're in any way dependent upon the powers of human pain, mind you. It's just that once our desires our satisfied, they seem to grow."

Zeldan gestured toward delta bank, behind Rathand, who shrugged. He didn't seem to know what the answer would be either. "Morrigan, I have a bank I'd like to send you—"

"*Zeldan!*" she shouted, cutting him off. "A single bank? *Four* would not be enough, at this rate."

Zeldan resisted a strong urge to smash the faceted image on the crystal, while seriously debating whether it was worth dealing with this demon. He quickly calculated how much of the Dream elixir they had, how long it would last, and what they might do if their supply were cut off.

"I don't know what to tell you," Zeldan said, trying without success to conceal the edge in his voice. "I am, I believe, keeping my end of the agreement. Do you wish to renegotiate the terms?"

A long, uncomfortable pause followed, so long that Zeldan started to assume their pact had been terminated. The Unseleighe began taking inventory of his defenses if an outright battle broke out between their two factions, and quickly decided that such a move would help neither of them, not to mention postponing his primary goal of defeating the Avalon crown.

"Excuse me a moment," Morrigan said. "I wish to confer with my staff."

She vanished momentarily, and when she returned, her expression was victorious.

"Well?" Zeldan said impatiently. "What would you like to do?"

"First," she said, then paused as someone on her side distracted her again. "Send your bank. We can *always* use the power. Then we will send you a special vial of elixir."

Zeldan frowned, this time making no secret of his distrust by raising his eyebrows and giving her a disbelieving look. "Might you be a little more specific?"

Again that animal gleam in her eye, like a wolf contemplating a helpless lamb. "We have a project in mind for you, Zeldan. Tell me what you think. First, let me thank you for fulfilling your end of the agreement. We have been wealthy with human pain, and in no time in our recent history can I recall such prosperity.

"But . . . your harvest of pain simply doesn't seem to be enough anymore."

Zeldan felt empty, then cold, in response. *Does this demon want a war with me?* he fumed, glancing away momentarily lest he fling a levin bolt directly at the Terminal.

"We have a plan that I think you will be most interested in," she continued. Zeldan's anger leveled off somewhat, but still remained near the boiling point. "What I propose is a large-scale version of what you already have been doing. True, mixing Dream with the human weaknesses for certain drugs has its own naive charm, but I believe there is a more effective way of distributing the elixir."

Zeldan pulled an office chair up and sat, then leaned toward the Terminal attentively.

"Had it occurred to you that we might get more dramatic results if we added Black Dream directly to the humans' water supply?" she said casually.

The idea stunned him. The water supply? All humans, and animals, would have to ingest so much water for anything to even happen. . . .

Zeldan shook his head in annoyance. "Morrigan, I don't

think you understand. The humans draw their water from vast lakes in the area, and to produce enough Dream to make such a plan feasible would be beyond anything we've done so far."

"But my dear Zeldan, *you* don't understand," Morrigan said, her smile unwavering. "We understand the human society more than you realize. In the time since our last transaction, we have developed a new version of Black Dream. It will look the same as what you have been receiving, but it is thousands, *millions*, of times more powerful. We will send you canisters of the new and improved Dream, and you will enlist the aid of your minions to distribute it in the water supply. And in twenty-four hours . . ."

She left the sentence dangling, but Zeldan imagined the results. Slowly, a crooked smile spread across his saturnine features.

"You are *brilliant*," Zeldan said, and truly meant it. "I doubt any of our kind would have conceived such a plan. It will mean, good gods, all that power, in *one area.*"

"This is a special version," Morrigan continued. "We have engineered it to have a time release of one day. Everyone, or nearly everyone, will have a full dose of it before authorities realize what is going on. Water is everywhere in the humans' world, and once the supply is infected it will take a great effort to cleanse it—provided they can even find the agent. This I doubt."

"And the results?" Zeldan asked, though he already had a good idea what they would be.

"Well, what else? Terrifying hallucinations, irreversible brain damage, damaged organs, poisoned blood, insanity, glorious mass insanity. The list is endless. And you will be on hand to reap all of it, to transmit it 'live,' I believe is the human term, directly to us."

Zeldan shook his head. *She must be joking.* "All that power . . . the port would fuse instantly."

"With all that power," Morrigan countered, "we can construct a Gate to admit it to Underhill, a Gate that feeds and sustains itself with the very power it's bringing to us. In that quantity, Zeldan, negative energy forms *rivers*. We will bathe in the waters of a dying race. And we will change, Zeldan. We will both become whatever we want."

Zeldan shuddered at the enormity of it all. *All that power*, he kept thinking, and the more he contemplated the reward, the more he desired it for himself as well.

We would become gods.

As the chill of excitement left his body, he turned to Morrigan and said soberly, "Morrigan, you have a deal."

"You're working *where?*" Paul Bendis shouted at his son over dinner. "Doing *what?*"

"The fitness center," Daryl said, pretending to be interested in a stray pea that had fallen off his plate. *Maybe I should have said I was the new manager.* "I thought you'd be happy to hear that I had a job."

Of course, he left out the part about the coke, but everything else about his new gig at the New You looked legit. Daryl sighed and set about the grim task of finishing his dinner. His mother had run out of Valium the day before and mysteriously felt energetic enough today to fix a full meal. It was the first time in months they had eaten together, and Daryl was hoping to make his father proud of him. But that hope was quickly disintegrating under his father's harsh glare.

Justin sat opposite Daryl and ate everything put before him, obviously pretending nothing was wrong, occasionally glancing at his older brother with sympathy. It was the only support he had at the table; Mother stared ahead blankly, exhausted after her special efforts, as Father spat his usual venom. Looking for something to distract him, Daryl noticed the t-shirt purchased earlier that summer was already showing signs of being too small on Justin's growing frame. For a brief moment, Daryl wondered why his own body hadn't grown so dramatically, and wondered if his coke habit had anything to do with it.

"Only fairies work jobs like that," Paul said, dragging him back into the argument. "Why do you need a job anyway?"

A bottle of scotch sat next to the table wine, and Paul had helped himself liberally to both during supper. When Father spoke, Daryl caught a nauseating waft of booze-breath, killing what was left of his already shaky appetite. "Doesn't your allowance more than cover your needs?"

A hundred dollars a week? If only you knew, Dad. . . .

It was a no-win situation, as usual. Anything he said would be wrong. If he agreed with his father, Paul would accuse his son of being weak. If he disagreed, that would be "talking back." Both infractions were punishable with the back of Paul's hand.

Daryl kept quiet, hoping the matter would just go away.

"So when the hell are you going to get insurance for that goddamned car?" Paul said after a blessed period of silence.

Daryl sighed. "I have insurance, Dad."

Paul looked mildly surprised. "Good," he said. "You might keep your ass out of jail after all."

Paul stood abruptly and tossed his napkin on the table. "I have a business dinner with a client. Next time you bother to cook a meal, Yanni, how about letting us know?"

Paul had left the table, grabbed his coat, and was halfway to his car when Yanni yawned and replied, "Yes, dear."

Later, when Daryl had cleared the table, he encountered Justin on his way down the stairs.

"Wanna go out?" Daryl asked.

Justin seemed to consider this. "And do what?"

"What else? Get loaded."

Justin shook his head, continued down the stairs. "Naw. I don't think so."

Daryl frowned. "Why? I thought you wanted to?"

"Because I don't want to look like you, Daryl," Justin said, without emotion, before leaving the house.

The remark left Daryl speechless. As he got ready to go out, he decided Justin was just pissed off because he'd said no the first time, and this was his way of being defiant.

An hour later, Daryl was out getting loaded on Dream all

by himself, praying to the gods who governed his life that
Mort would not show up.

Paul Bendis was on his second martini when Peter
Pritchard decided to arrive, and he might have taken
offense at his lateness. But when he saw the waiter leading
his prospective client to his table, he immediately pegged
him as a high-tech, high-dollar drug dealer, and decided
Mr. Pritchard could be as late he wanted to be.

"Paul Bendis," Peter said, extending a large hand. "I'm
Peter Pritchard."

"Pleased to meet you," Paul said, wanting to dispense
with the mandatory pleasantries. He took in the Oxford suit
at a glance and decided Peter was very wealthy indeed. "I
hope this restaurant is to your liking."

Peter hardly glanced at his surroundings. "I did not come
here to eat, Mr. Bendis," he said, waving away the menu
the waiter offered. "My time is valuable. And in short
supply."

"Then we will get down to business," Paul said, as Peter
sat in the chair the waiter pulled out for him.

"A drink, then?" Paul offered.

"No," Peter replied briefly. "What we have to talk about
will not take long." When the waiter was gone, Peter continued, "Donald Wallbrook works for me. He sells things
for me, if you understand."

"I've been Wallbrook's lawyer for many months now,"
Paul said evenly, wondering if he should refer to his "prize"
client as Presto, like everyone else. "I assume he gave you
my card."

"He did," Peter said, with a subtle smile Paul found
unnerving. "He has told me what an excellent lawyer you
are. There are others besides Presto who work for me.
They may need your services, as well, in the not too distant
future."

Okay, here it comes, Paul thought, clearing his throat.
"My rates are not cheap. I'm sure Presto has already told
you."

"He has. I will need a lawyer on call, twenty-four hours a day. Do you carry a pager?"

Paul had given up his pager a year before, as it tended to go off at the most inopportune times. It was easier to explain an ignored cellular phone call, which did not store the caller's number.

"You can reach me on my carphone or at my office. An answering service will call me if it's an emergency. The system works rather well, as Presto has certainly told you."

However, Peter didn't seem pleased. "I suppose that will have to do, since you are the best. Soon there will be an increase in business, within the week. My people will be moving large quantities of product, if you catch my meaning. There may be complications."

Peter removed an envelope from his coat pocket and handed it to Paul. When he opened it, he found a cashier's check for ten thousand dollars.

"Is that sufficient for a retainer?" Peter asked softly, getting to his feet.

"Ten thousand? It certainly is," Paul said, getting to his feet. "Here is my card, again, with all pertinent numbers. How can I reach you?"

"That won't be necessary," Peter said, taking the card and putting it in a coat pocket without reading it. "I will call you if I need you. Good night, Mr. Bendis."

Peter Pritchard turned and left the restaurant as Paul watched, mildly confused.

Secretive prick, he thought, and shrugged. *But for a ten thousand dollar retainer, he can be as secretive as he wants.*

Sammi McDaris listened to the conversation between Peter and Paul with extreme interest, while a reel-to-reel recorder taped it all. Sammi and Roach monitored the radio equipment while a young rookie sat in the van's driver's seat, keeping a watch for surly types coming out of the restaurant. They'd parked in an alley across the street, but had a lousy view of the entrance.

Roach uttered a low whistle when Paul mentioned the

check. "Ten *grand?* For a lawyer? Must be some heavy shit getting ready to go down."

Sammi stared at the tape recorder, as if Zeldan's image would suddenly jump from it and tell her what was on his mind. "Wonder why the sudden interest in lawyers," she said, more to herself than to her partner. Then she turned and addressed him directly. "Roach, I think you're right. But do we have enough evidence for a search warrant?"

"On the basis of this tape?" He scratched his head and loosened his already loosened tie. "Doubt it. Did they ever mention coke? No. How trustworthy is that waiter you had plant that bug?"

Sammi was embarrassed to say that she wasn't sure, and regretted using a human for what an elf might have done more efficiently with magic. The waiter had a pending drug charge, and she had arranged for a little leniency if he cooperated. The waiter had put a tiny radio transmitter under the table when Bendis appeared. She knew that Paul Bendis frequented this restaurant, and they had hoped to get some choice bits of incriminating evidence on tape.

She had no idea Zeldan was going to be his dinner guest, even when they caught a glimpse of "Peter" going into the restaurant. True, he was in his human seeming, but as soon as she heard the voice and sensed the dark Unseleighe presence from within the restaurant, she knew who she was dealing with.

"No, I guess not," Sammi said, trying to sound disappointed. She knew that what they'd learned was better than any evidence they might have on Bendis; this indicated something major afoot, something that would happen soon.

Question is, how much does it involve Daryl, or Adam, and the Avalon elves?

Chapter Fifteen

Feeling depressed and gloomy, Adam pulled the Geo into the driveway, after having driven in silence from the New You Fitness Center. Marbann, apparently sensing his mood, did not attempt conversation. During the drive over, Adam had nearly formulated a plan of evacuation, which would take the clan to another continent, England, or even Ireland, where they might live in relative isolation from the Unseleighe in the humans' world. Or perhaps they might reenter Underhill and plead with Outremer or some of the other, larger clans for sanctuary. Avalon had been separated from the other clans by choice for so long that he didn't know if they would even be welcomed.

The force Adam had seen in the Unseleighe's eyes, however briefly, was enough to convince him.

Zeldan is too powerful to defeat. To confront him would mean certain death for myself and the clan.

Retreat was the only option, Adam decided. He kept this to himself, because he knew Marbann would violently argue in the negative, that the only chance they had was to take Zeldan directly. This he had already argued, and Adam had no reason to believe anything had changed.

Also, the nagging question of, *what would Father do?* kept at him. *Would Father run in defeat?* Hardly. He had had the opportunity to flee before Avalon fell and had fought to the bitter end.

Now, the new King considered fleeing before the battle had even begun.

Adam hated and feared Zeldan and his forces, but when it got down to it, what he feared the most was his own failure.

What to do? The question continued to roll around in his mind while he and Marbann entered the house and greeted the clan.

"You look grim," Moira observed when he and Marbann entered the living room. "What happened today?"

She sat in one of the couches next to Niamh, who was busy playing dual Gameboys with Petrus. Wenlann was crocheting something in the corner, smiled when she glanced up, and went back to her work. The complete lack of concern the scene presented was enough to help Adam forget his worries, at least for a moment.

"Is Lady Samantha home yet?" Marbann asked, though Adam already knew she wasn't. The older elf had yet to make the connection between the presence and absence of certain automobiles and what that had to do with where the owner might be.

"She's working late," Adam said. "On some stakeout work." *Involving Paul Bendis.* He didn't want to think about what this might have to do with Daryl.

The encounter with Zeldan left him with a total feeling of helplessness, and he hoped his body language didn't reveal this. But Moira was far more observant than he'd given her credit for.

Moira pursued the issue a little more aggressively. "Adam, *what happened?* We're involved in this too, you know."

Adam doubted that she'd meant that viciously, but it still dug. *Yeah, don't I know we're all involved,* he thought morosely.

"I saw Zeldan Dhu today," Adam said dismally, taking what had become his "throne," near the Sony. All motion ceased in the room; the Gameboys ran on auto, beeping and chiming as all faces turned to Adam.

"Did he see you?" Petrus asked, his voice quavering with terror.

Adam shook his head. "He did not see me, I don't think. But *I* saw more than I cared to."

He had yet to share this insight with Marbann, who regarded him curiously. "Do continue, young King," Marbann said. "You were rather silent during the journey over here. I sense you've come to some decisions regarding our future."

Damn his perceptiveness, Adam thought, but did not find it in himself to be angry. Even considering retreat felt like a failure, and Marbann's harsh look made it difficult to continue.

"Marbann and I followed my human friend Daryl to an establishment, which now appears to be a front for dealing Black Dream."

Moira sucked in her breath, while the others showed various degrees of concern. "We knew it was happening," Moira said. "This . . . establishment. You discovered the Unseleighe nest, didn't you?"

Adam nodded, shifted uncomfortably in the chair, and willed the room, which had become rather warm, to chill a few degrees. "Aye," Adam said dismally. "I got a glimpse of the power these elves have."

Marbann regarded him with amusement. "Is that what's been bothering you? I admit, I felt it too, but I didn't think their power *that* great."

"Tell me," Adam said, eyeing him directly, and for once Marbann's look wandered. "Do *you* think you can defeat Zeldan Dhu?"

"I don't know," Marbann said. "But if you're concerned about what you saw, or rather, felt, let me explain. . . ."

Adam was not convinced. "I saw the power that dwelled in their nest," he said, but Marbann waved him to silence.

"The power was stolen from human pain," Marbann insisted. "*That* much I know. And as such, it is unpredictable and difficult to direct. Do not think for a moment that it is greater than the forces *you* have at your command."

Marbann was being insubordinate, but Adam saw no

skillful way to call him on it. Instead, he decided to drop his proposal on everyone present.

"I think that we, as a clan, should leave this human city. We cannot survive another battle with Zeldan Dhu. We must begin to look for a new haven."

Having said that, Adam tried to look his clan in the face and found with alarm that he could not. *Why?* he thought frantically. *I have their interests as well as my own to consider. . . .*

Somehow, the argument didn't wash with himself.

"No," Marbann said. "Zeldan must die. We cannot rest until—"

"I am not running from Unseleighe ever again!" Niamh said. "I'm not, I'm not!"

"Do you really think he will just quit looking for us?" Moira interjected. "Running from him doesn't appeal to me, I'll have you know. I was looking forward to seeing his blood on my blade!" Already Adam was regretting his statement.

"Retreat. Before the battle even begins?"

All looked up at Samantha, who had just entered the living room. Adam hadn't noticed her arrival, and her sudden appearance made him quite uncomfortable indeed. Her look, a wintry glare that chilled his blood, reminded him why.

Gods, I haven't even considered her opinion on this. . . . he thought, wishing he might recall the words.

"And who have you consulted in this matter?" Samantha advanced into the room, her aura sparking with anger and something else—a tangible fury Adam usually associated with thunderstorms. She took a seat near him, but despite her wrath, she still looked weary. With a wave of her hand, she dismissed her human seeming and regarded Adam with her full elven features.

"I know that you are frightened of Zeldan Dhu," she said, softer than he had expected. "And to a certain extent I am also. He is an abomination to the entire elven race."

Adam felt his authority slipping, but in the presence of the elf who used to be his human "mother" this felt natural, if not inevitable. *There are still buttons she can push. She had years to install them.*

Samantha's expression seemed to soften, and she continued, "But you are the King, and it is wrong of me to criticize your decision." She walked over to the buffet, and among the antique knickknacks she selected a small wooden box and handed it to Adam.

As he examined it, he began to see what a delicate work of art it was. The rectangular box, small enough to fit in his palm, was a mosaic of inlaid wood, forming a dozen or so five-pointed stars. When he saw that the hinge was not metal, but carved wood, he said, "This is from Underhill, isn't it?"

"It is. Open it."

Inside was a light blue crystal, tipped with four facets. As it caught the light, a rainbow spread down his arm.

"It is a memory crystal, which your father sent with Wenlann before Zeldan defeated him. I was to give it to you when you were further along in your studies, but now your hasty decision has forced my hand."

Adam opened his mouth to ask, *How do you use this?* Then he remembered.

He closed both hands around it and reached for it as he would reach a node; the crystal pulsed in his hand, and he saw a deep blue light trickling between his fingers, illuminating his hands from within.

The images came swiftly, moving like the swift current of a shallow river, before he focused on what he perceived was the primary image in the recording; his father's last memories surged into his mind.

"Close your eyes," Samantha said. "The images will be easier to see."

As he did so, he dropped into a sea-vertigo, and relived his father's last thoughts. . . .

. . .this is the last message I will ever send you, dear son. All is lost here, as I record this crystal. Your mother has died and soon I will, too, but what is important is that you take the clan to safety. . . .

At the edges of the message Adam caught glimpses of the small room he'd last seen his father in, falling dust, the tremor of levin bolts. The memory sickened him, and saddened him, as this was the last thing his father saw.

Zeldan Dhu will pursue you until he finds you and kills you, and once that is done, he will kill the rest of the others, and there will be no Avalon.

Adam wrestled with himself, wanting to drop the damned piece of crystal and wanting to hear the rest. Grief welled within him as his father's thoughts mixed with his own; it felt, for a moment, like he was still alive, offering fatherly advice.

Do not misunderstand me, my dearest son. I want you to find safety in the humans' world, but once you've established yourself there, you must make yourself strong and attack Zeldan. Soon, and quickly. If you don't attack, he will surely kill you. That is the only way you will survive, and this request is the only gift I can give the elfhame, in my dying breath. Find Zeldan and—

That was all. The message ended abruptly, replaced by darkness.

"No!" Adam shouted, opening his eyes. He dropped the crystal and tried to stand up; dizziness and fatigue prevented him from going too far. *Father* . . . he thought through the tears, as the loss of his father once again tore an open wound in his chest.

"There, there," Samantha said soothingly, and he felt her arms close around him. He leaned into her and returned the embrace, fighting back the sobs, then surrendering to them completely.

Several minutes later, he looked up into Samantha's face, this time with fierce determination.

"I didn't think I had any tears left," he said through the anger that replaced the grief. "Those may be the last for a long, long time."

Samantha stroked his hair, a motherly gesture that had calmed him in times of human crisis in the past. The elfhame surrounded him with expressions of concern.

This is no way for a King to behave.

He stood, successfully this time, and went into the bathroom. There he washed his face with cold water, twice, as if this would sweep the grief away. It helped; at least his eyes weren't as red. He noticed something else, too, a change in his face that went beyond the tears he'd recently shed. He saw anger, and determination. Leadership, and an awakening.

I'm not afraid of Zeldan Dhu.

Then, *Zeldan Dhu murdered my family. I will not allow him to kill any more of us.*

And, *If we don't act now, he will.*

Adam returned to the living room, where a sea of hopeful faces greeted him. Composed, he seated himself in his usual chair. The memory crystal was in the wooden box, which was open and sitting on the coffee table.

"I think I might have made a decision in haste, without consulting the clan. As Samantha has pointed out." He paused, wondering briefly where this would go. His mouth ran on, seemingly on its own volition. "My father knew Zeldan well," he continued, eyeing the wooden box with a raised eyebrow. "As I should also have known, having seen his work so far.

"We must summon our energies and strike Zeldan and his Unseleighe with everything we have."

The resultant cheer drowned out his next thought. The reaction wasn't something he expected, and he blushed with pride.

Finally, I've done something *right,* he thought, grateful for his father's insight. He wondered if a bit of Father had just rubbed off on him during the memory transference.

"I'm uncertain where to begin. Suggestions, anyone?"

Niamh raised a hand tentatively, then spoke. "There is something I wanted to bring up earlier. It may make a difference when we confront Zeldan."

Everyone turned to Niamh attentively.

"Yes?" Samantha said. "Go ahead."

"Well," Niamh began, visibly flustered by the newfound

attention, "it's the weapon. Long ago, before there was ever a threat from Zeldan, Avalon appropriated—"

"Stole," Samantha corrected.

"Okay, *stole* this weapon from a human school. In California, I think it was."

"I recall the project," Samantha said. "The technicians in charge of it were killed in Zeldan's first wave, but this was what happened. The creator of the weapon, a college boy not much older than our King, had second thoughts about its use. One of the Seleighe, then doing a reconnaissance of that region of North America, came across the lad, and when they learned what he had, they made arrangements for its disappearance."

Adam was confused, and let it show. "What weapon? What does it do?"

"It was originally meant to amplify light. The humans call such a device a laser, and they are common now, used in medicine and the making of things. What made this device unique was that, with a few adjustments, the device was capable of amplifying node power."

Adam stared at her, then broke out of the mental fog the concept induced. "Node power? This made it more . . ."

"Concentrated. The Seleighe techs who came across the device were fascinated by its properties and were interested in a peaceful use for it. But when they brought it to Underhill, it refused to work."

"I know where they keep it," Niamh said smugly. "In fact, it was—"

"I remember it now," Adam said. *In the chamber. Where Mother's body lay.* "But why didn't it work in Underhill?"

Samantha shrugged. "Who knows? Perhaps there was a difference in physics between our two worlds that was slight enough to keep it from working. We do know that it worked before they brought it to Underhill."

Adam thought of the device, now a murky but substantial memory, and how much it resembled a rifle. He'd seen a movie, *Ghostbusters,* and remarked how much it resembled the ghost-annihilating weapons in that. But the weapon was more streamlined and did not require big backpacks, just a little one.

If it does what Samantha says it does...

"We need to go back and get it," Adam said suddenly. *Anything to swing the odds in our favor.*

"You and what army?" Moira said. "The Unseleighe captured the palace, remember?"

Samantha interrupted, "Now, wait a minute. Keep in mind that Zeldan is rather powerful at the moment. Our resources are limited, as well as our skills. We need something to give us an edge before we can even think about taking on the Unseleighe."

"Do we know how many soldiers Zeldan left at Underhill to defend the palace?" Adam asked.

A long thoughtful silence followed. Marbann spoke up. "For all we know, they've abandoned the palace. From what little we know of their strategy, they don't take positions for any reason other than killing whoever owns them. Our palace included."

"There wasn't much there *to* take," Samantha admitted sadly. "By the time I arrived, the palace was all but destroyed."

King Aedham Tuiereann batted the subject back and forth until a consensus had been reached: they would return to Underhill and retrieve the weapon. Adam asked for volunteers; everyone present raised their hands. Samantha regarded him with a look which seemed to say, *This decisions's yours to make.*

He considered the matter. Spence would be helpful on the other side, but he wasn't here to volunteer himself. He finally selected Niamh, who knew where the weapon was. Then, of course, his teacher, Marbann. Though not a mage, he did have a better grasp of magic, particularly that of Underhill.

"I move we go now," Adam said. "There is only one problem that I foresee. How can we guarantee that we will return to the humans' world within a reasonable period of time?"

"Yes, indeed," Marbann said thoughtfully. "To return in five human years or so and find the elfhame conquered would never do. Also, if the Unseleighe still have possession of the nodes, which is a certainty, I would have nothing with which to build a return Gate."

Samantha seated herself in the living room. "If we construct a Gate to remain open during your entire stay . . . you would return at the exact point you left," she said, crossing her legs and kicking off her high heels. "The drawbacks would be that your time to find the weapon would be limited. For any substantial length of time, a Gate would require more than the usual amount of node energy."

"This is not a problem," Marbann said. "Adam can reach all the power we need," he said, looking proudly at the King. "With his help, I can control what power he brings forth and build a Gate to remain active for the duration of our journey."

As Adam considered the plan, he became more excited over it. *A weapon to conquer Zeldan. We must have it. Provided they haven't destroyed it, of course. . . .*

"We can do this!" Adam said. "Can we construct a Gate directly into the chambers we fled?"

Marbann looked doubtful. "That would be too risky. Better to Gate to a remote location, then move in. The Unseleighe may detect it if it were too close; they may detect it anyway."

"With the nodes in Underhill in the Unseleighe's possession," Samantha continued, "any power you use must come from the nodes we have here."

The King was not certain, but Marbann seemed confident. "I believe we can do this. The sooner we return with the weapon, the more time we will have to make it ready for our use."

"Now wait a minute," Moira said. "Aren't you forgetting something?" To everyone's puzzled looks, she continued, "How about disguises? You want to go in looking like Seleighe, or Unseleighe?"

Moira pulled out a huge makeup case, and in the next

several moments converted their bright, healthy appearances to sickened, pasty ones.

"Here," Samantha said, holding up several bags of something. "Black clothing. I started stocking up when Gothic became popular."

Adam found himself in a black tunic, with even blacker hose; Marbann looked pale and sick, as did Niamh.

Wenlann recoiled in shock when she saw them, and Adam smiled grimly. "So. We look like the real thing."

"Well . . . well, yes," Wenlann squeaked. Moira went to her and put an arm around her shoulders.

"They're only pretend," Moira said, then, to the rest, "She'd never seen Unseleighe before the invasion."

"We will return soon," Marbann said to her. Then he said to Adam, "I think we should construct the Gate now."

The King nodded, closed his eyes, and *reached.* . . .

Though more distant, the nodes from the Marketplace appeared easily in his mental vision. Adam sensed Marbann as he entered the vision, a ghost of a being with the bright orbs as backdrop; he pulled the power toward him, and Marbann routed the streams, weaving them expertly, then directing the result to a location immediately before them.

"It's ready," Adam heard him announce. "Time for us to be off." When he opened his eyes, the Gate glowed brilliantly, an extension of arched brightness pouring out of the big screen Sony.

Wasting no time, Adam led the "Unseleighe" past the curtain of light into Underhill.

Midafternoon at the Marketplace.

The natural wood interior of the mall was a sharp contrast to the sterile, chlorine and sweat atmosphere at the New You Fitness Center, where Daryl had just left after a grueling day of towel handling. He'd almost forgotten what it was like to show up for a job, and he'd nearly blown it off like all the others, when he'd remembered that Dream was involved, and he would eventually start dealing quantity.

Since they didn't have anything for him to deal today,

they let him go early. He had a bit of Dream leftover from the cache Presto supplied him (the Man had told him his debt to Presto was paid), and he decided to see what he might be able to turn at the Yaz, Adam be damned. Or maybe he might turn some in the arcade, where no one had yet pegged him for a dealer.

Yet. . .

He stood in the entrance, trying to decide where to go, when someone tapped him on the shoulder.

"Want to go have lunch?"

He turned around to see Moira, whom he'd seen hanging around Adam a lot lately, and he'd begun to wonder if they were dating. She was part of the circle Daryl himself had once belonged to a year or so ago, but Daryl had only had a fleeting, personal acquaintance with her. He'd noticed her around the mall and thought about getting to know her a little better. Given the strange events lately, he'd had little time to investigate the matter, but here she was, talking to *him*.

The question startled him, but he tried not to let it show. "Sure," he said automatically. "Where to?"

"Upstairs would be fine," she said. "I've got a one o'clock coming in. A *perm*. I hate perms."

As they started up the escalators to the top floor, where a number of mini-fast-food places were located, he caught a whiff of her perfume. She was wearing leather today, and the scent of her perfume mingled well with the black studded miniskirt, wristbands, and black stiletto pumps. With dark makeup, she looked severe without the S&M overtones; overall, Moira looked and smelled incredibly sexy, and Daryl wondered if his love life was about to take a turn for the better. And without knowing why, the prospect terrified him.

"Adam told me there was some excitement over at the Wintons' the other day," she said after they'd ordered pizza and seated themselves at a tiny table. "What happened, anyway?"

She'd asked him in a completely friendly manner, but the

question caught him off guard. *What does she know about what happened?* Defenses snapped into place, and he began to wonder if he'd made a big mistake by taking her up on lunch.

"Looks like some bad dope got loose in the party," he said.

The counter called out their number, and in the short time it took Daryl to claim their lunch, he decided to change the subject.

Instead, she changed it for him. "So tell me," she said, her sexiness suddenly more alluring, as if she had a "sexpot" dial somewhere, and she'd turned it all the way up to ten. "I hear you're quite the broker in exotic chemicals."

"I can get it," Daryl said, opting not to mention the amount of stash, ten vials, he carried on him. "You want to get high?"

She shrugged, then shook her head. Daryl wanted to kick himself at his stupidity. *She knows Adam; Adam's mom is a cop. Too much association with the law there for comfort.*

Despite his gut feeling that she might be dangerous to his freedom, the words came tumbling out; part of him had no control over them, and another part of him wanted to impress her.

"I've been selling quantity for about a year now. That's how I got that Corvette, you know."

"Really," Moira said, playing with a strand of cheese that had refused to break. "I heard your father bought it for you."

Daryl nearly coughed on his Coke, but recovered in time. "That's the . . . cover story."

"So who do you buy it from?"

That's where he had to draw the line. "Sorry, trade secret."

"Doesn't it get a little, well, scary?"

Mort came to mind, and all the other strange things that had been happening to him. "It's worth the money," he said, wondering if it really was.

They ate quietly, and Daryl feared he might have turned her off by talking about his part-time work. As soon as he thought all was lost, she gave him a sly, sexy smile and nudged his ankle under the table. Daryl nearly jumped out of his skin.

What was that—an invitation? Or is she just teasing me? He desperately wanted to find out. *She doesn't get high, but she must have at one time. A recovering addict? Maybe . . .*

In spite of all the uncertainty, she turned him on something terrible.

Here goes. Balls to the wall . . .

"Would you . . . like to spend the night with me sometime?"

She regarded him with a look of incredulity. His soul withered.

"I don't know . . . I'm sort of dating someone right now." *Adam.*

"But let me think about it. I don't like casual sex. Perhaps a date, if things don't work out otherwise. Then, maybe, when we've gotten to know each other a little better."

Daryl had difficulty believing that such a sexy girl—no, despite her age, this was a *woman*—would make a pass at him, then pretend to be a prude.

"Okay," he said, his fire only somewhat diminished. "Yeah, I know, safe sex and all that."

"You don't sound terribly convinced."

"I guess I'm not. I've never known anyone with AIDS, or even HIV positive."

What was it about her that made him think she was reading his mind?

The moment became awkward, and Moira finished up her lunch. "It was nice having this little talk," she said. She gave him scrap of paper with her name and a phone number on it. "If you ever need help, give me a call. I mean, if you ever want to get off drugs. Try something different. Or anything." She turned and strutted off, the black stiletto heels looking like tiny stilts as she stepped onto the escalator.

Now he was really confused. *Does she want to boff me,*

or does she want to do a Mother Teresa routine on my drug habit?

The encounter left him feeling empty. Instead of impressing her with his position, he feared he turned her off. *But she wants to go out. Doesn't she?*

He even considered getting clean to go out with her. *How long would that take? A week? A month? Would it be worth it?* He doubted it. *She must be a narc. That would explain everything.* If she was, he hadn't told her anything the average kid in school wouldn't know.

Then, with startling clarity, he saw what his life might be like without the Dream. And he liked what he saw. For one thing, his relationship with his brother would improve. That insult Justin had thrown at him hurt far more than he realized; it still dug at him, like a splinter in a finger. No more Mort, or so he hoped. No Presto, no fear.

But getting there . . .

And once he was clean, then what? First, Presto, or even the Man, would have him killed. He had no doubt about that. He didn't want to go into a treatment center because it would just piss off his dad, and his dealer.

Dad can handle his drugs just fine, can't he? Isn't he one of the highest paid lawyers in Dallas?

He pushed the reasoning away. *It's just easier to keep things the way they are. I can handle it. I can go on forever like this. I'm still young.*

"I've got time," he whispered to no one at all.

Chapter Sixteen

"We must be in the wrong place," Adam said sadly, once the five Avalon elves had stepped through the Gate to Underhill, or what was left of it. "This can't be the kingdom."

"Are you still in touch with the nodes, Adam?" Marbann asked. He seemed disturbed by the sight before them, which apparently urged him to make certain they had a way back to Dallas before going any further. "If the power has weakened, I don't know if we should continue."

"I don't know if we should continue anyway," Niamh said, standing behind the others and peering furtively between them. "I don't like what's happened here. I don't."

What was once a lush, green landscape abundant with moss and fern was now a sterile wasteland. Dust rose as they walked; no plants, trees, or even grass greeted them. Nothing lived here, at least not that they could see, and the annihilation of what was once their home renewed the rage he felt for the enemy.

At least our disguise fits our surroundings, he remarked to himself, once his anger had subsided. "Marbann, do you know where we are?" Adam asked hopefully. Marbann seemed confused, turning his head right and then left, as if trying to get his bearings straight.

"I think . . . the palace is that way," he said, pointing toward the valley. "If not for that thrice-damned dust, we might even be able to see the palace in the distance."

"Or what is left of it," Niamh said distantly. Adam wrestled with the dark mood that fell over him, sensing that the same depression had fallen on his comrades.

"Then let us proceed," Adam said. "The Gate won't remain open forever," he said, glancing back at the portal, which glowed dully in the murky light. He feared the Gate would act as a bright beacon, attracting unwanted attention, but as they left it behind them, advancing cautiously down a slope, it dimmed until it was invisible.

"I can find the Gate again," Marbann said, apparently sensing the King's uneasiness. "And so can you, if you reach out with your mind."

Adam closed his eyes, and indeed the Gate appeared in his mental vision, and beyond the Gate he saw the tendrils of node power that kept it open. Before going too much further, he reinforced the power holding the Gate in place, which Marbann in turn used to strengthen the opening.

"I hope this weapon can deliver what we need," Adam said. "The less we are all down here the better."

"Aie, yes," Niamh said meekly. "The Unseleighe have ruined this land, they have."

Got no argument there, Adam thought as they descended into the valley. "Marbann, how long do you suppose it has been since the Unseleighe moved in?"

The older elf negotiated a cluster of boulders blocking their way, then helped the others over them. "No way to know," he said. "It may have been years. Or days. The same time distortion exists whether traveling to or from Underhill."

Years, Adam thought. *What might the Unseleighe have accomplished, if it has been that long?*

"We must hurry," Adam said, sensing danger somewhere near. "I'm afraid we—"

A rustle from beyond a ridge interrupted him. In seconds, a party of creatures on horseback surged over the hill, wielding bows with arrows, nocked and ready to fly.

"Elf-shot," Marbann murmured. "Those arrows would kill us instantly."

The creatures, which resembled gargoyles, circled their mounts around behind the Avalon elves and stopped. One gargoyle, with hideous reptilian skin, looking like a cross between a lizard and an elf, brandished a banner and wore a more elaborate tunic than the others. Adam surmised he was the leader.

"These are not Unseleighe," Marbann whispered. "But they may be in Zeldan's employ."

Adam glanced from one creature to another. Then he considered that they might be rogues, an independent band of critters looting what Zeldan's group left behind.

"Zeldan used gargoyles as mercenaries," Marbann replied. "But that is *not* Zeldan's banner. I don't know for certain what is going on here, young King, but I do have a suspicion. Let me do the speaking, if you please."

Adam had no problem with that, he thought, before motion from one of the creatures distracted him. "Perhaps we are about to find out," he said. The apparent leader approached them cautiously while the others looked on. Their arrows remained aimed and ready.

The gargoyle barked a series of unintelligible words in a language Adam had only a fleeting familiarity with. It sounded like well-formed grunts, hard hissing of consonants, followed by the snapping of teeth—or whatever incisors gargoyles had. Marbann replied in kind, to the surprise of Adam; he had no idea his mentor spoke fluent Gargoyle.

Marbann and the leader exchanged a few, harsh words, when finally he turned and shrugged.

"They don't believe me," he said. "But they would like to escort us back to the palace. We were in no position to bargain," Marbann said. "We stand no chance against arrows, and so many creatures."

But what about other protections? Adam thought. Discussion didn't seem to be restricted, and Adam ventured a few whispered words to Marbann. "Shields, Marbann," Adam hissed. "If I . . ."

Marbann snorted in annoyance. "Are you certain you can

have one in place, to protect all of us, in the split second it takes to let an arrow fly?"

Surrounded as we are, the shield would need to materialize instantly and perfectly. He remembered the misshapen shield he'd constructed in their garage and how pathetic a construction it actually was.

"I might try myself," Marbann offered. "But I have doubts. I'm not willing to risk our lives on that chance."

Reluctantly, the King admitted this wasn't such a great plan. Another gargoyle grunted at Adam and motioned for him to follow. The leader advanced ahead of them several paces, as the other gargoyles flanked them on either side.

"What did you *tell* them?" They were several paces from the nearest gargoyle, and going by their lack of reaction he doubted his words had reached their ears.

"I thought they might be working for Zeldan, and I was right. I claimed the Unseleighe lord sent us to seize some of the treasure in the palace."

Moments passed. "And?" Adam asked. "Did they believe you?"

"Well, we *look* Unseleighe. They will take us to the other Unseleighe already there to verify what I told him."

Adam stifled a groan. *They'll know for certain we're bogus,* he thought. *Or maybe not.* At any rate, there was little they could do to improve their situation, except to wait for an opportunity to act.

Presently, the palace, or rather what was left of it, loomed into view. Adam's heart sank when he saw the ruins, but he concealed his expression as much as possible. Large sections of the turrets and the outer walls had come down, apparently the result of well-placed levin bolts. This was the first time he had seen the palace remains, except for the vision in his dream; even the ruined bridge remained in place, as he envisioned, complete with vine coverage. He looked nervously in the sky for the black eagle which had attacked him in the vision, though he doubted such a creature truly existed. It was more a symbol of Zeldan's power, he had thought, than an actual beast. And Zeldan was Above now, in the human's realm.

He reached cautiously for the nodes of his homeland, but Marbann's warning look made him reconsider.

"Trying to reach the Underhill nodes would only alert the enemy," he whispered. "I doubt, even with our combined power, we would be able to wrest anything from them."

"But . . ."

"But nothing," Marbann said. "Until we know what's going on, it would be best to keep secret our abilities."

"Aie," Adam replied. "They may yet buy our story."

Marbann's stony silence suggested he didn't think this too likely. Then, his mentor asked, "What about the Marketplace nodes?"

The King felt the vague power just beyond the periphery of his mental sight and knew that it was still within reach. Adam nodded.

"Keep the power in sight," Marbann advised. "If the Unseleighe attack us with node power, unleash it. Right now we must convince them of our false identities."

When they reached the edge of the ruins, the gargoyles led them into a makeshift cavern; this had been an opening leading into the lower levels of the palace. The opening had been widened and improved over time, but it was still a grim example of how little the conquerors had tried to fix what they had destroyed. The wooden arch that framed the entrance was old and well seasoned, indicating a great deal of time had passed since the palace fell. That the Unseleighe spent so little effort to rebuild or improve the place sickened Adam as much as the loss of his home.

The gargoyles dismounted and gestured, using their arrows as pointers, for Adam and his party to follow.

"No Unseleighe yet," Marbann whispered. "Perhaps, beneath the ruins, we might have a better chance against this group."

True. Bows and arrows were not practical in close quarters, and Marbann's plan had merit, if no others awaited them below.

The gargoyles led them into a darkened chamber and barked a command to Marbann.

"We are to wait here," Marbann said. "However, young King, you will notice that their guard is down at the moment. Now may be our only—"

Before Marbann completed the sentence, the world turned silver.

Moments before, Adam felt a surge of power rising beneath them. The release of energy happened so quickly that time froze, and he was himself momentarily paralyzed. He knew this was a new threat, from an unknown source, but he found himself powerless to do anything about it.

"*Marbann, what the*—" Adam began, but the shield, or whatever had become their prison, snapped into place around them, sealing them in, like being trapped inside a Tupperware container.

Mute, they stared at their cage: a reflective, silvery surface. Adam touched it, saw his finger extend to the first knuckle in the mercurylike surface. Then he touched hardness, like cool concrete.

"Perhaps we might dig under it," Marbann said, getting down on his knees. He scooped several handfuls away, but soon they found that the silver walls encasing them curved down, probably completing the form of a sphere.

"We might keep digging," Marbann said, "but I suspect we're trapped beneath by whatever field this is." He stood, regarding the surface in puzzlement. Though Adam saw no obvious light source, the field glowed enough to provide dim illumination.

"Will it permit us to breathe?" Niamh asked, but no one had an answer for him.

Adam sat down on the floor, trying to think, while Marbann proceeded to inspect the interior of the shell to no apparent effect. He felt completely useless, not only because he was unable to help himself, but also because he had failed his clan.

"This barrier has completely cut off our power," Marbann said. "Can you sense any node energy?"

The shell proved a major barrier, but beyond it he did detect the vague impression of the Gate and the nodes supporting it. "It's there, but I can't quite reach it. This shell, it's like a signal scrambler." They all stared at him. "Never mind. That would take too long to explain."

Niamh stepped forward, addressing the group. "Perhaps if we combined our powers . . ."

"And focused, say, on a single spot," Adam continued for him. Then he turned to his mentor. "Would it work?"

"We must try," Marbann said. "First, let's form a circle. . . ."

Daryl stood against the fender of his 'Vette, smoking a cigarette, wondering if there was some way to kill a demon.

"Isn't it beautiful?" Mort said, and with a majestic sweep of his black arm, he presented Lake Tawekoni. The gesture reminded him of the sexy models on *The Price is Right*; but instead of a new car or a European vacation, the demon stood beside the largest lake that supplied drinking water to the city of Dallas, Texas.

"It's a lake," Daryl said, tempering his anger with nicotine. The cigarette burned harshly down his throat, as it was the tenth one that day. That afternoon, after "work" at the New You, Daryl imbibed some Dream, forgetting to offer his prayer to the gods that Mort would not show up. Halfway into the second rock, Mort *popped* into place in the driver's seat. To say that the demon suggested the trip to the lake was an understatement; when Daryl resisted, his 'Vette assumed a life of its own. A force beyond him, apparently under the direct control of Mort, took over the driving for him, cruising down Highway 80 at an even 54 miles per hour. Daryl had folded his arms, fuming, as his pride and joy committed treason by going somewhere *he* didn't want to go. This had never happened before. But then, this had not been an ordinary month.

Mort frowned, a strangely comic expression on his exaggerated features. For reasons Daryl hadn't figured, Mort had grown two short horns, which made him look like Satan. *No, not Satan. Satan's annoying nephew.*

"It's not just *a* lake, shithead," Mort hissed. "It's gonna be the lake you're responsible for baiting with Dream. Other lakes, too, but you won't have to worry about them. We've already got them covered." He surveyed the vast expanse of water from the graveled area the 'Vette had decided to pull off on. "Hmmm. I wonder what the fish will look like afterward."

Daryl only half listened. The Dream had become a Nightmare, and he wished it would just wear off. He considered scoring a bag of pot to numb himself into oblivion, something besides Dream, but every time he'd pursued such a venture he always wound up firing up a Dream rock. The task dissolved into nothingness and apathy, much like his life was doing, bit by psychotic bit.

Earlier that day he saw his little brother, Justin, riding with a truckload of football jocks, guzzling Bud and making fools of themselves. He didn't know if Justin had seen him; but seeing his brother partying like that left Daryl feeling confused. First he was relieved to see him playing the party game. It was a rite of passage, of sorts.

But his choice of company really sucked. *Why did he choose those jerks?* he'd thought. *Why doesn't he want to get stoned with me?* Seeing his brother out like that had dug deeply at his pride and occupied most of his thinking for about an hour. Then Mort had shown up.

"You should be honored, you know," Mort said petulantly. "More Dream will be assigned to this lake than any others. Which only makes sense, of course."

"I'm not honored," Daryl said hollowly. "Why do you want to spike the water supply, anyway?" Daryl wanted to know. The whole plan had never made any sense.

"For grins," Mort said, walking over to Daryl and reaching up with a thin arm and patting his shoulder. "Why should you care? You're getting a free supply out of it."

"I get a supply anyway," Daryl replied. He thought about all those people, those straight people who'd never touched a drug in their life. He was surprised that he didn't find the prospect amusing. And the children . . . how would they react to a little Mort in their lives? *Millions of people coming unwrapped at the same time*. This was something beyond his ability to imagine.

"Besides," Mort said, with a sly grin, "think of the market for Dream it will open up."

"It's no use," Niamh said from his cross-legged position. "We need a stronger source than that crystal."

They had tried every approach to breaking the sphere that imprisoned them, but nothing seemed to work. Adam was starting to think that without the node power, or any power, for that matter, their chances were slim at best in getting out. Then he remembered the memory crystal his father had left for him; some residual power remained even after the message had been delivered. They now tried it as a focus.

"Niamh," Marbann admonished. He sat cross-legged in the tiny chamber, trying to concentrate on the crystal before him. "You know better. No negative input."

Niamh shrugged and looked apologetic. They collected their concentration and focused again. Though the crystal was nothing compared to a stream of pure node power, it had some interesting properties, which may or may not have been inherent in the original matrix when it was mined. This came as no surprise, as the crystal was designed not merely as a message transceiver but as a storage depot for a small sliver of thought and feeling. A complicated device, to say the least, the construction of which visibly impressed Marbann—and apparently went beyond anything he might be able to construct himself, even here in Underhill, with unlimited resources. Adam found it difficult to skirt the powerful emotion his father had impressed on the crystal, but in so doing found it possible to focus a single beam of stored power on a point immediately above them.

The beam brightened, and Adam struggled to control it.

"Don't lose it," Adam muttered, more to himself than anyone. He sensed that Marbann was doing most of the manipulation, even managing to intensify the beam during Niamh's interruption. The light appeared on the silver dome's inner surface, immediately above them, and looked as if it were penetrating the mercurylike material that held them in.

That's it, Adam thought, not daring to shatter the concentration by saying the words aloud. He kept as still as possible, focusing with the rest of the Avalon elves on the crystal, the beam, the ceiling. Then the beam shot through the sphere, the edges of a perfectly round hole visible from their sitting positions. He held back a cheer that threatened to slip past his lips, closed his eyes, and concentrated.

Our captors will see that hole, he thought, *or will they?* The beam itself was silent, and he'd heard nothing when it pierced the shell.

Something else is going on. The shell began to fluctuate, the light it emitted dimmed, then brightened.

Is its matrix compromised because of the hole we've put in it? he wondered. Their prison appeared to become unstable, and in places it grew thin; for brief moments, he had a patchy view of the exterior. Glowing, throbbing, pulsing, the dome issued a low, dissonant hum, a discordant tone that sounded like the death of a magical creation. Which was, Adam reasoned, precisely what it was.

"Power is siphoning off somewhere else," Marbann whispered, his eyes still closed. "It's dissolving. . . ."

Focusing on the crystal with a vengeance now, Adam pushed the beam one last time. The matrix gave, and their prison shattered.

They sat on the floor of the stone chamber, surrounded by a ring of lambent, but dying, light on the ground around them. Two guards, minions of some low order, stood and stared stupidly at them, their swords at their sides, touching the ground before them. They were younger gargoyles, mere larvae. With what looked like green urine running down their legs.

"Hi, guys," Adam said as they got to their feet. "You look surprised."

As a pair, the two "guards" turned and fled, leaving the swords on the ground.

"That was generous of them," Niamh said as he retrieved the weapon. "I think we should leave now."

"I agree," Adam said. "Do we have enough time to do what we came here to do?"

Marbann brushed the dust off his black breeches and replied, "Can you still contact the nodes through our Gate?"

Adam sent his thoughts back to the Gate, which was now unobstructed. The power sources glowed brightly again in his mental vision, and he exhaled a sigh of relief.

"Good," Marbann said, as if reading his thoughts. "We have some time, but not much. We must hurry."

Adam turned to Niamh. "So tell us, where can we find that weapon we came to collect?"

The King retrieved the crystal, which continued to emit its own light; this proved to be useful as Niamh led them down dimly lit and unlit corridors. In time Adam began to recognize his surroundings, encountering a painting of a long-dead relative here, a piece of familiar furniture or a fixture there. Occasionally they found the skeleton of what had to be an Avalon elf.

Again anger stirred in his soul, but he kept it tamed, so as not to cloud his decisions. *Later is the time for revenge. Now I must reman clearheaded enough to acquire this weapon.*

And then hope it can do what Niamh says it can.

"We are near," Niamh said, several paces ahead of them. He stopped in front of an open chamber and peered into the darkness.

"Here," Adam said, bringing the crystal. He hesitated, knowing his parents' bodies might well be here as well as the weapon.

He aimed the crystal into the chamber. This was indeed the place he remembered. The table was upright in one corner. Various weapons lay around, both Seleighe and Unseleighe. Pieces of armor lay cast aside. As he entered the chamber, the light fell on a shrouded form, covered in a cloth with the Avalon emblem. *Mother.* He did not want to look, knowing he would likely find a skeleton here. *Father's skeleton must be here somewhere, but where?*

Then he saw where. Hanging by his feet from the ceiling was what had to be his father's remains. Marbann said nothing, his silhouette framed in the doorway.

The young King fell to his knees, the crystal's light flickering to the floor. In the darkness, he heard a scream.

"NOOOOooooooooo!"

The wail echoed in the tiny chamber, down the passageways, throughout the very bowels of the palace. When Adam opened his eyes, he realized the scream had been his own.

He sat there for several long moments, wishing the dark cloak of pain would just go away. Marbann said nothing, his silhouette framed in the doorway.

The young King moved to get up, and his hand fell on the hilt of a sword. Examination by crystal light revealed it to be bronze, with a tip of cold iron. *An Unseleighe weapon. Designed to kill elves.* He stood, keeping clear of the iron tip, and willed the crystal to brighten. The yellowed light flooded the room like a lantern. *If the maker of this sword wanted it to kill elves, kill elves it will.*

Unseleighe elves.

"They will pay," Adam said with a biting, acrid anger he had never felt before.

Niamh stood up. "I've found it," he said, holding up a rifle of some sort. Wires and odd bits of electronics dangled off it. It did not look workable, but then Adam was no technician.

Adam saw Niamh pulling the cloth back over his mother's remains; evidently, they had hidden the weapon with her.

"Then let's get back to the Gate," Adam said.

"Aie," Marbann said weakly. Then Adam realized he was grieving for his father. "We have what we came for. We must go now."

"Yes. It's time for the Gate," Adam said, feeling for its power. In the short time they'd taken to find the weapon, the Gate's power had decreased noticeably. "We don't have much time," he added.

Adam led them back the way they came, toward the chamber where the gargoyles had held them captive. Marbann questioned this, pointed out that was where the backup guards would go first to look for them. Then Adam countered with, "Do you know of any other way out of here?"

"Hmmmph," Marbann had replied, but that might have meant anything. Behind them, deep in the passageways, Adam heard others. *Unseleighe?* He sent a mental probe that way, found only the odd, reptilian minds there. But they were on the alert and coming their direction.

They found the opening to the outside, and Unseleighe surrounded them immediately. At first glance Adam counted eight of them, looking very much like his group did in their disguises. The Unseleighe elves in their black tunics stared at them with surprise on their pallid faces, evidently confused as to who they were.

Marbann stepped forward and regarded the eight with visible disgust. "Zeldan Dhu has sent us to inspect his property," he said, and to the startled gasp of some of the onlookers, added, "It would appear that it has not been well kept."

Niamh clutched the weapon closer to him. They stood at the mouth of the tunnel that led to the palace remains, with room on either side to escape. *But the Gate is that way,* Adam thought, looking past the Unseleighe. *We may have to bluff our way through this. We are out-armed.*

The sight of his father's murderers set his blood on fire again. He wanted to leap into the middle of them and start swinging, but he knew that would not be a wise move. For one thing, he would likely die. For another, well, there wouldn't be anything else. *I'd be dead. And my people would be less one ruler.*

One of the Unseleighe came forward, his sword still sheathed. He didn't seem particularly concerned that Adam and his two warrior elves brandished theirs. This elf, once he drew closer, seemed no older than Adam and wore thick leather armor. Though no insignia distinguished him, Adam felt this was their leader, come to parley. Before he had come too close, Adam smelled a horrible stench, one he remembered from the battle of his youth. Father had explained this was what the Unseleighe smelled like, rank and ripe, and with the hordes that lined the horizon that horrible day, the air was full of their stench.

The smell was horrible, and Adam tried not to let it show on his face. "I don't know you," the Unseleighe said. "You look like none of the warriors our leader took with him, Above." He glanced at the weapon Niamh held. "What have you there?"

"Zeldan Dhu sent us for it," Niamh squeaked, sounding anything but warriorlike. "He awaits its return as we speak."

A shadow passed over the Unseleighe's face, a mask of doubt, emphasized by a twitching of his right, pointed ear. He raised his nose and took a deep breath of the air. Then a wicked smile crossed his elven features.

One thing we left out of the disguises, Adam realized, too late. *We don't stink!*

He pulled his sword, as did his elves. "You are not Unseleighe."

"*Shields,*" Adam said, pulling at the Gate for the power to create the protection. Marbann carefully and quickly erected thin barriers around them, as much as the weakening power flows would allow.

The Unseleighe attacked, and Adam's group moved forward; the enemy didn't sense the shield in time and ran headlong into it. Temporarily stunned, the Unseleighe stepped backward.

Adam's vision turned red. The Unseleighe were targets now, and his hunter's instinct, long dormant, now surfaced.

He felt a change come over him, fueled by rage, but originating from something primal within. Something his ancestors possessed, perhaps, or something connected to his mage abilities. At any rate, he was no longer Adam McDaris, the civilized, mild-mannered human youth.

He was King Aedham Tuiereann, standing on the ruins of his clan's palace, where his father and mother had been murdered, his clan banished from what was rightfully theirs.

And he was *pissed off*.

"You will all die for this," Aedham said to the Unseleighe. Then all Hades broke loose.

It began as a distant thunder, like an approaching storm, but as it deepened and strengthened, the very ground they stood on shook; the Unseleighe looked at each other uncertainly.

Never seen a mage on the other side of a conflict, have you? Adam thought briefly, then reached for more of the node powers, seeking in his mental vision the mouth of the Gate and the power beyond. First he strengthened the Gate itself, to insure their return, then, like grabbing a rope, he pulled. The node power increased and surged toward him, reaching through the ground, then surfacing where they stood. Then he went to work on the Unseleighe.

The eight remained in place, but looked uncertain as to what was happening. Holding his father's crystal in his right hand, Adam found it easier to manipulate the node power, first by decreasing the resistance, then by channeling it into the nearest focal point—the sword he held. Bronze proved to be an excellent medium. The power flowed into it, a short broadsword that looked plain in the light of day, but as node power raced into it, it glowed white.

Adam stepped from the protection of the shield and lunged for the first Unseleighe, the leader who first approached him. Though visibly frightened, the elf held his ground, assuming a defensive stance with his sword.

As the swords clashed, it soon became clear they were

unevenly matched. A node-powered sword against a similar model that was not so equipped had an interesting effect. It melted the opponent's weapon.

Adam parried and thrust, then advanced toward the elf, who withdrew immediately. He seemed to sense something wrong with his weapon, which had begun to glow not with node power but with heat. The tip drooped, and Adam watched, amid the swordplay, the area of red hotness creep toward the handle. Pain registered on the opponent's face. A fitting distraction before Adam struck the final blow.

Adam's sword swung in a diagonal arc; it caught the other's sword and severed the blade in two. It continued its descent downward, through the elf's shoulder, severing the arm. The Unseleighe's expression was of disbelief and confusion, and Adam felt a brief twinge of sympathy against an Unseleighe who didn't know what he was up against.

"*You are a Tuiereann,*" the Unseleighe wailed before he fell backward, across his own severed limb. Life drained quickly from the Unseleighe's face, the pallid color turning to an ashen gray.

The others stepped backward slowly. Adam's sword had cut through his opponent's like a dinner knife through a stick of butter. This must have been a very discouraging image for the ones who remained; one turned and ran. The others backed up a little more quickly this time. His sympathy for the Unseleighe was short-lived. The fever of hate, fueled by the images of his father's skeleton, urged him forward.

He had no idea what he looked like right then, but had never seen such terror in anyone, friend or foe, before. The ground around him was illuminated, and at first he assumed it was from his sword. But it was *all* around him.

From his soul Adam generated a levin bolt, pulling on the full force of the largest Marketplace node. The power suddenly turned red, like the setting sun, as it reached through the ground, through his feet, and simmered within his body. Using the sword as a sight, he aimed the power at the retreating Unseleighe.

You designed this sword to kill elves, he thought. *And kill elves it will.*

Adam let loose the power, which blasted from the sword with a brief flash of red. The concussion knocked him backward, and he nearly stumbled; arms caught him from behind, friendly arms. When he looked up, it was Marbann.

"King," he said, breathlessly. "You have defeated them. Turn loose the node power now, before it *kills* you."

He barely heard the words. His head and body were drunk with the power flowing through him. When he looked up to see the attackers, he saw six vague outlines of black, in the shape of a shadow, extending away from them. Then, six long, molten puddles of metal, bubbling and hissing—probably their swords. Beyond that, a blackened path, like a giant scorch-mark left by a fifties vintage spaceship, reaching to the arid horizon.

Adam blinked, and turned around. "Where . . ." he said, then tumbled to his knees. "The Gate. We must . . ."

Then, his world went black.

Chapter Seventeen

"She's already online," Rathand said, glancing furtively toward the door as Zeldan barged into the New You's basement. The Unseleighe was not happy about the interruption; each call to him through the Terminal put a strain on the entire system, including the stored energy he had in the crystal capacitors. Not to mention the time he spent scurrying down here to heed her calls. In general, her presence was annoying. It reminded him of the deal he'd entered into, perhaps in haste, the advantage from which he had yet to see.

Zeldan tried not to wince at the hideous image. "Yes, what is it?" he barked into the Terminal. He made no pretenses; he was mad, and he was going to let her know it.

"Did you send a party of Unseleighe to Underhill for any reason?" she asked accusingly.

The question took Zeldan by surprise. "Well, no. Why?"

"As I suspected," she said, and whispered to someone off screen. "A group of what looked like elves of the Unseleighe court showed up at the Avalon palace today—"

"It no longer belongs to the Tuiereann family," Zeldan pointed out icily.

"And claimed to be sent by you."

Zeldan scratched his long, pointed chin thoughtfully. "Not I, my dear Morrigan. I do hope you've imprisoned them."

She nodded, with some relief evident on her obese

features. "They are now in a node shell, on the palace grounds."

"Node shell?" Zeldan said. "But that means, if you made this transmission, you had to pull away power from the prison. Are you certain they're still secure?"

For the first time Zeldan remembered, Morrigan looked uncertain, threatened, even. "What?" she finally said. "Certainly that won't mean . . ."

"Who knows," Zeldan said with an air of resignation. *If she's slipped up, and these intruders have escaped, it would really make my day.* "My elves are down there. Nagas, if I remember, is in charge of patrolling the area. He is young, true, but he has a firm understanding of leadership." *And torture. And maiming.* "Have you even bothered to contact him?"

"Of course I have!" Morrigan snapped. "They are on their way to the palace as we speak."

"Find out who the intruders are," he said, wondering who would do such a foolhardy thing. *Certainly not the Avalon elves, gone to reclaim the palace? Since we've already sacked it, I'm tempted to give it back to them, so that I can have the satisfaction of taking it from them again.*

"One moment," Morrigan said, and left the screen temporarily.

Zeldan sighed. The idea behind communicating with Underhill in this fashion was to keep the messages brief; dead space like that took as much power as dialogue. He glanced at a dial on their bank of storage cells, watched it drop ever so slowly, and resisted a temptation to break the connection. "Hanging up" on Morrigan would give a certain amount of satisfaction. But her wrath would be difficult to deal with later.

She returned to the screen, this time more shaken than before. "It was a mage," she said. "And they've escaped. Nagas intercepted them as they were trying to leave."

"Ah, excellent," Zeldan said confidently. "Then we have nothing to worry about. Nagas will deal with them." *A mage? That might only mean . . . certainly not.* "Have

Nagas report to me immediately. May he use your terminal?"

After a pause, during which Morrigan had a difficult time maintaining eye contact with Zeldan, she said, "He can't, Zeldan. He's dead. The group, whoever they were, killed the entire patrol."

Zeldan stared at her image. *If there were some way to wrap my hands around your neck, I would,* he thought in the confused rage that followed. *Dead? The entire party?*

"No witnesses?" Zeldan finally sputtered. *This can't be.* "Survivors? Anyone?"

She looked distressed, not smug. Zeldan gave her credit for that much. "None. Except, the group of mercenaries I had watching the fields."

"Mercs?" Zeldan asked hopefully. *They would have to be formidable to be any match for a mage.*

"Gargoyles," she explained.

Zeldan groaned. *The weakest creatures in Underhill. I'm surprised they subdued the intruders in the first place.*

"Whoever they were, they are long gone," Morrigan said. "Tell me, Zeldan. You'd said that Aedham Tuiereann was no threat. Is it possible *he* was this mage?"

He withheld a snarl. "Perhaps, but I doubt it," he managed to say.

"You don't sound convinced," she said. "But no matter. Once our plan is completed, we will have *all* the negative power we need, and then some. Avalon and any other Seleighe clan that happens along will have their hands full with our mayhem. I am not worried."

You should be, Zeldan wanted to say, but that would only make things difficult for himself. "As for the Avalon pestilence, we will have that under control as well. We have a lead that should take us directly to the Tuiereann rat's nest. The McDaris residence, I believe," he said proudly. *She probably doesn't care that much about eliminating this particular King, but I certainly do. It was just a matter of simple detective work. Mort has proven his usefulness three times over.*

Zeldan continued, "We have already met with our human minions. They are ready to deliver your concentrated Black Dream to the human watering holes."

Morrigan's face turned blood-red. "Then why hasn't it happened already?"

"These things take time," Zeldan replied. *And planning, and patience, neither of which you have experience with.* "The logistics involved, the different layers of security we must penetrate to disperse our product in the water system. It's more complicated than you realize."

Her face darkened. "*Details!*" she screamed. "I want action!"

The screen went blank.

Zeldan gazed at it for a long time, then got up, put on his Peter Pritchard human seeming, and went back among the cattle, and their pain.

And with the death of Nagas, Mage Japhet Dhu thought, with no small amount of satisfaction, *dies the remaining obstacle to my plan.*

The mage had sensed the Gate in Underhill the moment it formed, but instead of intercepting whomever came out of it, he watched from a distance. It was, to his surprise, the former Prince of Avalon.

The Seleighe have returned to Underhill. Come to claim your kingdom, have you? he thought. Nagas was the last remaining Unseleighe leader who had remained faithful to his father, so it was only natural that he seek out this new threat to Zeldan's territory. The others in Japhet's organization remained quietly loyal to Japhet, while his father made a fool of himself chasing down Seleighe children. Japhet had considered approaching Morrigan in hopes of making an arrangement beneficial to both of them, but as it stood Zeldan was providing a substantial amount of raw power, energy which was lacking in this Underhill wasteland. *Better to wait until Father is less useful before approaching the bitch.*

This new development with the Avalon clan was completely unexpected. At first the mage didn't know what to make of it. The Seleighe King didn't seem to be particularly powerful, in fact had not even bothered to construct any kind of shield. And when the mercenary gargoyles captured them, they had put up no fight whatsoever. *Their actions are curious*, Japhet thought. *What do they expect to gain among the ruins of their former elfhame?*

Mage Japhet grew bored with the proceedings, returned to his stronghold, and summoned his fellow mages. While Morrigan's attention was focused on these new intruders, he reasoned, they had the perfect opportunity tap into Morrigan's fresh load of harvested human pain.

My father will pay for his folly, Japhet thought. *His obsession for ridding the universe of the Seleighe plague will be his undoing.*

And I will be waiting, patiently, until he fails. Then I will claim for myself what is rightfully mine. I am, after all, the sole heir to Zeldan's kingdom.

One of his mages brought a crude oracle to him; it was a construct of one of Morrigan's crystals, stolen from her mines. On occasion they were able to eavesdrop on the transmissions between Zeldan and Underhill, and do so without detection. They used the oracle sparingly.

This had better warrant my special attention, Mage Japhet thought as he took the fist-sized crystal from the cowering Unseleighe elf.

Interesting, Japhet thought, as he took in Zeldan's and Morrigan's conversation. *The King of Avalon is a mage. And he is returning to the human's world to destroy my father!*

How very kind of him to simplify my life for me.

Daryl returned home from the trip to Lake Tawekoni, in part because he hoped he might shake Mort. The little demon had appeared nearly everywhere else in his life but here, in his house. So here he came, hoping to be alone, at least for a little while.

The house appeared to be empty when he pulled up. Both cars were gone, which meant Mom was probably at her bridge party, and Dad was out God only knew where.

Only the porch light was on, but that came on automatically at sunset; the rest of the house was on a computer, which automatically turned on certain lights, but lately hadn't been working right, so Dad had shut it off. The house was dark when he entered, but he didn't find anything peculiar about that.

The Dream had worn off somewhat, but he didn't really want to do more of it right away, for fear Mort might reappear. He knew he had to slow down, he was doing too much of it, and since he wasn't an addict he had to show himself that the stuff didn't have control of him. That meant leaving the Dream alone.

He went into the kitchen in search of a beer or a cooler, found a half-consumed six-pack of Bud, and opened one. The cold suds burned a comfortable path down his throat, and as its numbness spread, he decided he wasn't so anxious anymore.

Maybe I should just switch to beer and leave it at that, he considered. But somehow the thought reminded him of Justin, guzzling suds with those football jocks in the pickup, and the prospect didn't have as much appeal to him.

Maybe scotch. That is the civilized way to imbibe, after all.

On the kitchen counter he found a note, with a twenty-dollar bill. It was from his mother, who was letting him know that she would be out playing bridge, as he'd already guessed. The twenty was for him to use "any way he liked."

A twenty. Mere pocket change, compared to what he'd been making at the New You. That day he'd made the first drop, a whole ki of Dream, and took his cut for that day, one grand, in cash. It was the easiest thousand he'd ever made in his life, and despite his reservations about working for this strange outfit, Mort included, he looked forward to more of the easy money.

The light buzz the beer gave him told him he'd hadn't had any garden-variety coke in awhile. *Hell,* he thought, *I guess that would be okay. It's Dream I'm slowing down on, not coke. Dad has some in his bedroom. He always has*

*some. Might even be able to snatch a few Valiums from
Mom's bottle to help me sleep later.*

He went into the master bedroom, turned the light on,
and reached for the silver tray under the bed. It was an
antique, probably about a hundred years old, but was so
finely polished that it worked just as well as a mirror.
There was enough coke leftover from the last time to make
two healthy, go-for-it lines. He took the twenty, rolled it up,
and snorted both lines in two deep breaths.

Use it any way I liked, he thought whimsically, regarding
the twenty. *Mom can occasionally be helpful, if only by
accident.*

The coke burned for a moment in his sinuses, then
became a mild itch, which had just been scratched. The
numbness originating with the beer deepened.

Just coke, he thought, as the clouds of heaven descended
on his brain. *No Mort.* Part of him realized that cocaine
reduced his thinking to two-syllable snatches. *No prob. I'm
fine.*

He put the tray back, turned off the light, climbed the
stairs.

Music from one of the Alan Parsons albums, Daryl didn't
know which, poured out of Justin's room. There was no
light under his brother's door. The door to his own room
was open, leading to darkness. Daryl frowned, vaguely
annoyed at this intrusion to his personal space.

He turned the light on, and saw his brother lying facedown on the floor.

"Justin?"

Justin didn't move.

He's playing games. Or he's passed out. I'll just ignore him.

With the intention of taking a shower, he stepped over
Justin on his way to the bathroom.

He noticed the five black-stoppered vials, all empty, and
his glass pipe, next to Justin's left hand.

"Justin, just what the hell are you doing?"

The words came out weakly, a mere whisper. Daryl's
heart thundered in his chest.

"Justin?" he said again, as he knelt over his brother.

As he reached to roll him over, his hand recoiled from the cold arm, the cold shoulder, the cold neck.

No. He isn't. He can't be.

The image of his birthday party at Steve's flashed through his head. His dead friends, and those not so dead. But this was different, this was his brother.

Justin is not dead.

Stars filled his vision as he became light-headed, but he grabbed Justin by the arm anyway, and rolled him completely over. He had never had much of a tan, but now Justin was very pale and very cold.

Justin's eyes were open, unblinking, and filled with terror. His mouth was frozen in a scream.

Justin!

Daryl stared at him, reached for his wrist, found no pulse there, looked for one in his neck. Nothing.

Shaking, he picked up one of the five empty vials. *Five? Did he smoke all five of these bottles of Black Dream? Oh, God. He must have. He's so cold. But where the hell did he get it?* Sticking out from under the bed was a shoe box, filled with vials. This was also where he'd kept *his* pipe.

He had no strength to move, so he sat there, staring at his lifeless brother. The pleasing numbness from the coke drained away from him. *His face is so horrible,* Daryl thought vaguely. *I wonder what he saw?*

His stomach's contents rose to the back of his throat. As he ran to the toilet to retch his guts out, he thought briefly about D&D, and all the good times he'd had with his brother. And all the times he wouldn't, now.

After he'd completely emptied his stomach, he reached for the telephone and dialed 911 for an ambulance. "Just *send one.* My brother overdosed. I think he's dead," he said, to the dispatcher's repeated request for details, and hung up.

Without being fully aware of what he was doing, he pulled his wallet out and began looking for something. The piece of paper with Moira's phone number fell out.

Call if you need help.

Through the tears, Daryl picked up the phone and dialed.

Adam woke from a sound sleep on the living room couch. He sat up with a start, then closed his eyes against the headache that threatened to rip him in two.

Holding his head with both hands, he looked around; around the Sony TV he sensed the remains of a Gate recently dismissed. Evidently, Moira had eliminated his Unseleighe glamorie, as he now wore his usual attire: jeans, running shoes, a tank top.

The Unseleighe sword lay on the couch. *A fitting trophy,* Adam thought, pleased as well as a little sickened at the memory of the levin bolt. The rage that had consumed him earlier, when confronting the Unseleighe, was gone now. He felt a bit queasy, remembering how totally he'd annihilated them. He began to question whether he'd be able to do the same thing again, when confronted with Zeldan. Either answer disturbed him.

He stood up and instantly wished he hadn't. *This must be what a hangover feels like.*

While in Underhill, he must have overdone the magic bit, he suspected. That would explain his headache, which far surpassed the one he suffered while healing Niamh. He looked around and saw a track of dust leading from the living room to the garage. *Our feet must have been covered with the dry soil of Underhill. But why did everyone go into the garage?*

He shakily made his way in that direction, which passed through the kitchen, where he grabbed a cold, canned Gatorade.

"Hi, guys," Adam said from the open kitchen door as he popped the can open.

Spence, Marbann, Moira and Niamh stood around the wooden worktable, which had been dragged to the center of the garage floor. A bank of fluorescents lit the garage up a little too brightly for his headache.

"Your Majesty," Marbann said, looking up from the worktable. "How do you feel? Are you well?"

"Uh, no," he said, sipping the Gatorade. "My head's about to burst open. But that's the only damage I suffered. I think."

Marbann nodded, but looked disturbed. "That will pass, in time."

"I'm less than convinced," Adam replied, but what they were doing roused his curiosity more than a cure for his headache. Spence was working on the weapon they'd liberated from Underhill. The mechanism was clamped onto the portable worktable, with a rectangular metal plate removed from its stock, revealing a spaghetti mess of wires and circuit boards. In its present condition, the weapon looked completely harmless. Spence patiently soldered a wire to a circuit board, his face a mask of unbreakable concentration.

Niamh, who had tried to fix the weapon years back, looked on, visibly confused.

"I'm not sure what they had in mind here, when they made it," Spence said. "From what I can tell, it's not steel, but an aluminum magnesium casing, and may have originally been designed for mining or some other industrial purpose. It's missing something, though." He pulled some wires aside, revealing a compartment. "There's a space here. Looks like a battery went there, or something. Damned if I know what kind it was. Doesn't look like anything I've seen."

"Weren't the engineers in Underhill modifying it to use node power?" Moira pointed out. "Instead of a battery, maybe it used something else?"

Spence looked doubtful. "It must be something else. Down in the stock here are chambers for two nine-volt batteries, and they've already been replaced. In this other compartment, there are traces of node power. I wish I could talk to whoever was working on it." He paused to wipe sweat from his forehead. "But all the engineers died in the first wave."

Moira looked up at the King. "Adam, what do you think?"

Adam shrugged, still weary from the ordeal in Underhill. "I'm not sure I can think anything," he said, then he leaned over the table. Indeed, there was a space there, but it didn't look like a place a battery would go. The contacts were cupped, not smooth, like the inside of a flashlight, and were faceted. As if they held something that . . .

Then he saw what it had to be. "A crystal," Adam said. "It must be."

He searched his pockets for what he hoped might work. His father's memory crystal was still in his pocket, and he pulled it out and handed it to Spence.

"I used it in Underhill," Adam explained. "When we were sealed off from the node energy, it was the only power source we had."

Marbann spoke up, "It acted more as a way of focusing the energy we already had among us. The crystal had a minimal amount of power stored in it."

Spence pointed at the weapon, gazing on it admirably. "This mechanism is one big lens for node power, whether by accident or design. Perhaps this crystal is just what we need. Everything else about the weapon appears to be operational, now that I've reconnected some of the loose wires."

He inserted the crystal, which was a bit small for the space. With a screwdriver he loosened one of the contacts, which slid against the crystal, clamping it in place. When he tightened it back, the weapon came to life.

A row of LED lights Adam hadn't noticed before came on, and a tinny, electronic whine, like the sound of a PC booting up, was emitted from somewhere in the stock.

"Now what?" Moira asked, as she stepped back from the weapon. "Do we dare try it here?"

Adam gave Moira a distressed look. "I know it's probably dangerous, but we have to know if it works or not," Adam said. Then, to Spence. "How do you use it?"

Spence pursed his lips, licked them nervously. He

looked like he'd been out here a long time and was getting twitchy. "There's a safety near the trigger." He looked around the garage.

"What is that over there, in the corner?"

He was pointing to the big smoker that had been sitting there unused for years. "So far as I'm concerned, it's a big hunk of useless Cold Iron," Adam said.

"Perfect," Spence replied, taking the smoker by the wooden handle and pulling it against the garage door. He flinched from it, evidently feeling the heat all Cold Iron gave off to elven senses. "I see what you mean."

Target practice. "I think everyone should go back in the house. We don't know what this weapon is going to do."

Niamh looked hurt. "But I've been trying to get this thrice-damned thing to work for so long, I have!"

Adam sighed. "Okay. Just stay by the door, would you? Everyone else, out."

As his clan complied, Adam hefted the weapon. The aluminum-magnesium alloy made it somewhat lighter than if it were steel, like most human firearms. It looked and felt like an assault rifle should, and might have passed for one if it'd had a clip. The barrel was short and square, resembling a policeman's radar gun. When he brought it up to aim, the stock was a little awkward. *I guess you can't have everything.*

Once the garage was empty, he thumbed off the safety. A green LED light near the barrel came on. *Nice features.* Then he aimed at the smoker and pulled the trigger.

Nothing happened.

"Well?" he heard Spence call.

"Got a problem," Adam replied.

Spence came back in and examined the weapon. "It's a focus for node power," he said. "Why don't you tap into the nodes, and direct them to, say, the crystal. That may be why it *needs* a crystal."

"I'll try it," Adam said, but he was already beginning to think the trip to Underhill to reclaim this hunk of metal was a waste of time.

Spence stepped back. Adam brought the weapon up again, this time reaching for the Marketplace nodes, keeping his eyes open, and on the target. Their power reached though the ground, through the soles of his feet, coursed through his body and into the weapon's crystal, which was beneath his left palm.

He pulled the trigger.

A tight beam of node energy shot from the barrel of the weapon and bore directly into the smoker. Sparks flew as the beam tore into the Cold Iron, impaling it, then proceeded into the garage door behind it. A half second later, an explosion shook just on the other side of the garage door, which threatened to shake off its track.

"NO!" Adam shouted, as he released the trigger and brought the barrel down. He already had an idea what the explosion was.

"Adam, what was . . ." Spence said, then stared at the garage door. "Oh, no. We didn't."

"I think we did," he said, feeling ill, giving Spence the weapon. "Hide this somewhere, quick. Before the fire trucks get here. And tell everyone else to hide, too. We're going to have human visitors real soon."

Adam tried to open the garage door via the automatic opener, but it would not budge. *The explosion must have damaged the door. Damn.* He grabbed a fire extinguisher off the garage shelf and ran through the house to the front door.

My ears! I'm still in elf mode! He paused for a full five seconds, cast the glamorie, and inspected himself in the hallway mirror. Satisfied he was presentable to the humans' world, he ran out the front door to deal with the fire.

As expected, his little Geo was engulfed in flames. The beam had shot through the door and struck the car's gas tank. Adam started spraying madly, hoping the extinguisher had enough of a charge. In the distance, he heard the wail of fire engines.

Great, he thought as he sprayed. *My tapes! They're history now.*

The car was completely engulfed in flames. His extinguisher did little against the fire, which had spread to a few places in the front yard. When the car exploded, pieces of Geo had blown into the street, but the car was still basically intact. Broken glass littered the driveway. *Looks like the car's history, too.*

As he beat back the fire, he felt strangely unmoved at the demise of his car. Under his frantic struggle to put the fire out was the unrestrained joy at finding something, anything, to use against Zeldan Dhu and his Unseleighe Court. In the flames of his burning car, he imagined Zeldan's face.

A fire truck, followed by a second larger one with a ladder, pulled up in front of the house. Firemen poured off with more extinguishers and started hosing the car down with white fog. They soon had the fire under control, and as they put out the last of the flames, Samantha McDaris pulled up in her cop-issue Chevrolet Caprice.

She had her badge opened and displayed as she walked up to the fireman who appeared to be in charge.

"This is my house, and this is my son. What in the world is going on?" she said, casting a brief questioning look toward Adam.

The fireman looked apologetic. "Perhaps you'd better ask him. A neighbor called in the fire, and when we got here, the car here was burning."

"I . . . don't know how it started," Adam said. "Honest."

"This car's a hazard," the fireman continued. "A tow truck is on the way. And we'll have to call the police."

"I *am* the police," Samantha said impatiently. Then Adam sensed a change in the man's attitude.

Sammi's using magic on him, Adam thought, but kept his mouth shut. *She knows what she's doing.*

"On the other hand," the fireman said, "since *you're* here, we won't need to call the police. The fire's out. I'd still have it moved, if I were you."

"Very well," Samantha said, and the firemen declared the job finished and left.

"In the house," Samantha said shortly.

Once inside, Adam found that everyone had done as he'd said—everyone was so well hidden he didn't even know where they were.

"Now tell me, what the *hell* happened?" Samantha said, dropping her purse and keys on the kitchen counter.

Adam told her.

"You've got to be kidding."

Adam smiled weakly and tried to sound apologetic. "Well, at least it works. It went right through that old smoker."

Samantha rolled her eyes. "At least we've found something useful for that thrice-damned waste of space."

Moira and Spence appeared, Spence holding the weapon, as the others came out of various hiding places in the house. Petrus startled everyone by popping out of the cabinet at their feet.

"So the damned thing works," Samantha said, holding it up. "Not very heavy. Aluminum?" Spence nodded. "Good thing. I wonder if that college kid from Berkeley had elves in mind when he made this."

The phone rang, and Moira picked it up. As the caller spoke, her face darkened.

"What is it?" Adam asked, but he sensed who it might be.

"Okay, okay . . ." Moira said. "Call an ambulance. You already did? Good." She looked up. "It's Daryl. His brother overdosed. He thinks he's dead."

"Let me talk to him." Adam reached for the phone, and heard sobbing on the other end. "Daryl? It's Adam. What happened?"

"Adam?" Daryl said, after a moment. "It's Justin. He got into some stuff. Black Dream."

For a moment, the King didn't know what to say.

"Don't hang up," Daryl said. "I need to talk to you. You know how you've been telling me about the drugs. How they're going to kill me? *They killed Justin instead. . . .*"

More crying, into which Adam spoke, uncertain if his words were getting through. "It's okay. . . ."

"No, it's *not* okay. Hold on." A long pause followed.

"What's going on?" Moira said. "Do we need to go over there?"

Daryl came back on. "Adam, some really weird shit has been going on. And I'm not talking about the drugs."

"I'm listening," Adam said, aware that Moira and Samantha were discussing whose car to take.

"I'm in deep, real deep. I've been selling quantity through my other job at the New You Fitness Center. There's something weird about that place. . . ."

Tell me about it.

"I've been seeing, like, ghosts and demons and shit. I think they're aliens."

Adam became acutely aware of his own pointed ears. "Really?" he replied, trying to sound like he cared. Still it came out sounding like he thought Daryl was nuts.

"There's something big going down. With my dealer. Your mother is a cop. I think . . . she should know about it."

"Okay," Adam agreed. "What's going to happen?"

"I'm not sure. Mort said they were going to call me here tonight."

"I see," Adam said. *I'll ask who "Mort" is later.*

"The ambulance is here," Daryl said. "I gotta go."

"We'll be there in a few minutes." Adam hung up the phone.

"Well?" Samantha said. "What did he have to say?"

His mother sounded hostile toward Daryl, but then he didn't really blame her. "It sounds like he's ready to turn in some people."

Samantha raised her eyebrows. "Oh really? His suppliers?"

"Yeah, his suppliers. And I think he knows his suppliers aren't exactly humans."

"Gods," Samantha groaned. "Just what we need. Daryl involved with the Unseleighe."

"I think he needs protection," Adam continued, reaching for his car keys. Then he remembered, they didn't go to anything anymore. "Once he starts turning people in to the police, the Unseleighe are going to be after him."

"I think we should all go over there," Marbann said. "It sounds like the young human needs our help."

The only operating vehicle left for them was Sammi's cop car, the '93 Chevy Caprice. It was built to move fast, and had ample room for passengers, and proved to be the perfect vehicle for Adam and his clan to migrate to Daryl's house. Marbann, Moira and Niamh piled into the rear seat, careful to cast glamories before leaving the house. Adam, Spence and Sammi, who drove, took the front after carefully stashing the secret Avalon weapon in the trunk, among the other cop bric-a-brac.

Definitely nonissue, Adam had smirked as he closed the trunk.

Sammi had left Wenlann and Petrus with instructions to "guard" the Gate. This was only to give them the illusion they were doing something important; the two littles were simply not combat ready, and possessed only the rudimentary skills of elven magic.

They'll be safe here, Adam thought as Sammi sped out of the driveway.

When they pulled up in front of Daryl's house, they found an ambulance, a coroner's station wagon, a black-and-white, and the white van Sammi and her new partner did surveillance in. The front door of the house was open, and Adam saw someone standing just inside.

"They must have called Roach," Sammi said, explaining the van. "Depending on how far Daryl is willing to go on this, the gear in that truck might come in real handy." She opened her door and got out.

"We leave the situation in your most capable hands," Marbann said from the rear of the Caprice. "Summon us if you require help." The others stayed behind while Adam and Samantha went inside.

"We'll do that," Adam said, casting a brief but longing look at Moira. *Gods, she looks sexy when she's tense,* he thought before following his "mother" up to the house.

What struck Adam as being strange was the absence of interest from the neighbors. All along the richly appointed neighborhood block, lights had been turned out or shades drawn. It was almost as if the other humans wanted to shut off what was happening at the Bendis' home. Adam doubted this was the first time police had shown up at this address.

A uniformed officer met them at the open door, and Sammi presented her credentials. It didn't seem to be necessary, only a conditioned reflex, as the officer seemed to already know her.

"The body's upstairs. The coroner just arrived." He looked down, looking disturbed. He was young cop, and apparently had little experience in death.

"Where the hell are the parents?" Samantha said.

"Not here," the cop said. "Kid doesn't know where they are, either."

Adam saw Daryl, crying his eyes out, in the dining room. A suit was questioning him, an older cop he assumed was Sammi's partner.

"This is my son," Sammi said briefly. "He's riding with me on this one."

"It's pretty bad up there," the cop warned, but they were already on their way up the stairs.

The coroner and his assistant waited in the hallway with their gurney, looking annoyed. Another cop was taking pictures of the boy when they came into the room. Justin lay on his side, staring upward. He looked terrified, his face frozen in fear, and Adam wondered why.

"There was a crack pipe and five empty vials of the stuff. It's already bagged for evidence."

Sammi exhaled loudly. "Five? I don't believe it." She stepped around the body, looking down in detached but sincere sympathy. "Did they have black stoppers?"

"Oh, yeah. Black Dream, I think the street name is." The cop snapped another picture, a closeup of Justin's face. "His heart must have given out on the fifth one," the cop commented. "The coroner will let us know for sure if it was heart failure."

"Has the room been searched?"

The cop shrugged. "Not really. We wanted the pictures, first."

"Of course," Sammi said as her foot hit something just under the bed. It sounded like glass bottles. She reached down and pulled out a shoe box, which had twenty or thirty vials of Black Dream. The cop whistled.

"There's got to be more," she said.

Adam took a long look at Justin's body, the whiteness of the skin, the total lack of movement. The only thing animated about him was that hideous face, and Adam wondered what he might have seen. Then he looked away.

I knew this boy. I played D&D with him, countless times, in this very room. And now he's dead. It might have been Daryl.

It might have been me. . . .

He shuddered, feeling suddenly unclean. The cop called the coroner in, and Adam left the room.

"We've got to talk to Daryl," Sammi said from behind him. She had the box of Dream with her, which rattled loudly as she walked.

They joined Roach in the dining room, where Daryl sat on one of the chairs, holding his head in his hands. He quivered as he sobbed.

"Let me talk to him alone," Sammi said. "My son here . . . he knows him."

Roach nodded and left the room. Behind them, the gurney rattled as the coroner wheeled the body down the stairs.

"Daryl," Sammi said. "You need to start talking to us."

Daryl didn't respond at first. Adam felt at first uncomfortable, then anger grew and spread as he considered the forces responsible for the drugs in the first place.

Zeldan. My enemy is now your enemy, he thought.

Daryl sat up slowly in the chair. Not, as Adam first

suspected, from reluctance, but from weakness. He looked deathly ill, and Adam was as shocked at his appearance as he was at seeing Justin's body. His face was sunken and hollow, like a skull. Dark rings dwelled under his half-closed eyes, and for a second Adam thought his father had hit him. But it was only the darkness of someone who'd been up too long, not the purplish welt caused by a fist. Adam had seen enough of those on Daryl over the years to know the difference.

Adam had half expected to see a calm but defiant human child who thought he knew everything and wasn't about to let the authorities rattle him. Instead, he found this shivering mess, whose tail had been decisively kicked.

"Good God, Daryl," Samantha said softly.

Daryl looked up at her slowly, blinking. "Yeah, I know," he said, and did something that passed for a laugh. "The stuff finally caught up with me."

Adam sensed surrender in the flat statement, which he'd never heard before.

"Where are your parents?" Samantha asked.

"Who the hell knows," Daryl said slowly. "Mom's playing bridge somewhere. Dad's probably out getting loaded somewhere." He looked at Adam. "Who cares?"

"We care," Adam said, pulling a chair up. He still felt awkward, but he meant what he'd said. He hoped some of that sincerity had leaked through.

Instead of a rude retort, Daryl said nothing at first. "We used to be good friends," Daryl finally said. "What happened?"

"You don't know?" Adam said, but he saw that Daryl did.

"Yeah, I know. All I hafta do is look in a mirror, right?" Adam said nothing. Then, after a brief silence, a tear ran down Daryl's face. "He's dead, isn't he?" he sobbed.

Adam didn't know who reached out first, but the next second he was holding his friend, who had wrapped his arms around Adam. He cried into Adam's shoulder and neck without restraint. Adam felt a tear squeeze between his own shut eyelids. "Oh, *God*," Daryl moaned into his ear. "How did I get so deep in this crap?"

"Do you want out?" Adam heard himself say.

They withdrew from the embrace, Daryl looking slightly embarrassed. "Hell, yes, I want out. But there's no getting out, don't you see? I'm trapped."

Evidently he'd been doing some thinking about his situation and wanted to backpedal on his earlier remarks.

"There is a way out," Sammi said. She had left the room and reappeared with a Coke in a glass of ice.

"Yeah, right," Daryl snorted, but took the drink nevertheless.

"No, I mean it," she said. "Start talking to us."

Daryl shook his head, waving his arms shakily for emphasis. "No no no no *no*. You don't understand. They'll kill me."

Samantha held out the box of Black Dream and shook it. The loud rattle of glass indicated a fair number of bottles. "No, *you* don't understand. What I have here can put you away for ten years, even with parole."

Daryl glared at her.

"Mom, do you really . . ." Adam began, but he saw where she was taking this.

I get it. Good elf, bad elf. Right.

"You'll be almost thirty before you see freedom. If you don't start talking, right now, I'll push for twenty, with manslaughter."

"Do you really think threatening him will do any good?" Adam said.

Daryl looked as if his soul had been deflated. "Okay," he said lifelessly. "You win."

Over the next half hour Daryl told them the whole story, when he started selling bottles for Presto, to the job he had at the New You Fitness Center. Adam's skin crawled as Daryl described Peter Pritchard, a.k.a. Zeldan Dhu, of the Unseleighe Court, and his arrangement at the health club dealing quantity. He pulled out a wad of twenties thick enough to choke a horse. "Take it if you want. It's drug money." He started emptying his pockets, and before he was through had added ten more bottles of Black Dream to the cache. "There's a bunch of coke under my dad's bed."

"Go get it," Samantha said.

Daryl did as he was told, moving laconically, like a zombie. "I think he's finally had it," Samantha said when he vanished into the master bedroom.

I'll believe it when I see it, Adam thought. He hated to be skeptical of his friend's attempts to mend his ways, but he knew he was not only up against the power of the drug, he was against the Unseleighe Court.

"That's all that I know of," Daryl said when he returned from the bedroom with a large silver tray with a visible layer of cocaine on it. "Honest. I probably have stuff all over the house I've forgotten about. I know Dad does." He set the tray down on the dining room table.

"As long as we have your permission," Samantha said, "we can use it all for evidence."

"You have it," he said. Then, his expression became fearful. "Now. I have a few of my own requests."

Samantha waved at Roach to come back in. The cop had been lingering in the hallway ever since she'd shooed him away, and he returned with a big goofy smile on his face, apparently having heard everything.

"You heard the boy," she said. "Search this house." Then she turned to Daryl. "Go ahead," Samantha said. "You've been fair with us. What do *you* want?"

Daryl returned to the chair again, a little more steadily this time. "First, you need to get me into a treatment center. I'm so strung out on Black Dream right now I'm afraid I'll die without help."

Adam withered at the mention of the Dream. *My family did not stop the Unseleighe, and they followed us here, where we fled. We are responsible, if only indirectly.*

"And I need protection. Lots of it. From Presto, from the Man, and from my father. After tonight, they're all gonna want my head on a stick."

"You've got it," Samantha said, and they shook hands.

"And there's the big thing," Daryl said. "That's going to

happen tonight." He told them about the other little side project the Man and Presto had cooked up, and how it was about to happen real soon now.

He didn't make much sense, but Adam caught the gist of it. "If they put Dream into the water supply, I doubt it would have much effect. The water would dilute it."

"Unless," Samantha said. "Unless it's—"

"It's some sort of concentrate," Daryl supplied. They're convinced it will work. Lake Tawekoni is one of them. I don't know where the rest of it's gonna be dumped. Mort said something about it being millions times stronger than the original. . . ."

Samantha turned to Adam slowly, deliberately. "This is something we need to worry about. I don't like the sound of it one bit."

"And how much is it worth to you?" Daryl pleaded. "My life's on the line here."

"We will protect you," Samantha said. "You have my word. You will get everything you asked for, the treatment center, protection, everything. When is this water supply thing supposed to happen?"

The phone rang. One of the officers reached to pick it up, but Samantha waved at him not to. "Let Daryl get it," she said.

Daryl groaned, but went over to pick up the phone anyway. After a brief conversation with someone, he hung up the phone, paler than he was before.

"It starts happening tonight," he said, his words edged with panic. "Presto wants me at the New You Fitness Center in an hour. What do I do?"

"We've got to know exactly what he's going to do," Adam said. "Unless you can tell us more."

Daryl looked miserable. "I don't know any more than that. Honest."

"But all those people, possibly the entire population of Dallas, hallucinating gods only knows what," Samantha said. "It looked like whatever it was your brother saw, it scared him to death."

Adam flinched, hoping she hadn't just gone too far. Daryl shook his head slowly, said, "*I know what Justin saw.*"

Adam waited for him to continue. Instead, he started to break down and cry again.

"We need you to help us," Samantha said. "We've got to stop this."

"I know, I know . . ." Daryl said through the new tears. "Can't you just go in and bust him? Haven't I told you enough?"

Sammi shifted in her chair. "We need evidence. The kind we can take to court. Your father's a lawyer, you should know all about that."

Daryl rolled his eyes and looked disgusted. "Don't remind me. What do you want to do?"

Sammi waved at Roach, who had just come down from the upstairs. "Roach, do we have a wire in the van we can send in with Daryl here?"

"Oh, we got a couple," he said, glancing from Samantha to Daryl. "What do you have?"

"Daryl here, he's willing to help us collect some information," she replied evenly. Daryl scowled, and Adam wondered if he was even well enough to do the job.

"Guys, I don't know . . ." Daryl began, and Adam put a hand on his shoulder.

"You know, this isn't something you can do halfway," Adam said. "We either do this right or we don't do it at all."

Daryl frowned, but looked resigned to what he had to do. "Okay. I'll do it. We'd better get started quick. Presto is expecting me."

Chapter Eighteen

Petrus lay on his belly in front of the television, remote in hand. "You *said* you wanted to channel-surf," he said petulantly to Wenlann, who cowered in the corner of the couch. "I want to watch this. This human intrigues me."

Wenlann sighed. "So be it. I think I can put up with this grotesque display of human maleness." A frown passed over her elven features, signaling to Petrus that he had won the argument only for the time being.

On the big screen Sony, Rambo threatened to blow something away with a .50-caliber machine gun. It was the most heroic human Petrus had ever seen; if Rambo were an elf, he speculated, the man would truly be formidable.

This was the first time they'd been left alone in the human house, and Petrus had already decided he liked it. He knew enough to stay out of things he didn't understand, particularly in the garage, where all manner of Cold Iron waited to burn them. There had been the temporary excitement earlier, when the King had accidentally set fire to his carriage, but the danger of unwanted humans entering their new elfhame had passed. Adam had put him in charge of guarding Wenlann, but even now he was beginning to suspect that was only to pacify him, while the "adult" elves went off and did the important things.

"Petrus, what was that?"

The young elf scowled at the interruption. "What was what?"

She looked fearfully toward the front door. "That."

Petrus heard it that time. A thud, then footsteps. Since the big crane had already taken the burned carriage away already, he knew it wasn't that. *Was the King back already?* He doubted it.

"I'll go look," Petrus said, but he sounded braver than he felt. *I'm in charge. I have to go look. But I don't like it.*

He crept into the dining room, which had a window looking onto the front yard and circular drive. He saw the charred outline of the carriage, and behind it was another black, rounded carriage. It didn't move, and he didn't see anyone inside.

He observed the carriage for a time, as a sense of dread fell over him like a black shawl. *This was how I felt when the Unseleighe took the palace,* he thought. Then, *We're in danger. I know it.*

He ran back to the living room. "Wenlann, I think we should hide in our quarters."

She leaped to her feet. "Why? *What's wrong?*"

"I don't know," he said. "Just to be safe." She clung to his arm like the frightened child they both were, and Petrus suddenly felt like an adult.

As he helped her up the ladder, he heard the front door crash open.

"*Go,*" he said impatiently as she scampered up the ladder, then pulled it up behind her.

Without really thinking, he ran back to the kitchen and started going through the drawers. He recoiled from the drawer full of Cold Iron knives, but reached for them anyway, burning his fingers. *Too hot. I need . . .* Then he saw the oven mitt over the stove.

As he grabbed the knife clumsily with the mitt, he sensed a presence behind him. Petrus froze.

"Is this all I have to show for my efforts?" boomed an alien voice. Petrus turned to face the intruder. "A pathetic elf *child* with a knife?"

Petrus knew this had to be an Unseleighe, but it was unlike any elf he'd seen. Small and vaporlike, the creature looked more like a black rat, with a ragged tunic.

"What are you doing in our home?" Petrus demanded. Despite his best efforts to keep his voice deep, it squeaked, mouselike, on *home*.

Petrus flung the knife at the intruder; the weapon flew through him, as if he were a ghost.

"Care to try that again, child?" the intruder said. Petrus fled into the garage.

He sensed others in the house as he closed the door behind him. Of course, the lock was on the other side, but at least it gave him a few more moments to scavenge for some other weapon. His eyes fell on the staple gun, one of the items Adam had warned him against, because it spat Cold Iron. It was a large, heavy item, and took both hands to hold up. The Cold Iron the weapon was made of burned, but he still had the oven mitt on and relied on that hand to grip it. He squeezed hard, and out popped a piece of Cold Iron that stuck in the wall. Petrus stood, holding the staple gun in front of him.

"Petrus, what's going on?" he heard Wenlann wail above him.

"Quiet, or they'll hear you!" Petrus shouted back. Then the door burst open. In stepped the biggest Unseleighe he'd ever seen.

"Where are the others, little one?"

Though blond, and in a human seeming, Petrus recognized the face and, when he spoke, the voice.

Zeldan Dhu.

"Gone back to Underhill!" Petrus squeaked, holding the staple gun quivering in front of him.

Zeldan laughed, his voice booming against the interior of the garage.

"Where I have complete control?" Zeldan advanced a step. "Who were you talking to?" His eyes traveled upward, to the ladder. "So that's where they hide!"

"*NO!*" Petrus screamed, and squeezed the staple gun.

The bit of iron flew directly into Zeldan's forehead, where it stuck.

"YAAAAaaaargh!" the Unseleighe screamed, reaching for the iron that protruded from his skin. Two tiny flames shot out where the metal went in. Petrus fired again, and again, missing once, then hitting him in the arm, with the same fiery results.

Zeldan screamed something incomprehensible, and Petrus continued firing until his hands ached. The staples struck his opponent half a dozen times, but fell out, more often than not, leaving only small burns.

Two other Unseleighe charged in behind Zeldan, and Petrus kept firing. They had him by the arms before he realized he'd run out of staples.

Zeldan walked over to where the others had him pinned down. "I would kill you, if I didn't need you for hostages," Zeldan said. Then Petrus saw another Unseleighe with Wenlann, who was screaming and kicking as they came down the ladder.

To the others, Zeldan barked, "Take them to the center. We have a formidable task ahead of us tonight."

This is the beginning of the end of the nightmare, a part of Daryl realized during his grief over his brother. *I only hope that I've stopped in time.*

Despite the assurance from Adam and Samantha McDaris, Daryl was not convinced he would live past the evening.

Can't live with it either, not anymore.

Samantha and her cop partner had gone off to get the listening equipment, and Adam had gone back out to the car for something. He was alone in the dining room as the cops went over the house again. It seemed to be a pattern, sitting in a dining room, feeling like crap, as police searched the house. He liked it even less that it was *his* house this time.

And then Presto calls in the middle of all this. Terrific. Here I am, giving the cops evidence to put him away.

*And Dad, wherever the hell he is, will probably be
busted, too.*

*Presto says it goes down tonight. And it will go down
more ways than he thinks, when I go in there with the cops.*

What a way to die.

He kept looking at his watch, waiting for Dad or Mom
to show up. Would the police protect him from Dad? He
didn't know if they could; Dad would go ballistic, and Daryl
doubted an army would hold him back. It became very
important for him to get the hell out of there before one or
both parents arrived.

Adam came in with the wire, a thin black box with an
coax antenna attached to it. The wire would show through
his tank top, so they went looking for clothing to conceal
the electronics. Upstairs in his room Daryl tried different
shirts that wouldn't be conspicuous in the summer heat,
before they finally gave up and ran the rig inside the front
of his pants. They did a mike check in the van, and while
the sound wasn't exactly Dolby quality, it would do for evidence.

Thirty minutes later, Daryl pulled into the parking lot of
the New You Fitness Center. The van and the Caprice,
driven by Adam, were parked nearby, out of sight. The hour
was 10 P.M., and the fitness center parking lot was packed.

But not with the usual assortment of vehicles. Instead of
the sedans and station wagons, the lot bristled with faster
machinery: a variety of scooters and motorcycles, Trans
Ams, Mustangs, Camaros, Corvettes. It looked like a high
school parking lot. He didn't feel out of place, so long as he
forgot his purpose for being here.

Daryl sat in his car for some time, afraid to get out, and
even more afraid to stay there. It was a classic setup for
Mort to appear, and that he hadn't yet seemed odd, especially this close to the Man's hideout. Somewhere in the car
was a couple of hundred in cash, perhaps much more,
which would pay for a one-way trip to California. If he
turned the 'Vette back on, steered it onto the nearest highway, and took off, no one would catch him.

And by the time he reached Arizona, a million innocent people would be going insane.

He forced himself to get out. *I have to do this. If I don't, people will die. They may die anyway, but at least I would have tried. Even if I die in the process.* His knees felt weak when his feet hit the pavement, but he made himself go on.

I feel like crap. Maybe if I just had a little hit of Dream, just long enough to keep me going . . .

The thought horrified him. *I can't even stay away from it for a few hours anymore.*

I have no control over it. My life is completely unmanageable.

The thoughts echoed from somewhere in his memory, from a movie he remembered seeing. *Something about recovery. Treatment. Meryl Streep was in it. What was the name of that damned movie?*

When he reached the front door and entered the fitness center, the decision was made for him.

About twenty or thirty kids, some he recognized from school, most he did not, stood about just inside the New You, smoking cigarettes by the carton. Smoke drifted down the tiled halls, where earlier that day, healthy and near healthy people sweated and grunted away excess fat and calories. It seemed unreal, what he felt and saw then. But then, everything else in his life seemed unreal, particularly the events of the last several weeks. As Daryl stood watching his peers, he wondered if he'd overdosed at his birthday party and had been in a coma ever since; that all the events since were a series of nightmares, strung together in his sleep as he lay somewhere in a hospital bed, hooked up to tubes and wires.

Among them was every grunge bunny and dealer he'd ever known in school, plus a few others he didn't know. They gave him a long, slow, scrutinizing look, one that seemed to say, *Okay, so you're one of us.*

The air was thick with smoke. Cravings he never knew existed swept through his body. He bummed a cigarette, then a light.

"It's about time you showed up," Mort said, appearing at his side. He took him by the arm and led him down the tiled hallway. "Where the hell have you been anyway?"

Daryl mumbled a reply even he didn't understand. Mort looked him over suspiciously, so much that he thought the damned little demon was going to pat him down. Then Mort shrugged, gave him an evil grin, and led him to the free-weight room, the largest room in the club.

At one end was a portable stage. Behind this were two double doors. Everyone focused on Peter Pritchard, who stood on the stage in front of a big map of the city of Dallas. With a pointer Peter pointed to the surrounding lakes, which were highlighted in red. His loud voice carried clearly in the large room, and everyone seemed entranced by his presentation.

Peter looked directly at Daryl for a brief moment, during which Daryl's heart raced into overdrive. Peter continued, "Now that our lieutenants are *all* here, I will go into detail on what you will be doing tonight."

Peter addressed the map with the pointer. "You will all be given paper-wrapped packages of product. It is very important that you consume none of it, as it is of a potency that would kill you instantly."

Daryl looked on attentively, cautiously studying the others assembled. They were all acting like zombies, mindlessly listening to what was said on the stage. Granted, this wasn't that much of a change in this group. But it was enough to start him thinking. *What other powers are these creatures working on this gathering?*

There, he said it. *Creatures. Whoever is in charge of this operation, they are not human. Even Peter up there, he doesn't look the same, somehow. Or maybe this is just another hallucination.*

He looked around and gratefully saw that Mort had vanished.

"Daryl Bendis and his group will go out on Highway 80 to Lake Tawekoni. There they will deposit the product in the waters near the dam," Peter said. As he spoke, his appearance changed. A cloud of light flared briefly around him, then vanished, leaving behind a dark tunic, trimmed with silver, instead of the preppy workout clothes Peter always wore. Daryl looked on, transfixed, as Peter's skin darkened, his ears grew, his nose lengthened, until he looked like a giant rat.

Daryl stared, trying not to let his fear show, recognizing Peter for what he really was—something unhuman, perhaps from another planet. This didn't seem to faze anyone, and Daryl bit his tongue to keep from calling out. Then his feet wanted to run, but he wouldn't let them do that, either.

I sure hope they're getting this all on tape, he thought.

"Once the product has been delivered, I suggest you all go home, pretend this meeting never took place, and watch the news. Better yet, watch the people around you, first. Things should get very interesting."

Muted laughter rippled through the crowd. Daryl positioned himself so that he had a line of sight view with Peter, or whatever Peter had become. *A gremlin? Or a gargoyle? I want out of here!*

"And you, Cory, you'll take your group to Lake Ray Hubbard and do the honors there," the creature continued, indicating the lake on the map. "The Highway 30 bridge, along here, would be a good spot to deposit the product. And you, Monk, you and your men will go to Lake Lewisville, to the place we've already discussed." It paused, scanning the group, until he saw who he was looking for. "Ah, there you are. Mikey, you'll take your crew to Lake Grapeville." He regarded the gathering like a doting father. "I trust everyone showed up with a full tank of gas?"

The group grunted acknowledgment. Peter turned to the twin doors behind him as four other critters appeared, each holding a small pallet of paper-wrapped packages, about the size of liter bottles. The creatures resembled the giant rat Peter had turned into; these were smaller, like little gremlins. As one walked up to Daryl and gave him a package, its stench nearly knocked him over.

Daryl looked around as the little beasties handed out

the packages. No one seemed particularly alarmed that creatures straight out of D&D were strolling through the free-weight room at the New You Fitness Center, handing out drugs. Their lack of response lent a bit of normalcy to the scene, which made it all the more frightening to Daryl.

They must be under some kind of spell. Or they're drugged. Whatever it is, it's something I'm not.

Daryl took the package with shaking hands. Peter looked his way again, then stepped off the stage. The boy stared at the huge alien rat coming toward him and nearly dropped the package.

Offer free drugs, Zeldan thought, bemused at the sight of human cattle massing in the New You, *and they will come by the droves.*

Never before had he so brazenly assembled a group of human minions in one place, much less in a place used as a front for shadier activities.

Soon the drug will be coursing through the veins of Dallas, and there will be no stopping its effects. With the power of a city in psychosis, we will fuel the Unseleighe forces until they are satiated, then invade Morrigan's territory in numbers.

The raid on the Seleighe stronghold was a disappointment. They left a feeble shield protecting—what? worthless Seleighe children? He had come with enough stored energy to take everyone out, and then some; however, the two he did find would make suitable hostages should the Seleighe try to intervene with his plan. Down in the lab, Rathand was keeping them company while he spoke to the troops up here.

During his speech, Zeldan noticed something unusual about Daryl, something he found quite disturbing. The boy had changed drastically, but the Unseleighe lord was uncertain precisely how. He didn't seem as fogged on Dream. He looked like he might even have a mind of his own now, not one obsessed by Zeldan's gift from Underhill. He even looked, well, *suspicious*. The boy had always been nervous, worried about when his next voyage down Dream avenue might be, and who might supply it. Tonight seemed to be a different story; Daryl looked like he was going to run out of the building any second now.

Zeldan stepped off the stage and casually strolled over to Daryl. The gargoyles had already handed him his package of Black Dream concentrate, and he stood there holding it as if it were a bomb. Zeldan had made certain their conversation would not be heard by the others when he approached the boy, throwing up a concealing wall of privacy before addressing him.

"Hello, Daryl," Zeldan said. "I believe our human servant Presto called you over two hours ago. What took you so long to get here, I wonder?"

Zeldan gave the words plenty of time to sink in. *Human. As we certainly are not—or are you blind, stupid human child?*

"Uh . . . I got here as soon as I could," he said, staring openmouthed at Zeldan. "Is something wrong?"

Zeldan regarded him with undisguised hate. "I should ask you the same thing," the Unseleighe said, leaning forward. The human pulled back, flinching. "Do you find my appearance *alarming* in any way?"

Daryl made a pitiful attempt to establish eye contact, but furtively looked away. "No, of course not. The plan is going smoothly, I hope?"

Zeldan scratched his long, pointed chin. "Right now, young human, I'm not so certain. Tell me, have you spoken with Adam McDaris lately?"

Daryl's eyes widened. "Uh, no. Why do you ask?"

He's lying. Time to let him know what a bad idea that is.

With his claws extended, Zeldan took a long swipe at Daryl, making four bloody incisions down his stomach and cutting through the denim of the jeans. The boy shrieked, but no one turned, or even noticed. Daryl fell backward, and lay cowering. A small box with a wire had fallen out of his pants.

An electronic device, Zeldan thought, picking the instrument up with a single, extended claw. *An electronic* listening *device!*

Though disguised, the voice coming over Daryl's wire was no doubt that of Zeldan Dhu. There were others the tape picked up, but Zeldan's was the most recognizable.

He was going to hit all the lakes, she thought grimly. *And there would have been no way to protect them all with what we have. If we don't stop them all now, we don't have a chance. And neither do the humans who live in this city.*

Roach listened to Daryl's wire also, but his mind was distracted by the sleep spell working its way over him; Sammi decided early in the stakeout that this was *not* something the human police needed to be in on. If it looked like they would need help, they were always there to call, but she doubted the cops would be much help against what Zeldan would be throwing at them.

How does a riot squad prepare for a levin bolt? They don't.

From the sounds she'd picked up over the wire, there were quite a few individuals gathered for the occasion, though she was having trouble determining how many there were, how many were human, and how many were not. She'd caught a brief glimpse of the New You parking lot before they parked on this particular street corner and remembered seeing a large number of motorcycles and sports cars.

Most, if not all of those, belong to humans. Zeldan isn't using only humans to carry this off, or is he? The worst occurred to her. *He would if they were going to be expendable. That would definitely be his style.*

A knock sounded on the van door, then Adam let himself in. He'd spent the last several minutes handing out black t-shirts printed with the word POLICE in bright white letters to the rest of the elves sitting in the Caprice parked behind the van. Under these were Kevlar vests, in the highly likely event some of the humans wielded handguns.

Samantha herself had changed from her professional woman's dress to more appropriate field attire: jeans and a POLICE t-shirt.

She had told Adam to check in with her instead of using the radio, because the operation they were carrying out was less than authorized. It wouldn't do to have the dispatch listening in on an elf war, or have human police as witnesses. That would be too difficult to cover up. So the whole thing was being done on the sly.

Adam closed the door behind him and situated himself next to Sammi. The King made a striking young human cop; if Aedham Tuiereann hadn't already become King of Avalon, she would have to recommended him to the police academy for training.

"Anything?" he asked, but Sammi was paying more attention to the receiver.

Finally, she replied, "Daryl's in the center now." She regarded him with a dark stare. "I just heard their plan to saturate the water supply with Black Dream. Everything Daryl said was true."

Adam groaned. "I was hoping he had imagined the whole thing."

"No such luck, apparently. This may work to our advantage. If they're so distracted with carrying this out, they may not be ready for us." After a pause, Zeldan spoke again, much closer and directly to Daryl. Zeldan's deep voice reverberated too loudly over the speakers; Samantha dropped the bass a little on the receiver.

". . . have you spoken with Adam McDaris, lately?" Zeldan said.

"Oh, gods," Adam said. "Does he—"

"Shhh!" Sammi said.

After that came a rustle and a shriek from Daryl. Then the wire went dead.

"Sammi, he knows," Adam said. "We have to go in there!"

"Let's go," Samantha said, reaching for her Glock as Adam scrambled for the door. "The whole thing's blown now."

In the driver's seat, Roach snored loudly.

"Hold the fort, will you?" Sammi said to her sleeping human partner.

The Caprice squealed to a stop in front of the New You, the car's nose pointed directly at the entrance. Just inside the doors a handful of kids spotted them, then ran further in; Adam hadn't anticipated a complete surprise, but he was hoping for more lead time than that. Now they knew they were being raided, before the good guys had even set foot on the pavement.

"So much for the surprise element," Sammi said, pulling her Glock out as she climbed out of the Caprice. Marbann, Spence and Moira swarmed out of the backseat.

"Niamh, you stay here and watch these vehicles," Sammi ordered. "These little shits are going to want out of here in a real hurry, and I don't want them taking off with our car!" Niamh stayed in the front seat of the Caprice, looking altogether pleased about staying behind.

"Everyone, behind Adam," Sammi said, holding her Glock up with both hands.

Adam flipped the power on the laser weapon, and the LED display came to life.

"*Shields,*" Marbann said, and Adam felt a tug on the nodes as everyone simultaneously tapped into them, creating individual shields. They agreed earlier on this tactic to permit them individual freedom, should they be forced to spread out. If the Unseleighe started flinging levin bolts at them, which was highly likely, node shields would be the only effective protection.

"Door's open," Sammi said, pushing the doors aside, while the others entered. Further inside, he heard chaos erupting.

"*POLICE!*" Sammi shouted, leaping into the hallway in front of them, the Glock drawn and ready. "Put your hands up!"

There were five people in the hall; each of them dropped the packages they were carrying and started running. Which is what they wanted. As a unit, the force charged down the hallway, empty racquetball courts on the right, a free-weight room on the left.

Sammi and Adam rushed in, the others behind them.

"Everyone, put your hands up!" Sammi shouted, but no one obeyed. Paper packages fell to the floor as the crowd scattered. A few of the Unseleighe's human minions remained, however, watching the "police" warily as the rest of the group beat a hasty trail to the nearest exits. Others were going around Adam and his group to get out, the "police" not making any move to arrest them.

Zeldan Dhu, in his true elven form, stood on a short stage at one end of the free-weight room. An unconscious form, which appeared to be human, was draped over his shoulder like a sack of laundry. Hate burned in his eyes as he gazed at Adam, Sammi, the others. Adam raised his weapon, which seemed to puzzle the Unseleighe momentarily. As he took aim, he saw who Zeldan had over his shoulder.

Daryl.

The Unseleighe smirked at his hesitation, and he sent a levin bolt directly at them.

The concussion threw Adam backward. His shield, which was still in place, absorbed much of the shock, but the impact of the levin bolt pressed him against the wall painfully, squeezing him for a split second like a vise grip. His weapon made an uncomfortable crease against his chest, pushing the Kevlar vest's shock plate against his sternum; nothing broke, but if the bolt had been any stronger, he would be dealing with broken ribs now.

Stunned, Adam got up slowly from the floor. Sammi and Moira seemed equally stunned, but unhurt; Marbann and Spence had been thrown into the hallway, but it looked like Adam had taken the brunt of the levin bolt.

Zeldan had vanished from the stage.

The other human helpers, who had no shields whatsoever, were now lifeless forms, thrown into weight equipment and walls like limp rag dolls; one boy, who was no older than Adam, lay dead on the floor, his neck clearly broken.

This Unseleighe doesn't care who dies and who lives, Adam thought, his mind racing. *And I had a clear shot of him, if only . . .*

If only Zeldan hadn't used Daryl as a shield.

"They've gone through those doors," Sammi shouted. She ran onto the stage, motioned for the others to follow.

"He's gone to the Gate," Marbann said. "If he gets away, he'll have a chance to rebuild his forces. *We cannot let this happen, young King!*"

"I know," Adam said, stepping over the bodies. *Just like the palace,* he remembered. *Elven bodies everywhere. Only here, they're human.* "He's *not* getting away."

Adam didn't think he was retreating; at least, not all the way back to Underhill. *What is in there that he would need? Daryl must be with him still, which will present a problem if he continues using Daryl as a shield.*

Adam heard the roar of a dozen different motorcycles as they sped off, followed by the cars, tires squealing.

"We'll have to collect this poison later," Adam said, toeing a package of Dream over, as if it were a corpse. "The rest of you, stay behind me. How are your shields, Sammi?"

Her shield distorted her sardonic grin, then her voice, as she spoke. "It takes more than that bolt to do anything to mine." She glanced through the doors. "There's a stairway leading down."

A service hallway led off from the stairwell, through which Adam saw another open exit. Beyond these doors a swarm of taillights sped off into the night.

Before him a thick metal door, painfully warm with iron, led to a stairwell.

"A trap?" Marbann said, peering down the stairs. "Or was he in such a hurry . . . ?"

"Don't know," Adam replied. "Might go either way. I don't feel anything safe or threatening about this stairwell." *Which way did he go? Out the exit, or down the stairs?*

"Banzai," Adam said with a shrug.

Adam advanced down the stairs, stopping at the U-turn it made, then waved for the others to follow. Red lights glowed in the fixtures, bathing the hall in crimson light. Smoke detectors had been installed every few feet or so. *Strange.*

Dark, Unseleighe magic flowed up from the basement, wafting past him like the stench of a sewer. Adam upped the node flow to his shields, both to filter out the foul magical odor of the place and to see if his nodes were still accessible. It did, and they were. He wiped the sweat off his palms, his temples pounding.

On a certain level, he felt like he'd passed into Underhill. This was only an illusion, enhanced by the Unseleighe forces putrefying down here. There was something else waiting for him, something powerful and alien, something greater than Zeldan. And Zeldan had control of it.

At the foot of the stairs he found another hallway—white painted cinder blocks and a waxed floor, the scent of old office insulation, and something that had died. Red lights lit this passage as well, giving the hallway a squared-off blood-vessel look.

From a doorway stepped a small, black demon.

Ghostlike, the transparent apparition strolled to the center of the hallway, folded its arms, and stopped. Through the being, Adam saw the cracks in the tile, the edge of the wall; the critter itself looked like a cartoon character.

The creature said nothing as it extended a finger toward Adam, then drew it back in a hook.

Follow me.

This seemed wrong, dangerous. Adam looked behind him to consult Sammi or Marbann, but they were nowhere to be seen.

Instead he found Zeldan Dhu preparing another levin bolt, this one directed toward his unprotected back.

Chapter Nineteen

The elven King spun around, aiming his weapon at the Unseleighe. A levin bolt shot from Zeldan's right hand; Adam reached for the nodes and pulled the trigger.

The weapon spat a beam of red light, which caught the bolt head-on, splitting it in two. The halves caught the walls on either side; the bolt's concussion threw him backward, amid a shower of concrete fragments.

Adam landed on the floor, sliding a good distance on the waxed surface. Zeldan's laugh echoed down the hallway, but it seemed strained, as if he knew the victory was incomplete.

Adam checked his shields, found them intact, but weakening.

Where the hell are the rest? Then he heard a gunshot, which may or may not have been the Glock. *They may have problems of their own by now.*

He regretted coming down here. They'd had no idea what waited for them, and Zeldan had plenty of time to set traps. It was starting to look like one or more had already been sprung.

Agony ripped through his left arm when he moved. He looked down to find a long, bleeding gash in his biceps. *Damn,* he muttered, bringing the weapon up despite the pain. Though scratched and dented after the last bolt, the lights on the display remained lit. But Zeldan was no longer in the hallway.

Zeldan, where the hell are you? he thought, getting up. The sight of his own blood, Tuiereann blood, angered him; it reminded him of all the Avalon clan blood that had already been spilled. *And you are not going to spill any more!*

When he got to his feet, Adam discovered another injury; his right ankle was sprained, possibly worse. He hobbled down the hallway toward Zeldan's last position. Behind a door, someone pounded.

"Spence, is that you?" he shouted.

"We're locked in here," came the muffled reply. "Use your weapon to blast this thing open. Sammi's Glock just dents it."

Adam stepped away from the door, glancing behind him for any surprises there.

"Stand back," Adam said, and pulled the trigger. The beam arced from the mouth of the weapon and carved a narrow gash near the doorknob. He ran the beam across the bolt; something heavy and metal dropped on the other side, and the door swung open.

Spence, Sammi and the rest of the crew charged through. "I sensed Zeldan," she said. "Is he—"

"He was here," Adam said. "This way."

"Your arm," Moira said as she caught up with him. "We need to look at that."

Adam shook his head. "No time. It's not serious," he said, trying not to make the limp too obvious. "He has Daryl down here somewhere."

From the other end of the hall came a distant whimpering. Adam and Sammi exchanged looks.

"That didn't sound like Daryl," Sammi said.

Backs against the wall, they crept up on a doorway. A bar of white light fell on the opposite wall. Shadows passed through the light, a lambent, flickering illumination, not electric in origin. Adam clutched the weapon to his chest.

The whimper came again, louder, nearer.

Adam peered slowly into the room.

Daryl lay on a table, shivering violently, his arms and legs tied down with straps. He seemed to be asleep, or in a coma, and glistened with sweat. Behind him was computer equipment and a series of large crystals, including one the size of a computer monitor, in the center of the floor. The crystals glowed brightly, outshining the flickering bare fluorescents in the ceiling. A light source from within the computer equipment shone with the intensity of ten halogens; from within these, Adam felt a strong, concentrated power. Like a node, but with pain.

Against one wall was a Gate glowing a dull red, similar to the one Adam had used recently to travel to Underhill, but reeking of Unseleighe magic. Adam felt the Gate, which was of a rather inefficient design, pulling vast amounts of energy from the artificial nodes.

It's the stored agony that fuels the Unseleighe's Gate. And Daryl is the source. The crystals drew off tendrils of light, like fog off the surface of a lake, from Daryl and the table he was tied to. *A pain collector. And with Daryl in withdrawal, he should be a fine source of pain.* Adam shuddered as he tracked his weapon across the room, looking for Zeldan.

Has he already gone through the Gate to Underhill?

In one corner of the room was a large wooden pallet loaded down with more paper packages like the ones he saw upstairs.

Though Adam didn't see him, Zeldan's voice boomed through the room.

"The sky opened up, and Gabriel tore loose with horns of brass. And Armageddon was here. And the black Eagle saw the ruined castle, and all the dead within waited for the might to take the palace."

Zeldan stepped from behind one of the big computer cabinets. Adam brought his weapon around. The Unseleighe held a young elf by the arms, using her as a shield.

"King!" Wenlann screamed out. "They have . . ."

Wenlann? How did . . . we left them alone. No, no no . . Adam thought, and Zeldan brought her up to head level.

"What's wrong, King? Aren't you going to *shoot*?"

He hesitated before pulling the trigger. "Zeldan. *Haven't you killed enough of us?*"

The Unseleighe laughed hollowly. "I didn't think so." He walked over to the table Daryl was tied to and looked down in mock sympathy.

"Do you know what Armageddon is, young King?" Zeldan inquired. Adam didn't reply. "Armageddon is the end of your world. It has just begun."

The Unseleighe was making no sense, though he'd heard the previous few sentences somewhere else. *And all the dead within waited for the might to take the palace. I know that . . . but where is it from?*

"Ah. I see you've brought friends. Come in, please," Zeldan said. Adam sensed Sammi, Moira, Marbann and Spence behind him, hesitating in the hallway. "Rathand, please come in with our other captive."

Another elf came in from the rear of the computer room. Adam didn't see who they were until they got past the bank of computer equipment; tied and gagged, Petrus looked up in panic.

"These two children will also provide us with a nice source of pain. We will begin by replacing their bindings with steel wire. For starters."

"Damn you," Adam muttered. Behind him, Sammi gasped.

"Damn *me?*" Zeldan said, leaning on the table with both hands. "*You* are the one to blame in all this. You ruined our plan, which would have only destroyed human minds. Now I'm afraid you've just pushed me, *Tuiereann*." He regarded the Gate momentarily. "My Unseleighe helpers have already returned to Underhill. Mort, despite the delight he took in tormenting this poor lad, has also passed through. Reluctantly, I might add. Cruz is just going to have to find reliable help among the pathetic humans."

Daryl groaned loudly, and a wide tendril of light flared, shot into the equipment. Zeldan's expression turned to pure hate. "You've forced me to send my people back to our new home of Avalon. There we will regain our strength and come back and kill you, *all* of you!"

He's retreating. I can't let him take our people with him!

Zeldan continued, "You've forced me to take hostages, and what kind of an Unseleighe would I be if I didn't take advantage of the situation?"

Adam took a step forward, then brought the weapon up, aiming for Zeldan's chest. Wenlann looked away. "Release them. *All* of them." Adam said. *I know I can hit him. The aim isn't great on this thing, but I might get an easy shot.* "Or I'll blow you away."

Zeldan regarded him with amusement. "You have lived with the humans too long, haven't you?" he said, snickering. "'Blow me away'? What, precisely, does that *mean*, young King?"

The Unseleighe had dropped Wenlann to waist level. Adam had a clear shot at his head.

I'll show you, Adam thought as he pulled the trigger.

Nothing happened.

What?! He tried again, with the same results. On the weapon's stock was an liquid crystal display, which read, "Low Battery."

"Awww. It's *broken*," Zeldan said, stepping from behind the table. "I suppose I'm just going to have to kill this defenseless little elf. Or take you captive and hook you up to my crystals, like Daryl here."

Adam looked up in time to see power shooting from the crystals into Zeldan's hand. The equipment behind him blazed with intense, yellow light, outlining the Unseleighe like the setting sun.

He had only enough time to reinforce his own shields, hoping they would take most of the hit and protect those behind him; when it did hit, he caught a brief glimpse of the computer room, afire with node energy, moments before the levin bolt carried him out of it.

Adam came to sitting against the wall. The bolt had knocked ceiling tiles off, which had settled around him like a nest. The impact had also knocked out the lights; the hallway was dark.

Zeldan spoke to someone in the computer room, perhaps the other elf Adam had seen earlier. Adam looked at his weapon, which he'd somehow hung on to during the blast. *Low Battery. Great.* He opened up the plate that held the two nine-volt batteries, removed them, and started sifting through the ceiling debris.

Marbann lay a few feet away; his chest moved slowly with his breathing. *Alive.* Sammi and Moira were also making some attempt to move. Spence was some distance down the hall, not moving at all.

They're injured. But if I don't kill Zeldan now, we're all dead meat!

He found a smoke alarm, then another, on the floor. Several more of the detectors dangled from the partially destroyed ceiling.

The voices within the computer room ceased, and as Adam ripped the batteries out of the smoke detectors and inserted them in his own weapon, he sensed someone standing in the doorway.

It was the other elf. *Is he Seleighe? A traitor?* Adam did not recall his being at Avalon. Instead of the dark hair of the Unseleighe, he was blond, like an Avalon elf, and had the distinctive Seleighe nose. He just didn't look like one of Zeldan's clan. *Outremer, perhaps? What did Zeldan call him—Rathand?*

Rathand, the elf, looked directly at Adam, who slowly struggled to his feet.

"No, Zeldan," Rathand said, addressing the Unseleighe in the computer room. "They're still out cold. I hope you didn't kill them."

"And what would it matter if I *did?*" Zeldan roared. Rathand gave Adam another look, one he did not know how to interpret, then went back into the room.

The "Low Battery" message had gone away; with as much stealth as he could manage, and with the pain he was in after the new set of injuries he didn't have time to assess,

Adam crept over to the door once again. Pain shot through his right leg; he bit his tongue to keep from screaming, and tasted blood for his trouble.

We can't let him Gate, Adam thought, glancing over at Marbann, who was still out cold. *If Zeldan gets away, we'll have this to look forward to all over again.*

Adam closed his eyes for a moment and reached for the nodes. The thin flow he had used before changed somewhat, feeding him a much stronger stream.

Marbann, Adam thought, glancing back at his mentor, who still appeared to be unconscious. The King knew better. *He's down, but he's using everything he's got left to bridge more energy to me.*

The nodes came into his mental view clearly, cutting through his pain like an anesthetic; the power hummed through his body, healing his injuries, mending his ankle, and knitting the wound in his left biceps, which had reopened during the last impact.

The King sensed a change in the computer room. His manipulation of the node energy had apparently not gone unnoticed.

"Rathand. *Rathand?* What *was* that?"

Another presence, tugging at a corner of his mind. *Sammi. Bridging as well.* The stream of node power widened, and Adam started to wonder if he would be able to handle it all. He felt the power spreading out, between himself, Marbann, Sammi, and now Moira; the images were dim shadows in the hallway, but he knew they were aware, they were helping him draw on the nodes. A vast pool of node energy formed, waiting to be unleashed.

"Rathand, what is going on out here?"

Rathand was apparently elsewhere. Adam raised his weapon as Zeldan's shadow sliced across the doorway.

As the Unseleighe stepped into the hallway, he apparently didn't see Adam standing in the shadows. But the LED lights on the weapon blinked brightly; when these caught the Unseleighe's eye, he didn't react strongly. Instead, Adam felt the Unseleighe reach for more power. . . .

"Not this time," Adam said, pulling the trigger.

The power of the web surged a portion at a time. But it was energy like Adam had never felt before.

The intense beam pierced the Unseleighe's right wrist. Zeldan screamed, and as he pulled his hand away, the motion drew his wrist across the beam, neatly slicing his hand completely off.

"*Noooooo!*" Zeldan screamed. Adam stepped closer, into the light. The Unseleighe stared at him in disbelief. "I was going to make you a partner, you fool! I would have let you live!"

Adam pulled the trigger again, piercing the Unseleighe's right leg with light. Zeldan screamed as the tight beam cauterized its way through his flesh.

"That was for my *mother,*" Adam said. Firing again, he carved a chunk of flesh out of his leg. "That's for my *father.*" Zeldan screamed again, batting at the smoldering flesh. Adam raked the beam over on top of him, cutting into his shoulder. "That is for my people."

Adam raised the weapon and aimed between Zeldan's eyes. "And this one's for *me.*"

The King fired, blasting a hole the diameter of a dime through the Unseleighe's skull. The scream that tried to escape from Zeldan's lips froze as the elf's features petrified. The limp form that was once an Unseleighe lord crumpled to the floor.

Adam stared at the still form for several long moments, waiting for Zeldan to move, sit up, talk, do something.

Is he dead? Adam wondered. *Do demons like Zeldan really die?*

Well, he sure looked dead. Even elves, when shot through the head like that, tended not to live very long.

I've got to be sure, he thought, raising his weapon to inflict more damage. *If he's not dead, then none of us are safe.*

Before he pulled the trigger again, Zeldan's body lit up as if it were a lamp shade and the raising of his weapon had flipped the switch. Adam stepped back, uncertain of the light's source, or its meaning; light pierced through Zeldan's wounds, in head and body, then changed from white light to blue. The wounds grew, the light dissolving the Unseleighe's flesh, expanding, consuming. It emitted a hiss, like white noise, a radio tuned to static. Like a mutant bacteria, the light consumed the Unseleighe's flesh, his clothing, until only a cocoon of light remained.

The cocoon rose toward the ceiling, then dissolved into it.

"Where is he *going?*" Adam wondered aloud.

"Beyond," a voice said behind him. "Where else?"

"Marbann?" Adam said, turning around. Marbann stood a few feet behind him, his right hand over a bleeding wound on his chest. *He doesn't sound or look at all intact,* Adam thought.

"Wenlann and Petrus . . ." Sammi said frantically as she and Moira ran into the computer room.

Adam helped Marbann to a chair. Spence wandered in, looking lost, but otherwise uninjured. *Levin bolt shock, most likely,* he thought, turning his attention to Marbann, whose right eye had clotted over from a wound in his forehead.

"Marbann, you're in shock," Adam said. "Please, sit down."

"Is he really gone?" Marbann said, his voice distant and weak.

"Zeldan is dead," Adam said, urging Marbann to sit on a chair. "That was his soul. There is nothing else left of him." *I hope.*

Daryl squirmed on the table, then sat up, clumsily, on an elbow. His bindings had been cut.

"Adam?" Daryl said. "What just . . . what . . . your ears."

"My—" Of course. "I'll explain later," Adam said. "We need to get you to a hospital."

Daryl didn't reply. Instead, he stared at Adam, who was in full elf mode.

"Later," Adam said firmly. "Now you will go to sleep." The King closed his eyes and exerted a little magic over his friend, willing him to comply. When he opened his eyes, Daryl had passed into a deep, sound sleep.

"Where's Sammi and Moira?" Adam asked, and Marbann pointed absently toward the equipment.

That makes no sense. Wait, isn't that . . .

"Adam," Sammi called out. "I've found them." She stepped from behind some of the big blue cabinets, holding Wenlann by the hand. Moira and Petrus came out also, with the other elf Adam saw with Zeldan. The King instinctively drew the weapon on him.

"Stay right there," Adam said, gesturing the others to get out of the way. Then, to the elf, "Who are you?"

The elf looked defeated, but the more Adam studied him, the less Unseleighe he appeared.

"My name is Rathand. Formerly of Outremer," he said sadly. He looked around with a hint of fear in his expression. "Where is Zeldan?"

"Dead," Adam replied. "I am King Aedham Tuiereann of Elfhame Avalon. You're of Outremer? How did you come to be in the service of Zeldan?"

"I believe he's on our side," Samantha said. "At least, now. He was the one who released Daryl, then hid Wenlann and Petrus in a back room while you two had it out."

Rathand stepped forward, and Adam aimed his weapon directly at his face. Rathand flinched, but continued to speak. "The Unseleighe captured me, long ago. Outremer never knew what happened to me. I tried to escape, but when Zeldan learned of my engineering capabilities, he made certain I would be his forever." Rathand lifted a thatch of brown hair from his left temple, revealing a red crystal embedded into the flesh. "If I tried to escape, I died. Suffered and died, I should say. This thing he put into me is connected directly to my pain centers." He flinched, as if the crystal were already doing its work. "It is not possible to imagine the pain this crystal inflicts."

"But Zeldan is dead now," Adam said. "You're free."

Rathand looked down. "I'm dead. Already, my life is leaking away." He looked over at the two elven children.

"Thank you for allowing me to do some good before I died. I might never have had the chance to redeem myself otherwise."

Moira stepped over to Rathand and examined the crystal. "Why are you going to die? Is it because of this thing?"

"It's connected to Zeldan's life force. It was insurance to prevent me from killing my captor. I don't have long to live."

"Then we'll remove it," Moira said. "We must do something!"

Rathand shook his head slowly, resolutely. "There is nothing to do. Removing it will kill me."

Adam lowered the weapon, finding no threat in a dying elf. "Why did you help, then?"

"It was the only way to rid myself of Zeldan. Helping you provided me with that opportunity." Rathand grimaced, and he reached for the crystal in his head. "It's already started," Rathand said. "This isn't going to be pleasant." Rathand dropped to his knees in obvious agony. "Don't mistake me for a hero, Tuiereann. I am not. I stood by while Zeldan killed your father, and I aided him in the assault on the castle. Please, allow me to die. I have no right to live."

"Even after Zeldan is dead, he inflicts pain," Sammi spat. "What is all this equipment, anyway?" She looked over at the large crystal, which had started to flicker. Rathand glanced over at it with a wry grin of amusement on his face.

"It's Morrigan, calling in," Rathand said. "Zeldan's partner in all this. She won't know yet."

From his crouched position, Rathand crawled over to the crystal, looking directly into it. "I'm going to *enjoy* this." He fiddled with something below the crystal. A hideous face appeared. The facets distorted her features a bit, but even Adam saw she was no beauty to begin with. Crosseyed, hawk-nosed, she *looked* like someone who would do business with Zeldan.

She looked puzzled at first; then, as she took in Rathand's pained expression, worried.

"Well?" she snapped at Rathand impatiently. "Where's Zeldan? Where's my pain? Where's my power? The Dream should have been dropped by now."

Despite his own level of pain, Rathand managed to smirk at Morrigan.

"He's dead, you *bitch*," Rathand said, looking rather pleased with himself. "Your plan is history. You're not getting any more from us, not even what's in our banks."

Morrigan turned different shades of red and gurgled something incomprehensible.

Adam went over to one of the cabinets and opened one. Inside was a series of crystals, each glowing with power. And in each one, Adam felt the pain. He slammed the cabinet closed in disgust. *That's how Zeldan did it. He stored human pain in this thrice-damned equipment.* He regarded Rathand with equal disgust. *And he helped him do it.*

Can I really trust Rathand?

"Get away from there," Adam said, pushing Rathand aside. Rathand surrendered his place to the King without complaint. Adam regarded this new element with renewed hate.

I still have an enemy to conquer, he thought.

"Zeldan's dead. I killed him. Personally," Adam informed her.

Her eyes narrowed. "Who are *you?*"

"King Aedham Tuiereann of Elfhame Avalon," Adam said. "And I will return to claim my kingdom. And if I find any Unseleighe or agents of Unseleighe on our lands, they will die without question."

"You . . ." she said, sputtering. "It was *you* who returned. That levin bolt, Zeldan's men . . ." Her voice trailed off. She consulted with someone off screen for a moment, then returned.

"I have a bad feeling about this," Sammi said.

From the banks of crystals, a low, resonant hum emitted. The color of light leaking through the cabinets changed from light yellow to red; something had definitely changed.

"You didn't!" Rathand wailed. Then, to Moira, said, "Please tell me she didn't."

"Didn't what?" Adam demanded to know. "What's wrong?" He looked at the crystal again; Morrigan had an expression of mock fear, which turned to amusement. Then the crystal went blank, with only her fading laugh to remind him she had ever been there.

He turned to Rathand. *"What is going on?"* He cast a wary eye at the equipment, certain it had become a new source of danger.

"She's reversed the power," he said, crawling up to a console of other, smaller crystals. One glance at it and Rathand shook his head, and sank back to the floor.

"Okay, so she's reversed the power," Adam said. "What the hell does *that* mean?"

Rathand fell over on his side, then rolled on his back. He was lying on the floor now, looking up at the ceiling. "This station was designed for one-way power transmission. The ports were only built to handle a certain amount of power, and in one direction only."

"Yes?" Adam said, standing over Rathand. *"And?"*

"There's going to be a big explosion," Rathand replied, visibly fading.

"How big?" Sammi asked, in a monotone.

Rathand looked about the room indifferently. "Oh, big enough to convert this entire building to dust."

"How do we stop it?" Adam asked.

"You don't . . ." Rathand said, exhaling a long, final breath. His head lolled to one side; his eyes stared at the ceiling, and the crystal in his head had turned bloodred.

The low resonant hum raised a bit in pitch, and Moira glanced at it nervously. "Okay, guys. Reality check. Why are we still down here?"

"She's right," Adam said. "All of you, get out of here!"

"What about Daryl?"

"I'll get him," Adam said, slinging the weapon over his back. "Sammi, help Marbann. Moira, Spence is in shock." Though still dazed, Marbann seemed to know they were in danger again. With little urging, he started for the stairwell.

With some effort, he managed to throw Daryl over his shoulder. The boy was still sound asleep and showed no signs of waking.

"Everyone, out!" Adam shouted, as he started for the stairwell with Daryl. *"The building's about to blow!"*

The weight room was empty of all but those already dead. Packages of Black Dream lay strewn everywhere, and he hoped that whatever was about to happen would destroy all of it.

Beneath them, Adam felt the concrete floor vibrate. Panting, lungs heaving, he reached the outside right after the others. The Caprice was still there, but the parking lot was clear of all the other vehicles they'd seen when they arrived.

Moira and Spence crawled into the back. Niamh jumped out of the car and helped Adam lay Daryl across their laps. Petrus and Wenlann climbed into the passenger's side of Sammi's cop car, followed by Marbann, making a tight fit. Then Niamh dove in across them. Marbann reached over and pulled the door shut.

"Everyone, hang on," Sammi shouted from the driver's seat. "This is going to be a rough ride."

Now, if we can get out of here. He situated himself with Daryl's head on his lap as Sammi threw the car into reverse. The Caprice lurched backward, did a reverse fishtail, then sped out of the New You Fitness Center parking lot.

In the rearview mirror, Adam watched the building explode.

He wasn't certain what he'd expected. The explosion's origins were not terrestrial, but from Underhill, so the explosion might have taken many different forms. When the building erupted, a fireball instantly engulfed the structure, then pulled it inward; the shock of the implosion cracked the rear window and caused the Caprice to swerve, but Sammi's expert driving skills maneuvered the car back under control.

Adam exhaled a breath he didn't realize he'd been holding in. Moments later, Sammi pulled up behind the van, which was still parked where they'd left it.

"I sure hope everyone was out of that place," Sammi said. She looked down at Daryl. "What's wrong with *him*?"

In Adam's lap, Daryl had started to shake. Slightly, at first, then his entire body started to spasm.

"He's having a seizure," Moira said. "Adam, can you heal him?"

"I'll try. But I think we'd better get to a hospital," Adam said, glancing down at Daryl, whose skin had become cold and clammy.

"I'll lead in the van," Sammi said, getting out. "I have a light bar in the grill. Get us there in record time. I have to make sure Roach is still zonked anyway. Moira, you get up here and drive. Follow me to Parkland Memorial."

Sammi hopped into the van and took off, and Moira pulled in behind them, scratching the pavement with rubber.

"Nice pickup," Moira said. "You okay back there?"

I don't know, Adam thought. Daryl was still shaking, more violently now. Moira threw a Bic pen in the backseat.

"If he's biting his tongue, put this between his teeth," she said. Adam tried to force Daryl's mouth open, but his jaws were too tight. He checked his nose, found he was breathing shallowly, but freely, through it.

Come on, Daryl, Adam thought, holding his friend's head. *Don't die on me now. Not after what we've just been through.*

He reached for the nodes and focused their power on Daryl, imagining him well again. He kept it up for as long as possible, before his concentration gave out.

When he opened his eyes, Daryl was breathing normally. His body had relaxed, and the seizure had stopped. Slowly, he opened his eyes and looked up at Adam.

"What happened?" Daryl said weakly.

"I'll tell you later," Adam said, relieved. "Just relax. You're about to start that vacation we promised you."

Daryl smiled faintly, then went back to sleep.

Chapter Twenty

Daryl woke in what appeared to be a hospital room, on a reclining bed set in the upright position. A curtain had been drawn across the room, separating him from another patient, who sounded old and wheezed and coughed constantly. From a clear plastic bag hanging from the ceiling, a tube ran to an IV tube in his arm. The area the needle was inserted was sore, suggesting it had been in there a long time.

Then the memory of what had happened flooded over him. *I narked on Presto. I narked on the Man. And everyone saw me with the wire.* He looked over at the door, suddenly nervous for his safety. *If they find me, I'm dead.*

Then he saw Adam, sound asleep, curled up on an uncomfortable-looking chair.

A nurse walked in carrying a tray of something. When she looked down at Daryl and their eyes met, her eyes widened in surprise.

"You're *con*—awake," she said.

Daryl frowned, not liking the nurse's reaction much. *She's lookin' at me like I woke from the dead.* Then he thought about this a moment.

"It . . . it happens," Daryl said. His voice, at first, refused to work. "Where am I?"

Adam stirred, looked up with sleepy eyes. "Daryl?" he said, with a smile. "'Bout time you woke up."

"I'll get the doctor," the nurse said, and was gone.

"What happened?" Daryl asked. He felt horrible. When his jaw moved, it sent a shooting pain through his skull. "After . . . what happened? The cops were carrying me out of a building. That's the last thing I remember."

Adam looked pensive, and for an uncomfortable moment Daryl thought he might lie to him about his condition.

"You've been out for three days," Adam said. "Before that, you had a series of seizures. They had to sedate you. They did other things to you. You were coming off Black Dream, and they didn't think you were going to make it."

Daryl managed a laugh. "I don't remember any of it."

"Which is just as well. They have you on Librium. They said you would have died without it."

"Really?" he said. "Funny, I don't feel high."

"You'd probably notice it if you weren't on it," Adam said, rubbing his eyes.

He still looks sleepy. How long has he been here?

"Or maybe not. They say they'll have to take you off of it, soon."

Daryl thought about what that meant. "I want off it," he said. "I want off everything." He felt a tickling between his legs, and when he lifted the sheet to see what it was, he nearly screamed.

"It's a catheter," Adam said. "Don't worry, you're okay down there. They had to hook you up so you wouldn't pee all over the place."

"Oh," Daryl said, suddenly embarrassed. "Anyway, like I said, I want off all of it. Everything. Coke, Dream, booze, pot, everything."

Adam was gazing at him in wonder. "Are you sure about that?" he said. "I mean, really sure."

Daryl didn't have to think for very long. "I almost died. A number of times. I'm lucky to be alive." *Yes, I want off everything,* he thought. For a frightening moment, he was afraid no one might believe him this time. "Death has a way of getting your attention."

"It does that," Adam said, but his eyes had wandered off, as if his thoughts were elsewhere.

"What about . . . my dad? And Mom," he said, suppressing a groan. "What, if anything, do they have to say about this?"

"They're in a treatment center," Adam said. "Your father is being treated for cocaine addiction, and your mother checked in for Valium dependency. They're both at the Dallas Regional Chemical Dependency Center. They were kind of hoping you'd join them when you were well enough to get out of here."

The news stunned him. *Dad's in a treatment center?* "Was it his idea, or did the court tell him to go?"

"His idea," Adam said without hesitation. "He wants to get well, too."

"This is too much," Daryl said. "I mean, that's the last person I expected to—"

A doctor came in, a young man in his thirties, wearing a white coat. "Hello, Mr. Bendis," the doctor said, with irritating cheerfulness. "I'm Dr. Cochrane. How do you feel?" he asked, pulling a pocket flashlight out and shining it in Daryl's eyes.

"Like shit," he said, flinching away from the light. "But I guess I'm lucky to be alive."

Cochrane raised his eyes at that. "Yes, I'd say you were," the doctor replied, replacing the flashlight. "We'll be easing you off the Librium today. There may be some complications—"

"I don't care," Daryl said. Without realizing it, he'd grabbed the doctor's wrist firmly. "Take me off everything. Today. I don't care what happens."

Dr. Cochrane nodded thoughtfully. "We'll do it. I would suggest a treatment center, as soon as possible."

"Dallas Regional," he said automatically. "That's where my parents are."

"Very well," he replied. "We'll see what kind of shape you're in today. You might be able to go in this afternoon."

*   *   *

He went in that afternoon, after the Librium wore off, and from that moment on hated everyone and everything around him.

"What do you *mean* Adam can't come see me? He's the only friend I have in the world."

The nurse was firm. "No visitors. In the third week, maybe. But while you're in detox, no way, no how."

Daryl stared at her. "Detox? I've already been through detox."

The half smile she gave him turned his blood to ice.

Detox, for real, turned out to be a room, a bed, and a toilet, which he hugged for three solid days while he retched his guts out. When he didn't have his head in a toilet, he was on the bed, shivering and sweating under three layers of blankets, with no sleep. In the few moments of lucidity, he became a fan of Beetlejuice and Tiny Toons cartoons, mindlessly watching the images act out their insanity on a tiny four-inch TV.

He thought he was going to die. He wanted to die.

Nothing's worth this. . . .

He woke in the middle of the night, soaked with sweat, as usual. He made it to the toilet in time. As he was staggering back to his bed, he remembered the dream.

Elves? he thought. *Peter Pritchard turned into a monster. Long pointed ears. A long nose. Claws like an eagle.*

Remembering the claws, he went back into the bathroom, and looked at his pale and clammy face in the mirror. Across one cheek were the faint traces of a scar, four lines, as if caused by . . . a claw. He raised his gown up and saw another set across his abdomen.

I remember what happened, he thought. *Or was it a hallucination?*

. . . a hallucination that leaves scars?

He tried to go back to sleep, but lay awake, thinking about that night at the New You. *Black Dream. Water supply. The Police. The wire. Was Adam a cop? His mother was. He was wearing a shirt that said* POLICE. *What the hell happened back there?*

When dawn broke and touched the wall next to him with a ray of light, Daryl nodded off to sleep.

Death has a way of getting your attention, Daryl thought, watching the tombstones file past the limosine's window. *Especially when it's someone else who's died.*

Justin's funeral was simple, quick, and sparsely attended. Daryl didn't know if it was a closed funeral, or if the Bendis family had run through so many friends nobody cared anymore. A few kids from school showed up, but in the heavy downpour few others did. As the line of black cars pulled away from the gravesite, the rain let up some, but continued to fall in steady torrents.

Daryl rode with his mother and father. He had hoped their reunion might have been under happier circumstances, but somehow it seemed fitting they should see each other clean and sober for the first time at Justin's funeral. At least to Daryl, it drove home how important it was to stay that way.

He'd noticed a change in his father right way. Paul Bendis looked defeated, and Daryl didn't know how to react to that. *Father has never been beaten before. But then, neither have I. This is a new thing for both of us.*

Yanni, his mother, said absolutely nothing past the first greeting. Without her Valium, she looked as if she were going to unravel at the funeral. But as soon as they began lowering the casket into the earth, she looked relieved.

It's over, seemed to be the thought shared by all of them.

The whole thing hurt, more than anything he'd ever been through, but at least he was feeling it. His counselor at the treatment center said it would take time to get over it. For him, he was taking time just to feel the pain. And for the first time while in pain, he didn't feel the urge to reach for a chemical to change that.

Not over it, not under it, not around it, but through it,

the words echoed through his head. Now he understood what that meant.

Of course, Adam, Samantha, Moira and another tall guy he didn't recognize showed up at the funeral. Adam had his arm around Moira, and although she was quite a bit taller, they looked for all the world like the perfect couple. It was the first time he'd seen Adam since the hospital. His memory of that night still nagged at him, and he asked Adam to come by and visit that day.

At Dallas Regional, there was a simple garden maintained just for such visits. It had tall rock walls surrounding it, and it still looked like a prison, but at least the grass was green and not antiseptically white like the rest of his world had become. The earth and rotting vegetation smelled good after the heavy rain. He eyed the sky suspiciously, wondering if the storms would ever pass.

"Hello, Daryl," he heard, and he turned around. Adam was still wearing his black suit. He looked a little less formal now, having removed the tie, but he still looked stuffy. *Why do people have to wear black to funerals? Funerals are for the living, not the dead.*

"Thanks," Daryl said, going over to Adam, and giving him a big hug.

"For what?" Adam said, looking surprised.

"For being there at the funeral," he said. "You saw how many friends we had left."

"That will change," Adam said. Daryl looked him over and sensed that something had changed in him. He seemed older, more mature. *Guess some big things have been happening in his life, too.* "How long are you going to be here?"

"Another week." He looked up at the clouds, which had begun to break, revealing blue sky. "You know, I still crave it, sometimes. Cocaine. Black Dream. Drugs in general. I still have dreams about it." His eyes left the clouds, then met Adam's. "Does it ever go away?"

"I don't know," Adam said. "But I do know there's a difference between a thought and an action. You can think about it, but what really matters is what you do about it."

Daryl nodded, but something else was eating at him. "You know, I saw some pretty weird stuff that night we were at the New You."

They started walking down a concrete sidewalk with beds of flowers on either side. "Do you remember much of what happened, back there?" asked Adam.

"When I was in detox, I remembered everything," Daryl said, and paused. He looked Adam directly in the eye. "You're my best friend, Adam. You're the only one who stayed by me. You've helped me more than any friend ever has. You might even be the only friend I've ever had. . . ."

Adam smiled serenely and put his hand on Daryl's shoulder. "Thanks, Daryl. But what are you getting at?"

Daryl studied his shoes, as if he'd find the courage to say what he needed to down there.

"Are you and your mother, like, *aliens* or something?"

Adam smirked this time, then looked up into a ray of light that had just burst from the sky.

Daryl heard a light buzzing in his ears, like a bee or mosquito, but the sound came from everywhere. For a second he felt light-headed, but the dizziness passed, and he took a deep breath of humid summer air, cleansed with rain.

Sunlight flooded the garden as the clouds parted. And in moments, his mood lifted. He had, for the first time, a sense of a future. In that moment, he saw everything he could be, if he tried hard enough. Only moments earlier, he had a craving for something, but he didn't know what it was.

"What was I saying?" Daryl asked.

"Oh, I think it was something about how the present looks good right now. And the future. You're only eighteen, you have a whole lifetime and a whole world in front of you."

"I guess that was it," he said, but he still felt confused. "You know, I can't remember anything of those last few days. Is that what they call a blackout?"

"I think so. Oh, and I wanted to ask you."

"Yeah?"

Adam's eyes shifted as he glanced slyly toward the door where the nurse's station was.

"Do they let you play D&D in this place?".